ANY MEANS NECESSARY

ALSO BY LILA HERRON

Red My Lips

LILA HERRON

ANY MEANS NECESSARY

A NOVEL

EMILY BESTLER BOOKS

ATRIA

New York   Amsterdam/Antwerp   London
Toronto   Sydney/Melbourne   New Delhi

ATRIA
An Imprint of Simon & Schuster, LLC
1230 Avenue of the Americas
New York, NY 10020

For more than 100 years, Simon & Schuster has championed authors and the stories they create. By respecting the copyright of an author's intellectual property, you enable Simon & Schuster and the author to continue publishing exceptional books for years to come. We thank you for supporting the author's copyright by purchasing an authorized edition of this book.

No amount of this book may be reproduced or stored in any format, nor may it be uploaded to any website, database, language-learning model, or other repository, retrieval, or artificial intelligence system without express permission. All rights reserved. Inquiries may be directed to Simon & Schuster, 1230 Avenue of the Americas, New York, NY 10020 or permissions@simonandschuster.com.

This book is a work of fiction. Any references to historical events, real people, or real places are used fictitiously. Other names, characters, places, and events are products of the author's imagination, and any resemblance to actual events or places or persons, living or dead, is entirely coincidental.

Copyright © 2026 by Lila Herron

All rights reserved, including the right to reproduce this book or portions thereof in any form whatsoever. For information, address Atria Books Subsidiary Rights Department, 1230 Avenue of the Americas, New York, NY 10020.

First Emily Bestler Books/Atria Paperback edition March 2026

EMILY BESTLER BOOKS/ATRIA PAPERBACK
and colophon are registered trademarks of Simon & Schuster, LLC

Simon & Schuster strongly believes in freedom of expression and stands against censorship in all its forms. For more information, visit BooksBelong.com.

For information about special discounts for bulk purchases, please contact Simon & Schuster Special Sales at 1-866-506-1949 or business@simonandschuster.com.

The Simon & Schuster Speakers Bureau can bring authors to your live event. For more information or to book an event, contact the Simon & Schuster Speakers Bureau at 1-866-248-3049 or visit our website at www.simonspeakers.com.

Interior design by Davina Mock-Maniscalco

Manufactured in the United States of America

1 3 5 7 9 10 8 6 4 2

Library of Congress Control Number: 2025949113

ISBN 978-1-6682-1889-1 (pbk)
ISBN 978-1-6682-1890-7 (ebook)

Let's stay in touch! Scan here to get book recommendations, exclusive offers, and more delivered to your inbox.

To my fellow fat babes
who wish they could see themselves in the books they read—
you're hot, this is your main character moment.

Trigger Warnings:

- Death
- Use of guns and gun violence
- Knife violence
- Explicit physical violence including blood and murder
- Mention of drugs and drug use
- Fatphobia
- Mental health topics such as panic attacks and past trauma
- Threats of violence
- Organized crime
- Torture used in interrogation
- Kidnapping
- Child abduction
- Mention of underage sex trafficking
- Explicit sex scenes
- Mention of infant death
- Explicit language
- Mention of child abuse and neglect
- Alcohol consumption
- Mention of intended rape and date rape drugs
- Body dysmorphia

PROLOGUE

LEXIE

I stare at my shaking hands, watching them tremble. These skilled, useless hands. Even now, after taking the gloves off and scrubbing them twice, I can still feel the blood coating them like a sickening second skin. The frigid night air whips around me, carrying the shrill wail of the sirens and chaos of the incoming traumas. The breeze catches the blood on my scrubs, a chill reaching all the way to my bones. Huddled on the bench, I struggle to suck in shallow breaths against my breaking heart. Once the tears start, there's no stopping them. The floodgates open and the first sob comes out.

Bringing my hands to my middle, I wrap my arms around myself for support. My helpless, pointless hands. They're no good to anyone, they can't fix this—nothing can. What's the point if they can't help when I need them to the most? All I could do was sit and watch helplessly. And now all that blood—sweet, innocent blood—is on my hands.

My skilled, useless hands.

My eyes search the night air for a sign of hope, a distraction, *anything*. The blazing ambulance lights bathe everything in flashes of blue and red. My eyes catch on an object laying on the cracked concrete a few yards away, illuminated by the flashing light. Staring at it, something inside me fractures as a devastating sadness settles so deeply in my chest I'm not sure I'll ever be without it again. It's like the ground has opened into an abyss beneath me and I'm slipping into the darkness.

A child's lunch box is stained with blood until the light blue color is barely visible. On it, the cartoon solar system sits in a cluster of stars with a tiny astronaut floating blissfully near a small rocket. The name Jack is written clearly across the front in Sharpie. It sits there on the ground, trampled and forgotten—belonging to someone who will never come looking for it. The sinking feeling drags me deeper into the abyss.

"Lexie?" The voice saying my name behind me barely registers, even as a hand touches my shoulder. "Lexie, are you okay?"

"I can't." I shake my head with a sob. "I can't do it. I can't stay here." I need to leave, and I don't know how I'll ever come back. How will I ever come back from this?

"Come on, let's get her inside and clean her up." Several pairs of hands support me when I stand on unsteady legs, but I don't recognize faces past my tears and despair. I allow myself to be led away from the bench, away from the flashing lights and the noise from the tragedy.

Away from the blood-stained lunch box.

CHAPTER ONE

CALLUM

*S*mack.

The high-pitched buzzing in my ear persists as my palm makes contact with my neck. Pulling my arm away, I already know I've come up empty before I look down at my hand. We landed in Florida less than an hour ago, and I'm sure I already have half a dozen bug bites.

"I'm waiting three more minutes. That's all he gets." The threat in my tone is clear. I consider myself a patient man, but I have my limits. After a certain point, tardiness bleeds into blatant disrespect.

I don't tolerate disrespect.

Roscoe, my right-hand man, looks down at his watch to take note of the time. He nods in understanding, but says nothing as he widens his stance beside me. Stoic as usual, I don't miss how he tugs at his suit coat against the humidity that's unseasonably heavy, even for this climate.

Waiting on the runway—if you can even call it that—for my contact has my irritation growing. The sounds of the Everglades increase in volume as the sun lowers past the tree line. Plant life dots the unpaved airstrip as nature slowly swallows the strip until it appears abandoned—I'm sure that's the point. It's a tactic often used by smugglers, much like the man I'm waiting for.

Not for long. Two more minutes, then I'm gone.

Headlights shine through the trees as a vehicle breaks through the brush and approaches where we stand waiting. As the SUV slows to a stop a few yards away, my phone starts vibrating in my pocket. Pulling it out, a quick glance shows me an incoming call from an unknown number with a New York area code. As the driver's door opens, I silence my phone to send the call to voicemail. If it's important they'll leave me a message.

The man who steps out from behind the wheel is not the one I'm expecting. Clamping down on my irritation, I address the newcomer.

"You're not Antoné Batista," I state the obvious as he walks closer to where Roscoe and I stand. Louis offers a smile that's almost apologetic, his shoulders lifting in a shrug. If I didn't recognize him as one of Antoné's men, he'd already have a bullet in his head. Last-minute changes like this come with risks bigger than what I'm willing to accept. In my line of work, I like to be prepared.

"He got held up and sent me to collect you." Louis runs a hand through his salt-and-pepper hair, then readjusts the thick framed glasses on his sharp nose. The sparse white facial hair on his chin makes him look older than his late forties, and he's dressed like a Floridian tourist on a night out. The floral print of his teal shirt is one limping step away from looking like he bought it off the clearance rack in a Hawaii gift shop.

"I didn't come to be *collected*," I point out, gesturing to the folio in Roscoe's hands. "This was supposed to be a simple hand-off."

Just when I thought I was going to make my dinner reservations.

The best-laid plans.

"And it will be," Louis assures me, his eyes latching curiously on the black, leather-bound package before returning to mine. "Allow me to take you to him, you can do the exchange then."

"Where is he?"

"The Reserve." Of course he is. I look over at Roscoe as I weigh my options, but there isn't really another way. If I refuse to go meet Antoné, I don't get paid. The job is already done; this final meeting is all that's left of our contract. And the last thing I need is to be right back here in a few days waiting in the bug-ridden swamp.

"Tell the pilots to stand by until we get back," I instruct, holding out my hand to take the book. Roscoe nods before heading back to my waiting private plane.

"Don't even think about it," I say when I catch Louis eyeing the book in my hand for a second time. "This is for Antoné's eyes only."

"Oh, I know better than that." The way his tone falters belies the confidence in his words. He'd take this book without thinking twice if he got the chance—so I won't give him one.

Louis swats at a bug as it flies around his head, gesturing to the SUV. "You can sit in the car, the air is on. It's already hot as balls out here." As tempting of an offer as that is, I wait for Roscoe to return before approaching the vehicle.

Just because I can be flexible doesn't make me careless.

The drive through the Everglades is rough, as the SUV plows through the underbrush along the almost nonexistent road that tests the vehicle's shocks. I feel sorry for any passenger who might have a weak stomach; this back seat would need to be reupholstered.

Finally, the trees part to the open skies and water as far as the eye can see. The car slows to a stop at a private dock. Climbing out of the back seat, my eyes scan the surrounding area—not a soul in sight. Louis takes the lead as we walk to the speedboat waiting at the end of the dock.

The wind off the Gulf as we fly across the water is a welcome reprieve from the suffocating humidity. Louis navigates around the dense patches of weeds that float just off the coast—swerving and revving the engine like an overzealous teenager being allowed behind the wheel of the boat for the first time—until we're out in open waters. An island dots in the distance, slowly growing as we approach.

Antoné calling his private island the "Reserve" is like calling a dog-fighting ring an animal rescue. He's what they call a *collector*—vintage cars, rare art, limited edition designer watches, the list goes on. But his true passion, to the point of obsession, is animals. Exotic and endangered animals, specifically.

He bought this island and had it registered as an animal reserve to keep the public and local government oversight from stumbling across his little hobby. Then he built his massive compound here, housing more animals than a small zoo—most illegal to own.

But just because you have a private island doesn't mean government agencies like the US Fish and Wildlife Service won't investigate you for poaching and smuggling endangered species.

That's why I'm here.

Pulling up to the island, there's another dock and another SUV. Fortunately, this road is both level and paved, making the ride up to the residence a lot smoother.

At the end of the long, winding drive, Antoné's estate spreads across manicured lawns with imported palm trees and ornate fountains. Pulling up to the front door in the circular drive feels more like a small resort than a private residence.

If there's one thing to say about Antoné, the man lacks subtlety.

Louis escorts us inside the flashy mansion full of brightly patterned furniture, gaudy gold fixtures, and decorated with animal pelts and taxidermic game.

Just like everything else he does, Antoné's house makes a statement. Each element—between the peacock feather chandelier, elephant tusk archways, and bold Picasso paintings—is a visual assault on the senses. Spending more than ten minutes here could cause a seizure. Just walking through is giving me a migraine. I can hear Roscoe's huff of relief when we walk out the back door into the evening air.

The sound of bird calls carries across the garden as we walk past caged enclosures filled with colorful, exotic birds. I'm not an expert, but I do recognize the distinct blue of the Spix's macaw, and fluffed feathers of a yellow-crested cockatoo among them—both illegal to own.

Walking past a few more enclosures housing animals of questionable legality—I'm sure Antoné has permits for the rarer species in plain sight—we approach the densely hedged wall that marks the end of the garden. But instead of stopping or turning around, Louis leads us along the hedge until we've turned a blind corner where a door sits hidden in the foliage.

Punching in a code on the keypad beside the door, Louis waits for the lock to audibly unlatch, before pulling it open and stepping aside to wave us in. I enter first with Roscoe at my heels. The door clicks shut behind our guide as he joins us in the spacious, concrete tunnel leading down into the ground. Lights dot the walkway every few feet, illuminating the way. The tunnel stretches a quarter of a mile before ending at another locked door.

This time the door opens to a warehouse. Enclosures stretch as far as the eye can see, sectioned by terrain and species. The entrance is lit by the red glow of heating lamps. I stride past terrariums full of reptiles and amphibians basking in the warmth. Some are so small you can't see them hidden amongst their camouflage, but I spot the bright colors of dart frogs in the leaves. The Burmese python is impossible to miss, a snake that looks like a tree trunk stretching out the length of a car. Not to mention the Komodo dragon that's basically a goddamn dinosaur still roaming the earth.

As we move through the building, the enclosures grow larger—each professionally staged and fully equipped to rival most zoos.

I'd never admit it, but I don't recognize half of the animals we pass. As we move towards the back of the bunker, the enclosures suddenly expand to hold large predators—a panther, a leopard. Even a fucking tiger is pacing its pen, licking its lips like it longs for a taste of our blood.

Past a break in the pens, the animals turn aquatic. Tanks of colorful fish, eels, and a box jellyfish. Just like the land dwellers, these tanks grow larger, holding barracudas and sharks.

A short, doughy man stands at the last tank, his gold silk shirt gleaming with the moving reflection of the water. Despite being shaved bald, his dark hair follicles show his receding hairline. His thick goatee is black, with a patch of silver hair growing directly in the center of his chin like the stripe on a skunk. A thick, gold Cuban link chain flashes around his neck, matching the chunky gold rings shining on his fingers. His white boots are premium ostrich leather, no doubt.

For someone trying to avoid attention, he walks around looking like a fucking peacock.

"Ahh, you made it," Antoné announces, briefly pulling his eyes away from the tank he's standing in front of. His dark eyes turn back to the mammal gliding through the water, standing so close his nose might as well be pressing the glass. "She's a beauty, isn't she?"

"Impressive," I comment, coming to stand beside him. I've never seen one before; it appears to be a porpoise of some sort—with a large dark ring around its eyes and dark patches on its lips that form a thin line from the mouth to the pectoral fins. The small aquatic mammal moves through the water with the same grace of a dolphin, its movements charged with distress. It tumbles around the tank as if searching for an escape.

"There were some complications getting her here, but she'll acclimate soon enough. The vaquita is on the edge of extinction, there are less than a dozen left in existence." The pride in Antoné's voice matches the greedy glint in his eyes. "And now one of them is mine."

"Quite the acquisition. I trust you were discreet. You still have eyes on you, now more than ever."

"Of course, of course." Peeling himself away from his newest prize possession, Antoné turns to give me his full attention. "You have it?" His weathered face splits with a grin when his eyes land on the folio in my hands. I offer him the book, watching as he unties the leather cords securing it closed to thumb through the pages detailing every one of his illegal transactions. "I'm tempted to ask how you got this back for me, I doubt you'd be careless enough to say."

"If I told you, I'd have to kill you," I respond soberly. Antoné stares at me for a split second before his head falls back and he bursts into boisterous laughter.

"I'm sure you would." He shakes his head, and wags his finger at me, his voice flooded with amusement. His laughter fades as quickly as it came, his eyes sharpening. "And the witness?"

"What witness?" I ask meaningfully, making his grin widen. His hands rub together gleefully, like a villain in a Bond movie, his rings flashing.

It wasn't easy. The U.S. Fish and Wildlife Service doesn't take poaching and smuggling endangered animals lightly, and they're determined to build their case. Antoné hired me to recover his little black book that was confiscated during a raid on his home in Palm Beach. Disappearing a federal witness in protective custody isn't a simple task—it requires connections with deep ties and a fat stack of bribe money. Not to mention a chemist with a strong stomach and complete lack of morals.

Antoné is paying a steep price, and I've earned every cent. Tom Strickland—the man who was ready to spill all of Antoné's secrets to a grand jury—won't be heard from again.

There's nothing left of him to find.

"I heard you were the best." Antoné looks over at Louis. "Didn't I tell you he was the best?" Louis nods as the smuggler addresses me again. "The Fixer who can solve any problem. I'm impressed."

"Glad to hear you're satisfied," I accept his compliments graciously. "Once we finalize payment, our contract will be finished. It'll be like none of this ever happened."

"Ahh yes, your payment. I have this amur leopard pelt, extremely rare. Or maybe an albino crocodile. My buyer fell through and it's ready for transit."

"I'll stick with the payment we agreed on," I state. His offer is interesting, but I don't stray from the contract for *interesting*. The possibility of weaponizing the infamous jaws of a crocodile is intriguing, but I have enough cold-blooded killers to get any job done. I accept cash via secure wire transfer, art, or favors of equal caliber. Nothing more, nothing less.

"A traditional man. Not nearly as fun, but I respect it. I'll have the painting pulled from display. Institutions like the Met tend to take their time with these things. Come to my office, and we'll start the paperwork." Despite his particular obsession with animals, Antoné's collector habits extend past birds and reptiles. He likes finding anything rare—cars, art, even people. With the way he's looking at me, I assume he now considers me a part of his collection.

Not that I can blame him, there's not another man on earth who can do what I can.

"After you."

The sight of my waiting jet feels like a reward, I'm so ready to get the hell out of this lawless swamp. I like things clean and in order. Everything about my time in Florida so far has been messy and unnecessarily complicated.

Stepping out of Louis' SUV, I pull out my phone to see that my missed call from earlier includes a voicemail. Pressing play, I hold my phone to my ear as Roscoe and I stride towards the plane. The stairs lower as we approach, my staff already waiting for our arrival.

The man on the other end kept his message short and simple—a US senator is in desperate need of my services, it's urgent. That's all I need to hear.

"Off to Miami?" Roscoe asks, waiting for me to ascend the stairs first.

"Change of plans," I announce. "I have business in New York." My right-hand man makes a sound of confirmation behind me.

Walking up the steps and ducking through the door, my pilots, Paul and Michael, greet me from the cockpit. I head towards the small four-person conference table at the back of the main cabin. Past my seat, a sleek black galley kitchen leads to the full bathroom connected to the bedroom complete with a king-size bed that's calling my name.

Finding a plane with everything I need when I travel for work was difficult, especially one that had fixtures big enough for me to fit comfortably. So, when I wasn't able to find one, I had it made to my exact specifications. Money well spent.

After informing the pilots of our new destination, Roscoe comes to sit in the chair across from me at the table. "I never thought I'd miss New York weather," he grumbles, tugging at the black shirt that's clinging to his skin.

"I'm ready to go home," I agree. Words I rarely say, but right now I can't get back to New York City fast enough.

Dzzzt. Smack.

Fucking mosquitos.

CHAPTER TWO

LEXIE

"And when are you coming back, exactly? When you said the hospital let you out of your contract, I thought that meant I'd be getting my best friend back." Mia's attitude is broadcasted through the kitchen, her irritation echoing on speakerphone. "It's already been four months, how long are you going to play hard to get? It's rude to tease me like this." I roll my eyes at her dramatics, grinning only because she can't see me.

"Oh please, it's not like you're just sitting at home all day without me," I shoot back. "You're the busiest person I've ever met. I invited you to come visit me. But noooo, you're *too important* to take the time off to come to New York." I let the sarcasm drip from my voice. Now that the potatoes are sauteed and softened, I add the steak to the skillet. The recipe calls for two steaks—instead of halving the ingredients, I'll just have leftovers. The meat sizzles in the hot pan, spitting grease and butter onto the stovetop and counter.

Damn, I hate having to wipe up grease.

"You know I have surgeries; I can't just run around playing housekeeper for strangers like you." She's on the defensive now, but she has a point. That's what I get for picking a surgeon as a best friend. Her job is a lot more demanding than mine, but I'm not about to admit that to her.

"Are you trying to say that surgeons are more important than nurses? Wow, tell me how you really feel." I'm laying it on thick and she knows it. But she has to deny it, she can't help herself.

"You know that's not what I'm saying, Lexie," she insists, but I continue to wind her up.

"It's fine, whatever," I tease. "I'm just not important enough to you. Just abandon me in this big city all by myself." Opening the spice cabinet, I need to reach on my tiptoes to grab the seasoning I'm looking for. Fresh basil would taste a lot better, but that would've required thinking far enough ahead for this meal to buy ingredients.

Which I did not.

"Oh, shut up." Despite her best efforts, I can hear the smile in her voice. I'm about to laugh at her, but my teasing is cut short.

"Shit," I mutter, looking down to see that I leaned into a puddle of grease. Damn these big boobs.

"What?" Mia asks.

"I leaned on the counter and got grease on my new shirt."

"That's what you get for being mean to me."

I pull off the shirt and take it over to the sink, treating it with a dose of grease-fighting dish soap. I've done what I can to save it. Now all I can do is pray that my new top lives to see another wear.

Standing in the middle of the large kitchen without a shirt on feels wrong, especially since I'm not in my apartment. I walked around my place back in Oregon topless all the time, but the unfamiliarity of being in someone else's home creeps in and takes giant bites out of my comfort-based confidence.

The wall of floor-to-ceiling windows that offers a magnificent view of the New York City skyline from this twenty-second-floor penthouse, while usually impressive, now makes me feel like a goldfish in a bowl. Each light illuminating the view feels like pairs of eyes staring with an unobstructed view as I stand here in my bra.

I need to put a shirt on.

"I have to get a fresh shirt and finish cooking, so I'm going to hang up on you now," I announce, walking back over to where my phone sits by the stove, just barely out of the pan's spitting range.

The steaks roar loudly as I flip them, before settling into the pool of melted butter and herbs.

"Fine." Mia's voice brightens with excitement. "But FaceTime with me tomorrow so we can watch *The Bachelor* together. I heard from one of the interns that Brandi slaps someone, and I bet it's Ashlyn." Damn, that sounds awesome, I love petty drama.

"Are you serious? Yeah, we're definitely watching that tomorrow. I'll call you," I promise. "Bye, Mia. Love you."

"Love you too, babe. Talk to you later."

Music resumes playing over the house Bluetooth speakers when I end the call. Turning down the burner under the skillet and praying that I'm not about to ruin my dinner, I rush to my room in search of a clean shirt. The guest room I'm occupying is on the first floor. I chose the one closest to the kitchen on purpose.

"Come on, where is it?" Muttering in frustration, I dig through the pile of laundry next to my suitcase for my favorite lounge tee. This is what I get for letting this room get so messy—and I've only been here two weeks. I can't find the right shirt and now my steak is going to burn.

Giving up, I pull on a T-shirt from the top of the pile and head back to the kitchen. Walking down the hall, I can hear my steak hissing on the stove over the music playing. Humming along, I turn the corner and my breath catches in my throat.

I freeze.

A man I've never seen before stands at the stove, spooning butter over my steak after turning off the burner. His giant frame fills the expansive kitchen, his presence dominating the space. He's definitely someone who can easily overpower me in a heartbeat.

Shit, what do I do?

I stand frozen, my heart racing as the surprise wears off. Time seems to slow as my limited options run through my brain on a loop. I'm tempted to turn around and go lock myself in the bathroom. But my phone is on the counter next to him, and I'll have no way of contacting help. Staying to confront the man isn't my favorite idea either—dread has a painfully tight knot forming in my stomach at just the thought of it. Either way, I'm screwed.

I can see the moment he senses me. His head turns, and our eyes lock—mine looking like a deer in headlights, I'm sure.

Shit.

Intense hazel eyes move over me, reading and processing, as he runs a hand over his dark, immaculately groomed beard. The sharp black suit covering his massive frame seems both fitting and confining as he moves around the room—like it's a custom-tailored uniform he's itching to be free of. He regards me for a moment while my brain lags on something to say.

"Who are you?" That's the genius question I come up with.

Confrontation it is.

"I can ask you the same thing." His deep voice is calm and collected. He reaches into the cabinet to the right of the stove to grab two plates, completely at ease.

"I don't know what you want, but you need to leave. Right now." There's nothing I can do about his presence, and we both know it.

"Oh, do I?" His voice is edged with a challenge. "And if I don't?"

"I'll call the police." I'm bluffing. I have no way to call anyone; I'm just praying he doesn't realize that. But the way he glances at my phone next to him tells me that he does.

"That would be a lot more threatening if I didn't have your phone over here with me." He leans his hip against the counter, crossing thick arms over a broad chest and tilting his head at me. "And considering I own this apartment, I'm pretty interested in what the police would say. But by all means, call them." Moving my phone from the other side of the stove, he puts it back down and sends it sliding across the counter. It stops just inches from me, and I stare at the device blankly as I process what he just told me.

"You're the owner of this apartment?" His crisp black suit does say money, so does the gold watch on his wrist. He's a lot younger than I pictured, nowhere near the balding middle-aged man I figured lives here. Instead, he looks to be in his early thirties. And his thick head of dark brown hair is far from balding. How easily he's been navigating the kitchen is also a clue, but that doesn't mean he actually owns the place.

"I am. Which leaves the question: Who are you?" His movements are relaxed and controlled as he plates the steak, green beans, and potatoes. It's like he's preparing to eat with an old friend instead of standing with a stranger in his home—if he's telling me the truth.

He pauses for a moment to shrug off his suit jacket and drape it over the back of an island stool. Rolling the sleeves of his black dress shirt to his elbows reveals muscular forearms completely inked in full tattoo sleeves that end cleanly at his wrists. Suddenly he doesn't look like the same man I was just talking to a second ago. Like Clark Kent's glasses, by removing the expensive suit coat, he transforms. With his clean-cut professional facade gone, there's an air of danger about him, the intricate tattoos hinting at a darker story.

Who is this man?

"I'm a travel nurse. One of the guys I worked with set me up to watch this apartment when I quit my contract," I say, just stalling while I try to remember the name of the guy Tony said owns this place. Something Russo. It started with a C, I think.

Collin? No.

"Do you have a name, travel nurse?" He's pouring two glasses of red wine, placing them with the plates on the island next to tall glasses of water. Next comes the silverware—a fork and a steak knife at each setting.

This is looking more like a date than a home invasion. Which one of us is doing the invading has yet to be determined. But it's feeling more and more like it's me by the second.

"Alexandra West," I supply. "Lexie." What was that name? *Callum*, that's what it was.

Callum Russo.

"Can I see some sort of ID?"

He looks at me in consideration for a moment, his gaze moving over me as his lips lift in amusement. "I'll show you mine if you show me yours."

It's not an absurd request for him to ask the same of me.

"Deal," I agree.

He reaches into his discarded suit coat pocket, and I walk to where I put my handbag on the far end of the kitchen counter, giving him a wide radius as I pass. Pulling my ID from my wallet, I'm suddenly wishing I had a better license picture.

"I'll trade you." I offer him my card, and he hands me his.

There it is, printed in black and white by the state of New York. Callum Russo, with the penthouse as his listed address. I've never seen such an intense driver's license photo before; he's staring down the camera like he's daring every person who looks at it to question him, something I doubt happens often. And that's exactly what I did.

I glance up from his license to find him watching me curiously. Callum Russo stares with the same analyzing intensity in real life as he does in his photo.

I guess that's my answer, it's really him. Too bad this license can't also tell me if he's as dangerous as he looks—they don't exactly have a background check printed on the back.

"This doesn't look like you, Lexie West." He's commenting on my photo that's basically a decade old. I know exactly what he's looking at, the overly scrunched hair with curtain bangs flat-ironed into submission, round cheeks, and closed-mouth smile hiding a mouth full of metal braces. Overall, not my best look. My hair styling and skincare journey have really come a long way since then—it's just unfortunate *that* particular phase has been immortalized in my identification photo. I'm not the type to get embarrassed, but I can feel the blush warming my cheeks anyway.

"Hey, don't judge. I'm barely eighteen in that photo, that was eight years ago," I say in my defense. "At least my photo doesn't look like I'm threatening every person who asks for my ID," I shoot back, the words leaving my mouth too fast for me to think better of them. Dammit, I'm teasing him like he's the friend I was just on the phone with. I have a bad habit of being too comfortable around people I don't actually know.

Luckily, he cracks a small smile, apparently not offended in the least. The man is as devastating as he is intimidating, especially when he smiles. There's a small scar on his right cheek, and I can tell that his nose has been broken more than once, adding character to otherwise perfectly masculine features. He's tall, every bit the six-foot-four listed on his license. I have to tilt my head to look up at him; he stands a good foot taller than me since I'm only five-four. His presence matches his frame, and he fills the expansive kitchen until I feel crowded.

"I have that effect on people," he admits. "You're right, your picture certainly isn't threatening." The teasing edge in his tone laughs, whether *at* me or *with* me I'm not sure. Walking back to the place settings at the kitchen island, he pulls out a stool and motions for me to sit. I'm not sure that I'm comfortable sitting down to eat with this man, but I comply anyway.

"I didn't know you were going to be here," I say in apology. I wait as he cuts into the meat, admiring how it slices like butter, the center tender and bright red in the perfect medium rare. That's a beautiful steak if I do say so myself. As he chews, he nods in what looks like appreciation.

"You're not who I was expecting either," he says. "I wasn't supposed to be here, but there's been a change of plans."

"I'll go pack, I can be gone in thirty minutes."

"Don't bother," he states, the authority in his words leaving no room for argument. "I have some business to take care of, I'm only in the city for a few days." Suddenly I'm curious what kind of business a man like this does. But the last thing I'm going to do is ask. That's none of my business and I know how to mind my own.

"Okay," I agree, not sure what else I can say. Taking a bite, I chew slowly as silence stretches between us.

Glancing over, my eyes catch his as he regards me. This man stares a lot, but in a way I'm not used to. He's not gawking or ogling. His gaze is intentional, almost analytical. It's like there's some sort of calculation going on in his brain and I'm part of the equation. Those ever-seeing hazel eyes look into my very soul, reading me and tucking away that information for later use. He, however, shows very little of what he's thinking.

"What hospital do you work at, Doc?"

"I'm an ER nurse," I correct. "I spent eighteen weeks working at New York Presbyterian."

"But you don't work there now?" I shake my head, washing down a bite of steak with a sip of wine. This Cabernet Sauvignon is the perfect pairing choice.

"No, I took some time off." I don't need to mention that I'd planned to extend my contract at New York Presbyterian for another thirteen weeks but begged to be let out of the obligation.

Tony saved my ass from burning a few professional bridges when I was able to recommend him to my recruiter for a position they were desperate to fill. And all I had to do in return is stay in this penthouse for a few months? It was an easy deal.

"And someone else set you up to stay here?" He's more than just curious, he's solving a puzzle. "Tony," he supplies, looking for confirmation.

"Yeah, Tony." I nod. "He's an EMT I worked with. He took a contract at the last minute, so he got everything set up for me to watch your place instead."

Callum stares at the contents of his wineglass, processing and contemplating. Then he changes the subject.

"There will be people coming in and out while I'm here." He takes a sip of his wine, obviously not the least bit uncomfortable in the situation we've found ourselves in. And why would he be? It's his home, his wine, his say of what happens. I'm the one out of her element here, in a strange apartment, in a strange city, with a complete stranger. He's got the power, and he knows it.

Something tells me this dynamic isn't a one-off. Callum holds the power in most situations.

"I'll stay out of your way," I assure him. I plan on being seen as little as possible. But he shakes his head, hazel eyes meeting mine.

"Don't worry about that. The place is still yours to use how you want." Something shifts behind his eyes and the air around us turns more serious. "But from this moment on, you don't answer the door. Not while I'm staying here. And my office is off-limits."

I blink at him a few times, absorbing his instructions and the ominous threat simmering just below the surface. Then I nod, forcing back my nerves before I respond.

"I'll let you answer the door and avoid your office like the plague, promise." Great, Lexie, now it sounds like you're mocking him. My comment doesn't seem to irritate him. In fact, he barely registers that I spoke at all. He just stares at me, still solving a puzzle only he can see.

Hopping down from the stool, I carry my dishes to the sink and give them a good rinse before loading them into the dishwasher. I can feel Callum's presence behind me while I work, his tracking gaze giving me a complex. It's too bad a stranger appeared unannounced on a night that I'm not dressed for company.

"I didn't touch your bedroom." I address him over my shoulder as I clean up the mess I made while cooking. This silence is killing me, I compulsively need to fill it. "It didn't feel right to take the primary suite, so I'm staying in the downstairs guest room."

"Perfect." He sounds distracted, and when I turn around, he's typing on his phone.

"I'm going to my room, so I guess I'll see you tomorrow."

"Goodnight, Doc."

"I'm a nurse." There's definitely a dose of sass in my correction, and as I turn to leave the kitchen, I swear the corners of his lips quirk in a smug smile. Rolling my eyes, I'm heading to the guest room where I plan to read until my eyes close.

The clock tells me I've stalled as long as I can, it's time to go to sleep. Lying in the darkness, I will unconsciousness to come before my demons make their nightly appearance. Anxiety washes over me, hot and itchy. The silence in the large bedroom is deafening as my thoughts wrestle for dominance.

Just one night, I can survive just one night in the dark.

I peek one eye open to glance at the door for the third time to check if it's still closed. I can't see the door handle from here in the darkness, but I already double-checked that it's locked before climbing into bed. I'm not usually so paranoid, but my nerves are a mess right now. The last thing I need is to find a giant man looming over me in the darkness.

Callum didn't give me predator vibes earlier, but he seems like someone who knows how to hide his sins. Plus, he's still a stranger—and a man. I'm not gonna make attacking me any easier with an open door. Ted Bundy didn't seem like the predatory type either.

Forcing myself to relax, I roll onto my back, readjust my pillow, and squeeze my lids shut. The first face appears in my mind, curly blonde hair, wide brown eyes lit with pain, and two missing front teeth. She's so little, with so much life left to experience. But her light is already dimming.

Wrenching my eyes open, I sit up abruptly and try to regulate my breathing. Heart still racing, I reach for the tv remote on the nightstand. I click on the same show I choose every night, the familiar opening sequence playing. Comforting voices fill the room as I lay back down and try to relax.

"The best home bakers from across the country applied in the thousands. Just twelve have made it to our tent. Every aspect of their baking skills will be tested. Everything they create will be judged." Soothing English accents wrap around me, chasing away the shadows in my mind that threaten to swallow me. "Welcome to the *Great British Baking Show*."

CHAPTER THREE

LEXIE

The music playing in my headphones flows through me as I shimmy up to the cabinet, swaying my hips from one side to the other. Grabbing a glass from the shelf, I sing along to the song softly—I know better than to belt with headphones on. I save the Broadway-level theatrics for karaoke nights when I'm a few margaritas deep.

This fancy fridge dispenses the best pellet ice—the crunchy kind you find at gas stations—and perfectly chilled water. A glass of cold water from this fridge just hits different, especially after my morning workout. Going to walk on the treadmill, doing a few sets of weights, then coming back up and drinking a giant glass of water is my routine.

The first two gulps send a shiver through me, the cold shocking my system. The third swallow washes over me like a cool wave. I flip my high ponytail to the beat when the song changes, my long blonde hair whipping around me from one shoulder to the other. Needing another dance break, I place my glass of water on the counter so I can spin around.

My gaze collides with a pair of hazel eyes, and I freeze, letting out a breathy laugh of surprise.

Callum stands leaning in the doorway of his office across the open living space, arms crossed. His focus on me is intense, but the stoic look on his face gives away nothing about the thoughts that are brewing. Pulling the earbuds from my ears, I pause the music and offer him an apologetic smile.

"Sorry, I completely forgot you're here," I admit. His eyes flicker to my navy athletic leggings, matching sports bra, and white mesh crop jacket. The sports bra is one of my favorites with good coverage and decent support for my enormous chest. I left my jacket unzipped. Despite the amount of fabric on my body right now, my outfit makes no effort to hide my extra weight—apron belly included. I look cute for the gym downstairs, but Callum is seeing me when I'm not dressed to impress. Again.

"You've definitely made yourself at home." His eyes break away to look at the collection of houseplants I've added to the expansive windows in the living room, before returning to me. "Something tells me it wouldn't have made a difference if you had remembered," he says, raising dark brows in question.

I think about it for a brief moment. I always enjoy my music, feeling it in my body as I move, even in public. I'm not exactly shy.

"Honestly, probably not. Just let me know if I'm being too loud. I don't want to disturb your business." It's a sincere request, though probably unnecessary. Callum seems like the kind of guy who would bring up an annoyance the second it became an issue.

"I'd never allow you to disturb my business," he says simply, his face still giving no indication of how he's feeling. On one hand, I can't feel his irritation. But that just means he could be silently plotting my very slow and painful death and I won't know until it's too late.

I open my mouth, planning on asking him to warn me before he gets annoyed to the point of homicide, but I'm interrupted by the doorbell. Callum flashes me a look—a reminder of his rule—and moves to get it himself. I stay back, finishing my almost forgotten glass of water as he greets the newcomer.

"You look like hell," Callum says instead of a hello. Kinda rude, but okay.

"Staying up for twenty-eight hours will do that." The responding voice is deep and gruff.

The door closes and Callum walks back into the open living space. He's followed closely by a man who looks like he stepped out of a mafia movie casting call for *burly musclemen*.

Though a few inches shorter than Callum, he's still tall and wide, sturdy as an ox. His head is shaved bald, his broad face covered in salt-and-pepper stubble. If Mia was here, I'd bet her twenty dollars that his name is Boris or Ivan—something like that. When his eyes land on me, it's as if he's assessing whether I'm a threat.

"This is the house sitter." I don't miss the meaningful look Callum shares with the ox at my introduction. "Roscoe works my security." *Roscoe is close enough, I definitely would've won that twenty bucks.*

"Hi, I'm Lexie. Nice to meet you." I greet him like I would anyone else, offering him a smile, which seems to throw him off for a split second. He gives me a solemn nod, simply rasping a curt hello in return. Callum keeps his eyes on me during the exchange, his computer brain no doubt filing away everything he observes.

"You brought what I asked for?" Callum turns his focus to Roscoe. The bald man nods.

"Harris is an ass, but he's a well-connected, rich one," Roscoe grunts, producing a plain white envelope from his coat. Callum's face remains unreadable when he nods.

"Let's go to my office." They're both already walking, leaving me behind completely forgotten.

I'm not put off by it in the least—they can go about their *business*. I need to go shower and get ready for the day.

Wrapped in a towel fresh from the shower, I wipe the steam from the fogged vanity mirror and open my makeup bag while my phone rings. I can't help but smile when the line picks up and my best friend's voice sounds in the bathroom on speakerphone.

"Hey, bitch." The greeting is a term of endearment coming

from Mia. "I'm just filling out some paperwork, so I only have a few minutes. What's up?"

"I might not be able to watch *The Bachelor* with you tonight." Getting between Mia and her weekly reality tv fix is asking for trouble. I wince, bracing for her wrath.

"You better be joking." She's pissed, her tone promising terrible things if I don't take it back. Hopefully, my reason will be enough to smooth her temper.

"The owner of the penthouse I'm watching is here." I offer it like a golden nugget of prime gossip—something Mia lives for. Just as I was hoping, her tone shifts instantly.

"Shut up, who is it? Is he some crusty old businessman?" I can't help but laugh at the absurdity of her question. If she met this man, she'd have a field day.

"Businessman? Yes. But old and crusty are not words I'd use to describe him." My mascara wand pauses mid-swipe, my mind conjuring up the image of the man who owns the roof over my head.

"What words would you use to describe him?" She's begging me to paint a picture for her, so I oblige. Putting the tube of mascara on the vanity, I brace myself against the counter. What words would I use to describe the unreadable man I ate dinner with last night?

"Giant, beard, tattoos." Those are the physical descriptors she wants. But I can't help but add, "Intense. Complicated."

"He sounds hot." *If only she knew.*

"Hot? Yes. Someone I plan on spending any time with? No."

"Damn. So, hot-tattoo-guy is there. Does that mean you're coming home?" she asks hopefully, her voice sugary sweet. Nice try, Mia.

"He says he's only in the city for a few days on business, whatever that means. So I'm staying, apparently. I just have a slightly terrifying roommate for a while." And just like that, I've deflated her balloon of hope in one fell swoop.

"So, not only are you not coming back, but you can't watch

The Bachelor with me tonight? Hot-tattoo-guy sucks." She's pouting now, which I think is a step in the grieving process—right after depression and before acceptance.

"His name is Callum," I supply as I reach for my foundation.

"Fine, *Callum* sucks," she huffs indignantly. I let out a laugh, in total agreement.

"I might be able to watch, I just don't know yet. So, text me when you get home from the hospital, maybe I'll be free."

"Okay, okay fine." I can hear the switch in her tone, the added concern. "How are you, really? Are you sleeping?"

"Technically." I attempt a lighthearted joke to brush off her question. It doesn't work.

"Lexie—" I cut off her rant before it starts.

"I'm fine, I promise. It's just going to take some time."

"Is that what Julie says?" Julie is my therapist and my idol. She's seriously one of the best things that ever happened to me, after Mia and caffeine.

"Yes, Julie says taking some time away to refocus and heal is the best thing I can do for myself. Which is why I'm not at the hospital on contract right now."

"Instead, you're shacking up with rich, hot, bearded men. Maybe Julie's onto something."

"Yeah, I'm not sure this is exactly what Julie had in mind for me." I laugh, leaning forward to finish my makeup. A third voice sounds through the phone in the distance.

"Okay, I'm coming," Mia says, addressing the other person. "I gotta go, Lexie. But I'll call you later."

"Okay, bye. Love ya."

"Love you lots." With that, the call ends. Letting out a deep breath slowly I brace my hands on the vanity counter and stare into the mirror.

Eyes as blue as the summer sky gaze back at me over a delicate nose and soft, bow-shaped lips. All wrapped in fair skin that's never held a tan long enough to be considered anything other than porcelain—at least not without a good fake tan. Tilting my head to the side, light blonde hair tumbles over one shoulder and spills down to the small of my back in long loose curls. Other than the dark circles under my eyes, currently hidden beneath a little extra concealer, I look how I always look. But I don't feel the same.

Julie says taking time will help with the healing, and I trust her. She's gotten me through so much already. But so far all I've gotten is two weeks of sleepless nights and an overwhelming sense of feeling completely lost.

Helpless.

I'm twenty-six years old, with what I thought was a career path set for the rest of my life. But now I'm not so sure. After everything that's happened, I can't picture ever going back to how things used to be. I'm left teetering on the precipice of the unknown, dangerously close to plummeting into what could be total ruin.

Sucking in a deep breath, I push my shoulders back and finger comb my curls. I won't fall off the edge, my feet are firmly planted. There's no fucking way I'm going to lose myself—not with how hard I've worked to get here. I deserve so much more than that.

Touching up my gloss, I head into the closet to pick out an outfit. A short, soft pink sundress is the perfect choice for a day like today. Look good, feel good.

And, damn, do I look good.

I consider wearing heels, but that might be pushing it, especially with how much I'll be walking. The weather is nice, the late spring days warming up as we head into the East Coast summer. But I grab a sweater to wear later, just in case. I haven't quite figured out New York weather.

Taking my purse from the kitchen counter, I head out the front door. When I turn after locking it behind me, I collide with a solid frame. Stumbling back a few steps, I blink up at them.

"Sorry, I didn't mean to sneak up on you," the man apologizes, taking his own step back. His slender build stands at a modest height, but maybe I've just been standing next to Callum too much. Honey blonde waves fall across his forehead over soft green eyes. Compared to the other two men I've met in the last twenty-four hours, this guy looks friendly and relatively harmless.

"It's okay, I wasn't paying attention," I assure him with a smile.

"I'm here for Callum. But I don't think we've met." His eyes scan me as if to confirm before he makes his introduction. "I'm Enzo."

"Lexie," I offer. "I think Callum is in his office." An awkwardness settles over me as I struggle to figure out what to do next. Obviously, this introduction was an accident created by timing and coincidence. Not answering the door is one of Callum's rules, but I don't think literally bumping into someone outside counts. Should I just make an excuse to leave? I open my mouth but my response is cut off when the door opens behind me.

"Enzo, you're late." I turn to find Callum's irritated expression pointed at the newcomer. Enzo, however, doesn't seem the least bit bothered by the glare he's receiving.

"I was just meeting Lexie," he replies breezily, making Callum's focus cut to me. I can practically feel the accusation in his eyes, berating me for breaking the rules.

"I bumped into him on my way out." The need to explain the situation feels important, though I'm not sure why—maybe so he doesn't think I'm incapable of following simple instructions. My reputation for not being a complete idiot is on the line here.

Callum's gaze moves over me as if he just realized I'm dressed in something other than pajamas or workout attire.

"Out where?"

"I'm going to brunch." Glancing down at the time on my phone I realize I'm running late. "I have someone waiting for me, but it was nice to meet you Enzo." I flash another friendly smile before stepping around him. His head turns to watch after me along with the man in the doorway.

"You too, Lexie," Enzo calls after me. He then addresses Callum. "She seems nice, way too nice for you. Who is she?" I press the button for the elevator and wait for it to open.

"She's the house sitter," Callum replies simply. "Now get in here, we have shit to talk about." The elevator doors slide open with a soft ding. I step in and turn around to press the button in time to see Callum stepping aside to let his guest enter the penthouse. My eyes meet his for a moment.

"Alright, alright," Enzo complies. "Wait, the house sitter? What happened to Tony?" Whatever answer Callum gives is cut off as the elevator doors slide shut, closing in unison with the apartment door.

Walking up to the restaurant, Veronica is unmistakable. Her toned, willowy figure is accentuated by a colorful mini set, the sun kissing her rich, deep brown skin like an umber goddess. The colorful woman looks more suited for the runways in L.A. or Miami than the sidewalk in Manhattan.

"It's so unfair that God has such clear favorites," I speak up as I approach, making her turn.

"Stop pretending like you're not one of them." Ronnie grins, looking at me with a light squeal of excitement as she pulls me in for a hug. I breathe a laugh as we embrace, feeding off her energy.

"Hey girl, I missed you," she announces, pulling back to look down at me. We make quite the pair as physical complete opposites. Where I'm short, fair, and round, Veronica Price is tall, dark, and slender. But we share a love of margaritas and karaoke nights.

Ebony and ivory, as we were called around the hospital. And Ronnie made New York Presbyterian so much more fun. "I missed you too."

It's the truth, I've miss her. Ronnie doesn't take life too seriously, and her breezy attitude makes heavy situations feel lighter. It's the reason she works so well in the emergency room. When she's nursing everything remains on the surface, allowing her to leave work at the hospital instead of carrying it home with her. She doesn't let it weigh her down, not like I do.

The hostess seats us outside at a table with a cute white

umbrella, a beautiful floral arrangement in the center of the circular wrought iron table. The whole restaurant is aesthetically pleasing—with exposed brick, climbing ivy, and a charming macaroon station. It's the perfect place for brunch in the city, the kind of place where pretty people take photos to post on social media.

Maybe I'll take some photos myself.

The waitress is a friendly teenage girl on a mission, with a frizzy red ponytail and a green apron. She takes our order and speed-walks back inside, skirting around the other servers. Sitting back in the chair, Ronnie's dark brown eyes move over me in curiosity.

"So tell me all about your life," she says, crossing one long leg over the other. "You know I love to be in everyone's business. Just because you left doesn't mean that saves you."

"Not much to tell," I downplay, adjusting the neckline of my dress. "I'm house-sitting a penthouse uptown for some rich businessman for the next few months. The internet is supplying me with a bunch of recipes to try, and I've been getting back into drawing."

"That sounds very relaxing, now I'm getting jealous."

"It's been nice, not gonna lie." My fingers comb my hair back from my face. "So tell me what I've missed. It's only been a few weeks, but I'm sure Dr. Denton has done something asinine."

"Ugh, he has," Ronnie says animatedly. "He hooked up with one of the peds nurses, then snubbed her. She had a complete meltdown and went psycho on him in the cafeteria. It was crazy."

"Damn, I can't believe I missed that. Next time take a video for me."

"You know I will. I almost called you right after it happened, but then I got paged to deal with a woman who came in barefoot and ended up peeing in a trashcan." Ronnie rolls her eyes while I cringe at the mental image she's painted for me. "Damn girl, the unit isn't the same without you. Everyone is so boring and I have to deal with the crazies by myself."

"We handled a lot of crazies together." I laugh. The waitress walks up to deliver our food, placing my iced matcha and croissant sandwich in front of me before placing a spinach omelet, fruit salad, and latte in front of Ronnie. Next comes the pitcher for the bottomless mimosas—the real brunch necessity.

"We need a night out."

"Hell yeah, we do," I agree readily. "We need a girls' night out with karaoke and booze."

Ronnie is a bit of a party girl, and she definitely knows how to go out and have a good time. She might be a more surface-level friend but that's exactly what I need right now—light conversation, and distracting fun.

"Fuck, yeah! I'm so down."

"Okay, yay!" Taking a sip of my iced matcha, the caffeine greets me like a warm hug.

"Where's the apartment you're staying in?"

"Columbus Circle."

"Damn, girl! Central Park West? They don't just have money, they have *money*."

"It's a really bougie place, definitely out of my price range. I'm getting way too comfortable living in the penthouse, it's gonna be a slap back to reality when I go back to my place in a few months."

"You should come see my place in Harlem. I'm sure my one-bedroom makes your place in Oregon look like a palace."

I can't argue, I know what apartments are like in this city. The place I was renting before Tony set me up at Callum's was more like a closet than a studio apartment—plus it cost an arm and a leg. My home in Oregon, a comfortable two-bedroom, is more spacious and lacks the company of cockroaches and mutant rats.

Gross.

"So, who is this mystery businessman? Have you met the guy?" Ronnie asks, taking no time to pour the mimosas.

"His name is Callum. He's in the city for a few days for business, he showed up last night." I shrug, accepting the champagne glass and taking a generous sip. The bubbly goes down smoothly.

"But I don't know what kind of businessman he is, so my plan is to just stay out of the way."

"Probably a good idea." Ronnie drains her glass easily and reaches for a refill. "Leave the stuffy old guys to their business. It gives us more time for champagne." She lifts her glass towards me with a grin. I chink my glass with her, my head tipping back in a laugh.

"Cheers to that."

Spending three hours with Ronnie is the perfect little vacation from reality. Talking pop culture, discussing drama from the hospital, and sharing dating stories, fueled by carbs and mimosas—it's exactly what I needed. I'm bummed, and a little buzzed, when it's time to say goodbye and head back to the penthouse. But it's time to get back to real life.

Unfortunately.

The private elevator opens to the elegant corridor with black marble floors and cream porcelain tiled walls that reach up to the vaulted ceiling adorned with a magnificent crystal chandelier. Inside the oversized front door is an opulent entryway dressed in modern art that leads to the expansive grand room that makes up most of the first floor. A large waterfall island separates the impressive kitchen along the right wall from the rest of the open-concept space.

To the left is a dining room, with the living room taking up the corner along a wall of windows reaching up two stories that look out onto the terrace. A grand curved staircase by the living room leads to the lofted second floor with another guest room, laundry room, library, and a fully equipped home theater.

Dramatic light fixtures, chic art, and expensive finishes in neutral color schemes scream wealth and comfort. The entire space is a mix of modern luxury and traditional elegance. One of the best features of the penthouse is the breathtaking unobstructed view of the city and Central Park.

Callum is in the kitchen when I walk into the penthouse, and it seems like it's just us. My plan to ignore him and stay out of his way is proving to be impossible under the constant weight of his stare. I don't know why I thought I could pretend the man isn't staying here with me, he's built like a bull with an even more dominant demeanor.

"I thought you said you were going to brunch." His tone is calling me a liar, arms crossing as his hip leans against the counter beside me.

Is he always so serious? Must be exhausting.

"I did. I met up with a friend at Flora's on West 118th Street."

"That's basically in Harlem."

"I know, Ronnie lives in Harlem. It was perfect."

"So what's that?" Callum points to my shopping bag. The one holding my newest gold obsession. "I know restaurants have brunch promotions, but I didn't realize they started giving out gift bags with your meal."

"They don't . . . although they really should." Now that I'm thinking about it, getting a free purse with lunch would be too amazing for words. "I did some shopping on my way back. I'm a sucker for a pretty window display."

I didn't mean to take the long way back to the apartment, but then the sunlight hit a gold handbag in just the right way, making it sparkle and call to me from a store window. I had to stop, I'm only human—one who can't resist beautiful, shiny things.

"What is it?" He nods towards the bag.

"You ask an awful lot of questions." I tilt my head up and to one side. "Why so curious?" He doesn't acknowledge my question. Instead, he simply stands and waits for me to answer his. Clearly, trying to get out of telling him what he wants to know is pointless.

"It's a handbag. A pretty, mini, gold one. There was a purple one I almost got too, but I couldn't justify the price. Especially since I have nothing to wear it with."

Stepping around Callum, I open the fridge to reach for the

can of Mountain Dew that's been calling to me since I finished my matcha.

I'm the first person to admit that I'm attached but calling it an addiction would mean there's something wrong with it. I prefer the term *simple pleasure*.

The can pops with a hiss when I press down the tab. The first sip feels so comforting, the carbonation greeting me like an old friend. I know one sip isn't enough to start feeling the effects of the caffeine, but I swear some of the exhaustion weighing me down eases from my shoulders. Twelve ounces can't make up for the fact that I haven't slept more than a few hours a night for the last two weeks, but it definitely helps.

"Do you drink anything else?" Callum's eyes move pointedly to the can of soda in my hand. I shrug as I take a sip of my soda.

"Energy drinks. Oh, and margaritas." I smile prettily when he scowls in disapproval. "But it's too early for that."

"It eats you from the inside out," he grates. I look down at my soft, curvy body.

"You're right, I'm practically wasting away here." There's a healthy dose of sarcasm in my voice accompanying my nonchalant smile. His hazel eyes narrow at me, unamused.

"That stuff will kill you." Callum is glaring at the can I'm holding like it personally insulted his family. I bite back a smile, doing my best not to laugh in his face. He's so serious.

"So I've heard." I lift the can to my lips and take an exaggerated sip. "But until then, it'll keep me happy and caffeinated."

The sound of the front door opening and closing cuts off whatever Callum has to say; a male voice rings through the entryway. "I hope you have coffee in here, I've got the biggest fucking hangover of my life," the man announces as he appears in the doorway.

He's tall, maybe a few inches shorter than Callum's towering height. The term *pretty boy* comes to mind with his tousled black hair and playful whiskey-brown eyes. He's extremely good-looking; he almost doesn't look like a real person.

"You're letting yourself into my apartment now?" Callum asks flatly.

"You get pissy whether or not I ring the bell; this way I get to see that look of excitement on your face even faster."

"We have work to do now that you're finally here," Callum says, annoyed.

"It's too fucking early for this."

"It's two o'clock in the afternoon," Callum points out.

"Exactly, I woke up three hours early for you. You should be grateful." The newcomer's attention catches on me, his eyes lighting in curiosity. "And who is this?"

His gaze is lacking the hint of disgust and judgment I've learned to expect from a guy like this. The rakish player type who bed hops, using his looks and charms to get whatever he wants, staying out all night and sleeping late into the afternoon.

"He's about to tell you I'm the house sitter, which is apparently all the introduction I need nowadays," I say, watching the look of intrigue flash across his almost too-pretty, angular face. "Then you'll both look at each other and have a silent conversation about me like I'm not standing right here. It's fascinating every time." I laugh knowingly when the new guy shares a look with Callum. "Just like that."

"Ignore her, Liam." Callum's easy dismissal gets me fired up to piss him off. Let's see if I can pick at his control enough to get it to crack.

"Ahh, *Liam*. He was talking a lot of shit about you earlier; maybe you two should have a little heart-to-heart." I mock a serious expression as I lie to stir the pot, raising my eyebrows smugly at Callum's annoyed expression.

"Lexie." My name is a warning. Callum isn't amused, but Liam is. He poorly disguises his laugh as a cough, hiding his grin behind his hand when Callum's glare cuts over to him. I smile sweetly and keep bold eye contact as I move around the men to the living room.

"I'll leave you to it." I raise my can of Mountain Dew to them, picking up my bottle of glitter nail polish off the coffee table and shaking it in the other hand. Plopping down onto the couch to resume the episode of *Real Housewives* I was watching earlier, I begin to prep my toes for the polish. I've already watched every season, but the petty drama never gets old.

There's something about watching super rich people's ridiculous problems that feeds my soul. *Like, can you believe Lisa didn't invite Vicky to the fundraiser gala after Vicky invited her to the birthday party on the super yacht?* It's unhinged, I love it.

CHAPTER FOUR

CALLUM

"You look like you just stumbled out of bed," I remark, eyeing Liam's wrinkled shirt and unshaved face. Wavy black hair falls over his forehead in disarray, a five-o'clock shadow covering his usually clean-shaven face. His lack of presentation clearly not affecting his confidence, he smirks at me.

"Oh, I did just roll out of bed. It just wasn't mine." His dark eyebrows jump cockily. "It was a long night, I didn't get much sleep." Liam Caldwell spreads his arms along the back of the sofa, long legs stretched out in front of him. He looks like the cat after eating the canary. His toothy grin begs me to ask for more details like a high school gossip, but I don't have time to hear about his sexcapades at the moment.

"I hope you washed your hands. I don't want your STDs getting on my couch."

"What's got your panties in a twist? Does it have something to do with Blondie out there?" Liam asks, nodding his head towards the door that separates my office from where Lexie sits in the living room. She can't hear us. Soundproofing each of the rooms in my apartment was one of my top priorities when I moved in. I take my privacy seriously.

"Tony decided to test my patience and made a switch." The bastard thought he was so clever, sending Lexie in here like I wouldn't notice. She'd rounded the kitchen corner like the curvy, blonde complication she is.

I should've known when I walked in to find the steak sizzling on the stove that Tony wasn't the one living here. He can't cook for shit. He doesn't even try, instead leaving mountains of takeout containers to pile up by the trash. Drives me fucking insane, my place always smelled like day-old Kung Pao chicken when I got back into town. But Lexie's steak was cooked perfectly.

"He thinks that—what—dangling a juicy blonde in front of you will keep you from caring?" Liam tsks in disappointment. "I never figured he was that big of a fucking idiot to run out on a contract. Especially with you."

"He didn't. Technically." My grip tightens on the desk as frustration builds inside me. Tony is a coward for it, but he's not stupid. He knew what he was doing when he set Lexie up in his place. "There's an exigent circumstance clause in his contract that allows him to void the deal if he finds a suitable replacement who agrees to take over his position."

"Blondie agreed to work for you?" Liam asks.

"Lexie," I correct. "Lexie signed the agreement to take over Tony's placement as the house sitter." I created the house-sitting position as a front, a ploy for tax and payment purposes. "By legal definitions, he didn't break the contract."

Lexie is definitely a suitable replacement for watching my penthouse while I'm away. The house plants that now line the windows in sun-dappled greenery, and the spa-scented candles that are always burning, make that clear. She's turned this place into a home in a little over two weeks—something I haven't done in two years. It aligns with the contractual agreement exactly. And like the slimy snake he is, Tony slithered right through the tiny loophole.

"You don't go by legal definitions," Liam points out with a sarcastic laugh. He's right, I don't. I look at the details of every situation, identifying each one by weight of importance and consequence. If I feel cheated, no law will stop me. I'm meticulous.

"No, I don't. But Tony got away clean, even by my definitions." Tony's ability to wriggle himself loose from my legal bonds was unexpected. I'll never admit it, but it is slightly impressive. As twisted as it is, I almost respect Tony for his ability to screw me over in his act of self-interest. It's the only thing keeping him safe from my temper.

"So what does that mean for us? We're out a medic on payroll." Liam has a point, fueling my agitation. This isn't part of the plan, which is unacceptable. I never allow loose ends. I need to find a skilled medical professional that I can shackle with a contract and gag with an NDA.

"Lexie is a nurse. That's where Tony found her, at New York Presbyterian." I've already considered my options, and she has potential. There's just no telling how she would work out. The type of medical care that comes with my line of work isn't pretty and usually comes with a certain level of violence. The pretty pink nurse on the couch in my living room isn't what I'd call an ideal candidate.

"You really think Blondie is someone who wants to work for you?" Liam asks skeptically. "Or better yet, could you even work with her? She's in there watching reality tv, drinking a Mountain Dew, painting her toenails sparkly pink."

"It's not ideal, but it's an option. She's a nurse who worked in the ER of the best hospital in the city. But there's no way of knowing if our pretty pink nurse has the level of skill I need," I muse. Testing her seems riskier than it's worth; there's no telling what would happen when she's put under that type of pressure.

The memory of our introduction comes to mind. She'd been a deer in headlights when she rounded that corner and found me standing in my kitchen. She hadn't freaked out, screamed, or cried. Her instincts were to threaten me with the authorities, even when she had no way of contacting anyone. Her bravado was almost amusing when she ordered me to leave—even though I clearly had the upper hand in the situation. She'd handled herself calmly, blinking up at me while she processed everything before responding. Then she demanded to see my ID.

The thought of how she criticized my license photo makes my lips twitch with amusement. She's a grown woman who's easily distracted by sparkly objects and drinks like a college student, but something in my gut tells me there's more to Lexie than the shiny exterior she flounces around with.

"So what's this new problem that got you back into the city?" Liam changes the subject, leaning forward to rest his arms on his thighs. I sit back in my chair and smooth my hand over my beard.

"I don't know yet, Senator Harris was tight-lipped on the phone and insisted we meet in person. He'll be here in an hour, I'll have more information then."

"Do you want me to stick around for the meeting? Or am I just here for you to look at my pretty face for a while—though I have to say, you're no longer lacking in that department with your girl out there." Liam and I don't have a lot of things in common, our personalities are almost in complete opposition to each other. His habit of blurting out exactly what he's thinking and wearing his emotions on his face like an accessory goes against my every instinct for discretion and practiced control.

He's always found pleasure in women with more to their figure than skin and bones, one of the few things we do have in common. I'm not surprised Lexie's caught his eye, even if it's not something he plans to act on. He knows I won't allow it anyway. Letting Liam manwhore with people who work for me in any capacity has always been off-limits. Lexie's no exception.

"Your face doesn't even compete," I say, reaching into my desk drawer for the large manila envelope. "I need you to take these contracts to Ash Wilton's residence; it's a brownstone on fifth avenue. He's waiting there with his security. Have him sign both copies, then deliver the one in the red file directly to Jeffrey Lindstein at the Black-Moore club uptown."

"Ash Wilton, as in the hedge fund manager? Signing a confidential contract with Lindstein, the president of American Capital Bank? Sound the stock-market alarms."

"You're lucky you're better at keeping your mouth closed

than keeping it in your pants, Caldwell," I deadpan, earning a grin as he feigns a wounded expression.

"Ouch, slut shaming is hurtful." He stands, raking a hand through his tousled hair vainly before taking the contracts. Jokes aside, I know I can trust Liam with even the most confidential information. He's an ass about it, but he's been nothing but loyal. Not to mention he's the best wheelman in the country, which comes in handy in my line of work.

Opening the envelope, he thumbs through the files to familiarize himself with the contents. There's no need to double-check what I give him, he knows that, but he does anyway. It's one of the reasons I hired him in the first place.

Following him out of my office, we step out right as Lexie is ending a phone call over at the kitchen island. The room smells faintly like nail polish, and I can see her toenails are now pink as she swings her feet absently from her perch on the stool.

"Bye, babe," Lexie says, hanging up the phone as Liam and I walk out of my office. She turns to catch me staring, my gaze remaining steady on her as I observe and consider.

"You're dating someone?" I ask. If she's in a relationship, that might affect my business. Liam strolls over to the coffeemaker and helps himself to a cup, chugging it black like a frat boy at a kegger.

"Oh, no I'm single," she replies, tucking a tendril of blonde hair behind her ear. "I was talking to my best friend, Mia."

"You call your friend *babe*?" My tone is skeptical with an edge of challenge.

"What, you don't use terms of endearment with your friends?" she asks, her brows raising with a teasing smile. Liam turns to face us, leaning against the counter as he waits for the caffeine to counter the hangover he's fighting.

"No," I reply flatly. Liam's shit-eating grin spells trouble.

"Of course we do," Liam jumps in. "Right, bestie?"

My glare is withering.

"Fuck off." My growl only makes his grin grow.

"You have such a way with words." Seeing the urge to shoot him cross my mind, Liam holds up his hands in surrender. "As much as I'd love to stick around for this brotherly bonding, I'm leaving while I can still walk out on my own."

"Good idea," I state, watching him pick up the envelope of contracts from the counter.

"It was nice meeting you, Lexie. Don't let grumpy Cal here run you off." He shoots her a wink that makes my trigger finger twitch. Lexie's laugh is light and easy, a cheerful response that seems to be her natural reaction to most things.

"I'm not run off that easily," she assures him, turning her dazzling smile on me. Her attention radiates warmth and light, and I like being caught in those rays.

Liam downs one last gulp of coffee before taking a few steps backwards towards the front door.

"Alright, I'm gone. These papers aren't going to sign themselves." He lifts his hand to salute me with the envelope, flashing Lexie his best playboy smile, before turning to leave. The sound of the front door closing punctuates his exit and Lexie turns to gaze at me. The look on her expressive face is a mix of curiosity and humor—like we're in on a private joke together.

"What's that look for?" I should be irritated that she's practically laughing at me, but I'm tempted to smile with her instead.

"Oh, nothing," she teases. "You just have interesting friends, that's all."

"If you're hoping to get Liam's number, the answer's no," I inform her. "I don't let the people who work for me get involved with each other."

"Why not?" She seems genuinely curious, but her question doesn't confirm or deny my suspicions.

"It's not good for my business when things get messy. And getting involved with Liam is always messy."

"I guess that makes sense," she comments thoughtfully, her head tilting to one side as she regards me. "That's fine though, he's not my type. I don't date anyone prettier than me."

The idea that Liam is more attractive than Lexie in any way is laughable. But there's no need to correct her. From what I've seen, Lexie is very comfortable in her generously voluptuous body.

As she should be.

"I have another meeting coming in half an hour." I change the subject before I decide to ask her what her type is. Walking over to the fridge, I pull out a chilled bottle of water.

"I'm leaving to get my nails done, so you'll have the place to yourself for the next few hours," she assures me. Leaning my shoulder against the fridge, my eyes move down to her freshly painted toes.

"You just did your nails. Or do you just like the fumes?"

"I'm going to get a manicure," she says, wiggling her unpolished fingers at me. "So I had to paint my toes or else the nail techs will judge me for having crusty feet." Her tone while explaining the impractical logic makes it sound like the most reasonable thing in the world. I don't argue.

Lexie hops down from the stool, smoothing her pretty little dress over dangerous curves, and slips on a pair of sandals. When she steps around me to grab her purse from the counter, I'm surrounded by a delicious scent. It's light and citrus, and smells like heaven. Like a moth to a flame, I'm stepping closer.

She smells really fucking good.

Oblivious to the magnetism pulling me towards her, Lexie chirps a goodbye to me before heading out the door. My eyes don't leave her until she's out the front door, silently thanking whoever invented short pink sundresses.

My next meeting is due to arrive in less than twenty minutes, which gives me time to change. Normally I don't care to style myself for my clientele, but working with political figures comes with a certain dress code. And right now I'm not dressed the part.

Stepping into my closet, I'm greeted by black and white. Black pants, suit coats, dress shirts, shoes, socks. A small section holds the crisp white button-downs in stark contrast to the rest of my wardrobe. Black and white, the only colors I wear—save a stray pair of charcoal-gray lounge pants or workout shorts.

White is clear, unforgiving. It shows every flaw, every element that touches it—and in some cases what resides beneath it. White is disarming honesty, authority. It's a weapon I carry when it suits me.

Black is the opposite side of the same coin. Black keeps your secrets, sharing nothing but silence. The sharp darkness easily swallows the evidence of your wrongdoings—disguising your weaknesses, hiding your intentions. Taking over all other colors, black is domination and control.

Stripping off the black dress shirt, I replace it with a crisp white one, buttoning the front and the cuffs to hide my tattoos. If you look closely enough, you can see the dark ink on my skin through the light material. The only people who can get close enough to notice already know who I am. Everyone else gets to see who I show them.

CHAPTER FIVE

CALLUM

"Senator's here, boss," Roscoe says from the doorway of my office. I nod to him, ready for the men waiting to be allowed entrance.

"Bring them in," I say. Roscoe steps aside to let three men enter before following them in and closing the door. The two black suits are lackeys, glorified bodyguards who remain standing along the wall on either side of the door. Roscoe moves to stand diligently behind me as I rise from my office sofa to greet the man who brought me back to the city.

"Russo." The suit he's wearing is flashy, designer, and far more expensive than any elected official should be able to afford. US Senator of New York Richard Harris flaunts his importance any way he can. He extends his hand, the gaudy Rolex on his wrist catching the light—something I'm sure is intentional.

"Senator." I accept his hand, shaking it firmly. "I hear you have a problem." Walking around my desk, I get comfortable in my chair. "It must be a pretty big one if we couldn't have this conversation over the phone. So here I am."

Harris smoothly unbuttons his suit coat and sits opposite me, but I notice how his hand trembles ever so slightly. Something has him rattled, no matter how hard he tries to hide it. "I pulled a lot of strings to get your name, and I know your success rate.

The fact that no one talks about you tells me you're exactly who I need."

"Are you going to tell me about this problem? Mind reading has never been my preferred form of communication."

"My daughter Lottie—Charlotte—was taken." He clears his throat when his voice breaks with emotion. "She's sixteen."

"When and where?" I ask.

"Saturday afternoon. She told the housekeeper she was going to meet up with her friends to go dress shopping for her junior formal. But her best friend called our house an hour later to see if Lottie was still coming, because she never showed up. Her phone goes straight to voicemail, and I can't see her location anymore. It last pinged half a block from the store she was going to."

"You're sure she was taken? Sometimes teens run away."

"Not Lottie," Richard snaps, his stress getting the better of him. He reins in the emotion, smoothing down his tie. "She knows better than to do something like that. Someone has her."

"Any contact? Ransom demands?"

"None. We haven't heard a single word."

"Why not go to the police? Why come to me?"

"There's a chance that whoever took her doesn't know they have the daughter of a US Senator. I don't need the press getting a hold of this and making things worse. We're keeping it quiet until we know who has her."

"I don't have to tell you how girls usually end up when they're snatched off the street."

"I don't need a lecture about what happens in this city," Richard snarls. "They call you the Fixer because you do what you have to in order to solve impossible problems. And judging by how much political capital I spent just to get your name, you must be the man for the job. I need my daughter back, whatever the cost."

I stare at the man across the desk, contemplating. Snatch-and-grabs off the street come with a level of chaos that strategic kidnappings don't have. But that also means less red tape I have to avoid in my retrieval process. My methods work best when there aren't bureaucrats breathing down my neck. Men like this rarely approve of the lengths I go to for answers, or rather how it might make them look. It's only behind closed doors they're the first to endorse extreme measures and quick to demand results.

Harris is notorious for cutting corners and padding pockets to get his own way. His political career is a colorful one for people who know what they're looking at. And getting into bed with a self-serving official like the senator is a double-edged sword—his greedy arrogance both a tool and a hindrance. He's not nearly the most dangerous man I've dealt with, his status doesn't faze me at all. But having a senator owe me a favor could come in handy. And it all comes down to if he can pay. My results don't come cheap.

"My methods aren't up for discussion or negotiation," I state. Harris nods, but his eyes narrow.

"Agreed." I can hear the *but* coming before he continues. "But if I'm paying you, I expect you to keep me in the loop."

"Emotions make things messy, and you're too close to this," I say calmly. "I'll keep you informed of any progress, but you're only as involved as I allow you to be. You don't call the shots here, Senator. I do."

His jaw ticks tellingly, lips pressed in a straight line. A man like Harris doesn't enjoy being put in his place or told what to do. Power and influence mean he's used to being in charge. It's best he realizes right now—I'm the one in control.

"Fine," he grits through clenched teeth. "You'll do it?"

"I require half of my fee up front and the rest upon delivery. Get me every piece of information you have."

Harris motions for his man by the door to step forward with a thick file.

"This is everything we have. Lottie's photo, description, schedule, and medical history. A background on the housekeeper, Caroline. And our initial sweep of the areas she could have been taken from."

"Wire the funds, I'll find your daughter." I slide him the routing information with my fee, and he accepts it readily. Taking the file, I flip through it. As I scan the information to formulate a plan, Harris pulls out his phone.

"Don't just find her, Russo. Get her back for me, I don't care what it takes. I need her back." As he's speaking, my phone lights up with confirmation of his payment.

"I'll be in touch, Senator." I stand, holding out my hand. Richard Harris stands as well, his hand trembles tellingly against mine as he shakes it. I can see the tortured look in his somber eyes, even as he tries to present himself as calm and dignified.

He can make demands and throw his money and political weight around. But it won't allow him to be in control of this situation, and he knows it. We both do. Instead, he's forced to depend on a man like me to make everything better.

The moment the senator's gone, I'm memorizing every single detail listed in the file Harris provided. Roscoe's already on his way to the grab site, instructed to obtain security footage from the businesses in the area of the abduction. He's also carrying a wad of cash to grease the necessary palms to get the information we need to identify who took Charlotte.

The file reads like a scrapbook of Charlotte Harris' life—grades in school, extracurriculars, dietary restrictions, clothing size. She's five-foot-five and one hundred and fifteen pounds, with long black hair that matches her mother's, and round green eyes. She has a heart-shaped birthmark on her left shoulder, kiwi gives her hives, and she just got her braces off after a year and a half.

"It only took one camera to get a picture," Roscoe announces when he returns, placing the rest of the petty cash on the desk to be returned to the safe. "It was quick, but the man who took her is no criminal mastermind. I'm betting it was a moment of convenience, it didn't look planned. The fucker didn't even bother to cover his face, and in broad daylight."

"You got a name for me?" I accept the file Roscoe extends,

flipping it open. A grainy image stares at me, the screenshot from the security footage capturing the face of Charlotte's abductor.

Wiry frame, receding hairline, and an unfortunate crooked nose. His eyes are wild as he stands frozen in the photo, his hand clamped over her mouth as he totes her the few feet from the formal dress store to the delivery van parked in the shadows of a nearby alley. He looks familiar, a common criminal lackey hired to do the dirty jobs others don't want their fingerprints getting on.

"Kellen Gatz," Roscoe states, waiting for me to flip through the information he's dug up on our kidnapper.

Just as I suspected, the man's jacket is full of petty crime—shoplifting, grand theft auto, assault and battery. He's been arrested a handful of times, but usually walks due to "lack of evidence." Meaning he does the dirty work for people connected enough to keep him out of trouble. Too bad for him, I have my own justice system. No one can keep him safe from my due process.

"He's got a few outstanding warrants. Plus, he has a bad habit of putting money down on horses that don't win. His long shots never pay off, and he can't afford his losses."

"You know where to find him?" I glance up to see Roscoe incline his head in confirmation. "Bring him to the club. Felix is out of town, we'll have the place to ourselves to get answers. Take Enzo, I need this quick and clean." I don't need to remind Roscoe about discretion, he's the definition of tact. He could stab someone in a crowded subway car and be gone before they even felt it.

"You got it, boss."

It takes Roscoe and Enzo less than six hours to bag Gatz. They said it was easy; he was stumbling around in the dark after losing another race. Probably trying to sneak out on his commitments before anyone came to collect.

Coward.

I enter the building through the back door, avoiding the crowds of drunk partiers raving in the nightclub. Pulse is one of the top nightclubs in New York, owned by Felix Rivera. Our arrangement is mutually beneficial; I keep his reckless sons from being arrested and ending up in the tabloids for their drunken, drug-fueled rampages, and he gives me free rein over his clubs and their discreet backrooms.

"Our man of the hour," I say, stepping into the storage room. The pulsing sounds of the busy nightclub quiet as I close the door behind me and flip the lock. The beautiful silence that falls over the room speaks to the quality of the soundproofing that's gone into this building. Something I plan to take full advantage of. "Do you know why you're here?"

"I'm gonna pay it back, I swear. I have a big payday coming, you'll get your money," Kellen grovels, pulling at the restraints keeping him secured to the chair. His eyes are just as wild in person as they were in the photo, the overhead light casting dramatic shadows over his unsightly features.

"I'm not some bookie, Kellen," I say. "I am a debt collector, just not the kind you're used to. You took something I'm looking for. A girl."

"I don't know what you're talking about. I didn't take any girls."

"Even if I didn't have video evidence proving otherwise, you're a terrible liar. For someone who gambles so much, you really need to work on your poker face."

"I'm telling you, you got the wrong guy."

"Should I refresh your memory?" I hold up the picture. "You took Charlotte on her way into a store to try on prom dresses."

"Fuck you, I'm not saying anything."

"If she's not your big payday, that means you took her for another reason. For yourself. Do you like teenage girls, Kellen? Is that it? Couldn't resist her headband and training bra?" I lace my taunting with malice and disgust. "Maybe I should rid the world of a sick bastard who gets off on snatching young girls from the street."

"No, hey, I'm not into that!"

"Why did you take her?" His silence stretches until I lose my patience.

With a sigh, I take a step back and nod to Roscoe. He knows what to do. His fist lands a powerful hit to Kellan's temple, the force of it teetering the chair. I'm not going to lie, Kellen's cry of pain is satisfying. The second punch splits his lip nicely. If Roscoe wasn't holding back, our guest would be spitting out a few teeth right now. But Kellen is soft. I can already see he's ready to fold, two punches are all it takes for him to crumble. Roscoe can see it too, but he gears up to take another hit for good measure.

"She fit the list," Kellen grits out between clenched teeth. "White girl under eighteen, dark hair and light eyes." I nod to Roscoe and he steps back, lowering his fist. Stepping closer, I tower over my captive.

"Whose list?" I ask, running a steady hand over my beard. My stare drills into him, but he struggles to glare with his battered eye already beginning to swell. He presses his lips together like that'll keep me from getting my answers. I let out a heavy breath of disappointment. "You know I'm going to get the answer, Kellan. It's just a matter of whether or not you get to walk out of here once I do. Don't make me deal with killing you and just tell me who has the girl."

"She—" he stammers. "She's already gone." My expression darkens.

"Who has her?" Repeating the question, my voice cuts with the fury pushing against my control. The mask is slipping, and if Kellen doesn't give me a fucking name, he's going to feel my full wrath.

"It was just a job, good money. They gave me a list." The excuses are flooding from Kellen's mouth, his self-preservation kicking in. *Fucking finally.* "I got debts." His head falls forward in defeat. Roscoe walks behind him, grabbing a fistful of greasy hair, and yanks Kellen's head up to look at me.

"Your debts just got worse. You took from the wrong family, and now you owe reparations." My tone is ice cold. "A name. Give me the name of who has her." When he doesn't answer me, I nod to Roscoe, who brings a knife up to his throat.

"The Russians," he chokes out, "Anton Kozlov." I recognize the name. *Bratva*. The Russians are huge on the alcohol and sex trades. As head of the Russian Mafia, it's Viktor Mikhailov's territory. I've built a tenuous working relationship with Mikhailov over the years. This isn't the best news, but definitely something I can work with.

"That wasn't so hard now, was it Kellen?" Nodding to Roscoe, he reaches for the black bag—the bag that comes into play when some fucker has to pay for their sins.

"I gave you the name," Kellen stammers, tugging against his restraints. "So, you'll let me go now, right? You got what you wanted."

"Not quite." Those two words cut him off at the knees. "It's time you pay your debts."

"I don't have any money to give you."

"Oh, I know you don't," I reply evenly. "So we'll be taking something else."

Roscoe steps forward, the light glinting off the shiny metal hedge clippers in his hand. Kellen's eyes latch onto the tool, bugging almost out of his head. Something inside him snaps. Like a rat caught in a trap, his body heaves and wrenches against his binds, the chair rocking beneath him.

"Wait, I'll get you money! If you just give me some time, I can get you whatever you want," he sputters, seizing when Roscoe's approach doesn't falter.

There's no delaying his punishment, my mind is made up. He'll get what he deserves, my justice carried out by Roscoe without so much as a blink.

"Trusting you would make me an idiot. You're not leaving until you pay in full."

Roscoe cuts the red tape securing his left wrist to the chair. Kellen yanks against the other man's grip on his arm—eyes wild, yelping and begging.

Pitiful.

"What the fuck are you doing? No, stop!" Kellen shouts, struggling violently.

Growing irritated with handling our guest's panicked flailing, Roscoe slams his fist into our rodent's stomach. Caving against the power of the punch, Kellen folds in on himself like a rag doll. Suddenly, there's no fight when Roscoe lifts the hand to his clippers.

Slotting the pinky between the sharp blades, my enforcer looks back at me for the go-ahead. I hold up a hand for him to pause, stepping closer to bend over the man in the chair.

"Every time you miss your precious finger, you'll think about how much of a goddamn coward you are for taking children."

With that, I give the signal.

The wet crunch of slicing flesh and severing bone sounds distinctly in the silent room, punctuated by Kellen's scream of agony. Cut down to a nub, the pinky falls to the floor in a spray of blood. The yelling only lasts a few minutes before fading into mournful moaning and settles on catatonic silence. Job done, Roscoe steps back to wipe the blood from the clippers and tucks them back into the black bag.

My head tilts, feeling not an ounce of remorse as I gaze down at the subdued man dripping blood on my crisp plastic sheeting. I'm sure he's committed acts that deserve far worse, but Charlotte is the only job I'm here for. Letting my repulsion motivate me would only cause unnecessary problems; it's a lesson I've learned a hundred times over. Something my father and the rest of *The Family* have yet to realize. Violence has its place, but there are better ways of getting what you want—and they usually require a lot less sacrifice.

"They say confession sets you free. Do you feel any lighter now?" My taunting tone barely earns a slow blink against his swollen eye. The lights are on, but no one's home.

Standing to stare at the display of retribution sends a wave of satisfaction through me. I came here for answers and I'll be walking out with results. Watching Kellen Gatz the kiddie-snatcher bleed was a bonus. A pretty fucking good one.

After a few minutes of silence, I turn on my heel to head to the door. I got a name, it's time to keep moving forward. As much as I enjoyed watching the mutilation, I can't let Kellen leave with his bone exposed. Blood trails tend to bring unwanted public attention and questions from authorities I don't intend to answer.

"Where you going, boss?" Roscoe calls after me. I pause in the doorway.

"Without Tony, we need a new medic. Our pretty pink nurse is about to try out for the position."

CHAPTER SIX

LEXIE

Knocking turns into pounding as I shuffle my way through the darkness towards the bedroom door. When I open it, the light that spills in from the hallway practically blinds me. I can't help but squint up at the man standing on the other side in confusion.

"Callum?" He stares down at me, dressed and alert like it isn't the middle of the night. There's no reason for someone to look so hot at this hour; it's almost as blinding as the hall light. "What's going on?"

He scans me head to toe, from my long messy braid to my pajama shorts and bare feet, before his focus moves past me. A voice sounds softly behind me. "Who's in here with you?"

My eyes follow his gaze, brain lagging. "Oh, that's just the tv." The response is sleep-addled and delayed, but it's the truth.

"You're watching tv?" Those piercing hazel eyes are pinned on me now.

"I fell asleep watching something." Again, technically the truth. He doesn't need to know that I can't sleep without something playing, like a toddler needing a nightlight. Rubbing the sleep from my eyes, I change the subject. "Do you need something? Why are you knocking on my door at three-thirty in the morning?"

"I need you to come with me."

No idea what I was expecting Callum to say, but that's not

it. I blink a few more times—once, twice—processing. He waits calmly, observing and assessing while I absorb.

"What?" I need more information. It's too damn late for this. Or is it too early?

"Someone needs medical attention and I'm borrowing those skilled hands of yours." Again, not what I was expecting to hear. Someone needs medical attention? The questions are already forming.

"Is someone hurt?" I ask. His eyes roam from my face, looking pointedly at my silky powder-blue pajama set. I follow his gaze, barely registering my attire before bringing my eyes back to his.

"Put on your scrubs, Doc. We're leaving in five."

My brain still fighting through the fog, I leave Callum in the doorway and shuffle into the walk-in closet. Digging through my nightmare of a suitcase, the first pair of scrubs I find are pastel pink. Whatever, scrubs are scrubs. My braid is too messy to save, so a finger-brushed ponytail will have to do. Tugging on mismatched socks and shoving my feet into my ASICS, I'm still securing my hair into an elastic when I emerge from the closet.

Callum's large frame fills the doorway, muscled tattooed arms crossed. The sleeves of his crisp white dress shirt are rolled up to his elbows, something he seems to do often out of habit. As soon as his suit coat comes off, his sleeves are being rolled up. The intricate ink covering his muscled arms is in stark contrast to the crisp color of his shirt. I can see the shadow of where the ink continues up his skin beneath the fabric. Do his tattoos cover more than just his arms?

"Pink, huh?" There he goes again with those eyes of his, taking in every single detail.

I simply shrug, looking up at him expectantly. For someone who was in such a hurry three minutes ago, he doesn't seem too rushed to move out of my room now. The look I flash him is full of expectation.

"Are we going, or did you make me get out of bed for nothing?"

He looks at me for a while longer, almost as if just to prove that he can. Finally, he steps back into the hallway and sweeps his arm out in a gesture for me to walk ahead of him.

"After you, Doc," he murmurs, the nickname making me sigh in annoyance. But I relent and step out into the hallway anyway.

He walks closely behind me, almost too close. His tall frame towers over mine, looming and crowding. Hyper aware of his proximity, I glance up at him in the elevator, my shoulder to his chest. There's no way he means to stand so close to me, but something in his eyes when he looks down at me says he knows exactly what he's doing.

Nothing he does is by accident.

The private elevator opens up to the parking garage and I follow him to a car I've never seen before. A glossy, black vintage number that looks like a classic muscle car from the 1970s. I fail to recognize the symbol on the back as he holds the passenger door open for me.

The engine rumbles. It's the only sound in the car as Callum navigates the city streets. This silence is giving my mind too much opportunity to form questions I don't have answers to. Finally, I can't help myself, not knowing is driving me crazy.

"Where are we going?" I look over at him, the passing city lights flashing across his strong features. The white of his shirt catches the light, emphasizing his broad solid frame filling the seat to capacity. He stares straight ahead at the road, not sparing me a glance when he responds.

"Not far." He gives me nothing to work with.

"What kind of medical attention do they need?" I try again. The more time I have to prepare myself mentally, the better.

"You'll see when we get there." It's a non-answer, really.

"Really? That's all I get?" The agitation in my tone tells him just how fed up I'm getting with all this. He seems completely unbothered by my growing annoyance.

"Your medical expertise is needed," Callum says simply. "That's all you need to know."

Yeah, that's not how it works. If he thinks this conversation is over, he's dead wrong. I wish I knew what he was thinking, but I doubt it'll do any good to ask him. His lack of response almost keeps me from asking more questions. Honestly, I wouldn't be surprised if that's his goal.

"If someone is sick, I'll need specific medication. If they're injured, I might need to stop for supplies." I'm going to keep insisting until I get something out of the vault that is Callum Russo. But he doesn't even flinch, simply tilting his head to look over at me lazily. Here we are, driving through the city in the dark of the very early morning because someone needs a nurse for a mysterious reason, and he's acting like we're running an errand.

"You'll have what you need." His assurance does nothing to convince me. But instead of bombarding him with the other million questions on the tip of my tongue, I simply close my mouth. There's no point in wasting my energy trying to get answers he's obviously not going to give me. The only sign that Callum notices my resignation is another half glance in my direction.

He wasn't lying when he said we aren't going far; the drive takes less than twenty minutes. Out of all the places my brain imagined we would end up, a nightclub wasn't even on the list. Pulling up, the lights are still on, but there's no line in front of the door. Most clubs I know close around 3 a.m., which explains the lack of drunk partiers stumbling around the sidewalk.

"A club?" I ask, confused. "Why are we at a closed nightclub?" Parking right out front like a VIP, Callum shuts off the ignition and reaches for the door handle. Alarm bells ring in my head, anxiety clawing at me. Who could need medical attention in a nightclub that can't go to the hospital?

"I'm not going in," I say, my voice dripping with anxiety.

"Yes, you are." It's not a question. "Nothing's going to happen to you, Doc. It'd be too much of a waste."

The promise does little to soothe the dread pooling in my stomach like a ball of lead. Clearly, I'm not being taken seriously. Instead, he's climbing out of the car and leaving me alone in the terrifying silence. He circles behind the car, popping open the trunk momentarily, before slamming it shut. The passenger door swings open, and Callum stands expectantly, a large case in his left hand.

I look up at him from my seat, every instinct in my body telling me not to step from the safety of the vehicle. I highly doubt Callum would drive me all the way to a club to kill me. And seeing as he holds the literal keys to my only escape, I don't really have a choice here.

"No one is going to hurt you, you have my word." The conviction in his words matches the promise in Callum's eyes and his right hand extends to me. I stare at it for a minute, warring with my anxiety, my gaze sliding up to meet his. I'm here now, there's no way around it. So, I accept his hand and allow him to help me out of the car. His hand releases mine to close the door behind me with a resounding click and moves to the small of my back.

"Here you go, Doc." The case in his left hand lands heavily on the hood of the car. I lift my eyes to his face briefly, my tongue wetting my bottom lip in apprehension as I reach for the mystery case. His brows raise in a challenge, not offering any explanation. With hesitant hands, I unclip the top of the case and pull it open slowly. My jaw drops.

Calling this a medical kit is a gross understatement. This case contains everything I could ever need to provide proper medical care—gauze, suture kits, IV bags, sterile needles, local anesthetic, antibiotics, stimulants—it's a damn hospital in a box. All that's missing is the MRI machine.

My wide eyes search for his.

"Where did all of this come from?" There's stuff in here that I can't even find at the hospital. How did this man get vials of GHB? I'm at a loss here.

"I told you, you'll have everything you need." Reaching around me, he closes the case and locks it with a snap. "The man you're here to see is inside." With that, I'm being led through the front entrance.

The hazy, dimly lit interior is exactly how I expect it to be.

A few stray workers are moving to clean up the leftovers of the patrons' poor decisions. The heavy aromas of sweat, alcohol, and smoke cling to the air as a reminder of the night's lack of inhibition. I can see the door that leads out of the main room and back towards a more private area as we get closer. A sign reading "Private, no public access" warns me that I'm about to leave any witnesses behind.

I've always scoffed at the dumb, blonde sorority girls in horror movies when they hear a noise in the basement and decide to venture into the darkness in their underwear with nothing but a flashlight yelling *who's there?* Yet, here I am, allowing myself to be led into the dark with nothing but my scrubs and sarcasm to protect me. As good as a lamb to the slaughter, I might as well be wearing my underwear.

Either unaware of my reservations, or completely ignoring them, Callum presses his hand to the small of my back and propels me through the doorway. Once we're in the open and there's enough space, he steps beside me and grabs my wrist—his strong fingers leading me firmly. Then we're walking.

Moving down the long, dark hallway trimmed in blood-red LED lights, we pause at the very last door.

"Breathe," Callum murmurs beside me.

I let out a breath I'm all too aware I was holding. He reaches around me to turn the knob. I haven't exactly been trying to picture what's behind the ominous door, but it definitely wasn't a storage room. Roscoe stands along the far wall, his aggressive stance stiff. It's not the shelves of liquor and extra rags that has shock settling over me.

A chair sits in the center of the shadowy room, a man secured by one of his wrists to the chair's arm with red tape, his ankles secured to the legs. Spatters of blood spread across the plastic that covers the floor beneath him, filling the air with the heavy copper scent of violence. His left hand dangles awkwardly, his pinky missing after the first knuckle. I spot the rest of the finger discarded on the ground next to his foot in a pool of blood.

"What is this?" My question comes out barely more than a whisper. Callum's hand on my back pushes me into the room, the door closing behind us.

"Do your thing, Doc. Get to work and fix him up," Callum says.

The injured man's head lolls as he tries to look up at me. He looks so defeated, so broken.

"You're a doctor?" he asks, barely able to get the words out.

"I'm a nurse," I correct again, standing and assessing the situation. Callum walks around me, moving to watch from the other side of the room facing the door. His giant stature fills the corner of the room, making the space feel so much smaller.

Judging by the amount of blood, enough time has passed between now and the injury to allow some clotting. If the finger is still bleeding too much, I'll have to do a wet-to-dry. But hopefully, I can just stitch the wound closed and bandage it. That all depends on the instrument used and the state of the remaining finger. My eyes lock with Callum's as my assessment fully processes.

Then I'm moving.

"How long ago did this happen?" I ask no one in particular. I don't actually know who's responsible, so the answer could come from either of them.

"Forty-seven minutes," Roscoe supplies gruffly.

When I lower to my knees, I do my best to avoid the blood splatters. I'll kneel in the gore if I have to, but not if I can avoid it.

"What did you use?" I ask, placing my kit on the floor. When I move to get a closer look at the wound, the bloodied man jerks nervously. I can see Roscoe enter my peripheral vision, his muscles tensed and ready if he perceives the movement as a threat against me. But I don't flinch. "How was it cut off?"

"Don't ask that," Callum says, warning me off. "You don't want to know the answer."

He thinks I'm just curious—that I'm entertained by this display of brutality. Throwing him a look of agitation, I lift the mangled hand to inspect it.

"What you used to remove the finger might affect how I have to treat it," I say, pulling out the syringe of local anesthetic. No matter what they used, whether it was a surgical scalpel or a rusty kitchen knife, I have to touch it to patch him up.

And that's going to hurt like hell.

"I used these," Roscoe supplies a pair of handheld pruning shears. Taking the tool from his hand, my eyes catch with his momentarily. I'm struck with the sinking realization that the man of few words just used these landscaping scissors to remove someone's finger. But as quickly as the thought hits me, it's gone as my brain moves on.

"These don't look new," I comment, taking in the scratches and knicks on the sharp blades. Glancing at Roscoe, I can see the hesitance before he answers.

"Not new, but they were clean," he says.

There's no rust, which is a good sign, but they're not sterile. I'll need to make sure the laceration is cleaned thoroughly so there's no infection.

They cut the pinky off at a slight angle, so there's enough skin to fold over and close the wound. Just barely, and there will be lots of scarred tissue, but it will work.

"He's going to need stitches. But it's going to be tricky," I announce, sifting through the kit for the supplies to properly clean the wound.

"Can you do that, Doc?" The look of annoyance I throw at Callum just feeds the man's ego.

"I'm a nurse," I say, for what feels like the millionth time. "So, I shouldn't be able to, not for something like this. But luckily for you, my best friend is a trauma surgeon, and I've perfected my sutures on bananas over a couple glasses of wine."

Organizing the supplies I'll need and laying them out on the lid of the kit, I'm ready to get to work. Pulling the cap off the sterile needle, I flick the air bubbles out and give it a tiny squirt. Eyeing me warily, the man pulls at his restraints.

"No, what is that? Get that away from me," he rasps, yanking at his hand that's bleeding profusely. Roscoe takes a threatening step forward, but I raise my hand to stop him. Instead, I look the imprisoned man straight in the eye.

"I know you think you don't want me to touch you with this needle but trust me. You want what's in this syringe," I inform him calmly. Beaten, captive, tied to a chair or not he's still just another patient who needs to be treated properly. "If you refuse, I'll have to clean you up without numbing. It's your choice." I stare at him expectantly. It only takes three seconds for him to realize my syringe is his friend, and he nods his consent.

After numbing the area, I set to cleaning it thoroughly. The next step is trying to stop the bleeding enough to get a good grip for the sutures. It takes some time, and a lot of gauze, but I'm able to get the skin where I need to stitch it together. Once the wound is finally closed, I disinfect the area again and cover it with a sterile bandage.

"There." Finally sitting back on my heels, I realize how long I've been kneeling on the floor. Just like when I'm at the hospital, my focus kept me from feeling the discomfort in my knees. Not to mention the fact that I really have to pee. My legs complain when I move to stand and I struggle. Callum is at my side in an instant, lifting me off the floor. Damn, I definitely wasn't this tired a few seconds ago.

"You're finished?" Callum's question rumbles at my side. I look up at him, my mind racing as I look at the man I clearly don't know at all. Pulling my eyes away, I simply nod.

"He's gonna need to follow up with a doctor as soon as possible, and there's an enormous risk of infection. But he should be fine." I glance at Roscoe briefly before looking back at my patient. If he didn't blink at me with half-lidded eyes, I would think he was unconscious or dead, staying limp in the chair. What else did they do to him? There's no missing his swollen lip and the black eye that's still forming. "Are there any other injuries I need to look at?"

"No," Callum says firmly. "I'll take you home."

The exhaustion and shock from the events of the night allow Callum to pack up the medical kit and tote me back to the car without complaint. He practically buckles me into the passenger seat, stowing the case back in the trunk before climbing behind the wheel. My eyes can't seem to look at anything else but the terrifying man next to me.

Gazing at his profile, the distinct nose, sharp cheekbones, immaculate beard. When he's in a suit, he looks as distinguished as any high-power businessman roaming this city. But as soon as the suit coat comes off and the shirt sleeves are rolled up, I catch a glimpse at what he really is. A man with an edge that you don't mess with. I'd felt it the first time I met him—the danger just below the surface. But I never thought it was anything like this.

Who is he? Am I in danger right now?

"Are you just gonna keep staring, or are you gonna ask me what you want to ask me?" Coming to a complete stop at a red light, Callum meets my stare straight on. I refuse to avert my gaze. After what I just witnessed, I deserve to stare a hole right through his head if I want to.

"Why did Roscoe cut off that man's finger?" I've wrestled between asking and deciding I'm better off not knowing. But I'd be stupid not to ask just because I'm scared of what the answer might be.

"Because I told him to." Said so calmly, the answer is deliberately cagey, his eyes daring me to ask the next question he's leading me to. I need to know more, need to know what kind of man I'm living with.

So, I bite.

"Why did you tell him to?"

"Kellan took something that didn't belong to him. Now his debt is paid." He's watching me, taking in every blink and breath, reading me like a book. He's a lot harder to read, making my anxiety spike despite my best efforts.

"So, you're an enforcer?" I've pieced together a few things, like the fact that his "business" doesn't discriminate between crooked politicians or career criminals. But there are still some pretty huge gaps I need to fill in here. Because, after tonight, those gaps are starting to seem more like a black hole that'll devour me before anyone can stop it—and no one will ever hear my screams.

"I fix problems." Again, his response leaves me with nothing but more questions.

"What kinds of problems?" I ask. Callum leans back in his seat, flexing his shoulders to get more comfortable as we wait for the light to turn green. His eyes don't leave mine, observing, analyzing, calculating.

"That depends on who's asking." His focus momentarily moves from my face to roam down my body; taking in my messy blonde ponytail, wrinkled pink scrubs, and supportive footwear. Any sleepiness had fled the moment I walked into that back room. For better or for worse, I'm the picture of messy practicality tied up in a crumpled pink bow.

"I'm asking."

I'm not letting this go, not when I can get answers from him. The silence in the car stretches, making seconds feel like hours, the only sound coming from the engine. The light flashes green, but Callum takes his time pressing the accelerator. He's in no hurry to get home.

"Let's just say I fix problems that powerful people pay lots of money for me not to talk about." This bit of information is a step in the right direction, but it still doesn't tell me what I need to know.

"Fix them how?" I press, my voice shaking slightly. His grip shifts on the wheel to take a more casual hold with one hand.

"By any means necessary."

That tells me a lot and nothing at all. That could mean he skirts around the law by doing deals under the table, or he could be a psychotic serial killer. There's so much room for interpretation, which is probably exactly how he likes it. The black hole is slowly morphing into an endless gray area.

"Am I in danger?" The question leaves my mouth before I can think better of it.

"Not from me." It's a plain statement. And I believe him—maybe that makes me an idiot, but I do.

"So I don't need to be afraid of you?" It's a reach for clarification and—if I'm being honest with myself—a little comfort. But I don't get it.

"I never said that." His eyes slide over to find mine again. "Are you scared of me, Lexie?"

A knot forms in my stomach, heat spreading through me under his gaze.

"After tonight I would be stupid not to be," I shoot back. "I'm not stupid."

The car turns and we're entering the parking garage that belongs to the penthouse. Pulling smoothly into one of the private spots, Callum cuts the engine.

"You're a lot of things, but you certainly aren't stupid," he says. "And I know you're smart enough to realize that telling anyone about what you witnessed tonight is a very bad idea."

"I won't say anything," I assure him. I have enough self-preservation to keep my damn mouth shut. Besides, I don't even know what happened. Not really.

"Good. Because if you are stupid enough to tell someone, that might put you in danger. And I'll always know."

"I'm just gonna go shower and pretend like tonight never happened." When did my life turn into a suspense movie? I prefer my drama petty and through a tv screen.

"That's a good idea, Doc." Stepping into the elevator, he's watching me again. This time feels more intentional—like he's looking for something. I'll bet he's waiting for a meltdown with tears and trembling. Like the events of tonight might somehow break me. He can wait all he wants, the breakdown isn't coming.

The demons I'm currently fighting off are much more traumatizing than giving some creep a few stitches in a dark room. Tonight, as weird and confusing as it was, is just a drop in the bucket. I'm already keeping my head above water while much darker forces try to drag me under.

I don't wait for him when the elevator doors open, instead walking straight into the penthouse. Callum's only a step or two behind me.

"Good night, Callum," I say over my shoulder, not hesitating before walking through the kitchen towards the hallway that leads to my shower. And my bed.

"Sweet dreams, Doc," Callum's deep voice sounds behind me.
I wish.

CHAPTER SEVEN

LEXIE

"No dancing in the kitchen this morning?" Callum's voice has me glancing over my shoulder from my place at the stove.

It's been a day since he brought me to the nightclub. I thought it would change things but surprisingly it hasn't. I'm not shaken or traumatized, my life feels pretty much the same. And even as I stand here with the man who turned out to be even more dangerous than I suspected, I feel at ease. Maybe not completely, but close enough.

Callum looks immaculate, per usual, with his black dress shirt, slacks, and leather belt. I've never seen the man with a single hair out of place. Does he even own a pair of sweatpants? Or does he just wear his dress clothes to bed?

"I reserve dancing for mornings I have enough energy to pull myself out of bed without a caffeine drip," I inform him.

"Whatever you say, Dewdrop." His response makes me pause to actually look at him.

"Dewdrop," I repeat. "Isn't that a flower?" Callum's broad shoulders shrug as if it's the most natural thing in the world to compare me to a plant.

"Seems fitting. Dewdrops can be toxic when ingested, just like that poison you're so addicted to." He's referring to Mountain Dew.

"Do you have a thing for nicknames or something?" With a flick of my wrist I turn off the burner.

"I know how much you love your other nickname. What's one more?" He's winding me up on purpose, and it's working. "Right, Doc?"

"There are a few choice words I'd like to call *you* right now." If I'm not mistaken, I swear he laughs at that. My eyes roll dramatically to the ceiling as I turn away from him to focus on things more worthy of my attention. Like my food.

"What's for breakfast?" Callum eyes my spread like he doesn't know what to make of it. It's an unusual combination, but I like it.

"Oh, this is avocado, red onion, and a poached egg with some sriracha on a slice of toasted French bread." My finger points to all the different components on my plate.

After adding a drizzle of hot sauce and a sprinkle of salt and pepper, the spread is finished—and it's a beautiful thing. Maybe I'm just hangry, because my agitation melts away with each bite of food. It only takes five spoonfuls of cereal before I'm ready to do my happy dance—something I'm sure the man standing only a few feet away notices.

"And that?" he asks, nodding to the bowl. I flash him a smile and a small shrug.

"Cocoa Puffs."

"Isn't that a children's cereal?"

"What can I say, I go cuckoo for Cocoa Puffs." Swallowing the last spoonful, I reach for the box to refill my bowl.

"Are you at least going to put some fresh milk in there?" With the look I give him, he might as well have sprouted a second head.

"That's the best part. Do you seriously not know how satisfying it is to finish the second bowl and drink the chocolatey milk? Here, have some of mine." I extend the box towards him, but he just eyes the cereal like it's going to bite him.

"I don't eat that stuff."

"Oh, you're one of *those* people." I can't say I'm surprised. "Let me guess, you're a raisin bran and granola kinda guy."

Callum straightens to his full height, rolling back his broad shoulders and stretching his neck.

"Cereal doesn't cut it for me. I need protein and complex carbs. Sausage, eggs, beans, potatoes." Circling the island, he opens the fridge and starts pulling out ingredients. Looking at the machine of a man, it makes sense. I bet a guy his size needs to consume a lot of food for his body to keep running. He probably burns like a million calories a day just by existing, let alone working out. For me food is fun, and for him it's fuel.

"I'm surprised you don't have a cook." The thought has occurred to me a few times since he showed up. Watching a man as busy and formidable as Callum scramble eggs in the morning seems a little out of place. I mean, I know even dangerous people need to eat, but the task seems too commonplace and almost silly when he does it.

"Typically, when I'm in the city I have a chef that provides me with weekly meals, breakfast and lunch. This trip was last minute, I didn't get to some of the usual details." He flashes me a meaningful look, *case in point*.

"No dinners?"

"Dinner is usually for business. I cook when I can."

"Do you like cooking?"

"I'm good at it."

"Okay, but do you like doing it?" He turns to look at me as if I'm speaking an unfamiliar language, jaw clenched tightly beneath his immaculate beard. "You do know what liking something means, right? Finding enjoyment, having fun." I speak slowly, like an adult trying to explain something to a child with a soft smile on my face and a teasing lilt to my voice. The serious expression I receive in return simply stares at me intensely.

Why is it so damn hard to get to know this guy? What's a straightforward question for most people turns into a complicated equation with him. And I'm left sitting here with an incomplete answer trying to decipher all of the variables. Math was never my strongest subject.

The portion of food he piles on his plate could feed a small family. I sit patiently waiting for an answer, and after a long moment, he finally responds.

"Having fun isn't something I waste time on." Stepping over to the coffeemaker, he pours himself a cup. No sugar, no cream.

"That explains a lot," I comment, taking a bite of my toast. Next comes a spoonful of cereal, the perfect combo of savory and sweet.

"Meaning?" The man certainly has a mean stare, one I'm sure intimidates most people—it makes my pulse jump. My eyes trail down to how his expensive black shirt stretches taut across his broad shoulders. The sleeves rolled up to his elbows show off his strong forearms decorated in dark ink. There's no denying he has good hands—the kind every woman wants to grab her by the throat and work her into a frenzy. Those hands can be my undoing, and I'll gladly beg for more.

I haven't decided if I need to be afraid of Callum yet. The evidence is circumstantial at best and the jury's still out on this one. I know that people capable of violence aren't always dangerous, and he's never shown an ounce of aggression towards me. My high school best friend's dad was in a motorcycle gang. He liked to crack skulls and he had a habit of pulling out a switchblade, but he treated his wife and daughters like princesses.

Callum's grip on the coffee pot shifts and his brows raise marginally, his expression knowing. I'm staring, blatantly ogling him. And he noticed.

I avert my eyes quickly to focus on the food in front of me. "Just that you're all business."

"Speaking of business." He pauses to catch my full attention again. I drag my eyes from my plate to land on him—this time focusing as I fight back a blush. "Come into my office when you're done eating. There's something we need to discuss." With that, he's scooping up his plate and coffee and striding towards his office. I guess that means he doesn't plan to eat with me.

"Sure thing, boss."

"Don't call me that," he calls over his shoulder.

I smile to myself, bringing my bowl to my lips. I'm right, as usual—this chocolatey milk hits different. Callum really doesn't know what he's missing. What's the point in living longer if it means you can't enjoy a bowl of sugary chocolate cereal once in a while?

After taking my time to finish my food, I take a deep breath before walking into Callum's office. There's something ominous about this room. It feels like I might accidentally trigger a booby-trap if I make one wrong move. Maybe it's the man sitting behind the desk, inked arms on full display, who seems to always be watching and waiting. Or *maybe* it's the idea that anything can be lurking between these four walls, like a man missing his finger dripping blood onto a tarp.

"Alright, what's this business we need to talk about?" I ask, sitting in a chair across from Callum's desk. His eyes leave the computer screen to look at me, lowering briefly to my outfit.

"You changed."

I look down at the green dress that I replaced my pajama set with after breakfast.

"I got dressed. I don't want to be fired while I'm in my pajamas," I say, crossing one ankle over the other. Callum sits back in his chair, spreading his legs out in front of him while his eyes sweep over me in consideration.

"You're not being fired, Lexie," he replies, easing some of the worry gnawing at my stomach. "I was impressed the other night. The way you handled yourself at the nightclub surprised me, and I'm not surprised easily."

"Right, the other night when I sewed up some random guy's hand after his finger was cut off. You're surprised I did a good job?" I take a second to absorb what he's saying. "There's a compliment in there somewhere."

"There is," he concedes, his hand running down his beard. "I won't lie to you and say it was a one-off. But the person I used to call is no longer an option."

"Lucky me," I can't help but joke.

"In my line of work, I like to have a medical professional available to me at all times. Now that my previous arrangement is over, I'm looking for a replacement."

"You're talking about Tony," I guess, the pieces suddenly clicking together until it makes sense. Callum nods, the weight of his focus never leaving me.

"Tony did more for me than just watch the apartment while I was out of town. And now there's a position to fill. I want you to fill it, Doc."

"You want me to work for you long-term . . . as a private nurse?"

"Not specifically my nurse, but essentially yes."

"So this would mean, what?" I need to know exactly what he's proposing before I give him a response. Obviously having foreseen this, as a businessman, Callum slides a contract across the desk to rest in front of me. I thumb through it; it's a few pages long. Colored tabs mark the different spots to sign—blue for signatures and yellow for initials.

"You'd live here in the city permanently. I'd require you to be available to me at all times, but you won't always be working. You'll basically be on call, and act as a medical consultant on my behalf. You'd accompany me to certain meetings, and travel occasionally." He flips to the last page and taps on the paper. "And I require all of my employees to sign a nondisclosure agreement."

The NDA isn't shocking; I already initialed something similar when I signed the house-sitting agreement. Wealthy people, especially super private ones like Callum, don't like others knowing their business. I'm betting his actual business has something to do with it too.

"So if someone gets sick or injured, I'd treat them for you? Like a concierge doctor." It's not uncommon for people to hire medical care out privately. I know a few girls who got sick of dealing with the randoms in the emergency room and decided to work for wealthy old people who need a nurse to wheel them around and keep track of their many pills.

"Something like that."

"And the incident at the nightclub. Something like that could happen again?"

"It's possible." Callum's casual response is too vague. So I press.

"But is it probable?" The silent stare is answer enough. Damn, that's a yes. But is that something I can handle? Or even something I can live with?

Dealing with the aftermath of violence isn't a new concept to me; I saw gore walk through the ER doors all the time. You'd be surprised how many idiots think they know how to operate a chainsaw and end up detaching whole limbs. Not to mention the number of muggings and shootings that leave their victims riddled with gaping holes like bloody Swiss cheese. A missing finger is just the tip of the iceberg, small fish really.

But there's a big difference between seeing the result of violence and knowing the people creating it. I know myself well enough to realize that I can remain cool under pressure and handle any trauma, no matter how shocking. When I snap into gear, there's nothing I can't handle. My work ethic isn't the question here, it's my conscience.

"How long is the contract for?"

"Three years to start," Callum says, sliding a check across the desk to sit next to the contract. "You'll receive this first payment up front with a decent signing bonus."

There's no helping how my eyes widen at the absurd number written at the bottom next to my name.

Damn, that's a lot of zeros.

"And if I decide not to sign, I have to leave?" The initial rush of excitement is slowly fading as reality slides back in. This isn't just another few months exploring a new city; I'd be moving here permanently. Taking this job means leaving my apartment, my friends, my younger sister Samantha, and the job waiting for me back home. It means leaving Mia. I'd be abandoning the West Coast to become a New York resident.

"Not right away, I won't kick you out on the street tonight. But you could only stay until I fill the position."

"I'll need to read through this," I say, picking up the contract and leaving the check where it sits on the desk. It's calling my name, but the uncertainty in my head muffles the sound.

"Of course, take it," Callum agrees deeply. "I want you to think about it. But I need your answer by tomorrow morning."

I nod, holding the contract gingerly as I stand.

The walk back to my room has my heart thundering in apprehension. This is a big decision, one that dramatically changes my life. My first thought is to call Mia, my instincts are to talk it out with my best friend. But this is something I have to decide for myself, with no one else's opinions or judgment.

Plus, I know how Mia's going to feel about this. She'll do her best to be objective and supportive, but anything she advises is going to be tainted by her bias. And if there's anyone who can influence my decision-making, it's her.

Reading through every line of the legal document, it looks like a fairly straightforward contract, but it's air-tight. There's no wiggle room. Once I sign it, that's it—there's no changing my mind. The job sounds easy enough, definitely easier than what I did daily at the hospital. Plus, the pay is so much more than I thought I would ever make in my lifetime.

And the thought of having to leave, so much sooner than I thought I would, and having to go back to my regular life in Oregon has dread clawing at my stomach. I love my home, but the idea of walking back into an emergency room makes me want to curl into a fetal position. It's too soon, way too fucking soon—I need more time.

I can't go back to the hospital, to the emergency room. I can't go back to my regular schedule of twelve-hour shifts with patient after patient. Trauma after trauma. Just the thought has my heart rate picking up with anxiety.

Even after leaving the contract on my bed, my mind strays back to it throughout the day. The choice I have to make weighs on my mind for the majority of the day. Even as I bury myself in a new chicken recipe, my mind keeps falling back to the reality-altering decision.

Ignoring Mia's texts all day makes me feel guilty, but I can't talk to her before I've decided for sure. She won't hear from me until I've either signed the contract or started making travel arrangements back to the west coast.

Lying in bed to fall asleep, my mind is almost racing too fast for my demons to make their nightly visit. But it turns out the job offer isn't enough to keep the horrifying images from flashing behind my eyes. *Crimson blood trailing down the side of the gurney until it pools on the worn linoleum floor, mangled metal, and a child's lunch box covered in blood.*

Bolting upright in bed, I gulp for air as my heart pounds. Anxiety grips my chest tightly as a cold sweat breaks across my skin. Switching on the lamp beside the bed, light floods the room as I reach for the contract and the pen I keep in the nightstand.

It might be complicated, but this is a good job offer. The work is less tedious, the pay is incredible . . . and I can't go back to the hospital.

There's really only one choice.

Going through each page, my pen swoops across the tabbed lines in sparkly black ink. It might not be the standard practice to sign a legal document with a glittery gel pen, but it's what I have. And—let's be honest—it's who I am. At least it's black and not the hot-pink one I keep in my handbag.

And just like that, I've sealed my fate and changed my future.

CHAPTER EIGHT

LEXIE

I pause in the open doorway of Callum's office, my knuckles rapping against the door softly to announce my presence. "Knock, knock."

"Come on in, Doc." Callum gestures to me from his place behind the desk. Roscoe sits on the sofa along the wall to the left, silently observing.

Walking in, I place the signed contract in the center of the desk. "I signed it."

His eyes move from the stack of papers to gaze at me, read me. He seems surprised, but I can't be sure if it's because I signed the contract or the fact that I took so long to decide.

Maybe both.

Picking the contract off the desk, Callum flips through each page to double-check that nothing's missing. I don't blame him, I triple-checked every signature line myself before walking in here.

"You signed it," he confirms. "I'll make you a copy."

"Now what? When do I start, today?" I ask, glancing over at Roscoe. He's so hard to read. If I was a less confident woman, I'd probably assume he can't stand me. Between him and Callum, they're going to give my self-esteem a workout. Unreadable stares like theirs can give a woman a complex.

"Tomorrow we can go over the parameters of the job, and figure out scheduling," Callum responds thoughtfully, standing to place the contract into the large safe set into the wall behind his desk. "I don't expect to need you today, and I have meetings that can't be rescheduled."

"Okay." Sounds like I get the day off, which is fine by me. "Perfect, I was hoping to soak up some sun and use the pool today. The weather is beautiful."

Callum's eyes move down my body, most likely taking in how pale I am. I'm sure he thinks I just need a few hours in the sun to get some color, most people do. But my skin is always this fair, the only color I'll be getting from the sun is bright red—not that it'll stop me. I can't wait to load up on SPF and roast like a sun-dried tomato.

"Go ahead." With that, he's dismissing me. Hopping up from the chair, I can feel two sets of eyes on me as I exit the room. Leaving them behind, and any worry about work or the new life I just signed up for, I head to my room. I'm so ready to lounge and relax by the pool.

Looking in the full-length mirror, I pose to show myself the best angle in this swimsuit. The light pink structured top is the best I think I've ever found for my body type. With panels of mesh and a full underwire, it looks more like lingerie than swimwear. That's what I need for my boobs—full support. My girls need to be hoisted up and strapped in. Though, like almost everything else with structured cups, they are just a bit too big to be considered "the perfect fit." But they look fantastic, large and propped up in this top.

The periwinkle bottoms are high-waisted, with enough coverage for my stomach and thigh brows, dipping in the front to show my belly button. But they're also high cut on the sides, sitting high on my hips and creating a cheeky fit on my ass—and I've got a decently sized ass. The bottoms make my defined waist look snatched, my thighs look thick, my legs look long, and my ass voluptuous. The pastel colors perfectly complement the rosy hue of my fair skin and long blonde hair.

I look hot.

Giving my best angles and face, I snap a few pics in the mirror with my cell phone. These might not end up being posted anywhere on social media, but I want them for myself either way. It's important for me to capture this moment when I'm feeling sexy. An assignment from my therapist, Julie, to destigmatize embracing anything that brings me joy. I'll decide what I want to do with them later.

Damn, I look good.

Until I turn and catch the reflection of my side profile. Then I see how my soft stomach slightly overhangs a fupa, and the back of my thick thighs are decorated in cellulite and the faint silver silhouettes of stretch marks. I have more curves than I know what to do with. But to hell if I'm not going to wear what I want to wear.

Stay straight on, Lexie. How you look from the side is something to think about another day. You look good from any angle.

The terrace of the penthouse probably costs a fortune on its own, with manicured landscaping, a large rectangular infinity pool and Jacuzzi, and an outdoor dining area complete with a full bar, grill, and fire pit. Stepping into the ridiculously large pool, the water is heated to perfection.

Nothing beats swimming in a private pool. I could get used to this.

Soaking up the sunshine beneath the heated water, the time passes quickly as I swim laps, float, and breathe. When my fingers have turned into little prunes I know it's time to get out. I make a mental note to buy a house with a pool someday soon, one with lots of privacy so I can lounge in my bikini, or even topless, without straying eyes.

Slowly walking up the steps out of the pool, water runs off my body. The sun is warm, but the wind sends a shiver through me as I reach for my towel. Not wanting to drip a trail of pool-water across the apartment, I do my best to dry my body. Wrapping the towel around myself, I glance through the windows leading into the living room and pause.

A group of four important-looking men in suits stands just

inside the glass door with Enzo, deep in conversation. And judging by their expressions, the topic of discussion is a serious one.

As comfortable as I am lounging by a private pool in a bikini, I have no desire to walk through a heated business meeting full of complete strangers while I'm half-naked and dripping wet. I probably wouldn't pull too much focus otherwise, but in this situation every set of male eyes would be on me.

Yeah, no thanks.

Instead, I pad over to the door on the opposite side of the terrace—the one that leads into the primary suite. I breathe a sigh of relief when the door is unlocked and opens easily. Slipping inside, I close it softly behind me.

Just like the rest of the penthouse, Callum's bedroom is impressive. Natural light floods the room through the wall of floor-to-ceiling windows extending up two stories. Modern furniture and fixtures decorate the space in darker neutral colors. A sitting area is on my left facing a chic black fireplace, a beige sofa, and cognac leather sitting chairs paired with a coffee table made of lighter natural wood. The color palette matches the rest of the apartment and I can't help wondering if it was selected by Callum or some interior designer—black, natural light woods, beige, and cognac leather accents.

His bed is the biggest bed I've ever seen in my life; it must be a California king. It sits on my right against the wall opposite the door that leads into the hallway, nightstands with lamps on both sides. The black bedding covering the giant mattress on the sturdy wooden bed frame looks oddly inviting and comfortable. The two doors on the far back wall open into a spacious walk-in closet and en suite primary bathroom.

Even the air in here feels expensive.

I stop at the foot of the bed, my eyes scanning over the details of the room. I'm the first to admit that I'm nosy—not nosy enough to actually go around digging through drawers or poking around bookshelves—but definitely enough to take a good, detailed look when given the opportunity.

The room is beautifully decorated, each item adding to the masculine luxury of the space. But it's a little impersonal. From what I know about Callum, I wasn't expecting to find shelves of Little League trophies from when he was a kid. But I don't see anything sentimental at all, no personality. Or maybe this whole room is Callum's personality—masculine, expensive, clean, and devoid of emotion. The entire space is . . . controlled.

"Do you need something?" The deep voice makes me jump, ripping me out of my observations and forcing my head to whip around. Callum's large form fills the doorway that leads into the spacious primary bathroom, a black suit coat in his hands to match the black pants he's already wearing. The cuffs of his black dress shirt are buttoned at his wrists, his tattoos completely hidden.

"Oh, you are in here." Just like the first time we met, I'm a deer in headlights. But this time, my recovery is much faster. The towel shifts around me as I sweep my wet hair over one shoulder to minimize the amount of water dripping on the nice wood floors.

"That shouldn't be such a surprise since this is my bedroom," he counters, sliding one of his arms into the suit coat, then the other. Shrugging the jacket onto his shoulders, he straightens the lapels until his businessman camouflage is firmly in place.

"Right," I concede easily. "I'm not trying to invade your privacy, I just saw all the men in suits."

"So, you snuck in here thinking no one would notice?" His brows raise in question, and I'm suddenly starting to rethink my reasoning. It made sense in the moment.

"Sorry, there were a lot of people out in the living room, and I didn't want to be seen, so I came in through the balcony," I say, letting the towel fall away from my body to start drying my hair.

"And you thought you'd be safer in here with me?" His tone taunts the very idea of it. I didn't realize he was in here, but I don't think that would've changed my mind to walk through the crowd of strangers. At least with Callum I know where I stand.

"Well, yeah. There are just too many eyes out there. And

you're not gonna look, so . . ." I shrug, tilting my head to scrunch some of the pool water out of my hair with the towel.

"I'm not looking?" My hands halt at his question, eyes snapping to his.

"Are you?" I ask, blinking at him.

"I am." His eyes pierce through me, proving a point. His gaze settles over my skin like static electricity.

"Wait, what?" I gape at him now; my jaw might as well be on the damn floor.

Callum's eyes run over me from head to toe slowly, deliberately. His heated gaze takes in every inch of me in my bikini, and I can't help but wonder how the same eyes that have been watching me from the moment we met can suddenly make me feel so hot and desired.

"I have, I am, and I will." He takes three steps towards me, punctuating each phrase. My eyes widen up at him, not missing how his focus catches on where my breasts practically spill from my bikini top.

"I'm confused, you never—" He regards me like I'm a character in a children's tv show—something barely tolerable, maybe a potential source of mild entertainment, but altogether too bright and shiny to be taken seriously.

Or at least I thought he did.

Now he's looking at me like a man starved, and I'm a meal he wants to devour.

A wave of heat washes through me, my heart damn near doing backflips.

"Sometimes it's better to observe quietly. Don't mistake my silence for disinterest." There's no missing his interest in me now. "But now that you know, there's no reason to keep it quiet anymore. Is there, Dewdrop?"

"I—" The man has made my brain glitch, and I'm at a loss for what to say. "I thought you didn't like me."

"Wanting to fuck you has nothing to do with whether or not I like you."

"True." Heat pools between my legs. "You want to fuck me?"

"I want to bury my face in those gorgeous tits of yours while I pound into your pussy until I'm balls deep and you're screaming my name." He inches closer. "Yes, I want to fuck you."

Suddenly there's no air in the room. His dirty words have stolen the breath right out of my lungs and doused me in flammable lust.

The man is so unbelievably hot. Callum Russo could eat me alive and I'd offer him seconds. But he's officially my employer now—my dangerous, very serious employer. Not to mention he's only supposed to be in town for a few more days. So instead of responding how my throbbing pussy is begging me to, I say, "Sex would probably complicate things."

The hunger on his face remains, but he doesn't make any attempt to argue with me.

"Probably."

So that settles it, there will be no sex with my extremely attractive, giant, bearded boss who's covered in tattoos and looks like he could shatter me into a million pieces.

It's the right decision, we both know it. But that doesn't stop the regret from clawing at me while I stand here staring at the man with promises of complete devastation in his hazel eyes.

"I should go shower before the chlorine turns my hair green." Changing the subject, I wrap the large towel around my body. The material is cold now, the wet fabric having cooled from the air-conditioning. Callum doesn't miss the goose bumps that raise across my skin as he tilts his head towards his bathroom.

"Use mine," he says, surprising me. "I'm leaving, and I'll be taking the eyes in the living room with me. There's a robe on the hook."

"I'll think about it." We both know I'm about to go poking around his bathroom. "Have fun at your meeting." The look he flashes me says he noticed my choice of words. I give him a bright smile in return.

The towel slips around me slightly when I reach up to tuck a strand of wet hair behind my ear, allowing him to catch another glimpse of my cleavage. I'm not in a hurry to pull it back up and ruin his view.

"We'll talk tomorrow morning," he says, running a hand over his perfect beard—he has some seriously good hair genes. "Meet me in my office at eight."

I nod in acknowledgment. "I'll be there."

Callum stands there for a beat, gazing at me like usual. Only, now that I know how he feels when he looks at me, it's not like usual. It's hot and unnerving at the same time.

When he turns to stride out of the room, I'm left trying to make sense of what just happened between us. There's so much to process, especially from the last few days. My mind is still scrambling when I walk into Callum's bathroom.

It matches his bedroom: large, modern, and luxurious. And freakishly neat. There's no shortage of hygiene products between his face wash, beard oil, and musky, robust soap—which is no surprise. Callum is a very well-groomed man. Each item is lined up perfectly in place, keeping the counters clean and organized. The entire room is an odd combination of lived-in and pristine. It looks like a well-staged photo from a luxury interior design magazine.

To give some semblance of privacy, I don't rifle through his cabinets. Turning on the rain shower, I wrestle myself out of the damp swimsuit. When I step under the steaming water and look out of the floor-to-ceiling window with the spectacular city view, I'm sure this is going to be the best shower of my life.

CHAPTER NINE

LEXIE

Sitting in the back seat with Callum while Roscoe drives us through the city is a foreign feeling. In my mind, only celebrities and "important people" get driven around by a bodyguard chauffeur. Apparently, Callum is one of those important people, and I now have certain privileges simply by proximity.

The luxury black SUV was custom-made for Callum's large frame, with extra-wide seats and more legroom than I thought was possible in the back seat of a car. The limo tint on the windows offers as much privacy as possible, and I have a sneaking suspicion that the vehicle is armored.

Callum's focused on his phone, probably typing three emails at once. We went over the expectations of the job earlier this morning, which basically boils down to three things—be available, be reachable, and follow instructions. Simple enough. He didn't exactly sync our calendars, and I get the feeling I'll never actually know what he's up to until we're already on the way. I'll just have to be ready for plans to change.

Leaning back against the cognac suede seat, a notification sounds in the car and the vibration buzzes over my skin. Callum looks over in time to see me reach into the V-neck of my scrub top and pull out my cell phone. A text notification from my sister, Samantha, lights my screen.

"Did you just pull that out from . . . ?" Callum's deep voice sounds beside me, his tone equal parts amusement and bewilderment.

"My bra? Yeah." I shrug, unlocking my phone. Feeling his eyes on me, I turn my head to meet his gaze. Hazel eyes glance down at my breasts without discretion.

"You keep your phone in your bra?"

"All the time." It's really no big deal. "It's like having two large built-in pockets and women's clothes never have them so, why not?" His eyes on me are processing. Or maybe he's just taking this opportunity to check me out.

"People don't notice you reaching into your top all the time?" he asks, unconvinced.

"You couldn't tell it was there. Mission accomplished."

Callum eyes me curiously. "What else do you have in there?"

I suppress a smile, turning my attention back to my phone to read my text. "Wouldn't you like to know." Samantha is giving me life updates, complete with screenshots of the cat she wants to adopt. "Where are we headed?"

"I have a meeting with a Russian." His answer is short, as if that bit of information is everything I need to know. I'm still confused.

"What do you need me for?"

"The Russians aren't known for being friendly," Callum responds vaguely. "Some of them have a problem with my history with the Italians. You're here in case things get heated."

"Your history with the Italians," I repeat, trying to make sense of what he's saying. "I thought you were Italian. Isn't Russo an Italian last name?"

"It's Sicilian."

"So, the problem is with your family?"

"It's complicated." The steel edge in his voice ends the line of questioning.

The car pulls to a stop in front of a bar. It's only ten o'clock in the morning, and the place looks appropriately deserted for such an early hour. I doubt they're open yet.

Roscoe and Callum both exit the vehicle, and my door is opened for me. Callum holds out his hand to help me down from the tall car. I leave the medical kit in the back seat as instructed. Apparently walking into a tense situation looking like you're ready to start cleaning up blood isn't the best move.

Ignoring the "closed" sign on the door, Callum enters the building like he owns the place. The vintage feel of the dark interior seems like something out of a burlesque movie, with dark woods, red velvet-topped stools, and backlit counters. Pausing just inside the door, Callum scans the room until his eyes land on the booth in the far back corner. A man, who appears to be in his mid-thirties, sits at the table with a phone pressed to his ear. The large man that's standing guard next to the booth steps away to approach Callum.

"Wait for me here," Callum says, looking first at me, then having a silent conversation with Roscoe. The bald man gives a short nod, but widens his stance and folds his hands in front of him like he's ready for war. For all I know, I should be gearing up for battle too. Instead, I sit on a bench against the wall near the door—I'm not in the mood for war right now.

The bodyguard watches as Callum lifts his arms out at his sides and spins, visually patting him down to make sure he's not armed. I didn't notice the paper bag in Callum's hand until he's opening it to show the bodyguard the contents before following him back to the booth and greeting who I'm assuming is the Russian that Callum mentioned in the car.

I can't quite hear what they're saying from across the room, but I watch the two men greet each other with a handshake that's all business. Since there's nothing else to do, I follow Roscoe's example and just watch and absorb.

The Russian man is clean-shaven with a very square jaw and a cleft chin. His wavy hair could be either light brown or a very dark blonde, but there's so much product slicking it back that it's impossible to tell. When Callum pulls two bottles of liquor from the paper bag and presents them to the other man, I can catch a glimpse of the tattoos on the back of the Russian's hands that creep down to his fingernails. The ink makes them look like he has skeletal fingers.

Kinda creepy.

It's impossible to decide which man is more terrifying; I wouldn't want to meet either of them in a dark alleyway at night. But there's something about the way Callum's danger is so expertly camouflaged under a suit coat that makes him seem far more threatening. With the Russian, you know exactly who you're looking at when you meet him. Callum's true nature isn't revealed until his sleeves are rolled up and his metaphorical fangs are out. Between the two men at that table, my guess is that Callum Russo is the bigger threat.

"What's his name?" I ask, glancing at Roscoe. He pulls his eyes from his boss just long enough to look down at me. "The Russian."

"Levi," he answers after a moment of consideration, having weighed the pros and cons of telling me and deciding there's no harm in me having this information. Maybe I should take what I'm given and be grateful I got any answer, but I've never been good at stopping when I'm ahead.

"Am I allowed to know his last name?" I ask, following his gaze back to the men.

"Mikhailov," Roscoe answers this time without looking at me.

Levi Mikhailov. Definitely Russian alright.

It's like he could hear me thinking his name, because his dark brown eyes meet mine. I can see him say something and nod towards me. Callum turns his head and our eyes lock as he says something in response. I'm tempted to sit up straighter under the weight of their focus, but their eyes leave me as quickly as they settled.

The meeting doesn't last too long, and it's only a few more minutes before they're standing up from the booth and walking over to us. Levi's bodyguard falls into step behind him and Roscoe steps forward to meet them. Callum's eyes find me briefly when I stand from my seat, but I don't bother to speak or walk any closer. My plan is to just stand here quietly until it's time to leave.

"You won't be needing your nurse when you meet with Viktor either," Levi's saying when they stop in front of us, his eyes catching on me momentarily. He doesn't look very impressed; I'm betting a man like him surrounds himself with equally scary people. That's definitely not me. "Just make sure you bring more of that vodka and Irish whiskey."

"That can be arranged." Callum nods, signaling to Roscoe it's time to go. "I'll see you then." Roscoe and Levi's man are watching each other like cowboys having a showdown in an old Western. The tension breaks when Levi turns back to his place at the table.

Callum motions for me to walk ahead of him as we exit and head back to the car. He opens the door for me and his hand on my lower back helps me in. Roscoe doesn't seem to relax until he's pulling into traffic and we're driving away—well, as relaxed as Roscoe gets.

"You get the meeting?" he asks, looking at the man beside me in the rearview mirror. Callum nods and settles into his seat.

"Friday night, eight o'clock at The Dining Room." A muffled buzzing next to me has Callum reaching into his pocket to pull out his vibrating phone.

The phone only buzzes in his hand once before he's pressing it to his ear. "Marcus . . . Yes, we're close by. What happened?" The way he glances over at me confirms I'm part of the *we* he's referring to. "We're on our way." He hangs up the phone, making eye contact with Roscoe in the rearview mirror.

"Where we headed?" Roscoe asks the question we're both wondering.

"Brooklyn," Callum responds, apparently giving enough information for Roscoe to understand.

"Who's Marcus?" I ask curiously. Callum glances at me before continuing to type on his phone.

"My older brother," he replies. He has an older brother. A small piece to the giant puzzle that is Callum Russo.

"What's in Brooklyn?"

He rolls his shoulders, jaw tightening ever so slightly under my gaze. He's not exactly looking forward to wherever we're going, and my interest is piqued. What could possibly make the unshakable Fixer uncomfortable?

"Family business," is the only answer he gives me during the rest of the car ride the few blocks to our destination.

Pulling up to a business in Brooklyn, Roscoe stops in front of a butcher shop. It's unassuming, looking like any other family-owned business in the city, something you see around every corner next to the bodega. It sits between a flower shop and a small Italian restaurant. The dark red signage that reads *Russo & Sons Butcher Shop* over a traditional beige awning is dated but well-maintained.

Callum opens the car door for me, and I let him lead me by a hand on the small of my back to the front door of the shop, medical kit in hand. The bell over the door rings when it's opened.

The interior is as traditional as I was expecting. Shelves of sauces and spirits stand inside the door. The entire back wall is made up of a refrigerated display counter filled with different cuts of meats and cheeses with so much variety I don't fully recognize the majority of them. Giant hams, racks of ribs, and other bulky cuts hang from the ceiling by large hooks. The walls are decorated with vintage signs and generational family paraphernalia.

"Ahh, there he is!" A large older man greets us enthusiastically when we walk through the door, his heavy Brooklyn accent mixed thickly with Italian. His hair is more silver than brown, his cheeks ruddy and smile wide. He looks like the friendly neighborhood Italian butcher, but the kind you don't want to owe money to. "The man of the hour."

"Father," Callum says, simply giving him a nod.

"Is that any way to greet your papà?" The older man's voice turns stern, switching to another language. *"Rispetta la tua famiglia."* He pulls Callum into a hug, patting his back firmly. Surprisingly, Callum hugs him back.

A door behind the counter in the back of the store groans as it opens and two more men walk through it. One looks almost identical to Callum, just as tall and dark. Only, he sports stubble instead of a full beard. And he looks like the rough way he's lived his life is starting to catch up to him. The second man has jet-black hair, a severe, angular face, and wears all black—like he's using it to hide his sins. They both greet Callum like family.

"And who is this?" Callum's dad turns, bringing all eyes to focus on me. "Giovanni Russo, you can call me Gio." His hand reaches for mine, shaking it firmly with a strong calloused palm. Looking between him and Callum, I can see the family resemblance. He's not as tall, but Gio is a large man—sturdy and broad. He carries the extra weight of a middle-aged man who eats well, but he looks solid. His energy is loud and a little harsh—rough around the edges. And like his son, the friendliness only stays on his face with his smile.

"Lexie." I introduce myself with a smile. "Nice to meet you."

"I'm Marcus, Callum's brother. But don't hold it against me." I could've guessed he was the other Russo brother. "This is Lucciano Grassos." He nods to the intense Italian man next to him. Both men look tempted to reach out and shake my hand, but Callum steps between us.

"Lexie is the medic you asked for."

Gio addresses Callum with a question; the switch is so smooth it takes me a second to realize he's no longer speaking English. I don't hide my surprise when Callum also responds in what I'm assuming is Italian, my gaze meeting his.

I don't understand his words, but his tone hints at his agitation as he fights to remain cordial.

Marcus chimes in, speaking the same language. I do recognize the words *Barbie* and *Tony*, his eyes regarding me almost as intently as the way his brother does. His face is far more expressive, and he's clearly very curious about me. And more than a little skeptical. All of the men are looking at me like a fairy princess who just walked into a boy's birthday party when they were expecting Batman instead.

Whatever Callum says in response doesn't make any of the men stop staring. When the stoic Lucciano speaks up, his words make Callum's eyes flash with annoyance.

Callum's voice grows irritated, the beautiful language coming from his mouth turning harsh and unforgiving. It sounds like a threat.

That seems to shut everyone up. I think now is as good a time as any to speak up.

"Who am I here to help?" I ask, looking around at the men expectantly. None of them look injured.

Finally, Gio steps forward.

"*Scuse*," he says largely. "He's back here." He gestures for me to follow him through the door behind the counter and into the hallway that leads to the back rooms. Callum is right at my back, walking closely behind me with Marcus and Lucciano taking up the rear. And I'm being led through the plastic slats past the cool room into a refrigerated storage room. "Ricky's been shot in the left arm, seems like a through 'n' through. No bullet."

"Internal damage?"

"Not that we can tell. He can move everything just fine. We just need you to clean him up and stitch him closed until we can get our usual doctor to look at him."

"Usual doctor?"

"Yeah, ya know. Family guy. Usually, he'd be here to deal with this, but he's stuck uptown." The way they keep saying *family* sounds a lot more like a crime syndicate than mom-and-pop. I simply nod in response. "He's over there."

Ricky sits on a metal chair against one of the walls of the industrial processing room. Whole pigs and slabs of cow lay in various levels of dismemberment across metal tables scattered with knives and cleavers. Just like the other men, he looks to be Italian too, with dark hair slicked back with too much gel. His olive skin is pale as he holds a wad of blood-soaked rags against his left arm. As we walk closer, his eyes move over me like I'm an animal in the wrong zoo exhibit—not what he was hoping to see, but better than nothing.

"Ricky, this is Lexie. Cal brought her to fix you up," Gio introduces, pulling a second chair over beside him so I have a place to sit.

When Ricky speaks it's in Italian, the words coming out sounding slimy and unsettling. I'd bet money that whatever he's saying is a combination of derogatory and explicit. His gaze moves over me again, making my skin crawl. Even his eyes are handsy.

In three long strides, Callum's in front of him. His large hand clamps around Ricky's throat, forcing the injured man to look him in the eye. Callum's expression is dark—murderous—as he leans in to speak.

Responding in kind, Callum's words are spoken with a tone of violence. I wish I had a translator right about now. I'd love to know what he's saying. Giving the injured man's throat an extra squeeze, Callum switches to English before continuing. "Now shut your fucking mouth and sit still so the doc can stitch you up."

I'm tempted to clarify that I'm a nurse instead of a doctor, but a sharp look from Callum has the correction dying on the tip of my tongue.

Ricky's jaw tightens, but he nods against the hand on his throat. Callum releases the mobster roughly with a shove, forcing him to slump back against the chair. Still staring him down, Callum reaches his hand out for me. When I walk closer, he barely steps back—instead standing over the patient.

Over me.

Sitting on the empty chair, I place the medical kit on the floor. Ricky watches as I roll up his sleeve, peeling the blood-slick fabric from his skin. Unfortunately, the material only goes so high and my view is still obstructed.

"I need you to take off your shirt," I inform him.

"You want a better look at the goods?" Ricky asks with a

smirk, despite the giant man looming over him with promises of violence.

"Do you want me to close the holes in your arm or not? If you prefer to bleed out, it makes no difference to me." I meet his stare evenly, waiting patiently like he's a child who can't follow simple instructions. I don't miss how Ricky's lips twitch in contempt before he gives me a cocky grin and moves to comply. He doesn't like women talking back. Or maybe it's just the fat ones.

Reaching forward to assist him, my arm bumps Callum, who seems to have inched closer.

"Can you give us some space?" Easing the wounded arm from the sleeve, I pause to meet the gaze I can feel burning a hole through my skull. Callum's eyes connect with mine heavily, his laser focus intent on me. "I'm fine, Callum. I need more room to stitch him up." When he doesn't budge I flash a sugary sweet smile. "Pretty please."

"Nobody's gonna hurt your nurse, Cal," Gio says behind us. Callum stares me down for another minute, his serious expression set in stone as his eyes search mine. Finally, he backs away until I feel like I can breathe again.

Turning my focus back to the task at hand, I inspect the gunshot wound. The bullet entered the front of his left bicep and exited through the back. By the placement, it looks like his arm was extended outward when the bullet passed through, only affecting the fleshiest part of his underarm.

"Do you know what kind of bullet it was?" I ask, glancing up at Ricky as I set up my supplies.

"What does someone like you know about bullets?" Ricky's tone is mocking.

"Twenty-two? Forty-five? Nine-millimeter?" I ask, listing a few calibers. "Semi-jacketed, hollow point?"

The laughs that sound behind me match the surprise on Ricky's face. "What are you, some sort of undercover cop?" Marcus asks behind me.

"I've spent the last four years working in emergency rooms all over the country. Including Manhattan." Ricky hisses against the alcohol swab, but my eyes remain focused on cleaning the wound. "Plus, I dated a guy who worked in private security when I was in nursing school. I know a lot more about gunshot wounds than you'd think."

I learned a lot of life lessons from Jared. Like the different types of bullets, how to escape a car trunk, and not to trust a guy when he tells you not to worry about the bitchy client he's spending all his time with.

"It was a forty-five," Ricky says. "Lead round nose." He grits his teeth against my probing. That's a relief, the wound is pretty clear. A hollow point would've been another story—a bigger exit wound with fragments embedded in the tissue. Not pretty to clean up, and far more damaging.

"Do you want local anesthetic?" I ask, collecting the supplies for his sutures.

"Save it." Ricky's response is dripping with bravado. "I don't need it."

"Let's go to the office, we have things to discuss," Gio announces. "We'll leave your nurse to her work."

"Are you good with that, Doc?" Callum asks.

"Go ahead." I wave him off over my shoulder, not bothering to glance in his direction.

"Don't worry, I'll be real nice to her," Ricky says smugly, stirring the pot.

"Lexie." The steel edge in Callum's voice forces me to pull my eyes away from my work. I look up at him, our gazes colliding.

"I'm fine. This shouldn't take too long," I assure him, letting him read the truth written all over my face. Seemingly satisfied with my answer, if not reluctant, Callum turns to Roscoe.

"Stay here." Roscoe nods and remains diligently in place behind me as Gio leads Callum, Marcus, and Lucciano back into an office along the far wall. I can see them glancing at me through the window that looks into the larger room, but I don't bother to wonder what they're talking about. Instead, I focus on what I'm here for.

As soon as we're alone, Ricky shifts back in the chair, his stance cocky and dominant. There's no doubt in my mind that Callum's absence has everything to do with his change in attitude. Chin tilting up, his eyes run me up and down as a string of Italian leaves his mouth.

"Watch it." Roscoe's warning rolls right off Ricky's back, making his lips twitch arrogantly.

"You know I don't speak Italian," I say. "But whatever you just said was obviously an insult if you waited for Callum to leave before you said it."

"Was it?" It's not a denial.

"I would hope not. It's never a good idea to offend the person in charge of making sure you don't die from infection." I add a little more pressure against his wound than necessary to make a point, making him wince. His jaw sets, but he regards me with interest and a hint of respect.

"Where did Cal find you, anyway? You two fucking?" Ricky seems to flip between being a cocky insulting asshole and curiously amused by my mere existence. He doesn't find me pleasing, I'm clearly not what he prefers to look at. But he's enjoying the fact that I don't make sense. I'm an unknown variable in Callum's equation, written in sparkly pink gel pen amongst all the gray area.

"You can ask him that when we're finished here if you're feeling brave enough."

"Ah, you're no fun," he grumbles, making me smile.

"Not for you."

"So you *are* fucking."

"I didn't say that. I can't imagine Callum has a habit of mixing business with pleasure."

"Never," Ricky confirms with a snort. "He used to be so much more fun before everything happened with his mama. Now he's a fucking machine." He looks at me thoughtfully. "Although, none of his employees have looked like you, and he's not gonna fuck someone like Tony. But you? You're just his type."

"Oh really? And what's that?" I ask, bracing myself against the potential emotional scarring from whatever crude answer he's about to give me.

"Fat, blonde, big tits." The way he purses his lips while his eyes move over me says he doesn't get what Callum finds attractive about fat bodies. "Even before, he's always had a thing for big bitches."

"Hmm," I hum in a simple response, completely unoffended. Ricky not finding me attractive is almost laughable, especially considering I wouldn't let him touch me with a ten-foot pole.

"What did he threaten to do to you when we first walked in?" Curiosity has the question leaving my tongue before common sense can rein it back in. I guess I can relate to the cat who died of curiosity because it turns out I have just as little self-control.

"To put a bullet through my head if I don't play nice." As Ricky shrugs against my hands, his tongue runs over his teeth in contempt. He doesn't take that threat as lightly as he's letting on. Probably a good idea on his part. It's oddly flattering that Callum cares about my well-being enough to threaten someone's life. And horrifying.

"You get shot a lot?"

"Once or twice." Ricky's shrug is causal, but the scars over his torso say it's happened more than that. This guy is riddled with marks, both from knives and bullets. I'm sure he gets into quite a bit of trouble.

CHAPTER TEN

CALLUM

"You think she can handle it?" Marcus asks, looking at Lexie through the window.

"She's got the skills. She'll probably stitch him up faster than Dr. Morelli. And it'll be cleaner too." Morelli's gotten sloppy; his handiwork has started slipping with his age. The Family will need a new physician on payroll before too long.

"Lots of people can stitch up a little bullet hole." Lucciano says dismissively with a wave of his hand. "It takes a lot more to deal with a business like this. She seems sweet. Soft."

"You'd be surprised." Hell, I have been. I had Roscoe stay with her for both Lexie's protection and mine. Leaving her alone with Ricky is dangerous, not just because he tends to have wandering hands and doesn't like hearing the word *no*. I wouldn't put it past Lexie to get a few too many answers from the flashy idiot—things I don't want her to know.

"Tony's a cocky asshole, but he's good. And his family ties make him reliable," my father points out, crossing his arms. He's speaking like he has any say in my business, like any of them do.

I was over this topic of conversation when they expressed their unwanted opinions the moment we arrived. Introducing Lexie was as irritating as I anticipated—Marcus called her "nurse Barbie" for fuck's sake. Even after knowing me for thirty-one years, they question my decision-making. Assuming that I would ever hire someone less than capable is insulting, and it pisses me the fuck off.

They're questioning my decision as if they get a vote. That's not how it works. Not anymore. This whole conversation is really starting to chip at my control.

"She's better than Tony." My tone darkens, but Marcus breezes right past my warning with his typical shit-eating grin.

"Better than Tony at what, exactly?"

"I didn't have to bring her here. But you called and I came. Lexie's staying, it's not up for discussion."

"I'm sure her giant tits have nothing to do with your decision either." Marcus' grin widens, the fucker. "You always did like 'em big and blonde."

My jaw tightens, shoulders tensing slightly. I don't like him looking at Lexie's breasts, let alone talking about them. "I don't let my dick make my decisions. That already happens enough in our family. I'll leave that tradition to you."

"Enough." Our father cuts off Marcus before he can say whatever insulting bullshit is about to come spewing out of his mouth. He turns to Lucciano. "Are the authorities clued in to Ricky's little fireworks show today? I'd like to know if I need to be worried about the police raiding my shop looking for him."

"Don Rafael already spoke to the chief personally. They're not going to bother us about this. No one witnessed anything, so we don't need to worry about exposure or taking care of loose ends," Marcus replies, pulling out a cigarette. He lifts the lighter, but my father snatches it from his mouth before he has a chance to light it.

"Keep this shit outside and away from my office," he demands in disgust, tossing it in the trash can next to him.

"Whatever you say, Pop." Marcus isn't the least bit put off, having heard that exact phrase leave our father's mouth a hundred times over.

My brother never learns.

"There you are, *il mio amore*," my father says, looking past me.

"Who's in there with Ricky? I heard he got shot." My mother speaks behind me, her words lilting with her soft Irish accent. I turn to face her in the doorway. She looks up at me from her wheelchair and smiles warmly. The woman who raised me was strong, and beautiful. She's still as lovely with the white strands of age highlighting the red hues in her dark hair. Her deep green eyes are just as astute and all-knowing. But fragility has crept up on her over the years, leaving her thin and tired. "Callum, come give your mam a hug."

"Hi, Mom." I step closer, stooping down to hug her and press a kiss to her cheek. "That's Lexie. She works for me."

"Tony's gone?" she asks, her auburn eyebrows raising. "I would say that's a shame, but then I'd be lying." My mom never did like Tony. "An arrogant asshole who's only out for himself," as she called him. She wasn't wrong; she rarely is.

"Blondie's plugging the bullet holes until Dr. Morelli can get here," Marcus answers.

"Is she a doctor?"

"She's a nurse."

"If he hadn't barged into the Russian's territory like a bull in a china shop, he wouldn't have gotten shot in the first place," she says, frowning in disapproval. Her energy matches my father's—loud, unfiltered, and very opinionated.

But where my father is harsh and unforgiving, my mother is the picture of warmth. Despite her caring disposition, she's not someone you want to cross. She might not hold on to grudges like some, but she never forgets, and her temper surpasses even my father's Italian blood. Tara Walsh-Russo is tough as nails.

"Are you surprised?" I ask, earning a warning look from my father. I ignore it. "Ricky always acts first and thinks later. If at all." Every member of the *Cosa Nostra* does, something I've seen firsthand. Hell, I used to be that way too. Leading with emotions in the moment, consequences be damned.

It's the way the Outfit operates. Putting the Family above all else—including rationality and reason.

"He was doing what needed to be done." My father's voice has a familiar hard edge to it. The same one it gets every time this subject is broached in my presence.

"And did he? Did he put an end to it?" I remain calm, my expression giving him nothing—something that infuriates my father to no end. Not when his face gives away everything he's thinking like a flashing neon sign. Like the tic in his jaw muscles right now as his eyes narrow at me.

"We'll get them," Lucciano speaks up. "We'll figure out a way to repay them for what they've done."

"You always do." The cycle is exhausting and fucking stupid. Hundred-year-old feuds fuel rivalries that cost lives and money. All a never-ending domino effect of action and violent retaliation.

I've seen my fair share of family business. I've carried out enough of that retaliation to know exactly what happens. My undying loyalty to the Outfit is what used to drive me—and my trigger finger—to act first and let the Family think for me later. Until that same loyalty almost got my mother killed and put her in a wheelchair for the rest of her life.

That day—the day of what my parents only ever refer to as *the incident*—was the day I realized that there's a better way to get what you want than charging around with guns blazing. Emotions cloud judgment and get in the way of rational thought, leading to stupid decisions that cause nothing but more problems.

My brother went the other way, becoming a hothead who acts on impulse in a way that *Papà* considers loyalty to the Family. Something my father likes to berate me for every time I refuse to engage in any crisis regarding "*family business*."

My willingness to act with blind loyalty disappeared with my mother's ability to walk.

"Where are you going?" my father asks, watching my mother maneuver her wheels to swivel her wheelchair back towards the door.

"I want to meet her," she announces, rolling herself swiftly out of the office. No doubt on her way to pass judgment on whether or not Lexie gets her stamp of approval. Tony didn't make that cut, not after the first words out of his mouth at their introduction were insulting the Irish.

Asshole.

There are no second chances after the first impression with my mother.

I move to follow her, relieved to have this excuse to get away from the conversation in the office. It's getting a little too personal in here for my liking, I'd rather get back to my own business. And back to the pretty pink nurse I left with the trigger-happy mobster.

"Got shot again, aye Ricky? Why am I not surprised, always making a mess," Mom scolds as she wheels her way across the industrial space to where the injured man is being tended to.

"A small price to pay to set those Russian bastards straight." Ricky's not the least bit repentant. Lexie pulls her eyes from Ricky's arm to look over her shoulder at my mother, long blonde ponytail swinging like a shampoo commercial in the process. The stunning smile that graces her face at my mom's approach is magnetic.

"Hello," Mom says, rolling to a stop beside Ricky's chair. "Tell me who you are and what makes you qualified to work for my son." In typical Tara fashion, my mom doesn't mince words. It's her way of seeing who someone truly is, by catching them off guard. Her Irish accent is heaviest when she's demanding something, or angry, and it makes her sound sterner.

Lexie blinks at her a few times but remains otherwise unfazed.

"This is my mom," I say. "Tara."

"I'm Lexie, I've worked as a traveling ER nurse for over four years. I just finished an eighteen-week contract at New York Presbyterian. Between that, and the fact that my best friend is a trauma surgeon, I've basically seen it all." Lexie lists her qualifications easily, like it's just friendly conversation instead of an interrogation. "I'm really good at what I do. But honestly, I think

Callum only hired me because he needed someone after Tony left and I was convenient."

I can already see on my mom's face that Lexie's response was exactly the right answer. She hates bullshit and can't stand cowards. The way Lexie carries herself, self-assured and unbothered by the opinion of others, is exactly the right kind of personality to get along with my mother.

Mom looks Lexie over, sizing her up, before turning to look at me. I give away nothing, even when Lexie's questioning eyes look to me with brows raised. When Tara's lips twitch in a smile, she might as well have pressed her stamp of approval on the pretty pink nurse's forehead.

She likes her.

"Alright." Mom nods, keeping a straight face when she turns back to Lexie and the man she's been tasked with fixing up. "Let's see this work of yours."

Lexie backs away from Ricky, allowing everyone in the room to examine her needlework. My father, Marcus, and Lucciano, who followed my mother and me from the office, step forward to get a good look too.

Just like with Kellen's hand, Lexie's work is clean and tight. I've seen a lot of gunshot wounds, and there's no doubt Ricky's arm will heal quickly and with barely a scar. The caliber of work on this wound makes the other scars marking his body look crude and sloppy.

Lucciano remains silent, but the look in his eyes when his gaze cuts to me acknowledges he was wrong to doubt my judgment. My father starts sputtering in Italian, his voice dripping praise. Marcus, however, admires her work openly, boldly.

Too fucking boldly.

"Damn, that's impressive," Marcus says. "What's your number? I might need you to stitch me up one of these days." I'm about to tell my brother to shut his fucking mouth and stay away from her—that he doesn't get her phone number because she's not his to talk to or think about—but Lexie beats me to it.

"I work for Callum. You know how to reach him." Her answer soothes some of the hostility raging inside me, and my shoulders relax slightly when she glances up at me. That one look calms me considerably. "Can I finish bandaging him up now?"

"Go ahead, Doc," I say, nodding towards the made man.

Ricky's been surprisingly silent since I walked into the room. He can keep glaring at me as long as he keeps his mouth shut. I'll be talking to Roscoe to see how well the trigger-happy prick behaved himself when I left.

Lexie looks at me for another second as she takes a deep breath, a flicker of vulnerability crossing her face. The way her eyes pull away from me to glance around at the other people filling the space is the only sign she's given that she might feel overwhelmed. But it's gone as quickly as it came, and she's back to work wrapping Ricky's arm in sterile gauze.

As soon as Lexie's finished cleaning up and giving Ricky care instructions—that go in one ear and out the other without penetrating his thick skull—I have Roscoe take her back out front to the car. My mother takes the opportunity to get me alone.

"Come with me," she demands, rolling ahead of me to the front of the shop. "I cooked yesterday."

It's all she has to say to get me to follow. She leads me to one of the coolers, where she starts pulling out a stack of food containers, four in total.

"Lexie does good work." I already see where this conversation is going, but I humor her anyway. "She's way fuckin' better than that asshat Tony."

"I agree." She bats my hands away when I reach to help, forever the independent woman, and stacks the containers into a large paper bag.

"Be careful with her though. She's still got that light in her; I'm not sure she's cut out for the life you're leading her into."

"I know the risks," I state simply. I weighed the risks and benefits before writing up the contract, I know what I'm getting myself into, even if Lexie hasn't seen the full picture yet. Mom places the bag on her lap and forces me to look her in the eye.

"I don't get to see you much anymore unless someone gets a hole blown through 'em, so I'm gonna take my opportunity now that I have it." I brace myself for the lecture coming my way. "You might not be involved with the Family business anymore, but I know enough about what you get up to. You've got it in your head that emotions get in the way of every decision, and you're almost right. But sometimes acting on your feelings is the difference between staying alive and living."

Holding back my frustration, I pull in a deep breath as I formulate a response. Telling her to keep her opinions to herself like I would my father and brother isn't an option. But I have no interest in having a one-on-one therapy session with my mother about following my heart. So instead, I give her a response that ends the conversation without being harsh. "I hear you."

Mom lets out a humorless laugh. "I don't think you do, but I'll let you leave anyway," she scoffs, holding out the bag of food for me to take. I accept it with thanks, leaning down to press a kiss to her cheek before heading to the exit.

Settling back against the seat in the car, I can't focus on the email displayed on my phone when my eyes keep straying to the woman sitting next to me. Feeling my eyes, she turns from the window to meet my stare head-on—something she does a lot.

She doesn't get flustered or cower under my gaze. Instead, she stares right back.

"What?" Her brows knit together slightly in confusion.

"What are you thinking?" The need to know what's running through her mind is too strong to resist. Reading the emotions as they cross her face isn't enough.

"That I usually make a guy at least take me to dinner before I meet his parents," she teases good-naturedly, making me suppress a smile.

"You're handling this really well."

"You know, you have a habit of sounding surprised when you

compliment me, Callum. Someone with a smaller ego might find that offensive." She's not offended.

"I would never want to offend you, Dewdrop," I assure her with an amused smile. "One of these days I might need you to stitch me up."

Noticing an errant hair on her cheek, I reach up to gently brush it from her fair skin. Lexie's eyelids flutter as she stills against my touch, her breath hitching ever so slightly. When I remove my hand from her face she blinks a few times before speaking again, not the least bit flustered.

"You're right, it's never a good idea to insult the person with the scalpel," she agrees. "Smart man, always one step ahead."

"You have no idea."

She doesn't, but she will soon.

CHAPTER ELEVEN

CALLUM

"I want the docks locked down. I don't want anything coming in or going out without my knowing about it." I stalk across my office from one wall to the other before turning around and striding back.

"You know I don't have control of that, Russo." The cavalier air in Sal's voice makes me want to strangle the cockiness right out of the fucker. "I told you, I'll talk to the higher-ups and do what I can."

"If you let what I'm looking for out of the country, no one you love is safe from me." Venom drips from every syllable that leaves my mouth, each word deadly serious. If Charlotte Harris is shipped out of the country because Sal's twiddling his damn thumbs, I will personally skin him alive.

And I'll enjoy it.

When a girl is taken to be trafficked, the window to find them is usually very short. Maybe ninety-six hours, if you're lucky. But with adolescents, that window extends for transit conditions. Younger bodies don't last as long without food and water or being in extreme temperatures. That means timing and weather conditions are huge factors in when a container of girls can be shipped overseas. Which adds days instead of hours.

The Russians aren't taking just any girls, they're shopping

from a list. They won't move any of them until the full shipment is fulfilled. That extends my window to weeks.

If they have a buyer already set upon delivery, that changes the security factor. Having someone waiting turns the girls from livestock up for auction to curated goods, driving up the price. Where there's more money, there's more security. And security means firepower and strategy.

"That won't happen." His assurances mean shit. "Look, I gotta go. I'll call you." My phone beeps softly in my ear to announce that that call has ended.

The motherfucker hung up on me.

My fingers curl tightly into fists, muscles bunching against the urge to smash everything in sight. The pressure from how tightly my jaw is clenched threatens to crack my teeth. My legs carry me from one end of the room to the other, each breath coming out harsh and ragged. It's taking every ounce of my restraint to contain the fury raging through me. My arms twitch and swing with the desire to cause destruction and violence.

It's several minutes before I've reined in the fury enough to walk past my safe without pulling out a few guns and going to pay Sal a visit. He's not safe from me, especially if he can't do what he's told, but that will have to wait until later.

Striding out of my office, I'm looking for Roscoe. I find him in the kitchen with blonde Suzy-fucking-homemaker.

The entire apartment smells deliciously like sugar and cinnamon, the scent as enticing as it is infuriating. Lexie stands at the counter in a cute little apron with a pan of baked goods. Roscoe's behind her, lifting the heavy mixer back up onto the top shelf of the tall cabinet by the fridge.

"When you're done playing baker"—the bite in my voice has my enforcer standing at attention—"Enzo is waiting for you at the warehouse for my cut of the Ortega shipment."

"I'll leave now, boss." Roscoe nods, but Lexie stops him.

"Oh, here." She lifts a plate carrying a large cinnamon roll in front of his face. "Take one with you."

I refrain from rolling my eyes when the grizzly man's face lights up, his lips twitching with a smile, as he takes the plate before heading towards the door. The look I flash him is more than irritated, and he swipes the ridiculous mushy expression off his face on his way out.

Either unaware or unfazed by my mood, Lexie turns to me with another dessert on a plate. With her hair spilling over her shoulders, girly apron cinched in at her waist, and a big smile as she presents the baked good—she's the picture of sweet perfection. And it's aggravatingly arousing.

"Do you want a cinnamon roll? Roscoe said they're his favorite, so I made a bunch."

"No, I don't want a cinnamon roll," I grate, frustration brewing inside me. Sal's incompetence has me grasping at straws, getting in the way of my meticulous work. I can't do my job if people can't follow through on their end, and it's my results that suffer.

"What's your problem? I was just being nice." Lexie's tone turns assertive, her arms crossing under her breasts.

She wants to be friends. We're not fucking friends. With Lexie, it's either more or nothing. And we can't be more.

There's something about this woman that rattles me to my very core. Every instinct in my body is roaring for me to lean in closer when my rational brain tells me I should get as far away from her as possible. And the warring urges fuel a resentment inside me, sparked by irritation and frustration.

"The problem is that we're not friends, Lexie. You work for me, that's it. I'll let you know when I need you, all you have to do is follow orders." My words come out coldly, betraying the anger simmering inside me. "I don't need baked goods with frosting and sprinkles."

A full range of emotions crosses Lexie's face—shock, outrage, confusion, defiance—before settling on hostile acceptance. She lets out a short humorless laugh, completely devoid of her usual warmth.

I hate it.

"Fine, if that's how you want it to be." She matches my coldness, plopping a cinnamon roll heavily onto a plate. "I won't bother you with any more baked goods."

With that, she swipes the plate from the counter and stalks out of the kitchen towards her room. I watch her go, frustration warring with a wrenching in my gut that feels almost like regret.

My head hurts. Every gritty detail of the Harris job—every question, strategy, and possible outcome—races through my mind in a thundering roar that pounds against my temples. I've been sitting for too long, focusing too hard. Shoving away from my desk with a harsh breath, I stand to stride across my office. Standing in the doorway, I fight to quiet my brain as my eyes wander across the penthouse. My gaze doesn't stop moving until it lands heavily on Lexie's blonde head in the living room. The Harris job fades away as my laser focus zeroes in on the captivating woman.

Sweet fucking silence.

She's barely looked at me since our confrontation in the kitchen yesterday. And true to her word, she hasn't offered me another cinnamon roll, or a slice of the banana bread she baked early this morning. I should feel relieved, but all I feel is irritation. Turns out, being on the receiving end of Lexie's cold shoulder bothers me more than I thought it could.

And it's only been one damn day.

I can't seem to keep my eyes off of her. Since we've met, Lexie's drawn me in like a moth to a fucking flame. Her energy is unapologetic and irresistible. With the way she collects admirers wherever she goes, I know I'm not the only one who feels it.

Half of me—the twisted selfish half—feels the primal urge to snuff out that beautiful light of hers when she's sharing it with other people. I want to be the only one who gets to bask in her rays. That smile should only ever appear for me. If I can't harness it and own it, it shouldn't exist at all. It's a possessive and sick way of thinking, but it's always a temptation residing just below the surface.

Luckily the other half, the one I tend to listen to, doesn't have it in him to steal that glow from her. Her lovely, addicting glow that radiates with everything she is. I have enough self-awareness to know this part of me is selfish too. If her light's gone, my life dims with it. Her ability to scatter the shadows lurking with my demons vanishes. I'm not willing to give that up. Not willing to give *her* up.

Lexie's laughter rings through the penthouse, filling the living space from her corner of the couch. *Christ, I can't stop looking at her.*

She's playing with the sleeve of her loungewear set, the sky-blue color matching her eyes, her focus trained on the usually unfeeling bald man sitting on the opposite side of the couch. But even Roscoe cracks a smile for Lexie.

When I walk into the living room and her eyes meet mine, her smile falters.

I don't fucking like it.

"Go get dressed, Lexie. We're leaving," I say before I fully think it through. This dinner with Viktor is just an excuse to go back to his office for a drink afterwards and talk about his territory. I hadn't decided to take Lexie along. Now that I'm standing in front of her, I want her with me.

"Am I putting on my scrubs?" she asks with a sigh. The fact that she assumes I only want her to come patch someone up chips at the wall around my heart. That couldn't be further from the truth. But I should just say never mind and have her stay home. She'll just be a distraction anyway.

Instead, I hear myself say "Put on a dress, we're going to dinner." The words slip through the cracks in my self-control far too easily. Her face floods with surprise and confusion, but she stands to go change anyway.

Telling her to put on a dress was a mistake, one I regret as soon as she emerges in a little black number that has my imagination running rampant. Thin straps lead to an open square neckline draping across show-stopping breasts and curves to accentuate her fleshy waist. The hemline, that stops just above her knees, is made less modest by the slit on one side that flashes her creamy thigh. Her glittery black heels click on the floor as she walks towards me, sleek ponytail tossed to one side while she struggles to clasp a gold necklace.

Fucking hell.

Not a distraction, she's a devastation. A tornado of beautiful chaos determined to leave my life in ruins. And I'm nothing short of a storm chaser praying for disaster.

Christ.

Once the necklace is secured, she centers the pendant on her sternum and looks at me—for what—approval? Running a hand over my beard, I'm staring at her dumbfounded. The woman has stolen all words. My breathing is uneven as I desperately grasp on to the mask of calm that's splintering under her expectant gaze.

It's all I can do to give her a short nod.

Stepping into the elevator, I avoid looking at her reflection as the doors close. The last thing I need is to take this meeting with a raging erection, and one glance at her like this will have me rock hard. Roscoe catches my eyes, his brows lifting to communicate that he notices my discomfort. My glower in return only feeds his amusement.

Fucker.

"Who are we going to dinner with?" Lexie asks, oblivious to our silent exchange. She fiddles with the ring she always wears on the middle finger of her left hand, twisting it in a sign of what I recognize as anxiety. She's nervous.

"Viktor and Levi Mikhailov will be there with their wives, along with Enzo."

The elevator stops.

Ding.

The car ride is spent in silence. Lexie taps on her phone, most likely texting her best friend, Mia. I do my best not to stare at the way her dress rides up when she crosses her legs. My eyes keep catching on thick thighs despite my best efforts.

Get it together, Russo.

I can't show up to meet Mikhailov tripping over my hormones like some horny teenager. This dinner, despite its casual front, is crucial to the Harris job. If I can't get Viktor's blessing to enter his territory, it could result in a turf war I have no interest in getting involved with.

My ties to the *Cosa Nostra* already have Mikhailov and his *Bratva* roots on the fence about me. Old family feuds run deep, even now. This dinner is an active minefield. One misstep and this whole situation detonates.

Tugging at the shirt cuffs clasped at my wrists, I roll my shoulders to ease the tension settling there. The restaurant comes into view and my resolve is set firmly back into place. I'll get what I need from Mikhailov tonight, there's no other option.

My hand finds its way to the small of Lexie's back when we enter The Dining Room, the heat of her body radiating through her little black dress. Enzo stands waiting at the host stand, giving Lexie an enthusiastic greeting.

"Reporting for duty, boss," he says to me, exaggerating his dutiful tone with a nod before his focus turns to the blonde. "And here I thought it would be a stuffy business dinner. But if you're here, there's hope for a good time. What a pleasant surprise."

"Hi Enzo, it's nice to see you again," she replies. The fact that Enzo's happily married doesn't stop my fingers from flexing against Lexie's back. She looks up at me curiously, but I keep my eyes straight ahead.

"Mr. Russo," the hostess steps forward to address me. "Your party is already seated and waiting for you. If you'll follow me." As the young woman leads us through the restaurant, my gaze takes note of each exit, every staff member on the floor, and each set of male eyes that follow the woman on my arm.

Viktor and Levi are seated towards the back of the restaurant, the best table in the place that seats eight with a view of the city.

The Dining Room is one of the more upscale restaurants in New York, with marble floors, floor-to-ceiling windows looking over the city skyline, and a six-month waitlist. This place couldn't be more different from the seedy, outdated bar Levi owns—which is exactly the point. When authorities are looking for Russian thugs, Levi's bar is the first place they look. No one expects Viktor, the head of the Russian Bratva, to frequent a ritzy place like this, let alone own it.

"Russo," Viktor greets, nodding to the other two men. "Who is this?" He indicates towards the woman on my arm.

"This is Lexie, she's with me," I state simply. "Lexie, this is Viktor and his wife, Vera. And you remember Levi, with his wife, Alina." Vera is a striking woman with severe features, like her piercing dark blue eyes that can cut you with a glance. Her black hair is cut cleanly at the shoulders and curled inwards in a sleek bob. The darkness of her hair stands in stark contrast to the fairness of her alabaster skin.

Alina has a much softer look with long dark brown hair and wide brown eyes. Her default expression seems to be a stoic pout as she watches quietly. Despite her docile appearance, I know Levi's wife is anything but passive.

Lexie greets the two women in her usual fashion, complimenting them with a smile. Levi and Alina sit next to Vera then Viktor at the large circular table. Roscoe takes the seat next to Viktor while Enzo sits next to his son. I place myself next to Enzo, with Lexie on my right beside Roscoe.

Conversation starts off mildly with politeness and pleasantries. Lexie comments on Alina's earrings, which starts a small debate about natural diamonds versus lab-grown. I think a diamond is just a sparkly rock, natural or not. The pretty pink nurse seems to agree with me. What we talk about here at the table is inconsequential—the only conversation that matters to me tonight is the one I'll have with Viktor later. Alone.

Everything is going smoothly until the waiter comes around to take our dinner orders.

"And what would you like to eat, Miss?" The waiter addresses Lexie with a little too much interest. My eyes narrow at the man, but he's too focused on the bombshell beside me to notice.

"I've never eaten here before. What's your favorite dish on the menu . . ." Lexie looks up at his name tag. "Blake." The smile she offers him is far too warm and inviting. And I don't miss the way Blake eyes her breasts. More than once.

"I would recommend the center cut filet. It's so tender, it melts in your mouth." My grip on my fork tightens. Could he be any more brazen with his come-on?

"Oh, that sounds delicious." There's no reason to smile so much while ordering food. "I'll do that in the six-ounce, with the loaded mashed potatoes and mixed greens salad."

"Excellent choice, you have good taste."

I swear, if this fucker looks down her dress one more time. Of course, Lexie doesn't care enough to notice.

"And to drink, perhaps the house red?"

My arm stretches across the back of her chair, fed up. I'm done listening to frivolous conversation—done letting him stare at her like she's the real meal. He doesn't get to taste her, no one does. Leaning across her, I force the server's attention to me while I stare down the pathetic man trying to toy with something that doesn't belong to him.

She's not his, and she never will be.

"We'll take a bottle of the Brunello di Montalcino Riserva." My expression speaks the threats that my words don't. His face pales at the murder in my eyes. Looking from Lexie to me, the waiter seems to finally register that he's made an error. Luckily for Blake, he's smart enough to take a step back. His posture shifts with a polite nod.

"Right away, sir. My apologies." With that, he excuses himself and scurries away like the roach that he is. Lexie watches him go, flashing me a look of irritation that says she knows exactly what just happened. Her annoyance grates against my nerves.

She wants to keep talking to him.

Keeping my arm across the back of her chair, I bring my lips to her ear. "Try to be a little less shameless," I growl.

Her gaze flickers to me before her eyes roll briefly to the ceiling.

"I was just having a conversation. Waiters are people too, they deserve to be treated like it," she says as if she blatantly flirts with every waiter she comes across. The mental image only works to darken my mood.

"Why do you insist on talking to everyone who gives you the time of day? Are you really that desperate for attention?" I snap. A breath in only fills my lungs with her delicious scent.

"Probably because I'm starved of good conversation at home." Her barb hits me dead center. "I've got to take every opportunity I can when I'm out."

"It's childish. You're just begging for people to take advantage of you."

"Maybe I am. Maybe I want someone to take *full advantage*, Callum."

Arousal floods through me with her innuendo, seeping into my anger and fueling the darkness inside me. She's looking for someone to fuck, and she's making sure I know it'll be anyone but me.

"No one respects ridiculous women who try so hard to be the center of attention." She blinks at me, taking a sip of her water as she holds on to her unaffected facade for dear life. I can see her shiny confidence slipping. I'm conflicted as to whether or not that's my goal—break her down, take away any ability to replace me, so I'm her only refuge.

Sick bastard.

"What people think about me is none of my business. I'm not gonna try to take up less space just because other people feel small." Something flashes in her eyes, something deeper and more fierce than I've ever seen in her. I've struck a nerve, one I wasn't looking for. One I'm starting to regret poking at. "How you're feeling right now is your problem, it has nothing to do with me."

My eyes hold hers, pinning her where she sits. The conversations coming from the other side of the table barely register, my attention laser-focused on the woman next to me.

Each breath I take is filled with the addicting scent of her perfume. She's everywhere, in my head, under my skin, in the air I breathe. Everywhere but where she belongs—in my bed.

Lexie couldn't be more wrong. What I'm feeling right now has everything to do with her.

As good as the food was, I'm relieved when dinner ends. Now I can get to the real reason for this meeting tonight. And a few minutes without Lexie clouding my every thought means I have a much better chance of focusing.

Viktor and I stare at each other across his desk, drinks in hand. Our casual posture belies the tension radiating between us, a tension that always exists between a Vor and a made man—even if it's been a lifetime since I've been in the Outfit. Family ties run deep, something I've learned to work in my favor, and tend to complicate matters. People let their emotions run hot, and things get messy. From our past encounters, Viktor is more level-headed than that—something I'm banking on being the rule instead of the exception.

"So what's this about you wanting into my territory?" he rasps. Aged leather and wood groan under me when I lean back in the traditional wingback chair.

"Anton shit the bed, I've been called in for housekeeping." That's as much information as I plan on giving. With jobs like this, the less you reveal the better.

"Kozlov?" He doesn't sound the least bit surprised. I nod a confirmation. "What do the Grassos want with Anton?"

I spot the lure easily. *He's fishing.* I'm not about to take the bait. Running a hand over my beard, I take a sip of the whiskey. It's a top-shelf single malt, one of the best. I expect nothing less from Viktor.

"If this had to do with the Outfit, I wouldn't be here talking to you right now. There wouldn't be a conversation, just a bunch of body bags and bribed cops." Lucciano Grassos and his men tend to let their trigger-fingers do the talking. Fucking hotheads like them are what keep people like me and funeral homes in business—always leaving messes to clean up.

"*Khorosho*," Viktor acknowledges, turning the tumbler of whiskey absently on the desk. Cold dark eyes regard me without blinking. "What do you want with Anton?"

"You know better than to ask me that, Viktor." Considering the work I've done for him and the syndicate, he knows I don't mess with discretion. It's what keeps me alive and my bank account growing.

"If you won't tell me what you want with him, then you can tell me what he's worth to you."

There it is, an opening for negotiations. Exactly what I'm here for. I lean forward, resting my arms on my knees. Like most chairs with arms, this one is too small for me to sit comfortably. My mask of control remains firmly in place, not hinting at my discomfort, my gaze remaining unflinching on the Russian.

Someone less seasoned would offer up something in exchange for what I'm asking. But I know how the Mikhailovs operate. I can see on his face that he came in here already knowing what he wants from me. He always comes prepared, it's something we have in common.

One of the only things.

"Knowing you, Viktor, you already have a price in mind. What do you want?"

The old man smiles knowingly, but it doesn't reach his eyes. It never does.

"Turns out both the Kozlov brothers have been more trouble than they're worth. Alek's been skimming from the arms shipments and doing side deals." Anger edges Viktor's tone sharply.

Ah, there it is.

"He's stealing from you."

The biggest problem with organized crime is all the criminals. They get it in their heads that they can get away with anything. That they're untouchable. It's not just stupid to steal from a man like Viktor Mikhailov, it's practically a death sentence if they're caught. They're always caught. And I've been the executioner on more than one occasion.

"He dug his own grave, all you need to do is pick out a casket." Disdain drips from his voice. Dealing with Alek is a small price to pay in exchange for the answers his brother can give me.

"You sending a message to make him an example, or are you looking for a more permanent solution?" I ask. There are a lot of ways this problem with Alek can be solved, and I have no problem pulling the trigger on any of them, metaphorically or literally. Viktor takes a minute to contemplate, clearly not a hundred percent on his decision. When dealing with rats in your own ranks, it's a complicated situation. You might be able to take care of the rodent, but each extermination comes with its own set of issues.

"His blood runs too deep, he won't disappear quietly. Maybe some hard time will teach him some respect."

I can feel the regret radiating through his anger. Dealing with family matters has to make the most sense in the long run, not just what feels good in the moment. With the murder in Viktor's eyes, he wants nothing more than for Alek to suffer a long and painful death. But when murder isn't on the table, a nice hard prison sentence can have the desired effect.

"Are we talking all day?" I offer, a life sentence. The option is tempting, but Viktor shakes his head.

"A dime should do the trick. I have some friends waiting to welcome him in Sing Sing. You fix my Kozlov problem, you can have yours." I can get a ten-year sentence, easy.

"Consider it done," I state.

I down what's left in my glass, the liquor burning smoothly as it goes down. Rising from the chair, I place the empty tumbler on the desk heavily and pull my suit coat together to button it closed smoothly. "I'll be in touch," I say, agreeing to his terms and sealing the verbal contract. Viktor remains sitting and simply nods before I turn to leave.

Lexie isn't where I left her. Instead, I find her at the bar with a young female bartender. The medical kit sits open on the counter, gauze wrappers scattered across the surface. Getting closer, I can see she's got the young woman's hand spread flat in front of her while she sutures a gash across the palm.

"What happened?" My voice doesn't pull Lexie's laser focus from her meticulous work. The bartender swallows loudly, clearly nervous in my presence.

"One of the bottles broke," Lexie answers, tying off the last stitch. Peeling open one of the iodine swabs, she applies the disinfectant liberally before covering it with a sterile bandage. "There you go. Try not to use that hand, and keep it clean. Usually, stitches can come out after a few days, but hands are tricky—healing might take a little longer. You should follow up with your doctor or urgent care in about a week." Lexie leans back, giving the other woman a reassuring smile as she pulls off the disposable gloves.

"Thank you," the bartender says earnestly, withdrawing her hand and cradling it to her chest. She casts a nervous glance over her shoulder. "I better get back to work or else Michael's gonna kill me. But seriously, thank you."

"It's no problem, really."

My pretty pink nurse, always so gracious.

Finally, she turns those bright blue eyes on me. "Are we leaving?"

"We are."

"Okay, just let me pack up and say goodbye to Vera and Alina." Of course she wants to say goodbye to her new friends, like this is some social event.

I watch in silence as Lexie says her goodbyes, hugging both of the women. Seeing her embrace the Russian mob wives looks oddly similar to watching someone tame attack dogs. Both Vera and Alina are well-versed in the Bratva culture of blood and money. And yet, adding Lexie to the trio turns them back into playful puppies.

The silence in the car on the ride home holds a noticeable tension. Lexie's acting like I'm not even here, refusing to say a single word or even glance in my direction. I let my temper get the better of me at dinner, and I hurt her. She won't admit it. She even tried to brush it off. But I saw the moment the verbal blow landed. Now her confidence is bruised, because I'm a jealous idiot.

Getting the silent treatment from her is unbearable. I have to fix this, make things right. Make it up to her.

"What I said at dinner was wrong." Some of the tension eases when she finally turns from the window to look at me. "I'm sorry." As a man in my position, I don't often find myself having to apologize. But with Lexie, it doesn't just feel necessary, it feels right.

"Thank you," she replies, her eyes steady on mine. "Don't ever talk to me like that again." As she says it, in the deepest most visceral part of me, I know I never will. I can't.

CHAPTER TWELVE

CALLUM

"Where's Lexie?" Roscoe asks when I climb into the car alone.

"She's staying here. I don't need her to be there for this," I state, grabbing the briefcase off the floor of the vehicle near my feet.

Clicking open the latches, I lift the top to check the contents. Four bricks of cocaine lay stacked in the case, ready to serve as payment. It's more than enough coke to bribe a truck driver to give up his employer, even if it means betraying the Bratva.

"You like her," Roscoe states, navigating the car onto the crowded city streets.

"I'm doing my best to see her naked." My agreement isn't enough for him.

"More than just trying to bed her," he insists. "The pretty pink nurse has gotten under your skin."

"She's made her way into my blood. I just need to get her out of my system." I'm not sure if I'm trying to convince him or myself.

"Sometimes the only difference between poison and medicine is a matter of dosage." Roscoe knows me too well. I understand exactly what he's saying—and he's right.

I'll never admit it.

"What, are you waxing poetic now?" I growl, irritated at the knowing look in his eyes. "Just drive and focus on what we need to do."

"Whatever you say, boss." His comment carries a smugness that pisses me off. Forcing my focus back to the plan, I mentally walk through each step with their potential outcomes.

Getting someone to turn on Alek Kozlov was easy. He surrounds himself with greedy, disloyal men—like birds of a feather.

And how fitting for Joey Finch to be that bird. As the driver of Alek's delivery truck, he knows the different routes and schedules. Just the mention of Colombian cocaine had him blabbing on about the time and location of his next drop. Information I'll be using.

Technically I already got what I want, so there's really no reason to pay Finch at all. Not too smart on his part, though I don't expect much from lowlifes like him. But I'm a man of my word, so Roscoe and I are on our way to deliver the payment. Half now, half after his information proves useful. Joey Finch might be dumb enough to give everything away without guarantees, but I'm not.

If there was a better alternative than attending a charity gala, I would do it. Hell, I'd pull my own molars out if it meant I didn't have to stuff myself into the confines of a tuxedo and play nice all night. Unfortunately, this event has everyone I'm looking for under one roof, and my name is on the guest list. I'll just have to grin and bear it.

A charming smile settles over my face as I step into the ballroom. Tugging on my cufflinks, my eyes scan the event's attendees—crowds of people dressed to the nines in order to flaunt their importance. A room full of city officials, each one sure their political reach extends farther than it does. They flock together, schmoozing and greasing palms as they scramble to lift themselves up higher than the person next to them.

People like this, in the political arena, are all driven by the deep-seated desire for one or more of three things: money, power, and influence. Greed. Getting what you want from each of these bureaucrats is simple once you've identified their driving force. When you give them what they want—what they really want in the deepest parts of them, what they'll do anything for—they become useful tools. They might deny it to themselves, but I see it.

My eyes connect with the man I'm here to see on the opposite side of the ballroom. Entering the crowds, a robust frame steps into my path.

"You clean up good, Russo," Russell Moore greets me loudly, his veneers flashing as a grin spreads across his ruddy face. His tuxedo looks cheap and wrinkled, probably rented. No doubt a result of being kicked out by his third wife six weeks ago after she found him in bed with the co-ed dog walker.

Keeping an easy smile on my face, I don't miss how Moore pushes back his shoulders and stretches his spine to compete with the seven-inch height difference between us. His need to feel large in stature and importance has always been Moore's biggest weakness, one I use in my favor.

Influence.

"First Deputy Mayor Moore." I use his full title, feeding into his need for recognition. His shoulders relax slightly, his grin broadening. "I hear your municipal budget hearing went well." It's light conversation, exactly something you hear at a function like this. Unless you know what I know. What Moore knows.

He laughs, eyes lighting like we're in on a private joke together.

"It did. Our funding was approved, we got everything we wanted," he boasts. Including the point one percent being funneled right into his offshore account. Point one percent of the hundred billion dollars per year city budget adds up. A hundred million dollars a year going straight into his fat pockets, and my ten percent is what makes it possible and keeps me on retainer.

And they wonder why there's never any funding for arts programs in public schools.

"Who's your date?" My eyes move to the redhead on Moore's arm who looks barely legal. Russell looks over at his date, his eyes flickering in irritation that they're almost the same height in her sky-high heels.

"Nina is an undergrad at Columbia. She's writing a paper on the mayor's office, I'm giving her an inside look."

"I'm sure you are," I say, making eye contact with Robert Crenshaw over the deputy mayor's head. Excusing myself, I get intercepted three more times before I'm able to successfully cross the room to be face-to-face with the commissioner of police.

"Good evening ladies, looking lovely as always." I greet the two women he's standing with, his wife, Mallory, and her best friend Trisha. I've met both on several occasions.

"Callum, you're such a charmer." Trisha is flirting with me, a common occurrence. "Flattery will get you everywhere." I flash her a non-committal smile, my eyes moving to the man I'm after.

"Commissioner Crenshaw." I nod, my eyes holding his meaningfully. "I'm on my way to the bar, I need a refill. Join me."

"I could use another too," he affirms, turning to kiss his wife on the cheek. "I'll be back."

Crenshaw follows me through the throngs of people, to a darkened back hallway meant for service staff. We both know why I'm pulling him aside, but I say it anyway.

"I need you to make an arrest."

"Name?" Crenshaw's eyes scan the corridor for other party-goers, but there are none. I scouted the location beforehand, and Roscoe locked the door leading out of the ballroom to this hallway. We're alone. I note the way his jaw clenches, the tic in the muscles telling. Crenshaw's quick to ask for my services whenever there's something in need of fixing. He's only hesitant when it's time for him to hold up his end of our arrangement. His attitude chips away at my calm control.

"Alek Kozlov." I hand him the envelope of information. "The drop is Thursday afternoon at two fifteen over in the canning district. The evidence log is in there, you'll have what you need to charge at the scene." He knows the drill. Unsealing the envelope, he takes a peek at the documents inside.

"Kozlov? That's Russian," Crenshaw comments, glancing up at me for my reaction. I give him none, and he knows better than to press the issue. "Fuck, arms dealing? You gonna give me the big fish in this minnow's pond too?"

"No. Kozlov's alone." Viktor is off-limits, Alek is a means to my end. A stepping-stone to Anton and the girls. All of which Crenshaw doesn't need to know.

"Arrest?"

"Conviction."

"Who's he going to?" he asks, putting the papers back in and resealing the envelope before it disappears into his coat.

"Just take care of processing. Judge Mitchell will handle the sentencing." His Honor Judge Henry Mitchell already has his instructions—delivered to him by his favorite call girl, Cherry. "I shouldn't need to say it, but Russian weapons dealers don't show up unarmed. Make sure your men are prepared, I'm not paying for casualties."

"Of course." Crenshaw scowls at the implication, but I don't miss the realization that flashes in his eyes. "Anything else?"

"I need this one alive. You lose a black and white before you lose Kozlov, understand?"

"Got it," Crenshaw affirms tensely. "You'll get your guy. I'll call you when we have him." My phone beeps in my pocket. Glancing down, I see a text.

Barlow
> Meet me outside the south entrance.

"Good." I don't bother to offer Crenshaw any type of pleasantness in consolation, instead giving him a dismissing glance. There's no need to pretend, I dropped the mask with him a long time ago. "Always a pleasure, Commissioner." With that, I'm striding down the hallway.

Roscoe steps out from one of the darkened doorways, emerging from the shadows to fall into step beside me. "Turns out my dance card is full tonight."

"Mayor?" Roscoe guesses as I shoot off a quick text in reply as we navigate to the back entrance of the venue.

"D.A."

It's perfect really, the district attorney is who I need to speak to next, he's saved me the trouble of tracking him down. Although, if he's the one reaching out, that usually means he wants something from me. Not the most convenient timing, but I'll do what needs to be done.

District Attorney Ford Barlow is leaning casually against the back of the building when we exit through the south door, a cigarette hanging from his mouth. Glancing over at us through black frame glasses, he takes a long drag and holds the smoke in his mouth before releasing it in a slow breath.

"I can hardly stand these indoor events. It's illegal to smoke almost everywhere nowadays," he comments, reaching into his tux pocket to pull out a box of cigarettes. He holds it out to me in offering, and I take one. I'm not in the habit, but a good smoke hits just right every once in a while. Roscoe positions himself in front of the door, and a quick look around shows Barlow's security stationed not too far away.

"You get lonely out here smoking by yourself?" I ask, taking a puff. I pinch the cigarette between my thumb and index finger, watching the end spark in the darkness. The security lights hanging over the exit doors cast long shadows across the back alley, our smoke clouding the beams until they're hazy. "Your timing is impeccable."

"Sounds intriguing. Knowing you, this'll be good," Barlow responds easily, one of his hands going into his pocket. "What've you got?"

"There's a case coming your way. Alek Kozlov, Russian arms dealer."

"You want him to walk?"

"I want a conviction. Ten years in Sing Sing."

"Who's on it?"

"Mitchell," I respond. "Crenshaw's on delivery."

Taking another drag, a buzz of energy settles over my skin as the nicotine amps my system. The sounds of the city echo from the street—white noise to my native ears as we stand in the cool night air. I feel at ease here in the darkness, the shadows stealing the need for me to put on a mask to appease an audience. My fingers itch to remove my tux coat and roll up my sleeves, but the urge is ignored with practiced control.

"You won't have any interference from my office."

"That's good to hear." Taking this moment for the constant racing of my mind to settle is a small reprieve. When my companion's eyes cut to me, I know it's a fleeting one. Back to business. "Either you really like my company, or you've got something for me." My tone informs him I'm very aware it's not the former. Barlow doesn't bother with pandering, instead giving me a nod.

"Someone's looking for you. He's using a lot of capital to get your name."

"Who is he?"

"His name is Preston Wells, he's the president of Welling Industries."

"Give him my name. If he can pay, we'll see if it's worth my time."

"Pleasure doing business with you, Russo." With that, he turns to re-enter the building to get back to the party. I don't follow him. Now that my business here is done, I'm leaving. The sooner I can get out of this fucking tux, the better.

CHAPTER THIRTEEN

LEXIE

What a beautiful day.

Stepping out of the apartment lobby, I breathe in the fresh spring air. I really need to get out more. Staying inside all day, even in ritzy penthouses, can't be good for the soul. The sun is warm on my face as I stride from the building, adding a little more pep in my step my eyes scan the curb for my ride.

Roscoe stands by the street with the car door already open for me and the engine running. A smile tugs at his lips as he greets me with a nod.

It's been several days since I've been summoned for the job. Things have been pretty quiet around the apartment with the men off dealing with business. But after receiving a text to be ready to go when Roscoe pulls up, I've got my game face on.

The air is tense when I climb into the SUV where Callum is already waiting. He's focused on his phone, furiously typing either a text or an email. As soon as I'm in the car, Roscoe climbs behind the wheel and we're peeling away from the curb. Looking between the two men, I feel like I've missed something.

"I feel like something's wrong . . ." I let my voice trail off, meeting Roscoe's eyes in the rearview mirror before turning my attention back to Callum.

"Things didn't go how I planned, so it's time to switch tactics." The darkness beneath Callum's words makes me pity whoever screwed him over. Feeling my gaze, he glances in my direction.

"You're bleeding," I say, startled, causing Callum to reach for his temple. His fingertips come away covered in blood. I scooch closer in concern, trying to get a better look. "Let me see."

"I'm fine," he argues.

"Let me see, Callum." I'm not taking no for an answer. When he finally relents, I lean in closer to get a good look. It's not life-threatening, but it's deep. "You need stitches."

"Alright, go ahead."

"You want me to do it here? Right now?" I look around the back seat, at a loss.

"Yes." Not seeing another choice, I lift the medical kit from the floor with a sigh.

"How did this happen?" I ask, rifling through the supplies for what I'll need to sew him up.

"We raided a safehouse." He's back to typing on his phone. "The Russians didn't go down without a fight."

I've overheard him talking about his deal with Viktor Mikhailov. Callum arranged for one of Viktor's men to be arrested—which all went down without a hitch—in exchange for a location. I'm guessing that location was for the safehouse. Callum's been a busy boy the last four days.

"I can't get the right angle sitting like this." I'm expecting him to realize the back seat of a car isn't the ideal place for medical procedures. What I'm not expecting is for him to put his phone down before pulling me onto his lap. I gasp, quickly shifting to make sure the majority of my weight is supported by my knees.

"Is this angle better, Doc?" he asks as I stare at him wide-eyed. My eyes move over his face, and I give a small nod.

Hot damn.

Sucking in a breath, I focus on the task at hand. Or at least I try to.

"I need you to hold still," I huff in frustration when a bump in the road has the needle I'm trying to aim at the deep cut on his left temple gets dangerously close to Callum's eye. Straddling his lap in a moving car is getting harder by the second as the burning starts in my thighs from my attempt to remain hovering. "Can we pull over?"

"We have somewhere to be," Callum responds evenly.

"If you want me to sew you up, I need to be able to use this needle without giving you a nose piercing in the process." My frustration is rising. If I could just remain steady and hover while we drive, that would be great.

With the gash on his forehead, I have a sneaking suspicion there are bruises and other injuries hidden under his suit. There's no doubt in my mind that the man who did this to him is no longer breathing.

"Sit on my lap, all the way." Callum's gaze on me means business, his grip on my waist tightening.

"I'm heavy, I don't want to hurt you." My attempt to brush him off isn't successful, and his hands slip to my hips firmly.

"I can take you. All of you."

Still shaking my head, I fight to remain raised. "You're injured, I'll crush you."

One of Callum's hands moves from my waist to guide my chin until my eyes meet his. The intent in his gaze leaves no room for argument when he speaks.

"So crush me." The hand on my hip adds pressure to lower me as I finally relent. He wants my full two hundred and thirty-two pounds on his lap? Fine, I'll give the man what he wants. Releasing my legs, I sit on his lap without any support. A noise of satisfaction sounds deep in Callum's throat as I situate my body on his lap.

"That's my girl." Strong hands grip my hips, locking me in place against him. His words, spoken so deeply, send a wave of heat through me. My eyes lock with his, the pools of hazel pulling me in and threatening to drown me.

The sight of blood trailing down his left eyelid is an alarming reminder of what I'm doing here. My heart skips a beat as I force a slow deep breath I hadn't realized I was holding. I have to get this man stitched up before he bleeds everywhere. Taking his chin in one hand, I tilt his head down for the best angle to address his wound.

"Now stay still," I order, dabbing the gash with an iodine swab. I'm not about to let this get infected, especially an area so close to his eye.

"Whatever you say, Doc." There's something in his voice, something primal and self-satisfied, that has me glancing down. In this position, my breasts are barely a few short inches from his face and he has a very clear view of my chest down the V-neck of my top.

I can practically feel his eyes devouring every inch of exposed skin, and I struggle to ignore the sensations his hot breath against my skin elicit. With steady hands, I get to work.

"There," I say, dabbing the blood from his face delicately. "You're all fixed up." The wound took four stitches and two butterfly bandages to properly close.

"Are you sure? Maybe you need to do a few more," he says, making me bite back a smile as I roll my eyes.

"These will stay in for five days. Just make sure to keep them clean. A scar might add character to your pretty face, but guys who lose their eyes to infection have a harder time getting laid. Or so I've heard."

"I plan on keeping my eyes exactly where they are."

The double meaning is clear when I lean back on his lap and his eyes rake over me. Every inch of me burns under his intense gaze, stoking the spark deep in my core. I can feel him hardening beneath me, and I know if I don't move now things are going to change between us.

Reading my mind, Callum's grip on me tightens, one hand remaining solidly on my hip, while the other trails up to the small of my back to play with the ends of my hair.

"Callum, you're hurt," I remind him. His hungry eyes move over my face and land on my lips as I speak.

"Then it's a good thing I have you here to nurse me back to

health." His arms flex, pulling me in closer until my mouth is just a breath from his. My eyes flicker to his mouth, so close and tempting. "Go ahead, Doc. Kiss it better."

It's a challenge, and I've never been one to shy away from a dare. I lean in ever so slightly and Callum takes my invitation without hesitation. His hand on my back closes the gap between us to take my lips in an all-consuming kiss. Our mouths mold together, passion taking over. The way Callum kisses is devastating, all hunger and need.

God, so much need.

A deep growl rumbles in his chest, vibrating against my hands, and then I'm being crushed against him until I'm not sure where my body ends and his begins. His hand slides from my waist to palm one of my ass cheeks greedily as he all but eats at my mouth. I let out a soft sigh, and I'm drunk on him.

"Fuck, you're delicious." His groan is primal, and he drinks me in like he's a man dying of thirst. I've never been kissed like this before.

Callum's everywhere; his hands on my body, his growls send pulses of heat between my thighs, his breath mixing with mine as our lips work into a frenzy. It's like Callum's only purpose in life is to be there with me, like his entire existence depends on invading every one of my senses.

"We're here." Roscoe's voice pulls me from our little cloud of bliss and yanks me roughly back down to earth. Callum lets out a displeased grunt, reluctant as he leans back to look at me.

I'm sure I look a mess, all kiss-swollen and disheveled. I can see it in his eyes before he speaks a "go around the block" and pulls me back in. He isn't done with me yet.

The feeling is mutual.

"Yes sir." Roscoe's verbal confirmation reminds me that I'm straddling a man's lap. I'm suddenly aware that I'm having a heavy make-out session in a moving car. And we aren't alone. Reading my mind, Callum's hold on me tightens, his lips pulling my focus back to him.

And fuck if it doesn't work.

A soft moan escapes me when his teeth catch my bottom lip and gives it a sharp nip before his tongue eases the tender pain. The heat building inside me liquifies, my hips rocking against the hot erection I can feel hardening against my ass. An overwhelming need to unzip his pants and feel what's hiding underneath—what's promising to completely unravel me—is almost too much to handle.

When Callum's fingers slip inside the back of my pants as he palms my ass, it's a slap back to reality. Callum wants to do this, right here, right now. And I want more than anything to let him in.

We're in a moving car. And we're not alone.

Palms flattening on his chest, I break away from his kiss and create a sliver of space between us. His lips leave mine abruptly, leaving an unsettling cold where there used to be heat. My eyes open slowly, delirious, finding Callum gazing at me. The naked desire in his eyes is the only thing I recognize in his otherwise unreadable expression.

"We shouldn't," I breathe.

This is not the time or the place. If I really think about it—without the need and arousal taking over my brain—there might never be a time or place. Realistically, Callum and I don't work and sex isn't a good idea.

The way he's looking at me says he knows it too. He just wasn't going to admit it.

Callum takes his time pulling his hand from my pants, his fingers skimming over every inch of skin along the way—ass cheek, lower back, side. His eyes keeping mine hostage, he tugs my shirt back into place but doesn't let go immediately. We stay there for a long moment, just staring at each other while his hand on my shirt keeps me on his lap as we fight to catch our breath.

The wheels are turning in his head, I can practically hear his thoughts warring while he stares me down. If only I could know what he's thinking. He's watching every thought cross my face as it comes, reading every emotion. And all I get in return is indecipherable intensity and a rock-hard erection pressing hot and heady between my legs.

When his grip on my shirt finally falls away, I'm climbing off his lap and sliding across the back seat to put as much space between us as possible. Callum's eyes stare straight ahead as Roscoe rounds a corner, his hands working to roll his shirt sleeves back down. The tension settles back into his broad shoulders as he buttons each cuff into place. And just like that, he's back to calm and controlled Callum, devoid of any warmth.

When he does shoot a glance in my direction, it's one that looks an awful lot like regret.

Callum strides through the weathered brick building on a mission, and I'm a step behind him. With the distraction in the car, I have no idea where we are—and the man in front of me isn't giving any hints either.

His large frame fills the narrow hallway, broad shoulders nearly touching each wall with only a few inches of clearance from the ceiling. With the giant man ahead of me blocking my view, I'm basically stumbling along blindly with Roscoe walking steadily behind me.

We take a left at the end of the claustrophobic hallway. The doors that dot the space are as dated as the rest of the building, with small windows of frosted glass yellowed with age.

Callum doesn't hesitate to open one of the doors roughly, and I'm barely able to read the word *Freight* across the window in peeling vinyl before Roscoe is crowding me into the room and closing the door.

The stench of cigarette smoke and stale coffee hangs in the air. The small industrial office is drab with stained brown carpet, metal filing cabinets, and fluorescent lighting. The room is messy and cluttered until it's claustrophobic—binders and stacks of paper taking over.

A middle-aged man behind the desk looks up startled when we enter, his eyes going straight to the bull charging right at him. His gray-streaked brown hair looks crunchy with gel, matching the patchy facial hair on his chin. He has a gut from a few too many beers that's obvious on his lanky body as he slumps in his chair.

Callum stops short at the desk, staring him down.

"Hello, Sal. You haven't been answering my calls." The steel edge in Callum's voice has the man behind the desk glancing at the door in hopes of finding someone to save him. Instead, all he finds is a blonde in pastel scrubs and the enforcer blocking the only exit.

"Russo." Sal's false friendliness falls flat in his attempt to put on a brave face. "I was just about to call you back."

"Were you." It's not a question. "And what were you calling to say?"

"I—uh—I went up the ladder. There's really nothing I can do for you."

I can't help but wince at the arrogance tinting his voice. The tension that settles over Callum's shoulders has a dark cloud falling over the room. This isn't gonna be pretty.

"That's the wrong answer."

Uneasiness creeps up my spine when Callum's hands move to unbutton the cuffs of his dress shirt—the same ones he just buttoned in the car.

"I told you, my hands are tied," Sal not stammering.

"You know, Sal, the easiest way to free tied hands is to simply cut them off."

The threat isn't directed at me, but my stomach drops just the same. My entire body stiffens at the violence in Callum's words, spoken so casually. This is definitely not the first time he's delivered a warning like that.

"Whoa, hey. Wait, there's no need for that—" Sal's sputtering doesn't register as Callum continues, rolling one of his shirt sleeves up past his elbow.

"We won't start there, of course, we'll work our way up." Callum's tone darkens, his head nodding to where Roscoe stands behind him. "My friend here likes to start with the fingers, he's actually quite good at it. The knuckles sever nicely. Then maybe, if you've decided to be a little more cooperative, I'll have my nurse stitch you back up."

Sal's wide eyes dart to the door frantically. He's gonna make a run for it, it's obvious to everyone in the room. When he scrambles from his chair, with the grace of a rhino, to dash towards the only exit he doesn't make it three strides before he's being lifted off the ground. Callum catches him easily by the collar and yanks him roughly backwards.

The man goes flying, slamming against the corner of a filing cabinet with a groan. The air isn't even back in his lungs before Callum's hauling him up and slamming a fist into his face—once, twice, three times. Blood spurts from his nose, coating his teeth when he howls. The strong hand that Callum clamps around his throat violently drags him to the wall next to the desk, causing stacks of papers and folders to scatter to the floor dramatically.

A gasp escapes me at the sound of Sal's skull cracking against the wall with the force of the blow, hard enough to fracture bone. Callum's eyes cut to me, his dark gaze cold and unfeeling.

Terrifying.

"That was the last stupid decision I'll tolerate, Sal." His deadly focus returns to the man he's choking out. "Do you understand?"

Sal's desperate nodding is restricted against the hand clamped beneath his jaw.

"When I call, you answer it. When I ask you a question, you what?"

"Answer it."

"Very good." Callum's powerful grip bleaches his knuckles as it tightens on the man's throat. "Don't make me come here again, Sal. Or I'll be paying your family a visit covered in your blood."

"I won't."

"Now." Yanking him from the wall, Callum tosses the older

man into the desk chair like a ragdoll. Sal grips the armrests for dear life when the chair threatens to tip over from the force of the impact, blood running from his bashed nose and battered mouth and coating his chin where it dribbles down the front of his shirt. "Because I'm feeling generous, I'll let my nurse clean you up before you start making more calls."

When the other eyes in the room turn to focus on me, I'm caught off guard. I stand frozen, at a complete loss.

"This is why you're here, Doc. Fix him up." Those are the same damn words he used the night he led me into that storage room to sew up a finger and ripped me from my reality.

My feet have already carried me halfway across the room before I register that I'm moving. When I kneel in front of the bloodied man in the chair, our eyes connect briefly. For a split second, we share a moment of shocked horror, both trapped in the violence brought by the hands of the fixer standing behind me.

Okay, you can do this, Lexie. You can handle this, he's just another patient.

Yanking my eyes away, it takes everything in me to keep breathing—in, then out—as I go about the task of tending to my patient. He needs three stitches, and his nose is very broken. There's nothing I can do about the concussion or the fractures I'm sure now decorate the back of his skull.

There's a heaviness in my chest that seems to grow with every beat of my heart until it's crushing me under its weight. Whatever conversation happens between the three men in the room as I work doesn't register past the blood pounding in my ears.

Even as I numbly follow Callum through the hallway back outside, I feel like a zombie. I'm no longer residing in my body when the back door of the car is held open for me to climb in. Is this what shock feels like?

Closing my door, Callum walks around to get in on the other side. My mind is racing, the world doesn't feel like it makes sense anymore. The oxygen has been sucked out of the car, and the thought of sitting in a confined space with Callum threatens to suffocate me. I can feel the vehicle shift with his weight as he sits down, the sound of his door closing behind him igniting my flight response. Without thinking, I open the door and hop out.

"Lexie, *shit.*" I don't register Roscoe's call as I walk. My feet move, carrying me down the sidewalk, as I force in deep breaths. I just need air, *what happened to all the air*? My brain is trying so hard to make sense of everything, but nothing is processing as my mind glitches.

Callum and Roscoe are violent men, ruthless and cruel. Callum does whatever it takes to get something he wants, and he uses Roscoe to do it.

And now he uses me too.

What have I gotten myself into? I signed the contract and NDA, an unsuspecting mouse walking straight into a trap. And like an idiot, I read the fine print wearing rose-colored glasses that made the boatload of red flags seem pink and harmless instead. And the trap snapped closed without sympathy. Now I'm stuck, completely at Callum's mercy.

What have I done?

The question echoes through my mind as nausea churns in my stomach. My feet carry me one step at a time, my body on autopilot. The SUV pulls up beside me, slowing to match my pace. The back window rolls down and Callum's dark expression acts as a reminder of exactly what kind of hell I'm living in now. I glance at him, but looking at his face proves to be too much. Averting my gaze, I look straight ahead as I walk.

"Lexie, stop." The authority in Callum's voice rolls over me without effect. My heart is racing too fast, my thoughts becoming too panicked—and I *don't* panic.

"Lexie."

"I can't do this," I say, my voice breaking on the last word. I feel breathless, why can't I breathe? I round a corner, and the car follows. Roscoe says something to Callum, making him curse under his breath.

"Get in, Lexie," Callum orders. I simply shake my head,

staring straight ahead. I barely see the people I pass on the sidewalk, barely register the eyes on me. Glancing down, I realize I'm still splattered in blood, my blue scrubs stained by the crimson color. *His* blood. The man Callum made me patch up after threatening his entire family—all for illegal dock access for some shipment.

"Get in the car, Lexie. Or I swear to God, I'll pick you up, throw you in the car, and buckle you in myself."

Something in Callum's voice makes me stop in my tracks. I finally turn to look at him, still struggling to catch my breath. I feel a little faint, like the blood was drained out of me.

Meeting Callum's eyes, I can see he means every word. He'll physically pick me up and place me into the car right now. And the idea of him touching me with the same hands that just held a man by the throat is enough to crack through my panic.

We stare at each other for a moment. I can practically see the wheels turning in his head as he reads me. And when I finally take a step towards the car and reach for the handle, I swear his face softens slightly in what looks like relief.

After I climb into the car, Roscoe locks the door the instant it's closed behind me. With shaky hands, I slowly reach back and grab my seat belt. I can feel both men's eyes on me as I slowly pull the belt around me, but I keep my eyes trained out the window. As soon as my seat belt clicks, Roscoe is pulling out into traffic.

Callum's eyes never leave me, burning a hole in my already crumbling psyche. I'm exhausted, physically and mentally. I stare out the window without really seeing the cityscape pass by. When the first tear rolls down my cheek, Callum's voice is barely audible next to me as he rasps out another curse under his breath.

"*Fuck.*"

CHAPTER FOURTEEN

LEXIE

I'm barely in my bedroom before I'm yanking the bloody scrubs off my body with shaking hands. My heart beats unevenly in my chest, making me feel unsettled in my skin. Stepping into the shower, I run the water as hot as I can, hoping and praying that the scalding liquid will wash away the guilt that's mingling with the man's blood.

The urge to pick up my phone to call Mia and tell her everything is almost unbearable, so I keep my hands busy instead. I towel dry my body, moisturize, and pull on a random gray loungewear set. I've just finished taking my makeup off and washing my face when I feel his presence.

"The food's ready, come eat."

"No thanks." Turning on my heel, I move to exit the bathroom. He blocks my path.

"It's not a fucking request, Lexie."

Standing in my bathroom doorway, Callum's giant figure fills the frame, blocking me in completely. This time when he looks down at me, I don't look away. His expression is one of domination and intimidation, but I'm not having any of it.

"You're going to sit down and eat a full meal," he states—like it's a fact.

"I'm not hungry." It's not a lie, my appetite disappeared the moment Callum slammed that poor man against the wall by the throat.

"I don't give a shit if you're hungry or not. You haven't eaten yet today, you're going to now."

"What, are you watching me?"

"I always have eyes on you. Don't doubt for a second that I know everything you do."

"I'm not eating with you."

"Either you walk into the kitchen, sit that beautiful ass of yours in a chair, and eat every bite on the plate I set in front of you . . ." He leans forward, getting closer to my level without breaking eye contact. The corners of his mouth lift into a taunting smile. ". . . or I'll put you in the chair myself and personally feed you every single bite. And you'll have seconds."

He sounds almost excited about this possibility—like he's hoping I choose to defy him. Like he *wants* to manhandle me and hand-feed me, be in complete control of me. He's getting off on this, the perverted control freak.

A chill runs down my spine, goosebumps raising on my arms. I bite my bottom lip as I consider my options. His gaze catches on my mouth, growing heated, and the air in the bathroom shifts around us. Suddenly the tension between us feels more sexual than angry.

"Fine," I grit through clenched teeth.

Callum's eyes move back to my mouth once more before he finally steps aside so I can pass. But he doesn't move nearly enough, forcing me to press my body against his to squeeze through the gap. He flashes a satisfied smirk at my glare as I shove past him and walk to the dining room. He's following closely behind me, and I don't even care that it makes me look petulant, I stomp a little before I fall heavily into a chair with a huff.

The table is set for two, the plates filled with seasoned chicken, mashed potatoes, and green beans. A tall glass of water sits next to my plate, laughing at me. Callum takes the seat next to mine casually and gets comfortable like he doesn't have a care in the world. He digs into his plate without hesitation. When I don't even reach for the silverware, he leans forward and rests his muscled forearms on the table. His eyes latch on to mine and dare me to challenge him.

"Don't test me, Dewdrop. You're an investment now, and I take care of what's mine." His deep voice sends a wave of lust curling through me, but I ignore it and throw him a withering glare. "You're going to eat everything on the plate and drink everything in that glass." There's no way out of this other than to obey. I'd rather die than give this man the satisfaction of feeding me each bite.

Triumph lights his eyes when I relent, reaching for the fork and taking a scoop of the creamy mashed potatoes. He watches intently as I eat the first two bites and cut a piece of the chicken. It's perfectly seasoned, *the son of a bitch*. He relaxes back into his chair while I chew, his eyes only leaving me once I swallow.

There are a lot of things I can say about Callum, but the bastard can cook. Reaching for the glass of water, I take a sip.

"Good girl," he murmurs deeply.

My eyes snap to his over the glass, his piercing gaze pinning me in place. The heat in his eyes sparks something inside me, warming my blood. His focus flickers to my pursed lips, his expression as unreadable as ever. I slowly put the cup back on the table, shaking off the desire and forcing myself to keep eating as if the room doesn't suddenly feel ten degrees hotter.

After dinner, Callum disappears and leaves me to stew in my emotional chaos. There's nothing to distract me anymore—not food, and not a sexy, controlling asshole watching my every move. No matter what I try to focus on, my brain loops back to the image of Callum slamming that man against the wall. Something that snaps in my mind that has me on a fucking mission.

His office is off-limits, but I don't give a damn. I stride in there with a purpose, making no attempts to hide my anger. Callum looks up from his computer and watches as I take a seat in one of the chairs across from him. His passive expression just pisses me off further. Callum doesn't think he needs to concern himself with me and my feelings. He thinks that my emotions are just ridiculous and inconsequential.

He's very wrong.

"I want out," I state, sitting tall as I glare at him across the desk. He leans back in his chair, black dress shirt pulled taut across broad shoulders, sleeves rolled up to inked elbows.

"There is no out, Lexie. If you read what you were agreeing to before you signed it, you'd know that." His condescension is like a slap to the face, sparking my temper.

"You think I'm dumb, Callum, is that it? That I'm some clueless girl who just didn't read the fine print? I did. I read every line of that contract. I just didn't know the kind of business you're in when I was reading it. So when I signed my name, agreeing to be the medical party that acts on your behalf, I didn't know that meant doing your bidding—even if it means watching you hurt people."

His focus stays fixed on me in an unrelenting stare. I feel like a bug under a magnifying glass. The way his eyes take in every detail about me and seem to climb right into my head to read my thoughts is unnerving.

His expression in return is calm as still water, his shoulders rigidly set in stone. "You think it's just that easy? That's not how it works, there's no leaving one of my contracts," he says, making me huff defiantly.

"I can find someone else to take my place just like Tony did," I argue. I've done my research, I know my options. His expression darkens, something deep and complex flickering in his eyes.

"No one can take your place, Lexie." His voice lowers, jaw tightening. "I won't let you go."

"So that's it?" I ask, defeated. A conflicting cocktail of dread and warmth swirls inside of me, exhilarating and exhausting.

"It's binding. I suggest you get cozy, this is your life now."

CHAPTER FIFTEEN

LEXIE

As much as I love my therapist Julie, some days retail therapy is the best kind. The instant serotonin I feel when I receive a package or open a shopping bag—it can't be beat. Especially now that I can't actually talk to her about what's really going on in my life outside vague expressions about my current emotions. I think she's starting to notice, so my time with her is probably running out. I've decided to put our sessions on hold until I can untangle some of the giant complications that have recently twisted up my life.

At least I have a box waiting for me at the front desk for today's dose of excitement.

Taking the sharp edge of the scissors to slice through the tape, I pull one of the box flaps to peek at what's inside. "It's here," I announce to no one in particular as I open the box. I lift the oversized panda from the package, hoisting its considerable weight.

"What is that?" Callum's voice speaks over my shoulder, closer than I expected him to be.

He's always standing so damn close.

"It's a weighted stuffie." Pulling the bear to my chest, I give it a test hug. The weight of it feels satisfying in my arms. Hopefully it's heavy enough to crush the anxiety out of me long enough to fall asleep at night.

"I didn't figure a girl like you would try to replace a man with a pillow when you're lonely at night." Callum's comment has a wave of heat washing over me, a mix of arousal and embarrassment.

"I'm not," I say defensively, frowning up at him over my shoulder. Despite my protest, he remains unconvinced. His hazel eyes take their time looking me up and down, his lips twitching smugly under his beard.

"That poor panda doesn't stand a chance when you need satisfaction, Dewdrop." There's a patronizing edge to his voice. His taunting pisses me off.

"It's not for that, Callum," I insist, growing exasperated. The smirk on his lips spreads into a self-satisfied smile.

"Then what's it for?" His brows raise, waiting for another explanation. He's not expecting there to be one.

"It's so I can actually sleep when—" Realizing I've said too much, my voice trails off and I press my lips together. All humor drops from Callum's face, growing intensely serious in the blink of an eye. His eyes narrow.

"When what?" he asks slowly, distinctly. There's no way out of this, I've dug myself too big of a hole. I let out a sigh and avert my eyes.

"When I have nightmares," I admit. A line forms between Callum's dark brows, his shoulders tensing.

"Nightmares about what?" He's demanding answers that I'm not going to give him. Callum's compulsive need to know everything I'm thinking until he's in my head is an exhausting game I'm not in the mood to play. All teasing aside, there are some things he doesn't get to know.

"That's none of your business." Toting my new stuffed friend, I skirt around his demanding stare and head to my room.

Placing the oversized panda on the bed next to my pillow, I mull over what to name her. If we're going to be cuddling every night, she deserves to have a name. And a cute one to match how adorable she is.

Buttercup. It's perfect.

My phone chimes as a notification from one of my dating

apps lights the screen—Eric C. matched with you! Opening the app, I click on Eric's profile. He's cute with a full head of dark curls, and dimples decorating his wide smile. His entire profile screams "golden retriever energy."

I'm in the bathroom getting ready to go out for the night when my phone chimes again, this time with a message from the golden retriever. I pause my makeup sponge mid-beat to open the message.

Eric
You are stunning

Lexie
Aww stop, you're making me blush. Thank you! You're not so bad yourself.

Eric
Oregon, huh? What brings you all the way to NYC?

Lexie
I've always wanted to know what it's like to get bitten by someone on the subway. This was my chance

Eric
And were your dreams fulfilled? I'd hate for you to miss out on the real NY experience haha.

Lexie
Absolutely, and I have the teeth marks to prove it. On another note, my tetanus shots are up to date in case you were wondering.

Eric

Good, I was worried about that. If you're planning on eating anywhere in Brooklyn, you'll probably want to get a rabies shot too. 🐻

Lexie

I have yet to eat in Brooklyn, but I'll keep that in mind.

Eric

We'll have to change that, won't we?

Lexie

I guess that depends on what you have in mind . . .

My chunky heels click on the floor as I walk into the kitchen. Tossing my curled hair to one side to put my small gold hoop earring in, my fingers struggle with the backing. Callum sits facing the tv on the other side of the living space, a newscaster displayed on the screen.

"I'm leaving," I announce, finally securing my jewelry.

"Where are you going?" Callum's deep voice carries from the living room. I look over as he stands from the couch. When he turns and his eyes settle on me, his entire body turns to stone. The man could be a statue if it weren't for his searing gaze moving over me from head to toe.

"Girls' night out." My brows come together in confusion. What's his problem?

"That's what you're wearing? It's a fucking napkin." The accusation in his voice has me looking down at my outfit.

My emerald top has an open corset front, the strings connecting the two halves stretching over a large gap that doesn't cover much past my nipples and ends right above my high-waisted wide-legged black pleather pants. This top cuts down the globes of my breasts and puts them on full display.

Too open to wear even the lowest of plunge bras, I'm taped to high heaven. This industrial-strength boob tape is a miracle worker, and it's definitely fighting for its life against gravity. Somehow, it's winning—because my giant boobs are currently defying the laws of physics. Best fifty-five bucks I ever spent.

"This *napkin* is gonna get me lots of free drinks tonight." There's not an ounce of apology in my voice. I have nothing to be sorry for, I look great.

"Drinks? Looking like that, they'll think they can buy *you*." Coming closer, his eyes keep finding their way back to my cleavage, his expression darkening considerably.

Grabbing my handbag from the counter, I saunter over to the door. Pausing with my hand on the doorknob, I throw him a taunting smile over my shoulder. "In that case, don't wait up."

"Are you serious?" Ronnie cries the instant I step out of the car. "Girl, your boobs! You look so hot, I can't even stand it."

"I was just going to say the same thing to you. You look so good." I mean it. Ronnie's vibrant orange monochromatic look pairs incredibly with her rich, dark skin. And she knows how to pull off a look, her mini dress matching both her bold orange lipstick and the shoulder-length, wavy orange wig completing the ensemble.

"You know I gotta show up and show out," Ronnie laughs, doing a little spin to show off the full effect. She then turns to gesture to the beautiful woman standing next to her. "This is my girl, Maya. She's my best drinking buddy, she knows how to have fun."

"I'm Lexie, so nice to meet you." I introduce myself with an excited smile. "I'm always looking for fun drinking buddies."

Maya is simply stunning. With thick straight, black hair

hanging to the small of her back. Her tan complexion and dark features hint at a Hispanic heritage, with a curvy hourglass figure to die for. "I've heard so much about you, I'm very excited to see you get on stage," Maya laughs.

"Oh, you better believe I'm getting on that stage." I grin, excitement buzzing through me. "Let's go in, I'm ready for a drink."

The bar is large, colorful, and packed with people in various stages of inebriation. A stage that stands along the back wall is lit by colorful spotlights that change with the music. The music playing over the buzz of the crowd has a pulsing beat that vibrates through the floor and makes me want to dance. This is the perfect place to get drunk, let loose, and forget about my problems.

"Lexie, I can't get over your outfit. How did I not know you have a body like this? You're doing the world a huge disservice by ever wearing a shirt."

"I mean, scrubs aren't exactly the most flattering." I laugh as we make our way over to the bar. "Besides, I try not to show off for the randoms in the ER."

"So true," Ronnie agrees readily. "Look at us, the blonde, brunette, and redhead." And between my top, Ronnie's dress, and Maya's skirt, we've got tits, legs, and ass covered tonight. We're a hot group of ladies. This is already gearing up to be a fun night.

The first round of drinks has us loosening up nicely. We dance, cheer for the drunken karaoke performers, and just laugh together. Maya is hilarious, and she's definitely as fun as Ronnie described. She's ordering shots and matching my energy on the dance floor.

Lots of male eyes are on our trio from the moment we walk in, and it's not too long before men are trying to join us on the dance floor. They think they're so slick, slipping behind us like we won't notice they're trying to grind on us. Each one is pushed away, but that doesn't stop them from trying.

If men have one thing, it's the audacity. Cue the drunken asshole who looks like he has at least one photo of himself holding a

Mmm, he smells good.

I don't bother tilting my head up, opting instead to peer up at him through my false lashes. Even in my heels, the top of my head only reaches the top button on his dress shirt.

Damn, he's so tall and his shoulders are so broad. He's a man who could ruin me and I'm sure I'd enjoy every second of it.

I wanna climb that tree.

"I've been trying to call you." He pulls his eyes away from me to look around, throwing a deadly glare at someone behind me. Probably the man at the bar who was just making eyes at me.

"I'm sure you have. I put it on silent." I take a sip of my fruity drink, dancing along to the music. His eyes roam over me as I move, fixating on how my breasts bounce in this top. My drink warms me from the inside out, the music buzzing over my skin.

"It's time to go home," he says, but I simply laugh and shake my head. His eyes narrow.

"You can go home, I'm having fun with my friends." The music lowers as the song ends. The emcee of the karaoke night hops on stage to address the crowd.

"Alright, alright people! It's karaoke night, and you know what that means. Next up we've got Lexie West working her best blonde bombshell with the queen Dolly." I perk up at my name, raring to go. Defiance flares inside me when Callum steps into my path.

"I'm not leaving here without you, Lexie," he states, but I'm already moving. Putting my drink in his hand as I pass, I lean in.

"Then here." A grin spreads across my face. "Have a drink and enjoy the show."

Whoops of excitement erupt as I take the stage, accepting the bedazzled microphone from the emcee with a playful wink. The cheers of the crowd wash over me, hyping me up as Dolly Parton's "9 to 5" starts blaring through the speakers. My body moves in time with the music, feeling it flow through me and back down into the stage, the bass thumping with my moving hips. This crowd is the best audience, eating up everything I give them. And if there's one thing I know, it's how to put on a good show.

The first verse comes to an end and the chorus approaches, I take a deep breath and put my whole chest into it, the rest of the bar dancing and singing along with me. I channel Dolly with my entire being, feeling the power of her lyrics. My focus lands on Callum, singing to him with all I have when the chorus plays.

CHAPTER SIXTEEN

CALLUM

The crowd pulses around me, following Lexie's lead as she enjoys the music. I stand rigidly, not moving a single muscle. I'm frozen in place, unable to take my eyes off the woman on stage for even a second. She might not win any of those talent reality shows she loves so much, but she's got a good singing voice—never straining to hit the right note with a tone that's as bright and alluring as she is.

Her stage presence matches the rest of her personality, pulling focus and shining brightly on everyone who lays eyes on her without even trying. Magnetic. Every pair of eyes in this entire bar is glued to her, as helpless as I am against her charisma.

The way her body moves, not missing a single beat in the pulsing music is hypnotic, her generous curves accentuated with every sway of her hips or shake of her shoulders. I know every man in this bar is staring straight at how her full breasts bounce and sway in that fucking scrap of a top, each movement erotically charged. She pays them no mind, but I do.

Her confidence is so damn sexy. The way she's comfortable in her own skin makes me want to get comfortable in her skin along with her. Jealousy surges through me at the thought of any other man looking at her the way I am right now, wanting what they can't have.

Her attention returns to me every time she sings the chorus;

her serenading switches between teasing and flirting, to powerful and heartfelt. When the song ends, she draws out the last note dramatically, the crowded bar cheering wildly. My eyes track her movements as she hands the mic back to the man acting as host, narrowing slightly at the way he grins at her.

Any anger melts away when she bounds straight over to me, my chest tightening at the look of pure joy on her face. Her cheeks are flushed, eyes sparkling beneath dramatic lashes. She's absolutely beaming, dousing me in blazing warmth until I'm nothing but ash.

Fuck, I want to be the reason she smiles like this.

"Didn't you like my song choice? You didn't dance." She doesn't actually care, she's still coming off the high from being under the spotlight.

"I don't dance." I can't take my eyes off her. Lexie gives a small shrug.

"If you're boring, just say that," she says breezily and takes back the untouched drink she gave me. "Dolly is a queen."

She hasn't stopped moving since I arrived, her body constantly feeling the music in some small way. Hearing her words start to run together, I know she's passed the point of buzzed into tipsy. She looks up at me curiously, sipping through her straw.

"You're really not leaving without me? It's gonna be a while, because my night just started."

"I'll wait." *And watch.*

"Can you at least stop glowering at people? You're scaring my friends."

My eyes move over her head to find her party-happy friends eyeing me curiously. I offer them a practiced smile before turning it on Lexie. Her brows jump in amusement, eyes laughing at me.

"Wow, that smile is almost believable," she teases, her straw slurping against the ice in her now-empty glass. The adorable frown she gives the cup is one of disapproval—like it's personally offended her by running out of alcohol. "Well, time to put this top to good use for a free drink."

I catch her by the arm before she can turn away, making her stumble into me. She leans against my chest in that damn outfit that gives her so much cleavage it should be illegal. "I'll open a tab."

I don't know what possessed me to fund the drinks for her and her friends for the rest of the night. But the idea of her flaunting around to other men, letting them think they get to take advantage of her voluptuous body, makes me want to start snapping necks.

She lets out a delighted laugh, and steps over to her friends for another round of shots. I can hear her tell them that I'm covering the tab and they lift their glasses to me before downing the tequila. I step back to lean against the bar, settling in to watch the whirlwind of *girls' night out*.

If I thought sober Lexie was a handful, drunk Lexie is in a league of her own. Her already confident demeanor is amplified by the alcohol and her inhibitions are almost completely gone. Dancing on the bar with her girlfriends, becoming friendly with the bartenders, and helping the emcee announce the karaoke lineup.

She even talked a guy into giving her his jacket because she got cold. She doesn't realize who he is and the significance of his jacket, but I recognized the NFL linebacker instantly. Despite the number of people in the crowded bar, she's the life of the party. And she never stops laughing.

When her shoes come off, it's time to go home. Ordering a car for her friends who live in Harlem, I help them into their ride before toting Lexie to where I parked. But not before she returns the jacket to the "nice, friendly, giant man with the cool ring."

Revving the Gran Torino engine, I pull into the 2 a.m. traffic. "This car is so loud," Lexie giggles to herself. I can feel her eyes on me. "You know what they say about men with obnoxious cars."

"No," I lie. "What do they say?" There's no telling what'll come out of her mouth next, but I want to hear it. I can't help myself.

"That they're overcompensating for their small dicks." She falls back against the seat, tilting her head against the headrest.

"You think I have a small dick?" I raise my brows at her.

She remains unbothered, smile turning lazy as she eyes me knowingly.

"Not from what I've felt. You've probably got a big dick to match the rest of you. You're a very big boy, Callum." Her words shoot straight to my cock.

"Maybe I'm compensating for something else."

She doesn't hesitate to voice her opinion and offer up a suggestion. "Like your compulsive need for control and complete inability to express your feelings?"

"Maybe." She's too astute, even when she's drunk. I run a hand over my beard, turning right on red. She doesn't notice my attitude shift.

"It's okay, what you lack in the warm and fuzzies you make up for in badassery. Although, you could flash that pretty smile more often," she states. "Plus, you're rich and super hot. That tends to make up for a lot of sins."

"You think I'm hot?" My lips twitch in amusement.

Her animated face moves and I can see her eyes roll in my peripheral vision.

"I'm not blind. Of course I think you're fucking hot. I thought we already had this conversation." She's right, we did. Doesn't mean I don't like hearing her say it.

Driving another block, the engine echoes off concrete walls as I turn into the parking garage.

"I think you're hot." *Understatement of the fucking year.*

"I am really hot. Not everyone likes fat babes, but some people also don't like chocolate. It's really their loss. Like, do you see my boobs? Ridiculous." I don't get the chance to agree before she's changing the subject. "Mmm, chocolate sounds good. Can we stop to get some? Oh, and garlic bread. I would kill for some garlic bread right now." She asks like we're still driving.

Climbing out, I circle around to lift her from the passenger seat. She smells like girlie pink cocktails and tequila shots as she clings to me, unsteady on her heels. "I'm getting you to bed."

She laughs against me, her hands fisting my shirt. "Sounds good to me. Who knew it would take a girls' night out for us to finally end up in bed together."

"We're not having sex tonight, Dewdrop." She has no idea the amount of willpower I'm using not to take her against the hood of the car right now. Instead, I'm guiding her towards the elevator. Or at least attempting to.

"Jesus, it's like trying to herd a cat," I mutter the second time we have to turn around to find her phone on the car floor, after already having gone back for her purse. Of course, Lexie and her smart mouth has something to say about that.

"What, you can't handle a little pussy? That explains a lot." She feigns a sympathetic look, her bottom lip sticking out in an exaggerated pout.

"That's funny, considering you were just offering yours to me a minute ago." When she inches closer, my jaw tightens. She's tempting fate, and the amount of power she holds over me is maddening. I punch in the key code for the penthouse and the elevator doors slide closed. Then we're ascending.

Fucking finally.

"What's the matter, you don't want me anymore?" Her hands slide down my chest, glassy eyes sparking with salacious intent. I catch them in a firm grip before she can reach my belt. Any lower and she'll feel exactly how much I want her.

"You have no idea what I want from you, Lexie. But not like this," I growl, irritation warring with the lust chiseling away at my restraint. I've never been one to fold to temptation simply because it was convenient. But *fucking hell*, I want Lexie and she's standing here literally begging me to take her.

"Oh, suddenly you're so noble. Won't kiss me because I've had a drink," she scoffs, her tone mocking.

She leans in, her generous breasts pressing my chest and giving me an unobstructed view down her already revealing top.

I can feel my control start to slip, my restraint fraying against her lush body. Fuck. Focusing on the potent anger that surges through me, I use my hold on her wrists to put some distance between us.

"You didn't just have a drink, you're wasted. I'm not interested in a sloppy make-out session in an elevator when you can't even stand up straight, just because you're a horny drunk." I use a little too much force when I push her to the other side of the elevator. She stumbles, grabbing at the walls to steady herself. When she slumps against the corner for support, she reaches into her bag and pulls out her phone.

"Fine, have it your way." Her tone has my eyes narrowing.

"What are you doing?" I demand. The smile she gives me when her gaze flickers up to mine is nothing short of sinful.

"Getting on Tinder. This *horny drunk* is getting laid tonight. If you're not gonna do it, then I'll find someone who will." Her answer has me seeing red. "Ooo, *hello Rafael.*"

"Give me the fucking phone, Lexie." Before I know what I'm doing, her phone is in one of my hands and the other takes a possessive hold of her throat, pinning her against the wall. "Get on a dating app again, and I'll leave a trail of asshats with their throats slit across the city leading to your door." I tower over her, fury radiating from every tensed muscle. Her breath hitches against my hand on her neck, eyes glittering with satisfaction.

"You're really hot when you're angry." She's not the least bit intimidated. Instead, she's turned on by my show of dominance.

Fuck.

"You're even more infuriating when you're drunk," I grate.

"You love it."

I hate that she's not wrong.

By the time we reach the top floor, Lexie's legs are no longer supporting her. She stumbles, reaching and grabbing for anything close enough to offer her support. Instead of watching her topple around like a newborn giraffe, I decide it's better to just carry her inside.

Scooping her into my arms with her legs wrapped around my

waist, the considerable weight of her feels satisfying against me. My hands sink into the flesh of her ass through the thin material of her pants, and it's all I can do not to grope her. The way her arms wrap around my neck as her head lays on my shoulder is foreignly intimate. I like the way she trusts me to take care of her, to keep her safe.

Laying Lexie on her bed, her breasts bounce on impact, practically spilling out over her top. They're enticing—promising to be soft and supple. And fucking delicious. I want to get lost in them, drown in them. A better man wouldn't look at her like this, inebriated and vulnerable. But I've never claimed to be chivalrous. And to hell if I'm not going to look.

"It's okay, you can look. Everyone does, there's no hiding them," she says, rising up to rest on her elbows. "I know you want to. You want a *nice, long, hard* look." Her eyes slide down my body and look pointedly at where my erection strains against my pants. I'm fucking hard as a rock right now, all for her. "You do want me. I knew it."

She falls back on to the pillows in a halo of blond waves. One step closer and I'm standing over her.

"I do want you, Dewdrop." Taking her chin in my hand, I turn her head until she's looking up at me with half-lidded eyes. She'll pass out any minute now. "But when I have you, you're not going to be too drunk to remember it in the morning. You're going to feel every hard inch of me pounding into your pussy while I enjoy every inch of you."

She smiles against my hand like I've said something amusing, her eyes closing.

"Promises, promises," she murmurs, her voice trailing off as she gives in and lets sleep drag her under. Out like a light.

I stand, looking at her while she sleeps. Trailing my hand from her face to her chest, my fingertips tracing the dramatic swells of her large breasts above her neckline.

So fucking soft.

Everything about her is soft, warm, and inviting.

She looks so peaceful like this, her chaos finally tamed by unconsciousness—when she can't challenge me with one of her witty retorts, or by doing something ridiculous like twirling around a stage with a sparkly microphone.

But as infuriating as her chaos is, I almost miss it. I hate the emptiness that creeps into the gap her missing presence left in the room. What used to be peaceful for me now feels an awful lot like loneliness. Standing here with her in the silence is almost disturbing.

Lexie lies, dead to the world, completely at my mercy. Brushing a tendril of hair from her face, I let my hand linger.

My fingers itch to wander and explore, but I keep my hand where it is modestly on her waist as I pull her until she's laying on her side. I can't let her choke on her own vomit while she sleeps, we have unfinished business.

CHAPTER SEVENTEEN

CALLUM

The sound of my phone ringing on the desk next to me pulls my attention away from my computer. Seeing the name on the device, I lean back in my chair to answer it.

"Father," I greet him simply.

"You answer the phone like a funeral director. Always so serious."

"What can I do for you?" The group chat that includes my parents and my brother has been awfully quiet lately. Too quiet—like a toddler in another room with a pair of scissors.

"Why do you assume I need something? Can't a man call his son just to talk?"

"So you don't want something from me, what a relief," I deadpan, not buying it for a second.

"Alright fine, the Grassoses hosting Lucciano's engagement party in the Hamptons, and everyone expects to see you there." I'd heard the news that Rafael finally selected a wife for Lucciano—and she's the daughter of one of the Grassos biggest rivals, Frederico Manici.

I've known Frederico, the Don of Chicago, since I was a teenager. Of course, back then he was enemy number one to the Grassos family here in New York. And with my loyalties tied tightly to the Family, he was my enemy too. It took several attempts over a few years for us to be able to work together. Now I'm indispensable.

"Why is it assumed that I'll be in attendance?" I'd received the invitation, but I wasn't planning on going. I have business here in the city, and the last thing I need to deal with right now is my family and syndicate matters.

"You might have left the Family business, but you're still *my* family. You'll always be a Russo, and Russos show up." Despite his best efforts, I'm leaning towards a refusal when my father adds something that tips the scales in his favor. "Your mama has made it very clear she wants to see you there."

I let out a heavy sigh, and he knows he's won. "I'll see what I can do."

"Ahhh that's what I wanted to hear! Don Rafael bought out the Walmont for the occasion; he's reserved you a suite." I can hear the satisfied grin in his voice.

"Send me the details," I relent, leaning forward in my chair and running a hand over my face.

"Already sent. Your mama will be thrilled, we'll see you soon." Ending the call, I check for his message and confirm the dates and time for my schedule.

I can see why they chose the Walmont; it's the best five-star luxury hotel in the Hamptons—with a three Michelin star restaurant, known for its panoramic ocean views and sprawling grounds. Not to mention it's far outside of the Grassos family's territory in the city. Perfect neutral ground.

The Grassos and Manici families called a cease-fire three months ago so they could focus on the threat of the Bratva, but a tenuous truce is only as stable as the most volatile member. So, a wedding is the best way to assure the alliance holds strong on both sides.

Stepping out of my office, I pause to quietly observe the scene laid out in the living room. Lexie is sitting on the floor, a three-course meal set up on the coffee table, a reality show playing on the tv.

Her meal consists of a plate with three types of bruschetta, sauteed asparagus, and a plate of curly fries. A can of Mountain

Dew sits next to a glass of what I'm assuming is her favorite red wine. There's something oddly sweet about the sight of her like this, a total mix of elegant and casual. Her eyes stay on the screen as she takes a sip of wine, puts the glass back down, then leans forward to grab her phone from the floor a few feet away when it chimes with a notification.

I knew kissing her would only make things worse for me, and I was right. I've gotten a taste, and now I need all of her. A taste wasn't nearly enough—I need to consume her, devour every part of her.

Lexie's laugh pulls my focus. But she's not laughing at the show playing on the screen, she's laughing at something on her phone. Another chime sounds and she smiles before tapping away. She's texting someone. Who is making her smile like that? A man? The thought churns dark in my stomach and my eyes narrow on her.

"The dining room table is behind you." Her bright eyes pull away from the small screen in her hand to glance at the formal dining room less than twenty feet behind her, before lowering back to her phone. My jaw tightens; she didn't even look at me.

Who the fuck is stealing her attention? My fists clench with the urge to rip the device right out of her fingers and force her to focus on me.

"I know. I like the floor," she says passively, tapping on the screen. Another laugh at her phone has me turning on my heel to stalk back into my office. The door closes soundly behind me, and I sit behind my computer.

I know exactly what's possessing me to dig into Lexie's phone records, and I don't fight it. I need to know who's making her blush and giggle like a schoolgirl. I'll find the man who thinks he can have what's mine. By the end of the night, I'll know everything about the fucker.

There's no hiding from me.

CHAPTER EIGHTEEN

LEXIE

"Why am I going tonight?" I ask, walking into the living room. I was surprised when Callum mentioned the party for New York's elite, even more surprised when he extended an invitation. Or rather, demanded my attendance "Are you expecting trouble at the governor's mansion?"

"I always expect trouble." Callum turns at the sound of my voice, his eyes running over me from head to toe. Disapproval flashes across his face, making my stomach drop. He reaches for the jacket I discarded on the back of a kitchen stool after pulling it out of the closet.

"What are you planning on doing with that?" I can't help but feel offended by his dirty look, the indignation coming out in my dry tone.

"It's cold, and that dress barely covers you," Callum states, like I'm not already aware.

"Are you saying I should change?" I challenge. I'm way past covering my body when a man takes me out in public, no matter who he is. The next words out of his mouth will tell me a lot about what kind of a man he is. Callum's eyes move over me, taking in every inch of my appearance—navy blue cocktail dress, strappy gold heels, gold mini bag.

"I'm saying you need to wear a coat." The demanding edge in his tone grates on my nerves, making my defiance flare. The ever-in-control Callum asserts his dominance every chance he gets. But having him tell me what to do simply makes me want to do the opposite.

"I don't *need* to do anything, Callum. But thanks for your concern." Even if I was planning to wear a coat, there's no way in hell I'm putting it on now.

"So fucking stubborn." Jaw clenched, he stares me down, his gaze meant to intimidate me into submission. Instead, I remain unaffected just to spite him.

"You do know you can't actually pierce me with your stares, right?" I deadpan as he peers down at me expectantly. Hazel eyes don't falter as he waits, holding my coat open for arms that will not be cooperating. He can keep waiting.

"I'm sure if you could really cut me with that sharp wit of yours, I would've bled out a long time ago," he replies evenly. The mask of calm is set firmly in place, but I can hear the tension in his voice. His annoyance only fuels my need to poke at him.

"Oh, you wouldn't die. I'd stitch you up." I offer him a smile that's sugar and spice and everything nice, batting my eyelashes. "But only once you said please."

Callum's shoulders set in determination, and I don't miss how his eyes run over me. The man is the definition of "tightly wound." And I'd like nothing more than to tug at the strings of his resolve and watch him unravel.

"Lexie, the only begging that's going to happen between us will have nothing to do with pain." He leans closer. "Now put on your fucking coat."

Liquid heat pools inside me, desire pulsing through my veins. The air in the room thickens, the tension crackling between us like static electricity. My breathing changes, I know he can see it. Just like how I can see the raw hunger in his eyes. But if he thinks that he can control me by simply turning me on, he's got another thing coming.

Pulling my eyes away, I look down and make a show of adjusting my breasts in my dress. My cleavage is unbelievable with this neckline. I don't have to draw attention to it to know he's looking.

He's always looking.

"I don't want to ruin my outfit. But if you're so bothered by the cold, you can wear it." I flip my hair over my shoulder before I step past him, and the coat, with a saucy smile. "I'll meet you in the car."

When I step into the elevator Callum is right on my heels, my coat still in his hands. Looks like he's determined to bring the damn thing with us, probably to try and force me into it later. Roscoe steps in after us. "Wow, you clean up nice, Roscoe," I say, taking in his custom black suit. "Very dapper, you're giving James Bond a run for his money."

"I hate monkey suits." He's incapable of taking a compliment, but I can see the smile twitch on his lips. I'm slowly wearing him down. "You look nice, as always."

"Thanks." I beam at him, using the praise to disguise my triumph over the small victory. I'll win him over yet. "I love any excuse to dress up."

Something tells me tonight's going to be very interesting.

Calling it the governor's *mansion* isn't an overstatement. Every intricate detail screams luxury born from old money. Stepping past the threshold feels like entering an alternate reality.

Everything about the atmosphere is too perfect to be real, the people more beautiful, the live music flawless, and the unnaturally white smiles too appeasing. Everywhere you look polished people dressed in designer clothes float around and converse in dulcet tones. The diamonds are real and no smaller than my fist, and Rolex is the most affordable timepiece adorning any man's wrist.

I'm definitely not in Harlem anymore.

Following Callum's lead, we move through the grand entryway into what can only be described as a ballroom. Ornate cream walls hold decorative paneling and detailed crown molding gives the space a decadent feeling. An impressive crystal chandelier hangs from the medallion in the center of the vaulted coffered ceiling, combining with the wall sconces to bathe the room in romantic light while the aggressively pretty people mingle around the room in clusters. Uniformed waitstaff pass around trays of appetizers and flutes of champagne.

"Mr. Russo," a man calls as he approaches, a woman by his side.

"Jack Stanza, CEO of Capitol Energy." Callum leans down to murmur into my ear, giving me a cheat sheet. "Margot Primm, governor's aide."

"Welcome, so glad you could come." Jack's silver hair is quaffed with gel until it's visibly stiff. Margot stands next to him poised with a sharp brown bob and a smile that doesn't reach her dull brown eyes.

"I never miss one of the governor's events when I'm in town," Callum comments, his voice taking on a light tone that sounds foreign coming from his mouth. I glance up at him, surprised by the amiable expression on his face. I've never seen him look so friendly before, it's intriguing.

"Peter Wilcox and I were just discussing those pony bets from last quarter. He was so sure that long shot was going to pay off," Jack says, nodding to a tall, thin man standing not too far away. "I believe we both owe you quite a bit of money."

"Oh, I remember," Callum says easily with a laugh. Who is this carefree man beside me? "I always remember my wins; that's the real reason I'm here. I came to collect before Wilcox tries to leave the country again." Jack chuckles deeply at Callum's joke, nodding largely.

"I don't blame you; I wouldn't trust us with our losses either." Jack gestures towards the human string bean. "It's time we paid the piper."

"I'll find you later," Callum murmurs into my ear, meeting my eyes. I look up at him and nod casually. Turning to address the older gentleman he says, "Lead the way."

I watch the two men walk away, leaving me with Margot. The governor's aide is rail thin, with a haughty air about her that oozes judgment and condescension. Her black chiffon dress cost three figures, easy. "I love your dress. Is it Ralph Lauren?"

"Thank you, it's Badgley Mischka." Something about the way Margot accepts my compliment doesn't feel anywhere as gracious as it should. Her eyes move over me in a way that makes my stomach knot. "Your dress is very bold of you. Such a brave choice, I applaud your confidence."

The underhanded insult is more aggressive than passive, hidden only under a fake smile. My kind smile turns knowing, making a show of smoothing my hands down my waist and over my hips.

"Wow, that means a lot coming from someone like you." I let my gaze move pointedly over her. "If you'll excuse me." With that, I'm walking past her, grabbing a flute of champagne off a tray as it passes.

I consider finding a quiet corner to hide from any more snotty comments about my body in this dress. But then a woman named Christine asks me where I get my nails done and I decide to mingle for a while instead. Every once in a while, I catch sight of Callum making his way around the room.

Even standing in a crowd of other important men dressed in expensive custom suits, Callum stands out. His size draws focus, standing a head above everyone around him. But it's his dominating presence that makes it nearly impossible to look away.

Callum commands respect, knowing exactly how to engage with each person in order to get it. Watching him charm his way through a room is fascinating—a box jellyfish easily navigating deep sea waters. Deceptively elegant and captivating to distract from the potent deadliness of his sting.

When Callum smiles, his whole face transforms. The storm clouds dissipate, leaving nothing but clear skies over a sea of charm. The edges of his angular, bearded face soften, any sign of danger melting into charisma. But when I really look at him, I can tell there's something missing—warmth, humor, enjoyment. It's a fake smile, a mask perfected with time to appeal to this intended audience. A tool to disarm and engage. And it's fucking working. The people around him are falling for it hook, line, and sinker.

Meeting his eyes over Christine's head, I offer him a very fake smile of my own. One equally as bright and full of sugary-sweet false promises. His eyes narrow slightly, and I know he can read exactly what I'm saying.

I see you, Callum. They don't, but I do.

Our eye contact is severed when a figure steps in front of me. My focus shifts to the blonde-haired, blue-eyed man smiling at me. The royal blue of his suit is a pop of color amongst the sea of black and gray covering the other men in attendance. His grin is friendly, if not a little cocky, flashing straight white teeth that belong in a toothpaste commercial. There's something about him, a cheesiness to his charm, that feels almost cartoonish.

"I don't think we've met, I'm Daniel Taylor," he says, his eyes flickering to my generous cleavage none too discreetly. "I couldn't go the entire night without learning your name." He's not exactly my usual type, but Daniel's a good-looking man. So I give him a bright smile.

"We couldn't have met, I'm new to New York." Taking a sip of my champagne, I peer up at him through my lashes. "I'm Lexie."

"Well, New York is lucky to have you, Lexie." He knows how to play the game, and he's decent at it. "Where are you from?"

"Astoria, Oregon. It's a coastal town."

"From one coast to the other, that's a big change. What brings you all the way across the country to our fair city?"

"I'm a travel nurse, I came for a contract," I answer. "Although, from my experience, concrete jungle is a more accurate description than *our fair city*." Daniel's blinding smile widens and his head tilts back in a hearty laugh. If he were a cartoon, he'd definitely be cast as the charming prince who gallantly comes charging in on his white horse to save the day whether you want his rescue or not.

"I can't disagree with that description," Daniel laughs. "Who do you know in the governor's office? Did you come alone?" His tone is asking if I plan on leaving alone. His eyes flicker over my shoulder, a look of recognition flashing across his face. I can feel Callum's presence behind me even before he speaks.

"Taylor, I see you've met Lexie."

"Russo." Daniel's eyes move between me and the giant now pressing to my back. The heat of his body mixes with mine. "I suppose I can't be surprised that this is your date."

I'm tempted to argue that I'm not Callum's date, but I guess it's technically true. I did come as his plus-one. And with the competitive air between the two men, a statement like that would be striking a match while soaked in gasoline.

Not a good idea.

"How do you two know each other?" I ask, changing the subject. Or at least trying to. My question fails to ease the tension. Instead it supplies Callum with more ammo.

"Taylor is legal counsel for the governor." There's something taunting in Callum's voice when he explains. "He deals with the less complicated matters."

I nod in understanding when realization hits me, making Daniel's eyes narrow ever so slightly. Callum fixes the messes Daniel can't; he's the one burying the skeletons that pile in their closets to keep their noses clean. Their relationship is based on respect built around fear and power. Callum's power. It seems like every relationship Callum has is very complex—a balancing act of nuance and intimidation. They need him, but they resent him for it.

Daniel looks like he's biting his tongue. He catches the eye of another man not too far away, gesturing to him in greeting. "Pleasure as always, Russo." The flat, sarcastic edge in his voice melts into warmth when his focus shifts to me. His hand reaches for mine, lifting it to his lips. "It was so lovely to meet you, Lexie. I hope our paths cross again soon." His lips are a whisper over my knuckles before he lets go, but not before Callum steps out from behind me to stand at my side.

"You too, Daniel," I say simply with a soft smile. With that he's moving on, his energetic charm reviving as he greets another man enthusiastically. Even as the blonde man is walking away, Callum's presence doesn't ease up.

"You go to one party and you're already getting cozy with one of the biggest tools in the state," Callum states roughly. "One with heavy baggage he's never able to carry for himself. Maybe I should cut him loose and see if he drowns." There's destruction in his voice, a desire to cause ruin.

"Are you jealous?" I ask, baiting him. Surprisingly, this time he bites.

"What if I am?" he counters gruffly, his mouth at my ear sending a shiver down my spine and liquid fire pooling between my legs. Looking up at him, I meet his eyes and take a sip of my champagne. He's so sexy I have a hard time pulling my eyes away.

"I'd be shocked half to death. Jealousy is an emotion." My tone is half teasing as I feign a concerned expression through the desire building inside me. "Careful, Callum, your humanity is showing."

"You haven't seen anything yet."

"Haven't I?" I counter, plastering on a fake smile so bright that it burns straight through his mask of calm. Callum's jaw clenches, his expression darkening until he's glaring at me. The thunder is back, his dark cloud dominating the space until it feels small.

"Stop." His low demand is all bite and no bark, sending a shiver down my spine and drenching my panties.

"Stop what?" My brows raise in feigned innocence.

"You don't want to play this game with me, Lexie. I don't lose." He steps closer until we're practically chest to chest. I look up at him, meeting his gaze evenly.

"I would never play games with you, Callum." I tilt my head

slightly to one side. "You're far too serious to waste your time on something ridiculous like having fun."

"I'd like to pull you into the other room and have some fun. I can think of a few activities I'd enjoy doing with you."

"Wow, do you really only ever think with your dick?" My voice comes out more breathy than confident, the sass draining out as desire hits me fast and hard. He's so close, and my eyes can't help but catch on his lips.

"Two heads are better than one." Callum's voice is deep, his eyes hungry.

"Mmm, so far I'm not impressed with either of them." My gaze slowly slides from his lips back to his hazel eyes in invitation. "I guess you'll just have to take me into the other room and prove it."

The moment my words register, we're moving. Callum's strong grip on my waist doesn't falter as he leads us out of the ballroom. We pause briefly in the doorway for Callum to find someone in the crowd. I follow his gaze in time to see his silent conversation with Roscoe, before I'm being pulled into the hallway.

Anticipation thrums inside me as we move through the house, his pace purposeful. He clearly knows where we're going, leading me down a darkened hallway meant to be off-limits for the party. Stopping at the end of the corridor, Callum opens a door and pulls me inside.

It's a home office, most likely belonging to the governor. I'm briefly able to see the built-in bookshelves that line the walls, completely filled with uniform books with decorative spines. The ornate furniture matches the rest of the historic house—wing chairs facing a brick fireplace, a carved coffee table, heavy drapes. A large desk sits opposite the door, framed by two tall, arched windows trimmed in crown molding.

As soon as I'm in the room, Callum's closing the door and pressing me against it. His hand reaches over to flick on the lights as his lips descend on mine. There's no preamble, the time for teasing is over. All that's left is domination and desire, his thick frame taking over mine.

Large hands are on me, fisting in my hair and sinking into the ample flesh of my ass. A sigh escapes my lips, lighting a fire to Callum's short fuse. The hand in my hair untangles to reach down and grab hold of my thighs, forcing my legs to wrap around him as I'm being lifted.

My sound of surprise as Callum pulls me off the door and carries me across the office is met by a grunt of approval, his mouth never leaving mine. He places me down on the edge of the desk, pulling back to remove his suit coat and toss it over the back of a chair.

Like a predator stalking prey, his eyes never leave me as he unbuttons each cuff of his crisp white shirt and impatiently rolls the sleeves up to his elbows, revealing the intricate artwork decorating his strong forearms. Just the sight of him like this is almost enough to unravel me, beard, tattoos, and the consuming desire in his piercing gaze. His dangerous intensity is like a pheromone, leaving me intoxicated.

I watch with bated breath, the hunger growing inside me with each beat of my racing heart until it's almost unbearable. The separation only lasts seconds, but it's far too long and does nothing to dampen the potent chemistry charged between us. And then he's kissing me again, touching me.

Strong hands are pulling my dress straps down my arms. His lips on mine are demanding, tasting and exploring in long, deep pulls. It's all fire, hunger, and need. As soon as the dress is down far enough, my bra cups are being pulled down next.

Callum's large hands touch every inch of my skin as soon as it's exposed, groaning against my lips. Electricity spreads through me under his touch, and I gasp as his fingers explore. His lips leave mine when he leans back to look at me, ravenous eyes taking in my bare breasts—rosy, giant, and heavy. My skin flushes under his gaze, lust licking through my veins as my heart hammers with anticipation.

"You're so fucking gorgeous," he murmurs deeply, his hands returning to my breasts like he can't help himself. I sigh as his lips join his hands in worship, arching into his touch. The scrape of his beard against my delicate flesh heightens every sensation. His breath is hot against my skin. "I've thought about getting my hands on these incredible tits so many fucking times. They're even better than I dreamed they'd be."

"You know me, I aim to please." My head falls back and I catch my bottom lip between my teeth to bite back a moan. His lips are sinful.

"Don't do that." Callum nips at my skin, sending a bolt of pleasure through me until I gasp.

"Don't do what?" I ask, breathless. His mouth moves over the sensitive skin of my left breast, tasting and appreciating every inch while his greedy hand kneads the other.

"Don't hold back." His voice vibrates against my skin, sending a shiver through every nerve ending in my body. "I want to hear everything—every moan, every gasp, every sound of pleasure. I want fucking all of it. It's mine. *I earned it.*" His mouth latches on to my nipple and a long moan falls from my lips. My hands reach for his head to thread my fingers through his hair and pull him closer. A hum of gratification ripples through him, his mouth sending sparks over my skin.

I'm so hot, so wet.

"I need more," I pant, overwhelmed by need. Callum doesn't hesitate to grant my request. His lips don't falter in their attention on my breast, but his hand is trailing up my thigh under my dress. I lift my hips to allow my hem to be pushed up around my waist. He tugs my panties down my legs and over my heels, allowing my thick thighs to spread open wide enough to bare myself to him. The breath hitches in my chest when his skilled fingers press my exposed pussy, his thumb strumming over my swollen clit in maddening circles.

"Oh, God," I pant, pleasure spreading through every part of my body. His fingers plunge inside me, stealing my breath.

"You're so wet for me, Dewdrop," he growls against my breast, his head lifting to meet my eyes. His fingers pump into me, hitting my G-spot until stars dance across my vision, his circling thumb driving me into delirium. "So damn responsive. Fuck." When he catches my nipple in his mouth and tugs it with his teeth, I shatter into a million pieces.

"Yes!" The word tumbles out of my mouth over and over as I ride the wave of pleasure carrying me away. "Oh, *Callum.*"

"That's the hottest fucking thing I've ever heard," Callum groans, withdrawing his hands to lower to his knees. "You're such a good girl for me. Look at this pretty pussy. I bet you taste as good as you look."

The first flick of his tongue makes my hips jerk, a soft cry escaping me. "Just what I thought," he murmurs, voice rough with primal gratification. My body is teetering on a cliff, climbing higher and higher with each touch. My hands fist in his hair passionately, holding him against me.

"What do I taste like?"

"You taste . . ." His tongue flattens over my slit in a long, smooth stroke. Savoring, torturing. "*Addicting.*" Strong hands grip my thighs as they try to clamp around his head on their own accord, holding me in place to allow his mouth to devour me without interruption. The roughness of his facial hair contrasts with the heat of his mouth, pushing me closer to the edge of bliss.

"Oh god, yes. *Callum.*" I chant his name, tugging on his hair. He growls against me hungrily, the vibrations making my nerve endings fire all at once. His tongue enters me over and over, the heat searing me from the inside out.

"When we leave here, I'm going to shake the governor's hand with you on my fingers, and my tongue." His thumb joins to rub my clit in slow, steady circles while he fucks me with his tongue. The stimulation is too much. It's all I can do not to scream as I fall over the edge, tumbling and freefalling into a sea of euphoria.

My thighs shake beneath his hands as I come. The orgasm lasts minutes instead of seconds, Callum lapping up every last drop like I'm his favorite delicacy. "My pretty pink nurse, such a dirty girl." He stands, using my hands in his hair to pull me closer. There's a look of primal satisfaction in his eyes, his beard glistening with the evidence of my pleasure.

Our lips meet sensually, panting for breath, and I can taste myself on his lips. It's surprisingly erotic and wildly arousing—something I'm sure Callum would agree with by the impressive erection pressing against my thigh through his pants. It would be so easy for him to step between my thighs, unzip his pants, and take me right here on the edge of the desk. And it seems like he plans to do exactly that, his lips urgent against mine.

Then his phone goes off.

Turning to pull it out of his discarded suit coat pocket, he curses when he reads it. "It's Roscoe," he says, less than pleased. "Apparently the governor's looking for me."

"We should get back to the party." I'm still struggling to catch my breath, but my hands are already moving to pull my bra back into place. "They'll see more than they bargained for if they send out a search party, and I'm not in the mood to give them a show."

When I move to fix the top of my dress, Callum beats me to it. His fingers trail up the skin of my arms with the straps, dragging them back where they belong on my shoulders.

Taking a step back, he holds out a hand to help me down from my perch. Hopping down onto unsteady legs, I can't help but lean against him for support as I regain my composure. Callum catches me readily, his expression one of frustrated satisfaction.

"I'm going to speak to the governor and say our goodbyes," he says, watching intently as I step back into my panties, navigating my heels, then shimmy them back up my legs and under my dress. Tugging the skirt back down, I smooth my hands over my dress to make sure I'm back to looking presentable. "Then I'm taking you home, Dewdrop."

Whatever Callum has planned for us is promptly shut down when we re-enter the ballroom. Roscoe stands waiting, leaning in to whisper something into his boss' ear the moment he's close enough. And whatever he says isn't good news, judging by the set of Callum's jaw. His eyes cut to me in consideration, hand running over his beard as he makes a decision about something.

After a long moment, he finally gives Roscoe a short nod, his expression deeply irritated when he leans in to murmur something to him. The enforcer's focus lands on me briefly, making me wonder if I'm their topic of discussion or simply a component of it. I'm half tempted to open my mouth and ask what they're whispering about, but I don't get the chance.

"There you are, Callum." Governor McCann approaches with his arms wide. There's an unsteadiness to him, which might have something to do with the empty glass in his hand. "I was beginning to think you snuck out on me." Callum's easy smile is instant as he seamlessly slips into character.

"You know I'd never do that to you, Harrison," Callum insists. "But I do need to be going, I have some business that can't wait until morning."

"Ah, well, business comes first." If I wasn't watching so closely, I would've easily missed the conspiratorial wink the governor shoots at the man beside me. Callum chuckles with a nod, the rich sound vibrating through me. "Keep in touch. And I expect to see you at the club next month for a rematch."

"I wouldn't miss it." With Callum's confirmation, Harrison McCann's glassy gaze moves to me.

"It was an absolute pleasure to meet you, Lexie. I hope to see you at another function very soon." Even buzzed, his charisma is smooth and eloquent. Spoken like a true politician. My smile in return is friendly.

"It was great meeting you, Governor," is my gracious reply.

"Duty calls, I won't keep you." Governor McCann extends his arm towards Callum. My eyes meet Callum's when he reaches out to clasp hands in a firm shake. The same hand that was just inside me less than five minutes ago. His words from the office echo through my head, turning my insides into molten lava.

With one last round of goodbyes, Callum leads me outside

to the town car waiting in the circular drive. The heat coursing through me has my heart pounding in my chest until I'm practically breathless. The feeling of the firm hand on the small of my back burns straight to the throbbing between my thighs. When the car door is opened for me and I slide in alone, the only thing keeping my protest from being spoken like a horny, needy sex addict is my pride.

Callum remains just a few inches away, hand clamped firmly on the top of the door as he stands staring down at me. The man is as rigid as a statue; he could be carved from marble.

He nods to the driver at the wheel. "Corbin will take you back to the penthouse. I have to put out a few fires." The regret in his voice is almost tangible, easing a sliver of my irritation.

He needs to put out the fire he started between my legs.

Biting the smart remark on the tip of my tongue, I simply nod in response. Pressing my thighs together to ease some of the pressure there does nothing to dampen my needs. It takes another long moment of passionate staring before Callum finally steps back and closes the door firmly.

The drive back to the penthouse is silent. I can feel the driver's eyes on me in the rearview mirror periodically, but I ignore his curiosity. By the time I'm in the elevator, the desire pumping through my veins is too much to ignore.

I'm home alone, but I switch the lock on my bedroom door anyway. The last thing I need is to be interrupted. Reaching for the top drawer of my nightstand, a comforting hum fills the air. My eyes close as I lay back on the pile of pillows, a sigh escaping me as some of the pent-up tension is eased by the vibrations. As I'm carried away, images play behind my eyelids—hazel eyes devouring me, impeccable beard building delicious friction, and strong fingers coaxing and demanding my pleasure.

CHAPTER NINETEEN

LEXIE

My teeth catch on my bottom lip to stifle a yawn, half-heartedly singing along to the music under my breath as I sprinkle flour to prepare my surface to knead. The sound of the front door unlocking and opening is drowned out by the music playing over the speakers, and suddenly there's a giant figure looming behind me.

Turning, my heart stops at the man standing just a foot away, my hands flying to my chest in a cloud of flour and startled curses. "Fuck, Callum!" I breathe when my heart finally restarts. "You scared the shit out of me."

"What are you still doing up?" His question has me looking at the clock on my phone that's laying on the counter next to me. Since when is it three-thirteen in the morning?

"I'm baking and must've lost track of time," I say with a shrug. It's technically the truth, but a strategic one so he can't read the lie on my face with those all-seeing eyes of his. His gaze pins me where I stand, narrowing slightly as he reads me.

"Baking what?"

"Oh." I pull in a deep breath of excitement that promises to overshare and go into painful amounts of detail. "I found a recipe for strawberry cake on Pinterest. The picture caught my attention, because it's pink cake—and who wouldn't stop to look at pink cake? I'm a sucker for it every single time. Plus it looked light and refreshing, kinda like strawberry shortcake but a little different since the strawberries are baked right in instead of just on top. And I knew we had that carton of strawberries in the fridge that was about to go bad. So I had to try it before it was too late."

"That's strawberry cake?" Callum asks skeptically, nodding to my covered bowl on the counter next to the floured surface.

"Of course not." The look I flash at him says *duh*. "The cake is in the oven." I point to the timer counting down the last few minutes on the fancy convection oven.

"This," I announce, pulling the cloth off the bowl with a flourish, "is bread dough that I found on the same page as the cake. It was the post right under it, so I just had a look at the recipe to see if we had all of the ingredients—which we do, by the way. It's an artisan bread, which is supposed to be super crusty and perfect for bruschetta. And you know how I feel about bruschetta."

While I'm rambling, I can't help noticing the way his white dress shirt—crisp and pristine a few hours ago—now hangs untucked and slightly rumpled beneath the jacket of his bespoke suit. And is that a drop of blood on his collar . . . ?

"Yes, I do." The deep rasp in Callum's voice has my train of thought flying off the rails as my eyes meet his. Despite the ingredients scattered around the kitchen, Callum's ravenous perusal remains solely focused on me. He's looking at me like I'm the cake that he wants to savor on his tongue, then fully ravage. A tongue I can still feel searing through me until I'm weak at the knees.

"Why are you looking at me like that?"

"Like what? How am I looking at you?"

"Like you want to eat me alive," I deadpan.

"I'd like to devour every edible inch of you. I remember exactly how good you taste." Dammit, if that isn't the hottest thing I've ever heard. My insides are quickly liquifying, despite my best efforts to reason with my own hormones. How can I feel like this from just a few words and a look from Callum? I need to shut this down.

Luckily, my battery-operated boyfriend took the edge off

just enough for me to remain skeptical instead of swoon like I'm tempted to.

"Really, this does it for you?" I look down at my pajama shorts and matching top, pink with a pattern of cartoon ice cream cones. The eyeful he's getting from me is probably a complete mess—curled blonde hair piled high on the top of my head in a messy bun, my full glam from the party still covering my face, and all with an uneven dusting of white bread flour. Yet Callum's gazing at me like an addict looking longingly at his drug of choice.

"I thought I made myself clear." His voice is rough and hungry. "*You* do it for me."

"Well, if you haven't noticed, I'm used to taking care of myself. Which is exactly what I did tonight. I don't need you." My eyes slide down his body to look pointedly at where his erection is pressing against his pants.

"Time to end that habit, starting now."

"Move on, Callum. We had a moment on that desk." His eyes darken lustfully at the mention of what happened between us earlier tonight. "The moment's over."

"You're lying to yourself if you think tonight was a fluke or a fleeting moment. That wasn't the end for us, Dewdrop. It was only the beginning." He steps closer, his hand surprisingly gentle as his thumb brushes a smudge of flour from my cheek. Eyes caught passionately, my breath hitches in my throat making his gaze flicker to my lips.

He wants to kiss me, I can read it in every tensed muscle in his body. And god, do I want him to do it. If I was thinking clearly, I'd probably have a little alarm bell ringing in my head right about now.

Callum is danger. But right now I'm feeling reckless without a cause.

If I tilt my head even a fraction, he'll take the invitation without hesitating. He'll swoop in like a predator pouncing on his prey. And just when I'm about to give him the green light, the oven timer goes off to announce that it's time to take the cake out.

Shamed by the bell.

"And just like that, another moment gone," I murmur, stepping away from his caress. "I should get the cake out of the oven before it burns."

"This conversation isn't over, Dewdrop." Facing away from him, I can feel the determination pouring from the man behind me.

I can't argue with him, because I can feel the truth of his words. So, I simply say, "Good night, Callum."

CHAPTER TWENTY

LEXIE

I have a date. A first date.

Take deep, slow breaths.

This will be good. I'll meet up with him, get a few drinks, have some flirty conversation. Maybe make out a little if the mood is right. It'll be fun . . . right?

At the very least I'll meet someone new and check out a cool bar in the city. Not to mention it's a few hours not spent fantasizing about the sexy man back at the penthouse that I'm trying desperately to maintain a professional relationship with—I could cut the sexual tension between us with a knife.

Agreeing to go on a date with the golden retriever boy from the dating app has me more nervous than I'd like to admit. I know I look good in my pretty periwinkle dress with a corset top and puff sleeves. I feel pretty and confident. The word *shy* has never been used to describe me. But I am a little jittery, just like I am before every first date. It's only natural.

My phone chimes with a location pin and a message from Eric. Waiting for you in the alley near the south entrance. Why would he want me to meet him in the alleyway behind the parking garage? Parking is ridiculously expensive in the city, especially in this neighborhood. I assumed we'd be taking the subway.

My hand tightens on the Taser in my purse as I round the corner.

Eric stands a few feet down the alleyway. I recognize his mop of black curls from his photos. He stands stiffly, dwarfed by the bulky frame of the man standing right behind him. I stare at the man, the air leaving my lungs. Hazel eyes stare at me over my date's head.

"Callum." His name is ripped out of me by the shock, my heart rate picking up speed. One large tattooed arm is wrapped firmly across Eric's chest, pinning him in place. The glint of gleaming metal catches the light, making me feel like I'm going to vomit.

"I'm surprised you'd meet us back here. I thought you'd be smarter than to meet a man off the internet in a back alley. People are found dead in places like this all the time." Callum's condescending tone is laced with something terrifying—a deadly intent that matches the darkness in his eyes as he presses the large knife to his captive's throat.

"Why are you doing this? Let him go." I inch closer, unable to focus on anything other than the sharp blade pressing angrily against delicate skin. Eric's eyes on me are a silent cry for help, his breaths coming out in harsh bursts through his nose. I stare back at him, just as powerless against the man holding us hostage.

"I don't like to repeat myself, Lexie. But you were drunk, so I'll make an exception just this once," Callum says. "I will slit the throat of any man who thinks they can have you." He means it, and even worse—he intends to carry out this threat while we're standing here.

"Don't." I choke on the word; the air leaving my lungs doesn't seem to be returning as I try to suck in. "Please, don't."

"You didn't take me seriously the first time. I'm sure you won't make that mistake again." He drags the knife across Eric's neck in an agonizingly slow, controlled movement. The skin slices easily under the sharp edge. "Get on a dating app again, I'll kill every man who thinks they have a chance with you. You'll watch as I split them open from ear to ear."

Eric's eyes widen in agony as blood ribbons from the clean

sever. The choking sound that slips from him echoes between the buildings, a sound that will haunt my dreams until the day I die.

"Stop," I plead, tears pricking behind my eyes. "I won't even look at another man. Please, just stop." It's a promise.

Callum's blade pauses its movement, leaving the job half finished. His dark eyes drill into me, a harbinger of death and destruction. Completely unrepentant for the carnage he leaves in his wake, demanding more when it fits his needs.

Any relief I feel when he removes the knife and steps back is squashed when Roscoe steps forward in Callum's place. In three long strides, Callum is in front of me, towering like the grim reaper. One of his hands is at my waist, the other gripping my skull, spearing through my hair roughly at the nape of my neck. I crane to look him in the eye like his hold demands.

"I don't know how I can make this any clearer to you. You're mine, Lexie. No one else gets to have you." His fury ripples in waves beneath his cold, calm exterior. "Understand?"

"Yes." My response comes out defeated.

"Good." Callum gives a quick nod and Roscoe allows Eric to slump to the ground like a bag of rocks, gasping and sputtering. He gapes like a trout floundering on land, clutching at his throat to stop the bleeding. It's no use. Callum stopped slicing halfway, but the cut is deep—probably hitting the carotid artery.

The blood is gushing too fast, spurting in the rhythm of his erratic heartbeat, and Eric is already fading. I move to help him, every instinct in my body screaming at me to save him. But Callum's punishing grip yanks me back, forcing me to watch helplessly as the man slowly expires.

"We're leaving," Callum announces, pulling me a step towards the garage. I dig in my heels, pushing against his hold in an attempt to resist. His hand in my hair tightens painfully, keeping me on a very short leash.

"I can't let him die. Let me help him." He leverages his hold on me until I'm looking up at him, his gaze demanding to be my sole focus. "Please, Cal."

"Once you're in the car I'll let you call for help and maybe they get to him in time." His hand in my hair turns my head to look at the man bleeding out on the pavement, the man who will die. Because of me. "Or we can both stand here and watch as he bleeds out."

In the close proximity, my chest presses against Callum with each shallow breath. His domineering presence engulfs me. I'm so overwhelmed with emotion, an eerie numbness settles over my body. I don't want to leave Eric like this, he's nice. But I don't really have any other choice, not if leaving with Callum gives Eric a chance to survive. I can't stand here and watch him die. I'll never get over it.

"Okay."

"Okay, what? Use your words, Lexie." The words are said in both taunt and triumph.

"Okay, I'll get in the fucking car."

"Good girl," he murmurs, his eyes lighting with victory. My loathing for this man swells, anger leaving a bitter taste in my mouth as I allow Callum to pull me away. Unable to help myself, I twist to cast a glance over my shoulder, trying to get one last look at Eric before we turn the corner. Roscoe's crouching over him, probably promising to finish the job if Eric breathes a word to the authorities when the ambulance arrives.

True to his word, Callum pulls out his cell phone once I'm buckled in the car and allows me to call 911. Keeping it short and vague, I inform the operator that a man is bleeding out and provide her with the location before hanging up.

"Do you think they'll make it in time?" I ask. Pulling out into traffic, Callum holds out a hand for his phone, his expression telling me he doesn't give a shit. Guilt gnaws at me, making me nauseous. My arms wrap around my middle, hugging myself in an attempt to stop feeling so sick to my stomach. Sirens sound around the corner and I pray that's Eric's rescue.

"Probably. If not, I'm sure his wife will make good use of his life insurance."

"Wife?" I couldn't have heard him right.

"Yes, *wife*." Callum overenunciates the word. "Eric and Jenna have been married for three years now. He never mentioned that?"

"No, of course not." Married? I'm gonna be sick.

"Then he probably didn't mention their one-year-old daughter, Lauren." My stomach rolls. "Seems like you both have a thing for wanting what already belongs to someone else."

"Pull over. I'm going to be sick." He has a daughter and a wife. *Cheating bastard*. Oh god, I'm not just a homewrecker. I probably just made some poor woman a widow and a baby girl fatherless.

"No, you're not," he says, weaving through traffic. "You're going to breathe slowly. In through your nose, out through your mouth."

"You're a sick bastard. The fact that you probably just killed someone in broad daylight doesn't bother you at all."

"No, it doesn't. His decisions led him there, just like yours led you here," he states, swinging the car into the parking garage.

"Going on a date with someone you met online doesn't mean you deserve to die. Cheater or not."

"That fucker deserves worse than what I did to him. I would say that you should really try to pick better next time, but there isn't going to be a next time," Callum says darkly.

As soon as the car is in park, I'm wrenching the car door open. Callum's getting out right behind me, slamming his door shut behind him. When his hand grasps my elbow to stop me, I whirl on him.

"There was no way for me to know he's married." I'm practically shouting, my voice echoing off the walls of the parking garage. "Eric isn't a monster, he's not like you. He was fun to talk to. It's next to impossible to find guys on dating apps that aren't total creeps, let alone ones who can carry a conversation. And he was nice."

"Nice." He snarls the word like it disgusts him.

"Yes, *nice*," I repeat, seething. "You wouldn't understand that,

Callum. You've never done anything for anyone that wasn't directly profitable to you in some way. But some people actually care about others without wanting something from them."

"Oh really? Here." Reaching into his pocket, Callum pulls out something and tosses it at me. I catch it, confused. It's a tiny ziplock about the size of my palm holding about half a dozen small white tablets.

"What is this?" I ask, agitated. He's trying to distract me from the point.

"That's Rohypnol. I found it in that asshole's wallet," Callum says. "I wasn't going to show you this, but since you seem to think he's *so nice*."

"Rohypnol?" I stare at the tablets, my mind racing.

"Apparently your date had a lot more planned for you than just dinner and drinks. He definitely wanted something from you, whether you were willing to give it to him or not. Still think he's not a monster?" he rumbles darkly. I shake my head, Eric's friendly smile flashing through my mind. There's no way. Callum could've gotten these anywhere.

"I don't believe you." I can't. But even as I deny it, my stomach begins to sink. A dark luxury SUV pulls into the parking garage, rounding the corner and turning expertly into a parking space. My hand closes around the bag, crumpling it tightly in my fist.

"You think I'm lying?" Callum challenges angrily. "Roscoe was there. Ask him." His words are punctuated by the sound of a car door closing. Roscoe steps out from around the driver's side, his eyes darting between us as he gauges the situation he's walking in on. He stops to stand warily a few feet from me and Callum, the third point in a triangle.

"Roscoe, what did you find in Eric's wallet?" I ask, my voice shaking. Roscoe looks at me for a moment before turning to his boss. Callum nods to him.

"Tell her." With permission, Roscoe's eyes cut to me again hesitantly.

"Date rape drugs," he states finally. "Roofies." The air leaves my lungs harshly, my brows coming together as I stare first at Roscoe then at Callum. Meeting his hazel gaze, I blink—once, twice, three times—as I process the realization of what might have happened to me tonight.

Eric had seemed so kind, the conversation was fun and flirty. In the years I've been on dating apps, I thought I'd mastered how to weed out the crazies and predators. How could I have gotten him so wrong? The man was married with a child, for god's sake. Sleeping with him wasn't the goal for tonight, the plan was to meet him and see where the night would take me. Apparently, it would've taken me to be drugged. Roofied.

Raped.

Taking the few steps to close the gap between us, I slap the bag of roofies against Callum's chest. "You're right, I sure know how to pick 'em." Stepping back, he catches the baggie before it falls to the ground. A line appears between Callum's brows as I turn to Roscoe.

"I don't want to be here. Can you please take me to Harlem?" I ask him, struggling to remain calm.

"Lexie . . ." I ignore Callum's warning, gazing at Roscoe expectantly. Roscoe looks between me and his employer, the muscle ticking in his jaw muscle.

"If you don't drive me, I'll take an Uber." My tone makes it very clear that I'm not asking permission to leave, just looking for a ride. One way or another, I'm getting the fuck out of here. Keeping my eyes on Roscoe, I watch him have a silent conversation with his boss. After a long moment, I get tired of waiting and turn on my heel to start walking towards the exit.

"Come back, Lexie. I'll drive you," Roscoe calls, making me stop halfway to the street entrance. I turn to look at him, ignoring the other pair of eyes fixed on me as I try to decide if I believe it. He jerks his head towards the car, his expression serious. If he's lying to get me back over there, I'm gonna lose my shit.

Relenting, I walk back towards the men, giving them a wide

radius as I head straight to the car. Callum and Roscoe exchange a few more hushed words before Roscoe meets me at the car.

Climbing into the passenger seat, I sit stiffly while I wait for the car to start. Even when the engine is started, we don't move. A large figure approaches my side and the window is being rolled down without permission. Callum stands on the other side of the door staring me down, tension coming off him in waves. I meet his gaze head-on, not even trying to hide my anger and contempt. He runs a hand over his beard, leaning into the open window to speak through clenched teeth.

"If you're not back by morning, I'm coming to get you," he states tersely.

"You got it, boss," I say coldly, pulling my eyes from his to sit back in my seat and stare straight ahead. Callum doesn't budge for what feels like an hour, then finally pushes off the window and takes a step back. Roscoe backs the car out of the spot and navigates us out into the city traffic.

"He admitted it, you know. Eric." Roscoe speaks up after twenty minutes of silence. "He told us what he was going to do to you." His announcement has my head turning to look at him. I knit my brows, my gut wrenching at the mere thought of it. His knuckles turn white with his death grip on the steering wheel, jaw clenched tight.

"Was that before or after Callum started torturing him?" We both know the answer, Roscoe's silence only confirms it. Callum might have stopped me from being assaulted, but he's no hero. "That's what I thought."

CHAPTER TWENTY-ONE

CALLUM

I fucked up. I let Eric live. I've never let a loose end go unfinished before. It goes against everything I am and how I've built my reputation. Callum Russo never had so much as a wrinkle in his plans. I was the Fixer who never had loose ends.

Until now, because I fucked up.

Letting that date-rapist go isn't the problem. It's her. I'm not an assassin or a serial killer, but there's plenty of blood on my hands. I don't hesitate to eliminate threats when the situation calls for it. It's the cost of doing business, a necessary step to effective problem solving. And my work is impeccable.

How many times have I been begged for mercy when my gun was pointed at someone's head or my knife pressed against their neck? And I never batted a fucking eye. I pulled the trigger without hesitation or remorse.

Until she asked me not to.

Lexie looked up at me with those bright blue eyes pleading, and I broke my own goddam rules like I would do anything to please her. I'm fucking pissed. Because in that moment, while lowering the knife and seeing the relief on her pretty face, I realized it's true. I will do anything to please her, give her anything that makes her happy.

Going after the son of a bitch from the dating app was bad enough. He wasn't part of a job. I'd found him for personal reasons.

Finding out he'd been flirting with my pretty pink nurse, that he thought she could ever be his, sent me into a jealous rage. Tracking him down was an action born solely from an emotional impulse—something I thought I'd gotten a handle on a long time ago. I wasn't planning on hurting Eric, the idea was to threaten the cheating bastard and make an example of him for Lexie. But then I found the little baggie of pills in his wallet—pills meant for Lexie—and I saw red. When he admitted what he wanted to do to her, my knife was suddenly pressing against his throat.

I won't lie, it felt good to slice him open for what he planned for Lexie. *My Lexie*. Thinking back, I'd do it all over again. But this time I'd finish the fucking job, instead of letting him live to see another day. Allowing him to survive is a threat to everything I've built.

But I did it for her.

Hurling my tumbler, it shatters in an explosion of glass and whiskey. *Lexie*. Just the thought of her name has my head spinning with messy emotions, my body buzzing with hormones. She is good, and decent, and simple. She's also stubborn, judgmental, and guarded. She thanks me for protecting her, and lectures me about violence against her attackers in the same breath. She's beautiful, and fun, and emotionally unavailable. She's complicated and wrong for me, and I'm completely obsessed.

The anger surging in me shifts towards panic, the realization unsettling every part of me. Lexie has me, and she has no idea. She's taken me without even trying, without meaning to. But she doesn't want me, doesn't need me. That's going to change, it has to. Because I *need* her to need me.

I'm going to own her, mind, body, and soul. I'll possess every part of her, the way she holds me in her sparkly manicured hand. It's not a matter of *if*, just a matter of *when* and *how*.

I'm not delusional enough to think it'll be easy, but that's never stopped me. I just need a plan—and if there's one thing you can say about me, it's that my plans always get results.

Awareness settles over me at the sound of the front door opening. I can feel Lexie's presence before she walks into the kitchen. Glancing over my shoulder, we make eye contact. She holds my gaze almost hesitantly, pausing in the doorway like a skittish doe at the edge of a clearing. I keep my movements small, not wanting to scare her off. After squaring her shoulders and taking a silent deep breath, she steps into the kitchen.

"Good morning." The greeting is simple and short but without hostility. A good sign.

Flexing my control, I resist the urge to reach out and grab her. She places her purse in its usual spot before her hand moves for the fridge, but her eyes snag on the counter where I've already set out what she's reaching for.

A chilled can of Mountain Dew sits waiting, next to a tall glass of ice water. Her eyes flicker to me as she rounds the island.

"You came back." My voice is low as I lean back against the counter a few feet from her.

"I had to." Those three words, so simple, carry so much meaning. She did have to. Because of her contract, and because of me. She was coming back, whether she decided to on her own or not. We both know it.

I say nothing as she reaches out, satisfaction coursing through me when her hand closes around the glass of water first. Her gaze catches on mine, the tension growing thick between us as my eyes say those two words echoing through my mind.

Good girl.

Tilting her head back, I watch as she drains the tall glass until there's nothing but ice.

"Where did you go?" I know exactly where she's been, down to the floor plan of the small one-bedroom in Harlem. Lexie's hands scoop her hair up, combing through yesterday's curls with her fingers before securing it in a high ponytail. My hands itch to wrap that silky ponytail around my fist and give it a good yank.

"I stayed at Ronnie's place," Lexie says, turning to face me. She braces herself against the counter, meeting my gaze steadily. The relief that floods through me just at the sight of her has the apology leaving my mouth.

"I crossed the line," I start, making her pause. "I didn't plan to hurt him, I went to make a point. But then I found what he had planned for you, and I snapped. You shouldn't have had to witness that." My voice is rough with remorse—not for slitting that asshole's throat, but for hurting Lexie in the process. The mix of emotions expressed through her eyes is too muddled to decipher. When she opens her mouth next, she takes me by surprise.

"Thank you, Callum." Her voice is soft. "With everything that happened last night, I never said it. But thank you for stopping what could have."

There's a vulnerability in her tone, a hint that she's surprising herself with every emotion as she feels it. She's not condoning how I handled Eric yesterday, but there's a recognition in her soft tone that settles between us. Acceptance.

"No one will ever hurt you, Lexie." My words vibrate through my bones. I'll kill anyone that tries, and they'll suffer.

Stepping forward, my hands grip her hips to lift her until she's seated on the island counter. It's bare of the baked goods and mess of ingredients that occupy it most mornings. There hadn't been any dialogue coming from the tv or music playing over the speakers in the kitchen this morning when I made my morning coffee, it was empty. The silence felt uncomfortable, wrong.

I missed her.

"Don't get any ideas, Callum," she scolds, even as her breathing changes. "This doesn't change what you did, and I don't want you thinking I'm okay with it." My hands go to her thighs, taking my time to feel her soft warm skin, before pushing them open wider until I can stand between them.

"You made yourself perfectly clear," I assure her. Standing over her, she looks up at me in consideration. Her thoughts are warring with each other, but I see the moment I win out. Her shoulders relax in a small sigh. My hand finds its way to her ponytail, wrapping the blonde strands around my fist once, then twice, giving it a firm tug. Lexie's head falls back to bring her lips to mine.

So damn sweet.

My mouth moves with hers, searing and sensual. Lust itches through my veins when her hands move up my shoulders, those pretty little nails scraping at the nape of my neck. Goddamn, this woman has a way of making me want her like I'll never get enough.

More. I need more.

A sigh escapes her when our mouths separate, so soft it settles deep into my skin. Leveraging my grip on her hair, I angle her head until her neck is bare to my lips. Trailing kisses down the column of her throat, I take my time to taste as much skin as I can. One hand still wrapped in her blonde locks, my other hand reaches into the water glass.

Pressing the ice cube to her neck, she startles at the extreme temperature. My hand in her hair holds her in place when she tries to avoid the ice sliding across her skin.

"*Cal.*" Her protest melts into a moan that shoots straight to my cock when I replace the ice with my lips, the heat of my tongue blazing against her chilled skin. Placing the ice cube back onto her throat, my eyes watch as it slides down the smooth skin, drops of water trailing over her chest into her cleavage. She squirms against the cold as I drag the ice across the exposed tops of her breasts, my tongue following the same path, licking away the cool water left behind.

With each drop that disappears past her neckline, the temptation to pull down her dress to follow it with my mouth grows unbearable. She's not wearing a bra, she can't be since the one she left in yesterday is sitting on the counter next to her purse. I want to bury myself inside her, drown in her. But first I plan to melt every ice cube in the glass across her heated flesh and use my mouth to ease the discomfort.

Pulling back, my gaze moves over her. Lexie's face shows me every sensation, she's so damn responsive. I'm a pyromaniac, soaking in every moan and sigh, adding fuel to the fire. The way her chest moves with each panting breath is thrilling. I've never met a woman so goddamn enticing in my life. She's like a piece of art perched on my kitchen counter—one I intend to study until I'm an expert. And those eyes—*fucking hell*. I'm going to stare into those eyes as she comes all over my cock.

A buzzing vibrates on the counter next to us as my phone starts to ring, something I ignore. Whatever it is can wait, and if it's important they'll call back.

"Are you gonna get that?" Lexie's question is breathless, and I can't help myself from reclaiming her lips.

"No." My voice is hoarse with hunger. "I'm busy." Drinking her in, I bite back a curse when my phone starts ringing again. Letting go of her hair, I snatch the fucking device off the counter to see Roscoe is calling.

Godammit.

"What?" The word holds a threat against his life.

"We've got a problem, boss."

"You're interrupting, so it better be a fucking big one."

"Joey Finch is coked up and making threats to start a war with the Russians." Roscoe's response has cold contempt creeping into my veins.

Motherfucker.

"Where is he?" My eyes meet Lexie's and I'm forced to take a step back to regain my focus well enough to hear Roscoe's response.

"We have him in the warehouse on the docks," Roscoe informs me, his voice grave. "He's rabid and demanding more supply."

"Keep him contained until I get there."

"On it, boss," Roscoe confirms. "He didn't go down easy. He's bleeding."

"We're on our way." Ending the call, I toss my phone onto the counter with a clatter and lean forward to capture Lexie's lips, kissing her deeply until she's panting against me. When I finally relent, I gaze down at her with so much fucking regret I'm sure she can feel it.

"Let me guess," Lexie breathes. "The moment's over." I hate those words coming out of her pretty mouth. This isn't just a moment, and it's not over.

Silently staring down at her for a moment, I force myself to focus on the new problem.

Joey fucking Finch.

CHAPTER TWENTY-TWO

LEXIE

I don't do well when I'm being rushed. It's not my best quality, but there's no getting around it. And Callum has a bad habit of announcing that we need to leave the penthouse with little to no warning. And I'm completely at his mercy. So here I am—in the passenger seat of Callum's car where I'm tucking the dress I slept in into a pair of scrubs because I didn't have enough time to actually change. I was lucky to put my bra back on before I was being herded into the elevator.

We crossed over into Brooklyn a while back, and the buildings passing outside the car window are becoming less identifiable and more industrial. Turning onto side streets, we move farther and farther from civilization, instead driving through alleys and remote driveways until we slow in front of a large rectangular building.

"Are you really going to make me go in there?" I ask, taking in the looming monstrosity as our car circles around back. By the size of it, I would guess this used to be a manufacturing plant of some sort. The old concrete structure with broken, boarded-up windows really paints the picture of neglect and decay. I've seen enough true crime documentaries to know that nothing good happens in abandoned-looking warehouses like this one. And by the state of this building, I wouldn't be surprised if it's haunted too.

"Yes, I am." He's clearly not giving me a choice. He taps something into his phone and suddenly there's movement. One of the old loading bay doors starts to roll upwards, and Callum inches closer.

Once the garage door is lifted high enough to clear the car, we pull forward. Two lights cast a dim glow over the small section where we park, the rest of the building disappearing in ominous shadows. My heart plummets when Callum shifts gears into park and turns off the ignition.

"I hate this place. No one should ever come in here without a death wish," I inform him, my eyes scanning the darkness like something might jump out at me if I look too long.

"That's the point," Callum responds simply. He's barely glanced at me since our little make-out session in the kitchen. Okay, *little* isn't exactly the word for it—not with the heavy petting and whole ice cube thing. I'm trying not to overthink it.

Callum's shoulders are tense when he exits the car, his expression menacing. The man I was with in the penthouse an hour ago is long gone, leaving me with the Fixer. I can practically see the wheels turning in his head behind those intense hazel eyes of his. He looks formidable.

My eyes are darting around the ominous building riddled with shadows. The industrial structure and use of steel tell me that this building was once a factory of some kind. But looking at the corrosion and disrepair, it's definitely no longer in use—at least for the building's original purpose.

I pause too long near a doorway and a strong hand grasps my arm to lead me forward. Judging by the fact that Callum seems to know his way around, he's been here before. More than once. There's a chill in the air that adds to the seriously sinister vibes this place is giving off.

"This building is definitely haunted," I say, looking into an empty office as we pass, fully expecting to see a demon's face peering back at me.

"Come on." Callum's hold on my wrist tightens ever so

slightly as he leads me through the shadowy halls. The fluorescent lighting is only so effective, especially since every third bulb works, allowing darkness to creep in between where the illumination of one ends and the next begins. I inch closer to his side, doing my best to keep up with his brisk pace. Right now, I'm not a big fan of Callum's penchant for secrecy. If this man doesn't kill me, the suspense will.

"I just want to go on the record and say that I don't like this part of the job. Walking around in places like this is how you end up the subject in a true crime documentary," I announce. Callum glances down at me, this time really looking as his lips twitch in amusement.

"Noted." The only response I get.

I was right, nothing good happens in a building like this. The long foreboding hallway opens up into an expansive room with ceilings over two stories high. Old industrial shelving sits empty and forgotten at one end of the space. But that's not what catches my attention.

I can hear them before I see them, the sound echoing through the warehouse. Shouting, incoherent and angry, spewing nonsense and profanities. Just like the night in the storage room that started all of this, a man sits tied to a metal chair. This one isn't comatose, but he's definitely broken. His eyes are crazed as he gnashes his teeth, his mouth practically foaming with his screaming. Roscoe stands in front of him, knife in hand. The blade looks clean, so the blood dripping from the psycho man's face must be from something else.

Three guys I've never seen before create a perimeter around the captive, looking like real goons. There's a small table set up a few feet from the chair the man is secured to, waiting for me to set up camp. It's a visual reminder that I have to get close to the deranged stranger, and the idea of having to touch him has dread settling over me heavily.

"I have a bad feeling about this." I'm fighting against the sinking feeling in my stomach as we get closer to the crazed man. He's absolutely seething, his glassy eyes manic. Callum pulls me closer and leans down to speak into my ear as he propels me towards the sinister scene.

"Roscoe has him secure, and that door leads outside," he says, nodding his head to a metal door along the back wall. "You're safe. You're not going to end up in any true crime documentaries." I believe that. A man like Callum knows how to get rid of any and all traces of evidence. If something does happen, no one will ever know that I was here.

Approaching the group, I stop a safe distance away and focus on setting up the small table for treatment. I'll have to get a better look to know exactly what I need to treat him, but I start off by laying out the basics—gauze, suture kit, local anesthetic, disinfectant. Callum doesn't hesitate to get closer until he's towering over the captive.

"Well, if it isn't the bastard we've been waiting for." The man sneers, glassy eyes gleaming. "You're a dead man walking."

"Big words for someone who doesn't even know my name." Callum's hand clamps under the man's jaw, forcing his mouth shut and his head up to examine his eyes. His pupils are blown out, and a thin line of blood trails down from his inflamed nose to his top lip.

"Is he high on cocaine?" I ask, staring at the captive man from my safe distance.

"Among other things," Callum says. "Fucking idiot, sampling your own product."

"That was some good shit you gave me. Colombian, right? You're gonna give me more or I'll destroy you. My name's Finch but I'll sing like a fucking canary." His tone switches from taunting to raging in a single breath, spit flying from his mouth on the last words.

"And who are you planning on telling, Finch? Mikhailov is the one who gave me the green light," Callum replies calmly, seemingly unfazed. He shoves the man's head back before taking a step, turning his back to him without a care in the world. He walks over to Roscoe, who leans in to mutter something I can't hear.

"Mikhailov might know, but what about the rest of them? I know enough about how this works. One right word and it's war. Once the Russians find out Alek's arrest was a setup, you're fucked." His maniacal laugh sends a shiver down my spine and his eyes land on me, pupils dilated. "Your fat bitch is fucked too. They'll have fun raping and torturing her after they kill you. Maybe I'll even take a turn, make you choke on my cock. I can't wait to hear you scream."

The man's profanities are silenced when his head jerks violently to one side, blood and brain matter spraying out the opposite side of his skull. Cold shock settles into my bloodstream, my eyes wide on the now lifeless man staring through me. Tearing my eyes away, I slowly turn my head to see the gun Callum holds aimed at the dead mobster, a silencer extending the barrel towards me.

He killed him, he fucking killed him. Callum shot him in the head, and now he's dead. Dread churns my iron stomach, threatening to make me sick.

We both know it's pointless when I reach down to check for a pulse. Glancing up at Callum's unapologetic eyes, he knows I won't find one.

"He's dead," I state the obvious to everyone in the room. Looking down at the body, I can feel Callum's gaze on me, burning. The feeling of his eyes on me doesn't leave as he barks orders to the other men. I watch numbly as two goons step forward to untie the bloodied body from the chair and haul it away.

Struggling to breathe through my pounding heart, I lean down to start collecting the medical supplies laid out on the short table. There's no use for any of this now. A dead man doesn't need stitches.

Dead.

I've seen death before, I work in a hospital. I'm a fucking ER nurse for crying out loud. But *this*, this is different.

Murder.

Callum is a killer. I've never seen that look in his eyes before, the emptiness. His blank calculation lacked any empathy or remorse. He pulled that trigger and ended a man's life like it was an item on his to-do list, like the next step in an equation where death was the clear and simple solution.

A cold calm settles over me as I close the kit and snap the latches closed. The panic and fear have twisted into something far more troubling—numbness. Acceptance. I turn on my heel and walk towards the door. Passing Callum where he stands overseeing the cleanup process, I can barely meet his eyes. I don't think I can stomach ever looking into that void again.

"I'm done," I state coldly, my declaration landing heavily in the air between us. I say it knowing I'm tempting fate. But instead of waiting to see what my announcement ignites, I continue walking quickly towards the exit.

I barely make it out of the building when a strong hand grabs my wrist and I'm being backed against the rough brick wall. The medical kit clatters to the ground, ignored and forgotten. Trying to catch my breath, I stare up at Callum, who has me pinned between his large frame and the building. Our eyes lock, and I can't help the relief that I'm not staring into the gaze of a calculated killer. Callum's heated expression emulates fury and passion, threatening to swallow me whole.

"What did you just say to me?" It's a challenge, a warning to change my answer instead of repeating myself. It doesn't work.

"I'm done." This time I say it slowly, purposefully enunciating each word.

"You're not done."

"You killed him. Shot him in cold blood."

"He was a threat, so I fixed it," he says simply with no remorse. Like it's just that easy.

"You fixed it," I repeat with a bitter laugh.

"That's what I do, Lexie."

"And at what point are you going to *fix* me?"

"I only fix problems. There's no running from it. You're in this now." Suddenly it feels like he's talking about a lot more than just a job. Something much heavier and more terrifying. "You're not done."

"Let go of me." The feeling of his solid body against mine should be sickening. The same hand that pulled a trigger to end a life not five minutes ago touching my skin should repulse me. Instead I'm fucking turned on. Our chemistry is buzzing between us as sparks fly and it's infuriating. Because I shouldn't want this man to be touching me at all.

But I do.

"Go back to the car and wait for me," Callum orders before taking a step back, making my burning blood boil. He turns his head to address the man I hadn't realized had joined us in the alley, his eyes never leaving me. "Roscoe, go with her."

"I don't need a chaperone," I snap, reaching down to snag the medical kit off the dirty ground. With the rage that's powering through me at the moment not even Satan himself could challenge me and win. Whatever's waiting for me in the shadows can do their worst.

Callum's struggling against his restraint, his expression flickering between cold indifference and fierce intensity. His hands start twitching at his sides, moving to reach out to me once or twice before he thinks better of it and pulls them back. I can practically see him wrestling with the urge to throw me over his shoulder like a caveman. His computer brain is glitching. I'd probably find it amusing if I wasn't so damn pissed.

"Have fun dealing with the *body*," I say bitterly as I step around him to stalk back into the wretched building. Walking straight past Roscoe, I shoot a glare at him when he attempts to open the door for me. He's not innocent in this either.

CHAPTER TWENTY-THREE

LEXIE

The inside of the warehouse passes in front of my eyes unseen as I stomp back to where Callum parked the car. I'll admit I slam the car door shut behind me a little harder than I should. There's no calming me down, even sitting alone in the silence. Wrestling out of my scrubs until it's just my dress, I whip the balled-up fabric into the back seat.

It's a good thirty minutes before Callum climbs into the driver's seat beside me.

The car ride is spent in an uncomfortable silence and the tension grows thicker by the second.

The elevator ride up to the penthouse is even worse.

I feel like I'm in a room with a ticking time bomb. I'm not sure which one of us will explode first, but it will be catastrophic either way.

Turns out the sound of the elevator *ding* when we reach the top floor is the last straw. Something shifts in the air that feels final and unforgiving—the point of no return.

As soon as the doors slide open I make my escape—rushing into the apartment and heading to the nearest door to close. I end up in the guest bathroom in the entryway. Callum is right on my heels before I slam the door shut in his face and flip the lock.

"Open the fucking door, Lexie. Don't make me break it

down." My heart hammers in my chest at the dark threat in his voice. He means it, he'll come in after me. Anger flares in me, my defiance mixing with dread. I have two options here: open the door myself or let him break it down. Both end the same—with me face-to-face dealing with the wrath of a furious Callum.

Hand trembling slightly, I flip the lock and slowly open the door. There's no way I'm gonna show him how rattled I really am, so I square my shoulders to face him. Callum's storming the door the second it's open, stalking towards me until I'm backed against the wall. He doesn't stop until we're chest to chest and I'm forced to tilt my head back to look up at him.

"You're a sociopath." My barb hits him without inflicting any damage. His eyes move across my face in dark possession, sending potent lust pooling between my legs as my heart rate jumps.

"What pisses you off more, hmm? The fact that I'm a killer? Or that it doesn't stop you from getting wet for me?"

"I hate you," I snap angrily, shoving against his chest to put some space between us. It's pointless, the man is as moveable as a mountain. He catches my wrists and pins them to the wall above my head, taking a step closer just to make a point. He's bigger than me, stronger than me, and a sadistic control freak who needs to assert his dominance. My pulse jumps, breasts heaving with each breath.

"You're a terrible liar, Dewdrop," he states, his observant gaze on me full of heated intent.

"I wish I never met you." This time it's not a lie. This man has completely taken over my life and turned it inside out. He's turned *me* inside out.

"Regret is a waste of time, there's no going back. You're mine now." His deep voice rolls over me as he presses closer, his knee pushing between my legs to spread them open and rub against me where heat is already starting to pool. Anger and frustration radiate from him, mixed with something in his eyes that I can't quite decipher. He's so close, leaning over me with his face just inches from mine. "There's no pretending. You want me as much as I want you."

"Don't." There's no conviction in my voice as it trails off, my eyes latched on his lips.

"Don't, what? Touch you?" Callum challenges, pressing closer. The intent in his gaze dares me to end this. "Tell me to stop." He leaves one hand to keep my wrists pinned against the wall above my head, the other slipping under my jaw to take hold of my throat possessively. Desire pulses through me from the pressure of him as my head tilts up just a fraction, bringing my lips a breath away from his.

"Would you even listen?" I ask, not even bothering to hide how aroused I am right now. I need him, every inch of my body is screaming to feel every inch of his.

"Abso-fucking-lutely," he says without hesitation. "I don't want a woman who doesn't want me." His meaning is clear, and if that doesn't make him even hotter, his eyes are roaming over my face like I'm a meal he's about to devour.

"Good." I'm practically breathless. "I don't want a man who doesn't take what he wants." This man is going to ravage me—rough, and hard, and without mercy. And god, I want him to.

"I'm going to do so much more than take you." His voice vibrates through me, tickling every nerve ending in my body. "I'm going to *own* you." When his mouth lowers to mine, he doesn't kiss me—he consumes me. His lips take mine in an all-consuming kiss that doesn't allow me to catch my breath.

The hand on my throat wanders down until he's palming my left breast greedily. Even through my dress and bra, his rough hands seem to burn straight to my skin. A moan escapes me when he squeezes my aching breast almost painfully. The discomfort just adds to my bliss with his assault on my senses.

Callum lowers his grip, running his hand up the back of my thigh, over my ass, then around to my center. His fingertips brush along the waistline of my panties, giving the elastic a little snap, before cupping my pussy firmly.

"*Fuck.*" The curse is pulled out of me. I'm not ready when his fingers push past the sheer fabric and straight between my lips. Arching against him, I'm breathless. "Oh god."

"Don't move." The order is muttered right into my ear as his fingers move, exploring for a torturous moment before plunging into me, hard and fast. My gasp is involuntary, and it takes everything in me not to arch into his touch. But I keep still as his fingers invade me in the most powerful and delicious way.

"Good girl." Those two words, said deeply into my ear, have me teetering on the edge of euphoria. Another moan escapes me, and my restrained hands push against his as I fight my body to remain still instead of giving in to the pleasure. "Fuck, you're so wet and responsive. If I had any patience left, I'd take my time sucking every drop from you."

"I'm so close," I pant, teetering on the brink as his fingers drive me to insanity. "Oh, yes."

"Not yet." The command is accompanied by a relentless pace as his fingers work inside me. My eyes catch his, the piercing gaze as unrelenting as his masterful hands. The wave building inside me intensifies, and I'm on the brink. I know he can see it in my eyes, can feel it. "Not yet."

"I don't think I can stop it," I gasp, overwhelmed by the sensations threatening to drown me.

"You'll wait." His tone leaves no room to argue. My body shivers as I fight against the orgasm looming, my breathing becoming erratic against the sensual torture. "Ask me nicely to let you come. Beg me."

The shivers turn into shakes, and I'm delirious against his hands. The agony is so delicious, I can hardly stand it. I need to come. "*Callum.*"

"Beg me," he repeats, his rhythm never faltering. If I don't come soon, I might die. My breathless pants turn into moans as I hold on for dear life. His hand moves from my wrists to lift my chin. The moment our eyes meet, I know I'll say anything.

"Please, Callum. Let me come," I beg without shame. The raw hunger in his eyes only intensifies, if that's even possible.

"Come for me." His hand on my chin keeps our eyes locked as I shatter into a million pieces. Wave after wave of pleasure crashes through me, until I'm seeing stars. And his fingers never stop moving, drawing out my orgasm until I'm breathless. "Fuck, you're such a beautiful, dirty girl for me."

"I am, oh god. Yes," I breathe. I barely have time to catch my breath before the need in Callum's eye forces him into action. It's like he can't stand and watch for another minute without being inside me.

"Turn around." Even as he says it, he's moving me and I'm being bent over the sink, my ass in the air. I don't have time for questions as he flips up my dress and tugs down my underwear.

I stand in delicious agony, chest braced against the vanity and my hand gripping the counter, as I wait. My level of anticipation rises with the sound of his belt buckle, then his zipper. I don't realize how far gone I am until I hear the crinkling of a condom wrapper.

Just like with his fingers, he gives no warning before he plunges inside me, deep and hard. There's no finessing or teasing, just need and domination. My back bows with the strength of my gasp, my hands keeping me steady as he drives into me.

"Fuck, your pussy is made for me." His grunts turn into growls as he slams into me. His cock is as harsh and unforgiving as the rest of him. He's stretching me, filling me so completely I feel like I'm in danger of bursting. My moans are a mix of pleasure and discomfort.

"You're so big," I all but sob. It's almost too much, his power is almost painful. I'm sure his grip on my hips will leave bruises as I hold on to the sink base for dear life.

"You'll take it. All of it." His pace is punishing, both brutal and delicious. My nerve endings fire rapidly, and the pleasure is almost blinding as it builds quickly inside me. "Fuck, you feel so good. You like that, my dirty girl?"

"Yes, god yes." The words are ripped out of me as he relentlessly pounds us both into oblivion. Still sensitive from my first orgasm, this stimulation is almost too much to handle. The edges of my vision blur as a new orgasm builds inside me. "I'm going to come."

"Not until I say so." I could cry at his demand. My body is wrecked from the pleasure and screaming for release. Holding back this climax is the hardest thing I think I've ever done.

"Callum, please," I plead, his cock so deep I'm pretty sure I can feel him in my throat. He's so powerful, it's all too much. "Please."

"Fuck, I love hearing you say my name. You're such a greedy girl, scream as you come on my cock." He barely finishes his words before I'm falling. This orgasm is even more powerful than the first, lifting me to heights I've never known before. *Fuck.*

"You're like a vise, gripping me so tightly with your perfect pussy." Callum grunts in my ear. "You feel so fucking good." I've barely come down from my climax before another is building. His angle changes, and I let out a cry as he hits a wonderful spot deep inside me.

"Oh Callum, yes. Right there, shit." He growls in satisfaction, his strokes possessive as he takes a fistful of my hair. He tugs my head back until I'm looking into his eyes over my shoulder while he slams in and out of me. He doesn't slow as his lips capture mine. His strokes become more intense as he kisses me.

"Who does this perfect pussy belong to?" He growls against my lips.

"You," I say eagerly, desperate for the orgasm that's building between us, growing bigger than anything I've ever felt. Bigger than even the two life-altering ones I've already had tonight.

"Say it." His teeth catch my bottom lip, tugging roughly.

"It's yours, Callum."

"Mine. Only mine." He pulls back, his hand in my hair keeping my head in place. His eyes hold mine, refusing to let me look away. His breathing changes, and I can see he's on the edge of his own release. "Come for me."

The release is immediate, a fire licking through me burning so hot and bright that I'm completely consumed. My back arches and lips part when my breath hitches with the force of it. Hazel eyes are all I see, stars floating across my vision. The pleasure pounds against me like the sea clashing against a cliff, wave after wave of euphoria hitting me until I'm spent.

"Oh, Cal. Yes, yes." His name tumbles from my mouth over and over, my pussy clenched tightly around him.

Callum's movements become more ragged, feral. He has me right where he wants me, where he needs me. His grip on my hair tightens sharply, his eyes never leaving my face as he explodes inside me, pumping roughly through the power of his own release. His arms shake against me, growls turning guttural.

"Fuck, Lexie," he groans, a deep primal rasp edging his voice. He slows and pulls my head back until my lips meet his in a languid kiss, his giant frame all but collapsing onto mine. Pulling my lips away, I struggle to catch my breath. Even being crushed beneath a tattooed giant, I'm floating. My body is in a cloud of bliss that I may never come down from. And I never want to.

"Damn." Callum's nose presses into my hair with a deep inhale, nipping lightly at the sensitive spot where my neck meets my shoulder, then soothing it with his tongue. "You're gonna be the death of me," he mutters deeply. My mouth opens, but no sound comes out as I lay in a daze. The man has fucked me into a stupor. Callum smiles against my skin.

"What, nothing to say?" he taunts, sucking on a pulse point that sends electricity rushing through me. "I've finally found a way to leave you speechless. I'll have to remember this." His chuckle washes over me, and it's comforting. More than comforting, it's strangely endearing.

I don't have too long to toy with the Pandora's box that is my tangled mess of feelings. Callum's using his powerful arms to lift himself and he's pulling out of me. I don't move, allowing him to discard the condom. He grabs one of the hand towels from the rack and gently wipes the mess from my thighs. He takes his time, giving special care in a way that surprises me. He's now in complete contrast to how roughly he just took me in this exact position.

Even after he's cleaned us both up, my legs are Jell-O as I lay limp across the vanity. I'm still shaking with the aftershocks, and I know my legs won't support me right now. Exhaustion is clawing at the backs of my eyes. Maybe I'll just take a nap right here and recover for a few hours. I doubt I'd make it to my bed as it is right now. The man has thoroughly fucked me into a simmering puddle of satiated pleasure.

Strong arms scoop me up into the air. Callum cradles me against his giant muscled frame, carrying me out of the bathroom like I weigh next to nothing. Where is he getting this strength? I'm over two hundred pounds, and with that pounding he just put us both through, I don't know how he has any energy left.

My eyes are half closed as he walks, the swaying lulling me closer to unconsciousness. When he lowers me onto a bed, something feels off. These sheets don't feel right. Opening my eyes, I realize I'm not where I expected to be. This isn't my bed, it's his.

While I'm looking around in confusion, Callum kicks off his shoes and tugs off his shirt before climbing into the bed next to me. What is happening right now? Why would he bring me to his bed, and expect me to lay in it with him? I open my mouth to ask him, but he rolls over to lay on me before I get a word out.

His arms circle my waist, his head on my chest, face burying into my breasts. I can't tell if he's trying to suffocate himself or use me as a pillow, but either way I'm stuck. My weighted panda has nothing on the solid weight of Callum's giant body. I can't remember the last time I felt so secure, being pressed into the plush mattress like this. I can already feel the tension and anxiety melting away.

"Fuck, I love how soft you are," he mutters against me, so quietly I can barely understand his muffled words. The edges of my vision blur as sleep starts to claim me. I can't fight it anymore, my body is completely spent. As my eyes close, I can't help the racing thoughts spinning in my head until I'm dizzy. But none catch before I'm being pulled under.

CHAPTER TWENTY-FOUR

LEXIE

Opening my eyes to an unfamiliar dark room, I'm confused. Looking around in the darkness, my eyes land on the large man in bed next to me. Staring at him, my brain slowly pieces things together and the memory of Callum fucking me roughly against the bathroom sink comes rushing back to me. I can't believe that really happened.

My mind is racing, questions spinning in my head as one thing registers. I have to pee. And, shit, I forgot to pee after the sex—but I really have to use the bathroom now, and I gotta try and avoid a UTI as much as I can.

Slipping out from under Callum's arm, I sit on the edge of the bed. My body aches, and I'm sore between my legs. Standing slowly, my legs tremble slightly under my weight. Shit, it feels like I did a million squats. I take slow, quiet steps, glancing over my shoulder to make sure I don't wake Callum as I walk to the door. I consider just using his bathroom, but I need to wash my face and do my skincare, so I go to my room instead.

Flushing the toilet and washing my hands, I look up and catch my reflection in the mirror. My blonde hair is a mess, the long locks in disarray without my usual middle part. My makeup is smudged, with mascara running under my eyes. But despite the mess, there's a shine in my eyes, and a flush to my cheeks. I'm glowing like a person that's been thoroughly fucked, because boy was I. It was by far the best sex I've ever had.

After removing my makeup, I realize it'll just be easier to take a shower and wash everything. I smell like sweat, and sex. As the water washes over me, I try to make sense of what just happened between me and Callum. He's infuriating, demanding, and dark. He's ruthless and dangerous. Someone I shouldn't ever have gotten involved with.

But he's also smart, strong, and he sees me. He's the most captivating and all-consuming man I've ever met. Not to mention that he's so hot he can melt my bones with a single look.

Looking down at my hips, I can see the bruises from his vise grip forming where I knew they'd be. Callum is a man true to his word—he hadn't just taken me, he owned every inch of me. Even my mind. I'd submitted to him, surrendered to his will. And the reward was so much more than worth it. I'd never felt such blinding pleasure in my life.

This could cause so many problems.

I have no intention of submitting to Callum in any way outside of that little episode in the bathroom. He doesn't get to own me. I've already gotten myself in way over my head with this damn contract, I don't need to let Callum's controlling ass think he has a claim on me.

I've lived a life under someone else's crushing control; I'm not going back. I can't. My parents did everything in their power to break me and my sister down into obedient drones. It's taken me years to release, relearn, and rebuild. Hours and hours of therapy to find myself and create the life I want to live. I can't give that up, I won't.

Not for Callum, not for anyone.

Stepping out of the shower, I towel dry off, slather on some body cream, and slip on a pair of panties before tugging on my cozy robe and going through my hair routine. Standing in my bathroom, I look around and decide I'm done.

Still in my robe, I walk barefoot to the kitchen. The under-cabinet lights glow softly along the length of the counter, illuminating the room in a dim, ambient glow. Instead of turning on the overhead light, I opt for the pendant lights hanging over the island. Grabbing a glass from the cabinet, I fill it to the brim with crushed ice before adding the purified water.

Three refreshing gulps in, there's a pounding at the front door. I glance down the hallway towards Callum's room, but it's all silent. I'm not supposed to answer the door, not since Callum first arrived at the penthouse. But it can't hurt to check who it is at least.

Placing my glass down on the island, I walk as silently as possible over to the door. Another round of knocks sound as I press the screen to check the security camera on the other side of the door.

Roscoe stands in the hallway near the private elevator, holding a large manila envelope. Seeing Callum's right-hand man, I unlock the door and open it. Roscoe looks at me in surprise for a moment. Probably not expecting me to be awake. Glancing at the clock on the security screen, I see that it's close to 2 a.m.

"Hi, Roscoe," I say simply. I'm not really sure how to go about this. The whole bodyguard-enforcer thing is new to me. What do you usually say to greet someone like Roscoe at two in the morning?

"Lexie," he greets with a nod as I step aside to let him in. "I've got something for Callum that can't wait until morning." His explanation is as vague as it is telling. Closing the door behind him, I slide the lock back into place out of habit.

"I think he's sleeping," I say. It's the truth, and I'm not about to tell Roscoe I just left Callum in his bed. Just when I'm going to suggest he go to Callum's room and wake him up, the man himself emerges from the dark hallway.

His eyes search until they find me, taking in my robe and wet hair. He's still shirtless, but he's changed into a pair of lounge pants. The look he gives me says that we're going to talk later, before focusing on the man standing in the kitchen with me.

"Roscoe." His tone is both a greeting and a question. I step over to the island to grab my glass of water while they talk.

CHAPTER TWENTY-FIVE

CALLUM

"What do you have for me?" I ask Roscoe, crossing my arms over my chest and widening my stance when we step into the entryway to speak privately.

"Enzo traced the money Anton was paid for his last shipment of girls through back channels to find the source. The trafficking ring is based in Colombia; they use several shell companies to cover their tracks."

"That could complicate things." I'm listening, absorbing every detail of what he's telling me. Yet, my eyes can't help but wander over to my pretty pink nurse in the kitchen.

"Their encryption was too tight to find anything. But the freighter company was a lot easier to hack. He traced the money to the port authority."

"What did he find?"

"He got the container number that the girls will be in. We can't be sure which freighter they'll be on, but we know which container it will be."

"Good, we can work with that." My hand runs over my beard in thought. Another piece to the puzzle. I need to make sure my timeline doesn't waste any opportunities with this job. "I'll have Liam dig into the freighter workers to find us an inside man. One of them will lead us to the cargo ship for a payday."

Roscoe nods, waiting patiently while my mind catalogs the info he gave me and files it away for later.

"Lexie and I head to Southampton in a couple days. I'll need you to arrange transportation."

"Your car is already scheduled," Roscoe replies with a nod. "Roger will be here at eight on Friday morning."

"Great," I say. "Thanks, Roscoe."

"You got it, boss. Have a good trip." With that, he leaves me alone with Lexie once more. As soon as the door is locked behind him, I move to be closer to her. Like a magnet, she draws me in with ease until there's no more than an inch of space between us.

"I don't remember saying you could leave my bed," I murmur into her ear, placing my hands on the counter to cage her in on both sides. Lexie's head turns to look up at me with those bright blue eyes of hers. It brings me back to how she looked over her shoulder at me while she came around my cock in the bathroom only a few hours ago. I want her again, and this time I want her spread out for me, completely naked, to devour and dominate.

"Don't think a round of angry sex in the bathroom means you can tell me what to do." Her sass only works at turning me on. I wanna fuck that attitude right out of her until she's submitting to me over and over again.

She thinks our time in the bathroom was a one-time thing, and she can't be more wrong. When I said I'm going to own her, I meant it. And more than just her body, I want her mind and soul too.

Pulling her eyes from mine, she resumes smoothing the fig spread on her toasted French bread. Who makes bruschetta with fig, goat cheese, and honey as a snack at two in the morning? It's fucking adorable.

Taking my hands from the counter, I wrap them around Lexie's waist. Her hands pause as I move to untie her fluffy little robe, but she makes no move to stop me. I take that as an invitation to slip my hands beneath the fabric to find her soft warm skin beneath it.

Fuck, she's not wearing a bra—my hand finding nothing between me and the soft heat of her generous breast. Even my very large hand overflows with the ripe weight of her chest. And shit if that isn't sexy. My other hand trails down to feel her frilly little panties, only slightly annoyed to feel the lace covering her perfect little pussy. I like lace.

The soft gasp I elicit when my hand slides under the lace to stroke her has me hard as a rock, making me squeeze her breast harder. I know the bite of pain turns her on, I can feel her getting wet against my palm. I insert one finger inside her, giving a few teasing pumps as she falls back against me for support.

I would do anything to have her laid out for me on this kitchen counter as I suck every last drop from her pretty pink pussy. The things I would do to her, making her come against my tongue until she can't remember her own name. But that will have to wait.

"I have some business to attend to, and you're coming with me. Pack a bag, we'll be gone for two nights. We leave at the end of the week." I inhale one last time, enjoying the delicious scent of her hair products—it's something citrus and smells delectable—before withdrawing my hands and retying her robe.

Taking Lexie's idea, I head to the shower. Running my hands down my face, I can smell her on my fingers. Goddammit she's perfect. Soft, but strong willed and intelligent. She works impressively well under pressure and remains calm in times of crisis. And her pussy is fucking Nirvana. I've dug myself into an insanely deep hole here, and I only plan to keep on digging.

CHAPTER TWENTY-SIX

LEXIE

My brain won't shut up.

Not even a good rot-session on the couch can stop the incessant noise inside my head. I can't seem to focus on the social media posts scrolling across my phone screen; my mind won't stop obsessing over the questions that repeat on a loop. When did my life turn into such a complicated puzzle?

I let my eyes wander from the device in my hand back to the man sitting next to me on the couch. Callum isn't working for once, there's a book in his hands instead.

Just looking at him makes me want to jump his bones. He's so sexy, strong, and thick all over. I'd like to lick every substantial inch of him. I'm sure he'd enjoy every second of it too—before returning the favor. As hard as he is to read, there's never a single moment he's not charged up and ready for any opportunity to have me.

Callum is an enigma with more complexities than I thought possible in one person. His family is part of the New York Mafia, obviously very close to the head family. With his connections and involvement, it's obvious that he was a member of the *Cosa Nostra* at some point too. But that doesn't seem right.

To be fair, my knowledge of the Mafia comes from true-crime documentaries and romance novels—so it's more than possible that I'm wrong—but leaving the Mafia isn't something you can do alive.

Live by the blood, die by the blood, and all that jazz.

"It's difficult to read while you're staring so hard," Callum says, turning his head to meet my eyes. I don't shy away from his gaze, staring at him in consideration. "Ask me, Dewdrop."

"You're a made man." I wait, and he lifts one shoulder in vague confirmation. "Tell me how you left the Outfit with your life." His brows jump in surprise, and he pauses to look me over thoughtfully.

"Knowing that information is dangerous," he informs me.

"Apparently so is knowing you," I point out mildly with a shrug. "What have you been looking for? Levi, Viktor, the guy with the finger. You're obviously hunting something."

"Not what, who. I've been hired to track down a sixteen-year-old girl." His answer knots my stomach. Sixteen? She's so young, just a baby really. I open my mouth to ask a follow-up question but think better of it. It's a rare occasion that Callum is open to questions. There's a bigger mystery that I want answers to. I can finesse more answers about the girl later.

"How did you get into 'fixing'? And how long have you been doing it?"

"So many questions, Dewdrop. But I have some of my own. I'll make you a deal—truth for a truth." Of course he's bargaining. It's just like him to turn a conversation into a transaction. He can't simply give something away without receiving something in return, that wouldn't benefit him. Callum is an expert at spinning every situation for his gain. But this request seems fair, so I agree.

"Deal."

He leans forward to place his book on the coffee table, before settling back on the couch. I shift in my place in the corner of the plush sectional, crossing my legs underneath me to get comfy.

"Before Marcus and I were born, my father was part of the *Cosa Nostra* with Rafael Grassos' father Don Salvator. He was a loyal soldier, working closely with Rafael doing Family business. At one of the street fairs, he met an Irish girl whose father was part of the Irish Mob. One thing led to another and—despite all of the reasons not to—they fell in love."

"Aww, that's so sweet." I can't help myself, it's a regular star-crossed lovers' story. Callum's lips twitch with a smile, and he continues.

"They wanted to get married, but the Italians and the Irish were at war over alcohol trades and territory on the docks. So they made a plan. They knew the only way they could be together was to get pregnant and force their families' hands. They got married, and my brother was born three months later. The wedding was more than tense, a few members from both sides even came to blows."

"That's crazy."

"It's not uncommon." He shrugs. "I grew up loyal to the Grassos family. I became a made man when I was fourteen. My initiation into the New York Mafia was taking care of a supplier who was stealing from Don Rafael. That was the first man I ever killed." My stomach drops at the mention of murder, so I change the subject.

"What about your mom's family?" Callum flashes me a concerned glance that says he notices the shift in conversation, but he answers.

"The Irish and the Italians made attempts to get along but turns out being civil proved to be impossible." He shakes his head. "I was twenty-one and my mother insisted we should get both sides of the family together for a Christmas party. My father thought it was a terrible idea, but trying to stop Tara Walsh-Russo from doing something is like trying to stop a hurricane—completely pointless. My father was right."

"What happened?" I ask.

"Exactly what you'd expect when you put members of rival mafias together in the same room. Old feuds sparked and things turned explosive. A fight broke out, and one of my mom's brothers pulled his gun."

"Someone got shot." My eyes widen, and Callum nods.

"The bullet went through my mom's spine, almost killing her. Because those fuckers lost their temper, my mom will never walk again." His hand runs over his beard as he thinks back. "That's when I realized blindly acting on emotions was dangerous. There are much better ways to get what you want.

"I slowly started to separate myself from the Outfit. I knew leaving outright would be a death sentence, so my moves started out small. I made myself indispensable to the Grassos family as a 'cleaner' of sorts, taking care of messes. I kept all the dusty skeletons from falling out of their closet. That's how I met the Manici family who run the Chicago Syndicate, along with politicians, officials, celebrities, and CEOs. Eventually I was valuable enough to step away from the family business relatively unscathed."

"*Relatively* unscathed?" I repeat.

"The Grassos felt possessive at first. They didn't like when I started working with outsiders," Callum explains. "The shift in power caused some growing pains, but ultimately Rafael learned his place."

"So what about your brother? He's still in family business, right?"

"That's a different question. It's my turn." I open my mouth to protest, but the look he gives me is a reminder that I promised.

"Alright," I agree, scooching forward on the cushion. "Shoot."

"Tell me about the nightmares." Callum doesn't bother with small talk; there's no beating around the bush. Instead, he plows straight to the point. This isn't something I was planning on sharing with him—or anyone outside my therapist's office.

I narrow my eyes as I mull it over. Callum sits patiently, watching and waiting. Taking a deep breath, I steel myself for the story.

"Two weeks before my contract at New York Presbyterian ended, I was scheduled for a three-day stretch of twelve-hour shifts. A trauma came into the ER, a bus was hit by a semi-truck. The wreck was so bad, they were carting some of the victims in pieces." I can't help the tears that mist in my eyes, so I pull my gaze away. Tilting my head back to look up at the ceiling, I will the waterworks to recede. When the first tear falls down my cheek despite my best efforts, I close my eyes instead. "I've seen a lot of carnage in my job, a lot of car accidents. But not like that."

A shaky breath escapes me, anxiety dragging at my stomach at the memories. Biting my lip, I force out a calming breath before opening my eyes and lowering my chin. Callum sits silently, patiently. His eyes never leave my face, and a line forms between his brows.

"There were eighteen patients: seventeen from the bus, and the truck driver. Fifteen of them were between six and seven years old. It was a school bus." I can't help the sob that escapes me. I close my eyes again and strong arms wrap around me. Then I'm being pulled onto Callum's lap. His body envelops mine, his solid frame settling some of the panic inside me as I'm tucked under his chin.

"A class of first graders was going on a field trip to the Museum of Natural History. It was their first real trip away from the school as full-day students." My voice trembles, shoulders shaking as I suck in shallow breaths. Callum doesn't say a word, somehow knowing that I need to get this out. "One of the little girls, Andie, was crushed from the neck down. Every one of her organs was affected, and she was bleeding out internally.

"She kept asking me when she could see the dinosaurs. She said she sold cupcakes for the money to buy her ticket. All of the operating rooms were filled with other children who had better chances of survival. Andie Brentwood bled out forty-three minutes after the crash, holding my hand. Her parents weren't there yet, they couldn't get to the hospital because of the traffic caused by the accident."

Andie's face flashes behind my closed eyes; curly blonde hair, wide brown eyes lit with pain, and two missing front teeth. I have to open my eyes before the image breaks me. "Three kids out of fifteen survived. Two of them are expected to fully recover, one will be in a wheelchair the rest of his life. The bus driver and the teacher died at the scene."

"And the truck driver?" Callum's voice is gentle, his nose pressing into my hair. I can't help the small huff of disgust at the memory of the man who caused the horrific massacre.

"He walked out of the ER that same day with just a few cracked ribs from the seat belt and a broken nose from the airbag." Hatred burns in my stomach at the thought. "He was high on opiates. He never tried to slow down, didn't even touch the brakes before impact."

"Was he arrested?" Callum asks. I nod against his chest.

"He was walked out in cuffs. But he shouldn't have been able to walk at all." I'd never considered murdering someone until I saw the balding man shuffled out of the ER with barely a scratch. "People like Carl Suco don't deserve to live after taking away so much life from this world."

"He'll get what's coming to him. They always do." There's something in Callum's voice, a dark promise, that settles the animosity growing inside me. "When you get nightmares, what do you see?"

Curly blonde hair, wide brown eyes lit with pain, and two missing front teeth.

"Every time I close my eyes, I see the life drain from Andie Brentwood's eyes. I see Tess Webb's body severed in half at the spine. I see Adnan Fasil impaled by a bus seat. I see so many bright young lives destroyed and ripped away too soon, and there's nothing I can do to save them. I can't help them."

I suck in deep shaky breaths to regulate my breathing and calm my erratic heart rate. Callum remains silent as I sit in his arms, trying to calm down before my panic attack can fully form. It takes several long minutes before I've pulled myself together enough to speak again.

"Sorry," I breathe, pulling away from his chest to sit up straight. Forcing in a deep breath, I let it out slowly in an attempt to regain my composure. "I'm fine."

Callum's hand takes my chin and turns my face to look him in the eye. "You don't have anything to apologize for, Dewdrop. You never have to apologize to me for how you feel." His thumbs brush away my tears tenderly. Gazing into his eyes, I'm being drawn into him. Our mouths are a breath away, and my heart stutters.

He's being so unbelievably sweet, it's overwhelming. The urge to kiss him is too strong, and when he glances at my lips I don't hold back. Leaning in, I brush my lips against his.

Callum takes the invitation like I knew he would, using his hand on my face to pull me into him. He doesn't rationalize that I'm emotional and vulnerable, he doesn't care. This greedy, demanding man will take everything I freely give him without question or pause, just as long as I'm sober and willing.

And god, am I willing.

His lips capture mine in a kiss so deep that I feel it all the way to my toes. Fire licks through me as our mouths move together, and I want more. I always want more with Callum; it's like we can never get enough of each other. I shift on his lap, sliding one of my legs across until I'm straddling him. Without hesitation his hand slides up my thigh to palm my ass.

He keeps it slow, drinking me in like he could kiss me like this forever. There's no hurry, no frenzy. Even when I feel him harden against my ass, there's no attempt to deepen things. He takes his time, exploring my mouth; nipping, licking, sucking. And I'm lost in him. Just as I'm getting dizzy, he releases me.

Pressing one last lingering kiss to his lips, I sit back on his lap. He brushes the hair from my face, cupping my cheeks in his large hands. "Is that why you're always in the kitchen in the middle of the night?" he asks. I nod against his hands.

"I've only gotten a few good hours of sleep in the last few weeks." The night I spent in Callum's bed comes to my mind—the only hours of restful sleep I've had since the trauma. Callum catches it before I avert my eyes.

"Tell me," he insists, lowering his head to catch my gaze. I might as well, I'm in too deep now anyway. With what I've shared tonight it's just a drop in the bucket at this point.

"When I was in your bed, and you laid on top of me," I admit.

Warmth floods his eyes, the edges of his face softening. And there's something else that flashes across his expression, something primal that looks a lot like satisfaction.

"I wore you out," he rasps.

"I felt safe." It's the truth, the realization hitting us both at the same time. He brings my mouth back to his, kissing me soundly. I speak against his lips, "You owe me at least five truths after all this."

"Deal," he replies without contest. "But not tonight." With that, he stands from the couch, taking me with him. My arms clasp around his neck, my legs wrap around his hips, clinging to him. He cups my ass, supporting my weight without faltering.

"What are you doing?" I breathe in surprise.

"Taking you to bed."

"Cal."

"You need a good night's sleep." His deep voice vibrates in his chest against me. "I'll keep you safe from the nightmares." He carries me into his bedroom, leaning down to pull back the covers before gently laying me in the center of the California king.

He steps away, his hands moving to unbutton his shirt and walk into the closet. I take the opportunity to get more comfortable and unclasp my bra under my top, pulling my arms out of the sleeves, I tug the straps down my shoulders and out the bottom of my shirt. Leaning over to the side of the bed, I drop my bra on the floor.

Callum emerges from his closet wearing a pair of pajama pants hung low on his hips and nothing else. He's a very impressive man. He's not a body builder with muscles just for show. His strong frame is thick and solid, built for power—a Viking ready for war.

Flipping the switch next to the bed, the room is doused in darkness save the soft glow coming from his closet. The mattress dips under Callum's weight, and I'm being pulled back to the center of the bed by a strong arm wrapped around my waist. I let out a breathless laugh, looking up at him kneeling over me. Being back in this bed, sinking into the lavish sheets surrounded by the scent of his musk, I can already feel the peace settling over me.

Without a word Callum takes his place lying on top of me, strong arms circling my waist with his head tucked between my breasts. The considerable weight of him sandwiches me between his body and the mattress. I feel so small with him, a foreign feeling in my fat body. There's something about being dwarfed against a Viking of a man that makes me feel so delicate.

When did Callum become my safe place? The thought terrifies me.

"This doesn't change anything," I yawn, feeling the need to clarify. "Between us, I mean." I'm lying to myself, we both know it. Because despite my declaration, it sure does feel like something is shifting between us.

Callum settles against me, letting out a heavy breath of gratification from his place between my breasts. "Go to sleep, Dewdrop. You can go back to wishing you never met me in the morning."

CHAPTER TWENTY-SEVEN

CALLUM

It doesn't matter how powerful or connected you are; when your mother expects you to attend an event, you show up. Especially if she's Tara Walsh-Russo. There are very few people on this earth who can give me orders, but she is at the top of that list. So I packed a bag, and a certain beautiful blonde, and we're headed out of the city.

The drive to the Hamptons takes a little over two hours. There are faster ways to get there, but I decided to use the time to get caught up on emails and other work details before spending the next few days immersed back in Family affairs.

I sit back and listen to Lexie chat with our driver, Roger—the man who drives me whenever Roscoe's not available—like they're old friends. When traffic grows more congested, conversation dies down as Roger's focus goes back to the road, bringing Lexie's attention back to me. "You employ some really nice people."

"Is that a surprise?" I ask, raising my brows in question. I nudge her bottle of water when she reaches for the mimosa in her cupholder. The woman seems to have something against staying properly hydrated, drinking everything except what's actually good for her.

"Yeah, sometimes," she responds, unfazed. "You're not exactly friendly."

"What am I then?" I lift my cup to take a sip of my coffee.

Lexie gazes at me for a moment in thoughtful consideration. She looks torn at whether she's going to answer the question at all.

"You are," she starts slowly, searching for the right words. "Omniscient."

Her description seems fitting, I am all-seeing. Especially when it comes to her.

"Not to mention ridiculously good-looking and a little terrifying," she adds lightly, ignoring the water and taking another sip from the champagne flute. My grip flexes against my cup when she bats those blue eyes at me in a way that makes my pants tighten.

The two-and-a-half-hour drive feels closer to twenty minutes, and everything goes smoothly as we navigate traffic out of the city. I've only stayed at the Walmont once before several years ago. From what I remember, it's private and grand—the perfect place for an engagement party.

Lexie sits beside me, quietly admiring the new scenery as it passes by the car window. I can see her eyes moving to absorb every detail in the architecture and landmarks, and I make a mental note to take her sightseeing before we leave if time permits.

She's not wearing one of her cute dresses, and her pink scrubs are keeping my hand on her thigh from touching skin. My hand inches up her leg, moving closer to the pussy I crave to be inside again. She squirms under my touch, her hand covering mine to stop my movement.

Her eyes leave the window to meet mine, gazing at me intently for a silent conversation. Then her hand slips under mine to interlock our fingers. With that, she turns back to the window with our hands still entwined.

"Here we are, Mr. Russo," Roger announces, pulling my attention from the text I'm writing to Roscoe. He stayed back in the city with Liam and Enzo to keep the Harris ball rolling while I'm away for the next few days.

The Walmont stands proudly at the end of a long, hedge-lined drive. Converted from the French neoclassical mansion on the Walmont family estate built in the early 1900s, the hotel spreads across acres of sprawling, manicured lawns and gardens. It's as expensive and exclusive as it looks, and far removed from the crime syndicate that's about to overrun it.

"Wow, this place is stunning," Lexie comments beside me when we walk inside, and she's right. The glossy, cream tile floors reflect the intricate blue and bronze coffered ceiling. Ornate paneled walls and detailed crown molding show the history of the building, decorated with gold leaf and carefully curated decor. A grand staircase leads to a landing with two elevators before splitting to either side and wrapping around the massive chandelier. The large cherry wood reception desk sits along the back wall of the reception area.

"Mr. Russo," the woman behind the front desk greets me without introduction. "Welcome to The Walmont. The Raymond Suite is ready for your arrival," she says with a wide smile, holding out the pamphlet with the room keys and hotel map. I accept it with thanks.

"Callum Russo, out of the city." Massimo Grassos's voice announces my arrival. I turn to see him striding across the lobby in one of his signature pinstripe suits in the classic 1920s gangster style—all he's missing is the homburg hat and black-and-white shoes. As Don Rafael's second-oldest son and enforcer, it's his attempt at irony.

"I never miss a chance to take advantage of an open bar," I joke with a grin. The banter is for our audience, we both know that. To the hotel staff, we're just two old friends visiting for a special occasion. No one would ever suspect that I've buried more than one body for this man.

"Nothing but the best for such a special occasion. I don't have to tell you how important this wedding is to our family." Massimo's eyes move past me and I know he's clocked Lexie. "And you brought someone with you."

"This is Lexie," I inform him, my hand going to the small of her back as they shake hands. I don't particularly enjoy watching

Lexie smile at other guys, not when I know exactly what kind of man they are.

"Massimo Grassos," he introduces himself, blatantly looking her up and down. "Welcome to the Family."

"Hi—" Whatever Lexie is about to say is cut off when her phone starts to ring. She looks down at it before glancing up at me. "Sorry."

"Go ahead." I nod, giving her permission. I know that she's been waiting for a call from Mia about one of her old nurse friends. She flashes me a grateful smile before stepping away to answer it. My eyes follow her movements as she finds a quiet spot to talk by one of the rectangular pillars a few yards away.

"So, it's true," Massimo comments with amusement. "When Lucciano mentioned your new nurse was different than Tony, he wasn't joking. She's not what I was expecting, especially for you."

"Her work is impeccable and she's loyal. That's what I needed."

"She's blonde." He laughs at the absurdity of it. "And pink."

"Yes, she is," I agree, my gaze catching on Lexie across the lobby once more. "You have a list for me?"

"This is the information you requested." Massimo hands me a leather folder. "Itinerary for the weekend's events, guest list with everyone's room numbers—all of it. Go get settled in your room, we'll meet later. My father and our people will be here tonight to discuss business. Your family and the others arrive tomorrow morning."

"Perfect," I confirm. Arriving before everyone else was part of my plan—if I have to be here I might as well make a weekend out of it. The engagement party isn't until tomorrow evening, so that means I have until then to enjoy the Hamptons before all of the complications get here. Massimo's hands clasp my upper arms with an enthusiastic nod.

"Good to have you here."

"I wouldn't miss it." Better make the most of it.

CHAPTER TWENTY-EIGHT

CALLUM

When I first hired Lexie, I was all too aware when she was with me. But at some point, I've gotten used to having her by my side—she's become a constant, an extension of me. And I'm realizing now that having her with me is the only thing that feels right. So, when it's time to go pick up my suit from my tailor here in the Hamptons, I bring Lexie with me.

She's changed out of her scrubs into a girly outfit. She called it a romper, which is apparently something that looks exactly like one of her sundresses but isn't. This one has pockets, something she gets very excited about every time she remembers. Even now, as we stand in the store where I buy my custom suits, Lexie's hands keep finding her pockets as she looks around.

My phone beeps in my hand with a text from Liam. He's found a lead on who's behind the shell companies in Colombia. If we can find that person, we can get answers about which freighter the shipment of girls will be on.

The sound of dress shoes clicking on the floor announces my tailor's arrival, pulling my focus back to my current surroundings.

"Your suit, Mr. Russo." Walter presents the sleek black garment bag. "To your exact specifications, as usual." He insists on addressing me so formally, even after all these years—and my periodic reminders to call me by my first name.

Walter is a true gentleman, one of the last of his kind. He takes his profession seriously, a master at his craft. Anyone coming into this store simply sees him as a distinguished sales clerk at a designer clothing store, but he's the best in the business. The only man I trust to clothe me, both for my reputation and my comfort. There's nothing more powerful than a properly fitted suit to make a lasting impression.

"Thank you, Walter," I say, without accepting the garment bag. We came for more than just my suit. "Just leave it up front for me."

"Would you like to try it on?" He asks me this question every time, and my answer remains the same with each visit.

"No need, I'm sure your work is as impeccable as ever." Walter's measurements are unmatched; his ability to custom fit a suit with only one consultation is impressive even by my standards. Finding suits that fit properly as a man my size is practically impossible without several rounds of tailoring, and Walter's attention to detail is what makes for the perfect fit.

"Is there something else I can help you with?" Walter's eyebrows raise. He's got a good poker face with the practiced amiable smile of a salesman. But I can see the surprise in his eyes; this isn't protocol for me—I'm usually in and out, taking as little time to run this errand as possible.

But not today.

"We're going to do some shopping," I say. Walter's eyes light with understanding when his focus moves to where Lexie stands admiring the silk tie selection, clearly not paying attention to our conversation. His gaze cuts to me briefly in curiosity, far too professional to say what's on his mind, and written all over his face. I've never brought anyone with me on my many trips to see him before, even after all these years. *So who is she?* Feeling our eyes, Lexie turns to look between us expectantly.

"Lexie, this is Walter. He makes the best suits in the country."

"Nice to meet you, Walter." The smile Lexie offers is full of her usual warmth.

"The pleasure is mine, Miss." Walter smiles back politely, his eyes scanning Lexie thoughtfully. The way he's looking at her body, taking in every inch intently, would make me want to snap anyone else's neck. Fortunately for him, I know exactly what Walter's really looking at—it's one of the reasons I come to him, why I brought her here. He's looking at her proportions, measurement, and body type. His gaze is analytical, calculating in inches and centimeters.

"Let me know if there's anything I can help you with," Walter says, nodding before turning to bring my suit back to the checkout counter. Lexie follows me away from the men's clothes to the women's section. Rows of designer dresses, skirts, and tops. Lexie's eyes never stop moving, fascinated at the array of pretty things surrounding her. But her focus never lands on anything in particular, missing the point of why I brought her here. Stepping behind her, the light scent of her perfume wafts towards me when I lean closer.

She always smells so good.

"Take a look around."

"For what?" She doesn't get it, something I wasn't expecting. For someone who loves all things pretty and girly, she seems to be having a hard time grasping a simple concept like shopping. For some reason, it never even occurred to Lexie that we're here to find something for *her*.

"We're going to a party, you need a dress." The statement is simple, but she frowns at me.

"A place like this won't have my size. I can just wear one of the dresses I already have." She's so certain. I guess that explains her lack of interest—she never expected to walk out of here with something that fits her deliciously full body. She's wrong.

"Take a look around, Dewdrop," I repeat.

"What size are we looking for?" Walter asks brightly as he approaches.

"I'm usually an 18/20 or a 2XL, sometimes bigger. Way too big for these brands," she says, sifting through the hangers of a rack and letting her hand fall in defeat. Her eyes look around, but I can tell that each dress she looks at she's not really seeing. She's given up before even trying, just assuming I would take her somewhere she can't shop. It makes me angry.

Little does she know, I chose this place because I know they can provide just what she needs.

"I'll pull a few options for you," Walter says, excusing himself. Lexie watches him go, her usual enthusiasm missing.

"I'm too big. Nothing here is going to fit me, nothing ever really fits me," she grumbles, toying with a dress as she walks by a display. "Fat bodies don't work for designer and high fashion. There's really no point in trying. I mean, look at these rolls. They're not gonna fit into anything sold here."

Fed up, I grab her arm and pull her until my chest is pressed up against her back, my mouth to her ear. "Keep talking like that, and I'll take you into the dressing room and show you exactly what fits with this beautiful body of yours."

"Cal." My name on her lips comes out breathless, sending pure lust rippling through me. It's taking everything in me not to make good on my word and drag her into the fitting room.

"I always know exactly what you need." Her breath hitches in her chest. If I don't step back right now, I'll end up fucking her right here against the display window. "We're not leaving here until you've tried on a dress. Stop putting yourself down and start looking. *Really looking*."

When I back away she acquiesces, even if it's reluctantly. Her energy is still lacking, but at least now when she slides a hanger from a rack she's actually looking at what's hanging from it.

Going through a few of the racks, Lexie pulls out a light blue dress. Just by holding it up, I can tell the color would be perfect against her skin. The urge to see it on her hits me in the chest, making me insist that it's the first dress to bring to the fitting room.

Walter approaches with a rolling rack full of options in various styles, fabrics, and colors. I stand and watch as he holds up two dresses at a time for Lexie to approve or veto while he gets a sense of her taste. When they reach the last dress on the rack, there are already multiple options selected to be tried on.

Despite the selection in her size, Lexie eyes the collection of garments with skepticism. Like she can't allow herself to get her hopes up, despite her options. Each half smile cements my determination to provide for her, earn back the radiant smile she usually gives readily.

"Fitting rooms are right this way." My hand on the small of Lexie's back firmly leads her to follow Walter through the store to the luxury fitting area. The row of smaller rooms sectioned off with heavy cream curtains looks out to a deluxe seating area with sofas, armchairs, and glasses with the option of champagne or wine.

Even in her gloom, Lexie's focus latches on to each detail around her as she takes in every part of the first-class treatment I've grown accustomed to. Something I plan for her to get used to from today on.

"I'll just leave these in here for you," Walter says, hanging the haul carefully on the hooks in the largest of the dressing rooms. "Is there anything else I can bring you? Champagne, wine?" He stands diligently by the door, hands folded in front of him.

"Actually, do you have Mount—" I cut off Lexie's request for Mountain Dew before she has a chance to finish the question.

"We'll both take some ice water," I say, turning to give the attendant a nod. "Thank you, Walter."

"Of course, Mr. Russo." Walter bows courteously. "I'll bring that right away."

"That was rude," she mumbles, her delivery lacking its usual sting. Eyes catching on the clothes waiting for her, she begins twisting the ring on her middle finger.

"They don't have that shit here." What's meant to be teasing, an attempt to wind her up, comes out sounding irritated and condescending instead. I take a step closer to her.

"How do you know, have you asked them?"

"You're stalling."

"You're bossy." When she turns away from me, I can't help but grasp her neck to pull her back in. And she lets me, without bothering to resist. Never in a million years did I think I'd miss her defiance, but I fucking do.

"You bet I am." I use my hand on her neck to tilt her head back, bringing her lips closer to mine. She gazes up at me, her breasts pressing against my chest with each breath. Those big blue eyes flicker to my lips, sending a wave of lust straight to my dick. Lowering my head, I take her mouth in a kiss, drinking her in. She tastes so sweet, and lush.

Peaches and cream.

Her hands slide up my chest to clasp around my neck.

She's been disturbingly subdued this whole trip, the smart mouth of hers too quiet and polite. The unease of shopping in a bigger body has dampened her spark, and I can't help but miss it.

Each comment I make that goes without one of her witty remarks or a one-liner paired with a saucy smile, digs under my skin and weighs heavy on my chest like a stack of bricks. This isn't the Lexie that's blazed into my life and chipped away at my control with her pretty pink nails until she's wedged herself permanently in my head. I want her smile to go back to its blinding megawatt status.

"Take off your clothes," I order against her lips. She lets out a breathy laugh, and one of the bricks falls from my chest.

"Nice try, Russo," she says between kisses. "I'm sure fucking in the dressing rooms is frowned upon in a place like this. I'd hate to get you kicked out of your favorite store, Walter would be so disappointed."

There she is.

I can't help but laugh, amusement flooding through me. "I'm going to be inside that perfect pussy of yours again soon, Dewdrop." My hand slides down to palm her round ass greedily, making her gasp softly against my lips. "But right now you have dresses to try on."

"You can't be serious." She leans back to look up at me, her expression questioning my sanity.

"I'm always serious," I remind her, pressing one last lingering kiss to her lips. Untangling my hand from her hair, I step back. The defiance that flashes across her face tells me she's about to protest, so I cut her off as I back out of the room. "Start with the blue one."

Closing the curtain behind me, I take a seat on the sofa facing her fitting room. There's no doubt in my mind that she's glaring at the closed curtain wrestling between the idea of telling me to go to hell or just trying on the dresses to get this over with. I'll gladly take either option. One way or another, she's putting each of those dresses on before we leave here.

It takes a few minutes before I can hear Lexie moving around and fabric rustling. Her voice carries out to me, only a few of her words meant for me as she speaks.

"It's so pretty, this color is stunning," she gushes, making me grin. Her appreciation for anything pretty or sparkly never gets old; it fuels my enjoyment more than I could enjoy something on my own. "Ugh, it doesn't fit. These damn boobs," she grumbles.

"Come out and show me."

"It won't zip, my boobs are too big."

"Let me see, Lexie." I can hear her disgruntled exhale before the heavy curtain is being pulled aside. The powder-blue silk dress fits her like a second skin, accentuating her dramatic curves. The elegant hem ends just above her knee with a generous slit up one thigh, webbed with delicate chains dotted with pearls. She holds the top to her chest, her breasts on full display with the open sweetheart neckline that leads to the off-the-shoulder sleeves made of tulle, dotted with the same tiny pearls. The soft blue color matches her eyes, enhancing luxurious long blonde hair and that peaches-and-cream skin that always smells incredible. She looks absolutely stunning, even without the dress zipping all the way.

"I'm buying you that dress." I can't take my eyes off her. *Fucking angelic.*

"What part of 'it doesn't fit, my boobs are too big' are you not understanding?" she asks, exasperation tinting her tone with attitude. I ignore her, waving Walter over instead. The attendant places the tray of ice water down on the table beside my chair, turning attentively.

"Walter, we want this dress altered. It needs to be ready by tomorrow afternoon."

"*Callum.*"

Neither of us acknowledge Lexie's protest. Walter simply nods to me.

"Of course, sir. I'll send our seamstress, Lauren, in to take her measurements. Are there any other dresses you'd like custom fitted?"

I look over at Lexie, imagining the possibilities. "Not yet, but we'll have our selection ready for alteration before we leave." Lexie looks at me curiously.

"What do you mean?"

"Go try on the next dress, I want to see it."

"You want a fashion show?" Lexie jokes, breathing out a skeptical laugh. I grin at her, my brows jumping.

"Absolutely. And this time give me a little twirl while you're at it." She just shakes her head at me and disappears behind the curtain. The shuffling inside the dressing room is accompanied by mumbling as Lexie talks to herself.

"This one doesn't fit right either," she calls.

"I want to see," I insist. She steps out, unable to maintain her frown despite her sigh. My eyes run over her, taking my time to admire the emerald-green color against her skin.

"It zips, but the top doesn't fit right." She gestures to how her breasts spill out of the molded cups of the structured bodice. My gaze roams past her beautiful chest to how the fabric nips in at her waist and skims over the fullness of her hips and soft stomach, then flows almost to the floor. I lift a finger and motion for her to spin.

"Where's my twirl?" She rolls her eyes, but spins for me

anyway. I don't miss how she bites back a smile, and I make no attempt to hide my own. My grin grows as she turns in a circle, giving me a 360-degree view of her lush body. "Add that for alterations," I instruct. "Next dress."

Five more dresses, five more times she emerges to show me with a twirl. Four of the dresses fit, while one of them is a hard no between design and color. Despite herself, Lexie's having fun—but not more fun than I'm having. Watching her step out in each dress, getting to see her full figure in different silhouettes, is one of the best times I've ever had shopping.

She thrills and gushes over the smallest details, whether it's the fabric quality or intricate bead work, and her joy is infectious. Making Lexie happy makes me happy.

Lauren, the in-house seamstress, takes Lexie's measurements and we hand off two dresses for alterations. Four dresses are boxed up to carry out with us, six dresses total.

Walking out of the store, my hand finds its way around her waist, and I realize I'm nowhere near ready for our shopping trip to be over.

I want to see more.

So next comes shoes. Lexie, of course, picks the pairs with the most added details—glitter, rhinestones, bows. Beaming at me over glittery pink stilettos, she says, "They're not really impractical if they make you feel pretty." A statement I have no intention of arguing with.

And damn, does she look pretty in sparkly shoes.

Each pair is the definition of sensual femininity as she puts them on and struts up and down like the aisle is a catwalk. Her little poses and bouts of laughter when she tries on a ridiculous pair just for the hell of it feed my ever-growing addiction. I could watch her like this all day, every day, and never get bored. And looking at how many hours have passed, I've already started.

Jewelry, handbags, perfume, cosmetics, I try everything I can think of to extend our day together, to keep her laughing. She protests every time I swipe my black card, but her frown of disapproval vanishes the instant she's adding a shopping bag to the growing collection.

Helping her into the car to head back to the hotel is oddly disappointing. I've never liked shopping before, and I still don't. But shopping for *Lexie* is different. I like that.

"I had fun today," Lexie says. "Thank you, Callum." The smile on her face is exhilarating, and I want more. She beams and I'm hungry to feel that warmth like an addict jonesing for a hit. If I can keep her smiling like this for the rest of my life, I'll die a happy man.

"You can thank me properly when we get back to the hotel."

"Is that why you did all this? So I'll let you fuck me again, maybe get your cock sucked this time?" She's curious instead of accusatory. My grip shifts on the steering wheel, tension settling across my shoulders. Her question is simple enough; it's the answer that's complicated.

"No." I don't bother lying, there's no point.

"Then why? You hate wasting time and money. Why did you spend so much on me today?"

"For you, it's never a waste." The truth is heavy on my chest. I pull my eyes from the road to look at her. There they are again, those messy emotions slowly unraveling my tightly wound control. "I'll always give you what you need, Dewdrop."

CHAPTER TWENTY-NINE

LEXIE

"I still can't get over this room," I say, looking at my reflection as I clasp the dainty pear-studded necklace around my neck. It's one of the pieces Callum purchased during our shopping spree. Something about the fact that he bought it for me, just because I like it, makes it feel special. Everything I'm wearing tonight was purchased by him—from my perfume to the silk platform heels on my feet.

The suite is incredible, equally as impressive as the lobby. With elegant, wallpapered walls, detailed woodwork, and marble accents. I could never afford to stay at a place like this, it's the definition of luxury.

"I expected nothing less from the Grassos family," Callum says walking out of the primary bedroom. My eyes catch on him in the reflection and my heart flutters.

Callum's tall, broad frame looks incredible in his rich black suit. Walter is a genius, because it fits him like a damn glove. His full beard has been recently trimmed and shaped to perfection, his thick, dark brown hair styled in tamed waves. Those smoldering hazel eyes meet mine as he straightens the cufflinks on his white dress shirt.

Hot damn, he's handsome.

As I'm checking him out, his gaze sweeps over me in appreciation—taking in my big, loose curls, full glam makeup, and the light blue dress he had altered for me. My tits also look incredible in this dress; the off-the-shoulder sleeves with the open sweetheart neckline puts my chest on full display with the help of my industrial-strength strapless bra. My high-waisted shapewear underwear is currently holding me in and smoothing me out beneath the unforgiving fabric.

I'm not sure what to expect at this party. Callum will be the only person I know there—outside of his family that I've met literally once—and I'll admit I'm a little apprehensive. I'm not sure whether Callum is attending this party for business or pleasure, but I'm guessing it's a little bit of both.

Turning to face him, the air between us grows heavy with sexual tension. I can feel his desire to rip this dress right off my body as his eyes move over me—a feeling I know is reflected on my own face looking at his sexy suit. "Speaking of the Grassos," I say, forcing a cleansing breath. "They don't seem like the kind of people who like to be kept waiting. Neither do your parents."

"They're not," he agrees, though his tone implies he couldn't care less. His shoulders roll back and I watch him shift into Fixer mode. "You ready?"

Back to business.

"As I'll ever be."

The Walmont's ballroom is straight out of a Regency film, with polished wood floors and massive crystal chandeliers suspended from hand-painted, vaulted ceilings. A series of French doors along the back wall lead out into a large terrace overlooking breathtaking French-style gardens.

Elegantly dressed round tables are set off to the left, with an expansive buffet to the right. Along the back of the building is a fully stocked bar, complete with three bartenders. But as gorgeous as the venue is, there's a tension in the air that sits heavy and unrelenting like humidity over the guests who congregate in clusters. There's a very tangible divide between the people in attendance, separated between the sets of tables.

Callum mentioned there might be a bit of hostility at this event since the engagement is between rival Mafia families. *Okay, so his exact words were "two families with generational animosity" and I read between the lines.* But since he's well acquainted with both Chicago and New York, Callum crosses the invisible line without a second thought as he makes his rounds.

With each new group he walks over to, Callum simply introduces me as "Lexie" but doesn't elaborate further. I'm not sure what else there is to say about who I am and why I'm here. I'm met with curious glances, but I mostly just stand off to the side and let him do the talking.

I can tell when his family arrives by the way Callum tenses beside me before he can catch himself. I look up at him, but he's already squaring his shoulders with his armor firmly in place.

"You came!" Gio Russo's comment seems pleasantly surprised, but there's a barb hidden in his words. Callum doesn't allow it to get under his skin, but his hand moves to my hip.

"Of course, we couldn't miss it." The double meaning in Callum's response is clear. I can see the moment *we* register as Gio's attention turns to me.

"Lexie, I almost didn't recognize you without the scrubs," he says with a grin, but I don't miss the way he glances at the hand on my hip.

"Nice to see you again, Mr. Russo."

"Call me Gio, please." Just then, Marcus strolls up with a glass of what looks like whiskey in his hand—he clearly made the bar his first stop. He greets his brother by raising his drink in *cheers* before taking a large gulp. But then his eyes land on me, and I watch as his flicker of confusion turns into realization. The grin that spreads across his face has Callum's fingers flexing against me.

"The nurse, right? Lexie."

"Hi, Marcus," I greet him politely, but he's already on a roll.

"You clean up real nice. I liked the pink, but blue is your color." His gaze moves to the man beside me. "Don't you think, Callum?"

"I think you should lay off the booze and wait for dinner, before this place turns into a powder keg." Marcus shrugs off his brother's suggestion and takes another gulp.

"You've made your rounds?" Gio asks, and Callum nods. "What's the temperature?"

"It's heated, but I don't foresee any fires starting."

"You don't expect any violence, but your nurse is on your arm," Gio presses, his voice lowering. "Why did you really bring her?"

Callum glances down at me, his jaw clenching as my gaze meets his. His father's question echoes in my eyes before he turns back to answer him.

Why did you really bring me here?

"It's a Family event," he states simply, giving no further explanation.

"Your mama's going to have something to say when she sees you both."

"Where is she?" Callum asks, his eyes scanning the vicinity. But Tara's nowhere to be seen.

"Oh, Ginerva had a wardrobe malfunction in the ladies' room. Your mama went in to fix it." It takes me a second to place the name before it clicks—Ginerva Grassos, Don Rafael's wife and Lucciano's mother.

I don't have time for the frustration and confusion to settle over me before I'm led to the buffet table. It's an impressive assortment of gourmet food, and there's enough to feed an army. Seafood, premium meats, salads, pastas—the list goes on. My plate is full within seconds before I'm headed back to my seat, Callum glued to my side.

"I just repaired a zipper using dental floss and a paper clip. No one can ever tell me that I need to clean out my handbag after that." Tara's soft Irish accent announces her presence as she rolls up to the table, stopping right behind us. She looks very elegant, wearing a chocolate-brown dress that complements her complexion. Callum stands at her arrival, and I follow his lead.

"Callum, let me look at you. I almost forget what you look like between sightings."

"Nice to see you too, Mom. You look beautiful." Callum greets her dryly as he leans down to kiss her on the cheek. But the annoyance in his tone is missing its usual sharpness.

"Well, aren't you a vision? Lexie, is it?" Tara's focus lands on me as she moves closer, and I nod. "That dress is lovely on you. Fits you like a glove."

"Thank you. Callum got it for me—my whole outfit, actually," I say, and her eyes light with approval. Her gaze cuts to her son, the smile she flashes him both knowing and telling.

"Did he now? He always did have excellent taste." Callum opens his mouth to discourage her as we sit back down, but she changes the subject. "You're eating already. I didn't think I was gone *that* long."

"We'll grab you a plate, my love," Gio announces from his place. Callum's mother waves off his offer like it's ridiculous, and I can't help the smile tugging at my lips.

"I'll handle it, of course. Callum, come help your mam," Tara announces, rolling her wheelchair back from the table. She heads towards the buffet table; Callum squeezes my knee before he silently rises from his chair and follows to assist her. I can definitely see where Callum got his stubbornness from.

"He's finally back where he belongs," Gio comments once they're gone, breaking apart a roll. "With family. You're never too good for your family." I pick up my glass to take a sip of my wine, but I can't bite my tongue any longer. And honestly, I don't want to.

"It's interesting that you think of it as Callum abandoning the family. It seems to me that breaking familial expectations to make your own path is what being a Russo really means. At least, that's the example he was born into." My eyes look from Tara's retreating figure to Gio's pointedly.

Callum's father looks at me startled, like he's really seeing me for the first time and he's not sure how he feels about me. But I can see my words sinking in as his eyes move back to where Callum stands beside his mom at the buffet table while she directs him on how to fill her plate.

Glancing across the table, Marcus is grinning at me like he just won a bet. His eyebrows jump playfully as he takes a large bite of his manicotti, completely entertained by my presence. Or maybe he's already drunk.

Bringing my gaze back to Callum, I watch how he interacts with his mother. The man is a giant—especially towering next to petite Tara in her wheelchair. And yet, when he looks down at her, there's something about his countenance that I've never seen in him before. There's a vulnerability as his shield softens in her presence. He's not a fixer, or a man in control of a situation—he's just a son with his mom.

They're discussing something, I can see how adamant Tara's being on the subject. I watch as Callum sighs, his shoulders falling like he's confessing something. Tara's grin is both triumphant and knowing before she turns to continue down the buffet towards the salads. Before Callum moves to follow after her, he turns, and his eyes find mine.

Holding his gaze, warmth blooms in my chest as his expression softens ever so slightly. I feel like I'm looking at the real Callum—without any masks or his impenetrable control—for the first time. Something worms its way into my heart—permanent and unforgettable. The exchange only lasts a moment before he pulls his eyes away to follow his mom, but the feeling has branded itself into my memory.

When the pair returns to the table with Tara's full plate, he's back to being the unreadable Callum I know all too well. After getting his mom situated at her place next to Gio, he reclaims his seat next to me and resumes eating his meal. And as he cuts into his beef tenderloin, I'm left chewing the questions on the tip of my tongue and swallowing my curiosity.

---　✻　---

Just one more hour.

It's still early, but I'm ready to call it a night. I usually love a good party. But, considering the only person I know here has been actively ignoring me to work the party at the insistence of his father, I've resigned myself to a stool at the bar while sipping a cosmopolitan. I spent the first two and a half hours at Callum's side, but I got tired of playing the silent observer. Not to mention my feet are killing me in these new heels. I know better than to wear them straight out of the box, but they were just too pretty to resist.

The only good part about following Callum around like a shadow was being able to listen to him talk to the Grassoses and his family openly. I've learned a lot about Callum's past with the Mafia tonight.

Callum has worked with both families for a long time hiding their indiscretions. The heads of both Outfits have met a few times to forge an arrangement that works for everyone. Now it's time to bring the families together to celebrate their alliance through the marriage of Lucciano Grassos and Chiara Manici.

Despite the happy occasion we're all here celebrating, the vibes are less than cheerful as both sides mix like oil and water. Each family sticks to their own side of the terrace, eating and drinking, save the parents of the couple who mingle together tensely, followed closely by their enforcers.

Massimo Grassos, Lucciano's younger brother, has been glancing at me a lot as he follows his father around like a bodyguard. I pretend not to notice and keep my smile polite.

As if my thoughts conjured him, the man himself appears at the bar beside me.

"It's not a good look for our guests to go thirsty." Massimo indicates the emptied cosmopolitan glass in front of me. He waves to the bartender. "Let's get the lovely lady a fresh drink."

"Thank you." I accept the new glass and take a sip, holding his gaze boldly. He's not subtle when he gives me an evaluating look, scanning me from head to toe. I'm not surprised when he gives my chest a second look.

"I can't decide what I like more, this dress or your pink scrubs." What Massimo lacks in height, he makes up for in confidence and authority. Looking at the Patek Philippe Grandmaster watch on his wrist and the air around him that screams *untouchable*, he's someone important in Callum's world. It makes sense if his dad is the head of the New York syndicate.

"The scrubs are more comfortable, but things tend to get more violent when I'm wearing them." He smiles, flashing a row of pearly white teeth that reminds me of a shark. Something about his toothy smile says *predator*.

"Sounds very thoughtful to me. We wouldn't want our pretty nurse to feel left out." It's my turn to laugh.

"Oh yeah, very thoughtful. I would hate for my skills to go to waste." It's a joke, but something I say has Massimo's eyes roaming over me again. I feel like I'm being eyed by a wild animal, one that might snap at any moment—one wrong move and I'm dead. So I stay still, forcing my body to remain calm and relaxed.

"Something tells me you have skills I need to see in action for myself." Massimo's demeanor shifts, and just like that—I know we're not talking about my medical training anymore. Our flirtation has taken a turn, and now he's propositioning me.

Alarm bells start going off in my head, and my instinct is to recoil. But rejecting him isn't an option here. This man isn't someone you say no to without losing something very important to you—like a hand or someone you love.

Shit, what do I say?

Taking a small sip of my drink, I casually glance around to give myself a second to think. Maybe someone will come to my rescue. But the only eyes I seem to catch are Callum's, and he's glaring at me from across the terrace. He looks pissed, for whatever reason, so he'll be no help. I'm on my own here, I guess.

"Maybe someday you will," I say vaguely. "But I'm sure a man like you is too good at what he does to need my skills."

Massimo looks over his shoulder to make sure no one is paying attention before leaning closer. That one action tells me he's the type of guy who fucks fat girls in private, but he's ashamed to be seen with them in public. I don't mess with shitty guys like that.

"Perhaps I'll see you later for a private demonstration. I've always been good at handling large assets," he says. Rafael beckons Massimo over from his seat at their table, so he flashes those pearly whites at me one last time before stepping away.

The breath of relief that leaves me once I'm alone again isn't long-lived. I feel like I just survived a close encounter with a shark, but unfortunately I don't get the chance to finish my drink before a dominating presence is over my shoulder.

"We're leaving," Callum asserts, making me look up at him in confusion.

"Aren't you supposed to stay? What about your parents?"

"I have it handled. Let's go." There's a commanding edge in his voice as he helps me down from the stool. He's pissed, his expression thunderous as he pulls me through the crowds inside and towards the elevator. I pretend not to notice his mood, playing it cool when he drags me by the arm into our suite. He's lost his damn mind if he thinks he can get what he wants just by manhandling me. If he wants something from me, he can talk about it like a normal person.

I stop just inside the door that's slammed shut and deadbolted behind us.

He's right behind me, crowding me. His broad chest is practically pressing my back, and I can all but feel his eyes staring a hole through the top of my head. "Can I help you?" I ask, unbothered as I look through my purse for my lip balm.

"Massimo Grassos?" His deep voice is harsh, and quite intimidating. But not scary enough to rattle me. He can have this tantrum if he wants to, but that doesn't make it my problem. "What the fuck was that?"

Finally, I find the small tube of lip balm I'm looking for; of course it was at the very bottom of my bag. Figures. "We were talking," I reply calmly, leaning closer to the mirror. Swiping the balm across my lips, I blot them with the pad of my finger.

"That wasn't talking," he states.

"I was being friendly." I press my lips closed and rub them together.

"He's not your friend."

"None of these people are my friends." I brush off his comment with a shrug.

"He wants to fuck you."

"What does that matter?"

"He doesn't get to have you."

"Why wouldn't he?"

"Because I don't share." His statement has me turning to face him. He's got me cornered against the entryway table, and my chest is just a breath away from his torso. Damn my big boobs, I can't breathe deeply without rubbing against him. He'd probably think it was an invitation—and he'd be right.

"I didn't sleep with him, there's no harm in flirting," I say, looking up at him like my blood isn't roaring in my ears.

"The hell there isn't." His deep voice is so low, I can feel it resonating in my chest. God, his voice is hot. But that doesn't make his entitled ass any less annoying. He doesn't get to stake his claim on me because he's made me come a few times.

Fuck that.

"I have nothing to apologize for," I respond to his silence. "The sex is good, and it might even happen again. But that's all it is between us. *Sex.*"

I care about him, more than I ever thought I could. He's become my rock, a steadying constant in the whirlwind my life has turned into. Callum doesn't just watch, he pays attention. He knows what dress size I wear, he makes sure I've eaten, that I drink enough water. Callum sees me, he makes me a priority. He makes sure I'm catered to like no one has ever cared for me before. With him, I never feel like I'm asking too much, or that I even have to ask at all. He's always there to give me exactly what I need the moment I realize I need it.

But he's also a domineering, possessive ass who feels entitled to me. That same attention that makes me feel cherished turns crushing in an instant. And I refuse to give myself up to a man who can't even tell me how he feels. A man who can't communicate outside of brutal acts born from his jealousy. So unless there's a drastic change in his choice of communication, my body is all he gets from me.

I take a small step to the side in an attempt to move around him, but he turns with me. His arms go to the wall on either side of my head, and his massive frame is looming over me again as he cages me in—this time even closer. His head lowers, asserting his dominance, but he doesn't touch me. He wants me to make the first move, to submit to him—like he knows I can.

"I've been staring at this damn dress all night, imagining every way I can get you out of it. I get so fucking hard just looking at you." A wave of desire washes over me at the raw hunger in his voice. I hate how attracted I am to this dark, twisted, brilliant man.

"That sounds like a personal problem," I say, doing my best to ignore the way my heart is racing and the heat is pooling between my thighs. And failing miserably.

"*You* are my personal problem, Dewdrop. One I know exactly how to fix." Breathing in his cologne is like inhaling pheromones that cloud my mind until I'm dizzy. Something shifts between us as our eyes lock, and I know what's going to happen next. My chin lifts as I lean in, and he pounces like a predator taking his prey.

CHAPTER THIRTY

LEXIE

*O*h god.

His lips on mine are angry and heated, demanding everything from me as his hands yank my body against his. My dress loosens as the zipper is lowered roughly. His pent-up frustration is being inflicted on me with every rough press of his fingers and nip of his teeth, and my body responds eagerly to all of it. With each article of clothing taken off me, I'm pulling away the fabric covering him until there's nothing left between us. Our movements are frantic and desperate, trailing clothes across the front room.

We don't make it to the bedroom, Callum's too impatient. His erection presses against my stomach, hot, heady, and hungry for me. Our lips are pulled apart when Callum pushes me down onto the couch. The condom wrapper he pulls from the pocket of his discarded pants is hastily ripped open by his teeth. His eyes don't leave me for a second as he rolls the latex down the length of his impressive cock. He lowers to join me, kneeling with one knee on the couch between my legs, the other stabilized on the floor. The potent desire on his face is really fucking hot, handsome and ruthless.

His large hands grip my hips, pulling my open legs around his waist to line himself up at my entrance. The first stroke is deep and hard, stealing my breath as we moan together. Then he pulls out and pushes back in, building a punishing pace. His piercing eyes drill into me as intensely as his big, hard cock.

"Do you have any idea what you do to me? Do you?" he demands, an edge in his voice that's punctuated with the rough pounding of his hips.

"Callum," I moan loudly at the feeling of him filling me, stretching me so completely.

"You've gotten so deep under my skin I will never get enough. You've fucking branded me. Every second of every day, it's you. Your wit, your laugh, how fucking good you smell. I can't have a single thought without you being right there in the center of it. It's maddening."

"Cal—" His name is ripped from me with a gasp. His pelvis rubs my clit roughly with each powerful thrust, sending sharp bolts of pleasure racing through me. His beard scrapes over my skin as his lips move across my throat, shoulders, breasts. He nips, licks, and sucks, marking my fair skin—branding me.

"You drive me crazy," he rasps. "With this smart mouth of yours, this gorgeous body, and that addicting smile."

"Oh, shit." He's stroking me so deeply, it's all I can do to ride it out and let him take me.

"Every time you defy me, all I can think about is fucking the attitude right out of you. Just like this." He hooks his arms under my thighs and lifts my hips to push in deeper, making me cry in pleasure. "Tell me you're sorry."

"No. I'm not." I shake my head, biting my lip against the sensations rippling through me.

"Say it, Lexie."

"No," I insist. "Oh fuck. *Right there.*"

"Maybe I shouldn't let you come. That should be your punishment."

"No, Cal. Please. *Please*, I need it."

"I know what you need," he growls. "And you're going to give me what I want."

"I'm not apologizing—" My back arches beneath him as his

angle changes and he strokes something so deep inside me that my lungs malfunction. He drills into me, relentlessly, his hard muscles hitting my soft flesh over and over again as I'm dragged into delirium.

"Come," he demands roughly, the order opening the floodgates. The waves of bliss overwhelm me until I'm nearly drowning. I come hard and fast, eyes latched to his as I'm overtaken. Callum's rhythm never changes from punishing, my body being pushed closer and closer to the edge of delicious agony as another climax builds inside me. "I want four more."

"What?" My eyes widen, back arching when he lifts one of my breasts to roughly suck my nipple.

"Orgasms. You're going to come for me four more times." It's a demand, not a request. A moan falls from me as his other hand moves to circle my clit. His thumb rubs smooth, slow circles, the sensation in total contrast to how harshly he's slamming into me with each demanding stroke. Callum is everywhere, the stimulation is almost too much. I'm already on the crest, we both feel it. "But not until I say so."

"I—" I pant, my eyes closing as my head falls back against the couch. "I'm so close."

"Eyes on me." His order rumbles against my chest, and I obey. My eyes open to look at him, his gaze locking possessively with mine. His body is so powerful, I'm being taken so completely there's nothing I can do but hold on for dear life. "Say my name when you come for me."

And I do. Callum's name tumbles from my mouth over and over as I shatter into a million pieces, my pussy squeezing his cock as he pistons in and out. He doesn't slow, even as the sweat begins to drip from his forehead. His eyes hold me there and he curses under his breath.

"You're fucking perfection. Every inch of you," he growls, jaw clenched. I'm not even put back together after my last orgasm before Callum's body is demanding another one from me. "Look at how good you take every inch of me. My beautiful, dirty girl."

My eyes break from his to look down at my lifted hips to where he enters me, his big, hard, cock pulling in and out vigorously. The sight of how fully and deeply he's filling me almost makes me come again on the spot. I've never seen anything so erotic. I gasp, the sensations overtaking me. "Fuck, Callum. You're so big."

He is so big, his body, his presence, his authority. He's overwhelming and all-consuming, since the moment he entered my life. Callum's there—in my mind, *inside me*—demanding things from me I never knew I could give. Things I never realized I want, things I *need*. He thinks I've invaded his life, but he's completely conquered mine.

"I'm coming. Please." I don't want to hold this orgasm back, I can't.

"Since you asked so nicely." Callum leans down to nip at my jaw, his facial hair scraping against my sensitive skin. "Kiss me when you come all over my cock."

The climax rolls through my body, every nerve ending firing at once. Callum's lips capture mine, swallowing my moans as his mouth explores. My hands claw against his back, wanting him closer, deeper. His breathing changes, becoming more feral and ragged. He's trying to hold back, but I know he's close. And I want him to finish inside me, want to bring him over the edge. I need to make him lose control, knowing I'm the one doing it to him. That it's me who's unraveling him, overwhelming him. I tighten my inner muscles to squeeze him as he moves inside me, and he grunts wildly, his eyes snapping to mine.

"We're not done yet. You owe me two more."

"I can't, I need you." I'm breathless. I scrape my nails up his neck into his hair, squeezing him again. A fierceness flashes in his eyes as something snaps inside him. His control dissolves right before my eyes, the restraint falling away to reveal the passionate beast inside. A thrill runs through me at the primal expression on his handsome face, elated with the knowledge that I put it there. That I'm his undoing.

Callum's rhythm changes, growing desperate. He's not driving, now he's chasing something. Chasing his own release. "Fuck, you have no idea how incredible you feel," he mutters, and I can only moan in response. His hands are everywhere, ravaging and worshiping. The light inside me is building again. "No. Fucking. Idea."

Callum's release hits him like a freight train, ripping a groan from deep inside his chest. The muscles of his powerful body ripple with the force of his climax, his arms shaking above me. Looking into his eyes as he falls apart with my name on his lips sends me over the edge. I shout his name, the light exploding inside me until I'm blinded.

My chest heaves as I gasp for breath, Callum's breathing as erratic as mine. Lowering his head, his lips taste the skin of my throat as I bask in the glow of satiated bliss. His arm wraps around my waist, pulling me closer as he pulls out of me, his lips never leaving my skin.

"Mmm," I hum. Callum's arms harden around my waist and he's flipping us over so he's lying on the couch and I'm draped across him. My breath hitches.

"Take it easy, I'm already sore," I admonish. It's not a lie, there's already a dull ache settling over my body with the sated exhaustion. The tenderness growing between my thighs is definitely going to make sitting difficult tomorrow, and the next day.

"Good." Gentle fingers brush sweaty hair from my forehead. "I want you to feel me for the rest of the week," he murmurs. My hand starts wandering over his chest, tracing the indents of his muscled torso. He feels so solid beneath me, his large arms enveloping me completely.

"After that, I'm going to feel you for the rest of my life." It's meant to be a one-liner, but there's a moment of silence as the joke misses its mark and settles like a Pandora's box between us. Neither of us are brave enough to venture a look inside, opting to ignore it instead.

"You owe me another orgasm."

"Not right now, I need a nap," I yawn. His laugh rolls over me, vibrating in his chest against my cheek. His hand runs through my hair in lazy strokes.

"Don't think I'll forget, Dewdrop. I won't."

"Don't think that wearing me out like this means you're the boss of me," I counter. This time his laugh is different, deeper—the way an adult laughs when they're dealing with a child. Like I'm simply in denial of the truth.

Maybe I am.

We lay in silence, just enjoying each other's company for a while—dozing in and out as we recover in our satisfied state—until I hear my phone chime with a calendar reminder. It's time to get up. Shifting against him, strong arms tighten to halt my movement.

"Where are you going?" he asks deeply, pulling me back down as if laying on top of him is where I belong. I lift up to look at him, pressing a soft kiss to his lips.

"To put my clothes back on," I say, gently brushing a lock of hair back from his forehead. Callum's gaze tracks me like a heat-seeking missile.

"That's a waste of time. I'll just have to rip off anything you put on." I can't help my laugh, even though I know he's serious. His hands roam across my skin, caressing and massaging every inch he can get his greedy hands on.

"Oh really," I counter. "Sounds a little counterproductive since we're supposed to start packing. Our ride is coming early tomorrow."

"The car leaves when I say." His tone is final, not in any hurry to let me climb off of him. His body is substantial and firm beneath me, it's actually really nice. I'm a little surprised he doesn't feel crushed by my weight on top of him, especially after getting all hot and sweaty. My hair needs a good scrub after being so properly and thoroughly fucked.

"It's your schedule," I concede without a fight this time, letting him pull me back down to capture my lips. His mouth moves against mine passionately, our tongues dancing together.

"But if you ever ruin a bra by ripping it off, I'll have to kill you." I mean it. "Good bras are hard to find in my size, and they don't come cheap."

"I'll buy you a million bras, as long as I get to see you in them. I'll unwrap you like a present." He trails a hand up my side to palm my breast. His mouth turns possessive against mine as he gives my flesh a rough squeeze, eliciting a soft moan from me.

"I can't argue with that."

Getting ready for bed consists of showering together. Callum watches as I shampoo and condition my hair before he washes every inch of my body, then his own. I can't help my yawns as the exhaustion from the day creeps in. After Callum towel dries me, I skip the blow dryer and follow him into bed with wet hair and completely naked.

He tucks me into the covers, then pulls out his phone to respond to messages. Sleep claims me after a few minutes listening to the sound of his typing; being fucked into oblivion tends to have that effect on me. But it's not too long before my demons come to find me.

I can't run from it, I'm forced to watch the devastation. Helpless, hopeless.

Suffocating.

"Lexie." A deep voice breaks through my subconscious. My eyes fly open with a gasp, I bolt up out of the bed, but a strong arm around my waist keeps me from going too far. My eyes search wildly in the darkness, confused and disoriented, as I try to regain my bearings.

"Hey, shhh. You're okay." A large hand cups my cheek and turns my head to meet a pair of warm hazel eyes. "You're okay, I'm here." Callum gazes down at me, his expression full of concern. I blink up at him, panting as I slowly claw through the fog back to consciousness. Callum leans over me in the bed, anchoring me back to reality.

"Oh," I breathe, and repeat, "I'm okay." Easing back down onto the pillow, I turn my head to face him as he pulls me closer.

He gently brushes a tendril of hair from my face, gazing at me in the darkness. "Tell me about it."

"Truth?" He nods as his fingers run through my damp hair soothingly. "I can't move. I'm staring at the patients dying right in front of me—children dying. And I can't move. Can't speak, can't breathe." The memory of it makes me breathless all over again.

"It wasn't real, I'm real. Let's breathe together. Can you do that for me?" I nod. "In through your nose, out through your mouth. Ready?" I nod again, and we breathe together. I suck in long, deep breaths through my nose, and blow them out slowly through my mouth. We do it four more times, until I've stopped shaking and my shoulders start to relax.

"That's my girl."

"Thank you, Cal," I say softly, inching closer. "It's your turn, I want a truth." But my brain can't conjure up a question. "I can't think of anything to ask."

"I want you to be mine." His confession surprises me, sending butterflies and confusion tumbling through me.

"You've already claimed me as yours," I point out. But his gaze remains unrelenting on mine.

"I want you to *be* mine," he repeats slowly. Softly.

"I can't give myself to you," I inform him, almost apologetically. *Not yet.*

"I know," he assures me, allowing relief to extinguish the panic slowly burning to life in my veins. "Get some sleep."

As my eyes drift closed, this time there's only one thing running through my mind on a loop: *I want you to be mine.*

CHAPTER THIRTY-ONE

CALLUM

Walking through the halls, none of the Grassos soldiers perceive me as a threat. They should. I left a gorgeous blonde bombshell naked in bed to come down here. I could be upstairs using that incredible body of hers as a fucking pillow, but instead I'm down here dealing with this. Massimo should know exactly who he's messing with, but it seems like he needs a little reminder.

"Open your computer, I want you to see something," I say, standing in Massimo's room. He takes his time following my request. It's a power play, trying to show who's really in charge here. But he's about to see. "I saw you talking to Lexie at the party."

"I might've had a moment with—what did Marcus call her again? Ahh yes, the pretty pink nurse." Massimo's grin has my trigger finger itching to reach for my gun. I have a suppressor just for this exact reason.

"Lexie's mine," I state darkly. Either Massimo doesn't hear me, or he's too stupid to listen.

"She must come in handy a lot. Forget about being able to stitch people up, she's got the most fuckable lips I've ever seen." His words have the edges of my vision blurring with rage as I see red. Clenching my jaw, I take a slow controlled breath to rein in my fury. I could put a bullet right between his eyes right now before anyone realizes my gun is drawn. If killing Massimo weren't an act of suicide, he'd have sucked in his last breath.

My anger ebbs when he finally logs into his computer and the first image I sent pops up. It's a photo of Massimo standing over a dead police captain with his smoking gun still aimed at the cop's head. He stares at the image, a flurry of emotions crossing his face before he has time to cover them. Surprise, confusion, anger.

Then the next wave of images pops up on his screen—dragging a beaten prostitute by her hair, a drug deal, the list goes on. The next batch of photos never seems to end, his computer dings repeatedly as image after image pop on to his computer screen. Each one a different indiscretion he or his family has committed. Each one something I fixed. Over eighty of them, and that's just the tip of the iceberg.

"What the fuck is this, Russo?" Massimo demands, the confusion quickly shifting into intimidation and rage. Both are wasted on me.

"You want to share what's mine, it's only fair that I share something of yours." I can see his tantrum rising; he doesn't like being challenged. "If you or anyone else in your family goes near my pretty pink nurse again, I'll bury you and the Grassos name."

"You think you can walk in here and threaten me?" His voice is rising as he stands from his chair, and he slams his hands on his desk angrily. "Have you forgotten who you're talking to?"

"Careful, Massimo. Don't say something you'll regret." My voice comes out calm and cold, the underlying threat clear. "I'd hate to get angry, that's when things start to get messy."

Having heard the shouting, the door to the office opens and Elio enters looking ready for a fight. "Everything okay in here?" He addresses Massimo with his eyes on me. He puts on a brave face, posturing to be tough and dangerous. But I know the truth about him, like how he prefers his cars stolen and his women carrying leather whips.

"I was just leaving."

The car sways slightly as it turns, redirecting back to the city. When I'd left Massimo's office and gone back to my room, Lexie was dressed and ready for the day—another mark against the asshole. We left less than an hour later.

A comfortable silence fell over the car, allowing me to get some clerical work done. My records are meticulous; each job logged in detail before being heavily encrypted onto a private server that's backed up in three separate locations. I know exactly who's calling when my phone rings. I'm almost looking forward to this call.

"Don Rafael," I say, pressing the phone to my ear.

"You threatened Massimo and my family. You have a death wish?" Rafael's dark tone is much more practiced than his son's, having been perfected over decades of delivering threats and other intimidation tactics. Just seeing his name appear on my phone would've scared me shitless when I was younger. It's pointless now though, I've already seen the man behind the curtain. It's proved impossible to fear a man once you've slain the demons that keep him up at night.

I glance at the seat next to me where Lexie's curled against the side of the car, a blanket tucked under her chin. Her eyes are closed, she'd drifted off listening to something—either her gruesome murder podcast or a raunchy romance audiobook.

"He forgot his place and went after something that belongs to me. I was simply reminding him where he stands. Maybe Massimo needs to be put on a shorter leash."

"You forget that everything you have on us also incriminates you." He has a point.

"I'm not considering taking the shell company I use to hide my illegal empire public, Rafael. Your five-year plan could turn into twenty-five to life with one phone call."

"You've been a valuable asset for many years, Callum. My son can be reckless, you know that."

"You should teach Massimo to respect the man who scares away the monsters under his bed and buries the bodies. It's not very smart to test me when I'm keeping the demons from haunting your family." Lexie stirs and her eyes open slowly—blinking the sleep away once, then twice—before her gaze connects with mine. "This isn't a conversation I'll be having again."

"You won't," he assures me before I end the call. Lexie stares at me, far too observant for her own good. As she pulls the headphones from her ears, I know she heard me.

"You're having a problem with Massimo." She doesn't ask a question, but I still answer.

"Yes," I say simply, watching as she lets the blanket fall to her lap. Her tank top is stretched so tautly across each of her ample curves, it leaves little to the imagination.

"Because of me." Smart girl.

"Because he's an entitled prick." My response is met with a put-off expression as she rolls those beautiful eyes at me.

"Oh please, you're mad because he hit on me and now you two are in a pissing contest trying to prove who has the bigger dick."

"You know exactly how big my dick is. Or do you need a reminder?" I offer her a salacious grin, my eyes heated with intent. Lexie laughs and rolls her eyes again, but not before I've seen the desire flash in them as the heat of need flushes her cheeks.

"You're such a horn dog," she scolds, making me want to lick the sass right out of her mouth.

"When it comes to you, always." I'm tempted to take her right here in the back seat. But the next time I have Lexie, I want her laid out for me on a bed where I can enjoy all of her.

"Massimo is repulsive. He's not a threat to you, he never was." Lexie's assurance rushes through me, untying a knot in my chest before traveling straight down to my cock.

"I know that. Now he knows it too."

The back seat calls to me, but there's not enough time left in this drive to fuck her the way she deserves to be fucked—so thoroughly and deeply that she's branded by me and I've ruined all other men for her. And after having her in my bed, I'm going to devour her perfect pink pussy like the feast it is on my pristine white countertops. I plan on having her everywhere I can get her, I'll figure out where the car fits on that list later.

If there's one thing you can bet on with low-lifes, it's that they'll be greedy motherfuckers who don't know how to stop while they're ahead. These freight workers should have taken their payday and done their fucking job. But they didn't. So now I have to send Liam out to pay a few home visits with envelopes full of photos that could make a grown man cry.

If I'd never left the Outfit, Liam would be armed with more than a few pieces of paper. And he wouldn't be alone. It'd be easy to beat the fear of God into these leeches, but that's not the smart play here. I need something more reliable. We can't afford to take any more chances.

The thing about fear is that it's unpredictable. Its power is only relative to proximity. The further away you get from the thing you fear, the less it controls you. Leverage, on the other hand, never fades. Paired perfectly with fear, leverage is the key to power and control. What they should really fear is me, and I'm everywhere.

Me

Call me when it's done.

Pressing send on the message to Liam, I tuck the phone into my pocket and focus on the scene in front of me. Lexie's set the table for two, one of her signature steaks plated between green beans and roasted potatoes. It's the same meal she made the first night we met. She'd walked around the corner and changed everything.

A force of nature.

"Dinner is served," she announces, drawing me from my spot leaning in my office doorway. I join her at the table, pulling her chair out before taking my own seat. The first bite melts in my mouth, just like the first time.

Just like her.

The phone in my pocket buzzes audibly against my chair, amplified by the silence of our chewing. Whatever Liam said can wait, I'm too busy enjoying this sirloin.

"Who's got you glued to your phone tonight? Roscoe?" Lexie asks.

"I'm waiting for Liam to report back on a job."

"The Harris job?" Her voice is curious.

"Yes." I don't lie to her, but I don't explain. She doesn't need to know the nitty-gritty details.

"If I'm coming with you, we're saving every single girl in that container. We can't let them be sold," she says, looking across the table at me, her expression determined. Her bleeding heart is written all over her pretty face, and I know exactly how this conversation is about to go.

"I've been paid for Charlotte, not any of the other girls," I state, taking a gulp of my water, looking pointedly at her glass that's still half-full. She rolls her eyes, but picks up her cup anyway. I track the way her lips caress the glass as she sips, more than pleased with her obedience.

"I'll pay you," she says naively. So sweet and considerate, my Lexie thinks that saving this shipping container full of little girls fixes the whole problem. Like there aren't fifty shipments of girls for every one saved. Like they aren't being stolen from their beds every day, never to be seen or heard from again. This girl just happens to have parents rich and powerful enough to make a ripple. One that led to me.

"You can't afford me, Dewdrop." I lean back in my chair, arms crossed over my chest as I gaze at her. Her pretty white top has little pink flowers on it that bring out the rosiness in her cheeks. The wide neckline displays her creamy decolletage and frames her gorgeous breasts.

My pretty pink nurse.

I can see her question before she asks it, and I know just what my response will be. I've led her exactly where I want her. And that look in her eyes tells me she knows too.

"Name your price. What do you want?" She leans forward, her breasts pressing together and enhancing my view of her already distracting cleavage. She knows exactly what she's doing and she's good at it.

"You." My eyes roam over her as the possibilities flash through my mind. The many ways I can have this woman. "Spread out for me wearing nothing but lace and a pair of heels."

"Give me your word that you'll save them all, and that can be arranged," she negotiates. I can pretend to mull it over, but there's no point. Lexie's won, there's no way I can deny her this.

I'll give this woman the world.

CHAPTER THIRTY-TWO

LEXIE

"I'm gonna have to start wearing pants more. Or at least longer dresses," I mumble, mostly to myself, shifting against the car seat. The leather sticks to every inch of the exposed skin of my thick thighs, making each movement uncomfortable. Not to mention a little sweaty.

Callum pulls his eyes away from the road to flash me a look of disapproval. "Why?" he asks, like the idea is offensive.

"My legs stick to the leather in my short skirts." Lifting one of my legs to cross it over the other, the seat clings to the surface of my skin like it's proving my point. So annoying. A line forms between his brows, but his cell phone rings before he has a chance to respond.

"Yeah," he answers mildly, listening to the person on the other end of the phone. "I'm pulling up to the gallery now. Meet me here in twenty minutes." As he hangs up, we're parking next to an elegant white brick building with tall arched windows accented in gold. How this man always manages to get VIP parking, I'll never know.

I wait for Callum to climb out of the car and open my door to help me get out—something I'm grateful for with my dress. I'm not sure when I got used to having men drive me around and open the door for me. Between Callum and Roscoe my hands haven't touched a car door in weeks.

Callum's hand presses the small of my back as he leads me through the door into the high-end art gallery. We don't stop to admire any of the displays or art pieces, instead navigating towards the back of the gallery. A series of hallways and frosted glass doors take us into a private room.

The room is both modern and serene, with cream walls, black velvet furniture, and gold and glass accents. The luxurious simplicity of this environment screams money, which I'm assuming is intentional. Nothing loosens purse strings like feeling the desire to belong.

"Mr. Russo, good to see you." A slender woman greets him, her red hair swept back into a classy French twist, professional dress perfectly tailored. I don't miss how her eyes move over Callum, sparking irritation inside me. That's not how a salesperson looks at a client.

"Genevieve." Callum's greeting is all business, but that doesn't seem to deter her in the slightest. The smile she flashes him holds something more than friendliness, turning sour when her eyes move to me.

"And who's this?" If Callum recognizes the condescension in her voice, he doesn't show it. But I notice, not even bothering to give her my friendly smile when her judgmental gaze moves over me. Instead, I hold her gaze boldly, lifting my brows in question. This bitch isn't going to make me feel bad about myself.

"She's with me." Callum makes the statement with an authority that leaves no room for questions. There's no denying the butterflies in my stomach when I look up at him to find his eyes already focused on me, his hand never leaving my back when Genevieve clears her throat.

"I have the piece you're here for." She motions to the doorway with the heavy black velvet curtain. The hand on my back has me stepping into the adjoining room with Callum only a half step behind. Genevieve follows closely behind, closing the curtain to give us even more privacy.

An ornately framed piece of artwork sits displayed on a stand in the center of the viewing room, multiple lights illuminating the piece from all angles. I recognize the painting instantly with its unmistakable composition. The romantic painting of dancers on pointe with full tulle tutus and floral headpieces, with visibly intricate brush strokes in rich tones, softening any harsh lines and creating elegant movement.

"This is a Degas." My surprised eyes turn to find Callum's. "I thought this piece was on display in the Met." The Metropolitan Museum of Art was one of my first stops when I got to New York, and this painting had stuck out to me. And here it is.

"It was." Those ever-seeing eyes are scanning every single detail of the painting on the stand, expression serious as he analyzes it. I'm looking at a piece of art, and he's inspecting a valuable piece of merchandise.

"All of the paperwork is taken care of." Genevieve extends a leather folder towards Callum, waiting a moment for him to reach out and accept it. "Congratulations on your new acquisition, Mr. Russo."

"Thank you." Callum's smile is charming, if a little cold and distant. It's his fake smile. "I want it packed for transit."

"Of course," Genevieve agrees amiably, trying again to flash him a demure smile with what I'm assuming are supposed to be her idea of bedroom eyes.

So unprofessional.

When we walk back through the curtain, someone's waiting for us. "Reporting for duty, boss." Liam mocks standing at attention, a cocky grin on his face. "Lexie, you're always a sight for sore eyes."

"I didn't know you were going to be here, Liam." I'm not mad about it either, he always brings the entertainment. Getting Callum and Liam together is always fun to watch—Callum tries to remain serious while Liam annoys the shit out of him. It usually ends with Callum threatening violence of some sort, something that never seems to keep Liam from coming back for more.

"I would've gotten here a lot sooner if I knew you'd be here too. Traffic is a real bitch." The way his eyes move over me makes me think he's not entirely joking. His appraisal is cut short when Callum steps between us, partially blocking me from view. Liam's smirk turns knowing and he shoots me a wink. I don't hide my laugh of amusement, irritating Callum even further.

"Once the painting is packed, I want it brought to the vault. Send confirmation when it's secured." Callum's tone carries the edge of violence that seems almost exclusively meant for Liam.

"You know I live to serve," Liam replies, unfazed. Ignoring the giant standing between us, he leans towards me as if we're conspiring together and his eyebrows jump mischievously. "Lexie, now that you're here I can tell you all of my favorite embarrassing Callum stories."

"You have stories? I'd love to hear them, especially the embarrassing ones." I could use a few humiliating stories about Callum right about now.

"Oh, I have plenty. Remind me later to tell you about the time he accidentally called a mobster's daughter a frog in Russian and almost had New York City going to war."

My laugh has Callum's arm reaching behind his back to grasp my wrist, keeping me tucked behind him as he walks us towards the door. "That's enough, Liam. Just do your fucking job." The warning in Callum's voice only has the playboy's smile widening.

"Bye Lexie, we'll have to do this again soon," he calls after me. I turn to flash him an amused smile over my shoulder as Callum tugs me out of the room.

"Bye Liam," I laugh. As soon as there's enough space, Callum pulls me against his side, his hand sliding around my waist as we walk back through the gallery. It's funny, but now that he's gotten me out of the same room as Liam we don't seem to be in such a hurry anymore.

"You shouldn't encourage him," he grates, his mouth so close to my ear it sends a shiver down my spine.

"I think he's funny. Plus, he always seems to make that vein in your neck pop out, it's kinda hot," I tease, reaching up to poke him in the neck. Callum's lips twitch in what I assume is amusement before he squashes it. When he looks down at me thoughtfully, his expression sobers instantly, his eyes intense as they search mine.

"Is that really all it is, you think he's funny? He would have you in a heartbeat if you let him."

"Oh come on, he was joking. We were just talking, and he was trying to get a rise out of you. Clearly it worked." The charming bachelor has been playful and flirtatious, but I don't take him seriously for a second. Giving me a little extra attention is obviously just a way for Liam to poke a little fun at his friend. "It's just harmless flirting."

"It pisses me off."

"I know, that's what makes it fun."

"You're insufferable."

"And yet, here you are. Suffering," I shoot back sweetly, batting my eyelashes. My eyes snag on a painting we're about to pass, the vibrant colors and detailed brushwork making my steps slow. "That's beautiful. Do we have time to look around?"

"Not today, Dewdrop." After toting me back outside, he helps me into the car before climbing behind the wheel. The engine roars to life, and I can't help but watch his strong hand grip the steering wheel. I never thought I'd find the way someone drives arousing, but the way he handles the classic car is unbelievably sexy. "We'll come back another time when I can arrange it to be just the two of us."

"Just the two of us?" I repeat, blinking at him as I process what he's saying.

"There are a lot of things I want to do with you, just the two of us. Starting with going to dinner."

"Are you . . ." I say, my brows raising. "Asking me on a date?"

"Yes," Callum responds simply, calmly watching me.

"You do know that we already live together, right? And we've had sex. More than once."

"Is that your final answer?"

"No." That's not the word he wants to hear, so I quickly clarify. "My final answer is yes."

"Good." Leaning closer to grip my chin, he draws me in to capture my lips with his. "Be ready tomorrow night at six."

"Do I get to know where we're going?"

"Where's the fun in that?"

"You don't do fun," I point out.

"No, but you do." There's no hiding his self-satisfied smile now. He's enjoying this.

"At least tell me what to wear." I'm basically begging at this point, but I have no choice. The man is giving me nothing to work with.

"Wear something impractical." With that, he's pulling out into traffic and zooming through the city back towards Columbus Circle.

CHAPTER THIRTY-THREE

LEXIE

I have a date with Callum tonight—our first date. How is it that we've had sex and live together before even going on an actual date?

Following Callum's instructions, I pick out one of the dresses we bought during our shopping spree. It's tight, low cut, and completely impractical. The moss-green, velvet corset top fits my chest like a dream—a miracle in itself. The velvet skirt falls right above my knee, the ruching on the front gathering the hem up higher on my left thigh and pulling the fabric to hug my curves.

The shoes I pick are strappy and black, with an open toe and beautiful monarch butterfly appliqués across the toes and scattered up the straps that wrap around my calves. They feel whimsical, even though they're not the most wearable with the four-and-a-half-inch stiletto heel. But they're so pretty, and I feel like I'm wearing little works of art.

Armed with a gorgeous outfit like this would usually make me feel unstoppable. But of course, today would be a bad body day. The dress feels too clingy and unflattering, and I can't stop picturing a hippo on stilts while wearing these heels. I feel too fat to wear this, and overall unattractive.

But I get ready anyway.

Callum knows what I look like, I remind myself, from every

angle imaginable. And he very clearly likes what he sees, brazenly and obsessively. And when I step into the living room where Callum is waiting, he proves it again.

He turns at the sound of my heels clicking on the floor, and whatever he was looking at on his phone is completely forgotten.

"*Fuck.*" There's a rasp in his voice, his eyes touching every part of me. "You're absolutely stunning." A blush warms my cheeks, and I offer him a sweet smile.

"Thank you." My eyes take him in, a vision in his all-black attire. He's not wearing a suit coat tonight; he's in his true form. Dress shirt, no tie, strong tattooed forearms on display with the sleeves rolled up to his elbows. He's not wearing his camouflage that's usually paired with his fake smile, and I like it. "And you look..." My eyes move over him in open appreciation. "Damn."

Something colorful catches my attention out of the corner of my eye. A large white vase sits on the kitchen island holding the most beautiful bouquet of flowers I've ever seen. Pink peonies, soft blue hydrangeas, yellow ranunculus, and white poppies. "Where did these come from?"

"They're for you."

"No way." I'm getting excited. "You got me flowers?" I look back at the arrangement in disbelief. "These are all of my favorites."

"I know."

I can't help but squeal in excitement, bouncing over to hug him.

"I love them so much. Thank you," I announce enthusiastically. I press my lips to his in a soft peck, careful not to smear my lip gloss. "Wow, you're really pulling out all the stops tonight, huh?"

"Just you wait." Callum gazes down at me, his eyes as passionate as ever. "If we don't leave now, we won't be making it out of this apartment tonight. Not with how you look in this dress."

"Lead the way." My eyes flirt with him, even when my tone shifts to taunting. "I wouldn't want you ruining all of the special plans you made for tonight because you're too distracted staring at my ass while I walk."

"Don't tempt me." Callum's large hand skims up my side before sliding into place at the small of my back. "Our night is just getting started."

We use the elevator to ride down into the parking garage, where Callum helps me into the passenger seat of his vintage muscle car. He says it's a 1972 Gran Torino. All I know is that it's loud, powerful, and sexy as hell. Maybe a little obnoxious too, but who am I to judge someone for being a little extra?

Riding through the city, I accept the fact that I have no idea where we're going and settle in for the ride. We're seventeen minutes into the drive when I notice it. Something is different, but I can't quite put my finger on what. But then I cross my legs, and it hits me. My thighs aren't sticking like they usually do. Looking down at the seat, I'm surprised to see it's made up of smooth black suede instead of leather. Am I going crazy, or is this different now?

"Is this a new car?" I ask, looking around at the dashboard and into the back seat. I feel like I'm missing something. Callum shakes his head and glances over at me.

"No, why?"

"The seats are different. I thought they were leather." My fingers run over the fabric covering the seats. It's smooth as butter and feels expensive.

"They were. I had them reupholstered."

"You did? Why?" I ask, surprised.

Callum's eyes look pointedly at my bare thighs. "Do you like your little dresses?"

"Yes, I love them."

"So do I. Now you don't have to stop wearing your short skirts." He places a hand on my exposed thigh, giving it a telling squeeze. I stare at him, shocked and touched by this gesture. I'm honestly at a loss for words. But when I finally open my mouth to say something, we're turning into what looks like an airfield. My eyes widen when we pull to a stop.

That's a fucking helicopter.

"Is that for us?" I'm in disbelief. Callum flashes me a grin that I feel all the way to my toes.

"Like I said, our night is only getting started." With that, he climbs out of the car and walks around to open my door. I accept his hand and step out, my eyes glued to the sleek black aircraft perched on the landing pad, the rotor blades already starting to spin while it waits.

For us.

Walking towards the helicopter, our fingers intertwine to lock our connection. My other hand wraps around his thick bicep, squinting against the wind caused by the propellers. Callum only releases my hand to grip my hips in support while I step up into the back door he opens for me.

The soft gray interior is really nice with two individual seats behind the pilot seats that face backwards across from the connected seats that face the front. I move in to sit on the forward-facing seat, making room for Callum to climb in behind me. The door closes behind us and I can hear the propellers picking up speed as the pilots prepare for takeoff.

Callum's insistent on helping me with my seat belt, making sure it's securely fastened before we lift off the ground. The flight is smoother than I would've expected as we fly over the city, weaving through skyscrapers and monuments. The view is spectacular of picturesque New York City in the golden hour of the sun getting ready to set.

I'm absolutely giddy, my eyes never stop moving. Callum points out landmarks and specific buildings that we pass over, after reclaiming my hand in his. When we touch down, I'm surprised that we're not back where we came from.

"That wasn't the date?" I ask, stunned. Callum looks down at me, his grip on my hand flexing on our way to the waiting car.

"No, Dewdrop. That was our ride."

"Then where are we going?"

"You'll see."

Jane's Carousel—a classic antique carousel with horses carved with incredible detail, encased in a sleek glass structure. When the driver parked at the end of a private road between brick buildings, and I saw it, the excitement was absolutely overwhelming. I've always wanted to experience Jane's Carousel, but this is so much more.

My eyes roam across what I can only describe as the most romantic setting I've ever seen. An incredible sunset surrounds the glass box in breathtaking colors, the approaching twilight allowing the lights of the carousel to illuminate every intricate detail. It's nothing short of magical.

My gaze moves to the table in front of me, taking in how picture-perfect it is from the flickering white tapered candlesticks to the cloth napkin by my cutlery folded in the shape of a butterfly. If Callum had climbed into my head and pulled out the perfect date, I couldn't have come up with something half this incredible.

Callum sits across from me, patient as usual as I gape in awe. Like a parent watching their child experience the magic of Disneyland for the first time. When my focus moves back to him, our eyes collide and I'm struck by the intensity of our connection. While I've been taking in every detail around us, he's only been watching me.

When he starts to speak, I know the question before it even leaves his mouth. "What are you thinking?"

"I don't think there's ever been anything more beautiful than this," I say, indicating to our surroundings.

"Oh, I can think of a few things." His eyes move over me slowly, stopping where my body disappears below the table, before lifting back up to my eyes. My teeth catch my bottom lip when I smile, drawing his attention to my mouth. The air around us buzzes with chemistry.

"You like it?" Callum leans forward in his chair, his eyes never leaving me. I tell him what I'm sure he can already read all over my face.

"It's... perfect."

"Good."

"I had no idea you were such a romantic," I tease, lifting my wineglass.

"There's a lot about me you don't know yet."

"Well, since this is a first date, that means I get to ask first date questions," I say, taking a sip of my wine. It's perfect, just like everything else tonight.

"I'll answer yours if you answer mine."

"Of course, truth for truth." I agree easily, it's only fair. I pause to look at Callum across the table, admiring the way he looks under candlelight and in the glow of the carousel. Damn, he's attractive. "What did you want to be when you grew up?"

"A butcher. I was going to work at the shop with my father." He takes a sip of whiskey, speaking over the rim of his glass. "That's the official answer."

"What's the real answer?"

"A Power Ranger." My laugh of surprise is immediate.

"That is really cute." *Super adorable.* "You wore a costume around too, didn't you?"

Callum doesn't lie to me, so his silence says it all. "You did! I hope your mom has pictures, because I need to see those." I laugh, delighted. The image of a little Callum running around in a Power Ranger costume is just too good.

"Remind me not to let you anywhere near my mother again," he says, making me laugh. His gaze is intense, smoldering. I can feel his eyes on my skin as he takes in every centimeter of my face, as if to memorize it in this moment.

"Have you ever been in love?" His question throws me for a loop, but I recover quickly. This is a question I've been asked on a first date before, so it's not too surprising.

"I thought I was."

"You weren't?"

"I was young, naive, and just happy not to be alone," I admit. "But in love? I don't think so."

"Who were they?"

"That's another question, and it's my turn. Besides, you don't talk about exes on a first date—major red flag." I take a bite of bread while I think up my next question. "What were you like when you were younger?"

"I was a loose cannon." Callum's answer is not what I was expecting.

"You?" The skepticism is dripping from my voice. "I don't believe it." Callum's brows jump in challenge.

"I was. I ran around without any sense of self-control or consequence." His expression sobers visibly, and he leans in like he's sharing a secret. "I even drank soda."

"Shut up, no you didn't." I grin and lean forward in excitement, soaking up this juicy piece of information. "What changed?"

"That's another question, Dewdrop. My turn," Callum responds, and I don't bother hiding my disappointment. He looks at me in consideration for a moment before asking his question. "What's a deal-breaker for you?"

"Cheating." There's no hesitation with my answer. "The moment someone is unfaithful, they lose my trust. That's the best way to lose me forever."

"Cheaters don't deserve to be trusted," Callum says deeply, the conviction in his voice settling something inside me that I didn't realize was restless. There's no question in my mind that this man is fiercely loyal to a fault—he'll kill and die for the people who are important to him.

And I'm important to him.

"So, is this what you do on dates?" I gesture to the candles and the beautifully lit-up carousel. "Lay on the charm and manufacture a little magic?"

"You're the only one I want to make magic with, Lexie." The hunger in his voice has pure lust simmering deep inside me.

Letting those words linger, I pull my eyes away and smile down at my plate. We sit in silence for a while as we eat. It's some of the best lasagna I've ever had, paired with fresh baked bread, Caesar salad, and roasted asparagus.

A middle-aged man appears as if out of thin air at exactly the right moment to clear our plates, catching me by surprise. I wait for him to place our dessert on the table and disappear before I ask any questions.

"Who is that?" Dipping my spoon into the small ceramic bowl in front of me, I scoop out the most flawless chocolate mousse I've ever seen.

"He runs this place and agreed to help make tonight happen." Able to see I'm about to ask more questions, Callum continues with more information. "He's associated with someone I've done work with in the past."

Okay, so someone Callum's done a job for hooked him up for our date, that's nice. As connected as he is, I'm sure Callum knows someone for most places in the city—probably in every major city in the country. My eyes drift to the glowing structure behind Callum, so beautiful and inviting. He notices my attention shift, yet again.

"You want to ride the carousel?" Callum's tone tells me he already knows my answer. I light up like a kid on Christmas morning at the suggestion, beaming at him.

"I thought you'd never ask."

"Go pick your favorite horse, I'll be right back," he says with a laugh. Standing from the table, my eyes start to scan the horses. I have to know all my options before I can pick a favorite. It only takes a few minutes for me to find the right one—but as soon as my eyes land on it, I know she's the one. She's a white horse with a gray mane and a gold saddle adorned with green ribbon and medallions in the shape of flowers.

Climbing up isn't too difficult because the horse I chose is stationary. Between the wine, my heels, and the hemline of my dress, climbing onto a wooden horse suspended from the ceiling that moves up and down while also spinning in a giant circle isn't the best idea. My horse is perfect.

I'm just getting situated when Callum reappears. As soon as he steps onto the carousel, things start happening. The bulbs blink three times overhead and the sound of the engine whirring to life is followed by the classic organ music playing over the speakers. Rows of light bulbs twinkle and flash in time with the playful tune as the carousel begins to turn.

And the magic begins.

I tilt my head back and let out a laugh of excitement when we start to move. Callum stands beside me, holding steady to the pole securing my horse to the spinning structure above my head. I can feel his eyes on me as I soak in the nostalgia and whimsy of the lights and music. I can't stop smiling, and when I look up at him, he's smiling too. But his eyes remain only on me, making butterflies tumble around in my stomach.

After a while the carousel starts to slow, the music fading as we drift to a stop.

"You haven't stopped smiling all night," Callum observes. "You're enjoying yourself."

"Thanks for stating the obvious." Even as I say it the grin never leaves my face.

"I like it," he informs me. It's a simple statement that says so much. This time, when our eyes meet, it feels weighted—heavy with meaning. I'm the first one to look away after a long moment, averting my eyes when his gaze proves too intense. I can feel the blush warming my cheeks as I change subjects.

"What's your favorite color?" I swing my leg around to sit side-saddle facing him. Callum's hands move to grip my hips, anchoring me to the horse.

"Black."

"You look *really* good in black," I inform him. "And white."

"That's everything I wear," he points out.

"I know." My response earns a laugh. Callum's fingers grasp my jaw to pull me in for a slow, sensual kiss.

"I look even better in *you*." His deep voice is rough with desire, flooding me with lust and making my breath hitch. Callum smiles against my lips before deepening the kiss. Our mouths move together seamlessly, heat pulsing through me as our tongues dance in a passionate tango until my head is swimming in an inebriating mix of pleasure and arousal. His hand on my jaw moves to fist in my hair, the other wrapping around my waist to pull me against him from my perch on the horse. "Come here."

He tugs me until I'm slipping from the wooden saddle back onto my feet, his grip never leaving me as he takes the three steps backwards to one of the two-person benches decorated to look like an elegant chariot.

"Callum, your friend," I remind him, but he remains unbothered. Lowering onto the seat, his hands move in sync with his eyes down my body.

"I had him leave after he set up the ride for us. It's just you and me, Dewdrop."

"I don't usually have sex on the first date." There's no conviction in my voice as it trails off, something I know he hears.

"There's nothing *usual* about us," Callum says, widening his legs and pulling me to stand between them. "You owe me an orgasm and I'm ready to collect. Right here, right now."

Gazing down at him, I'm overwhelmed by the desire and longing flowing through me. Callum's looking at me like a man starved. He's the only man who's ever made me feel like I could burst into flames at any moment.

"You want an orgasm?" Leaning forward to press my lips to his, my hand palms his dick through his pants. He hardens instantly beneath my touch, making me feel bold. Powerful. "I'll give you an orgasm."

Callum grunts against my lips as I undo his belt, then the button and zipper on his pants. My hand slips into his boxers to grip him. Big, hot, and heavy.

Fuck, everything about this man is impressive.

My hand moves in unison with my lips to tease him, stroking

and caressing. The tortured sound that comes from Callum's chest is beyond satisfying.

"*Christ.*"

"You're so hard for me, I want your big cock inside me," I breathe, my tone shifting. "But not until you say please."

I press a soft kiss to the corner of his mouth, nipping lightly at his earlobe before whispering, "Go on, Callum. I want to hear you beg."

Placing one knee on the bench on either side of his legs, I straddle his lap in a hover as I continue to pump his rock-hard erection. His mouth on mine grows more desperate with each pull. Strong hands grip my hips to drag me closer as Callum moves to deepen the kiss. But I pull back, evading his lips to build the friction.

"Lexie, let me have you. I need to have you." Callum groans deeply when my fingers tease the sensitive tip of his cock.

"What's the magic word, Callum?" I trail soft kisses to his ear. Leaning back, I take one of his large hands and place it on my breast. I'm growing breathless as the desire builds inside me. I'm just as turned on right now as he is. "Say it, and I'm all yours."

I bite back a moan when he gives my breast a firm squeeze—something I know will drive him mad. He can't stand when I hold back the responses he elicits from my body. It's the final straw, I can see it in his eyes.

"*Please.*" The word leaves his mouth like a Hail Mary at gunpoint, and I can't help but smile.

"Now that wasn't so bad, was it?" I tease, pulling his erection free from the confines of his boxers. His cock strains up towards me, desperate and hard as steel. A harsh breath releases through his nose as I slowly roll the condom he provides down his length. "How did that word taste coming out of your mouth?"

"All I'm thinking about is how you taste," he growls, jaw clenched tightly as I pull my panties to the side. Lowering slightly, I run the tip of his cock along my slit. I'm already so wet for him, the arousal is overwhelming.

"You know what I think?" My voice is soft as I slide back and forth along the length of his cock, agonizingly slowly. His muscles bunch as he fights against his need for control, allowing me to take the lead.

"What?" He barely gets the word out. The breath hitches in my chest when I line him with my entrance and lower myself down until I'm completely situated on him. We moan together—mine breathless and overwhelmed, his deep and primal. He stretches me, filling me to capacity. "Fuck."

"I think you like me." I lift myself until only the tip is inside me, then lower until I'm completely seated once more. My voice grows more breathless with each slow stroke.

"Now who's stating the obvious?" he counters. I gasp sharply when Callum jerks his hips upwards, powering into me once because he can't help myself.

"I think you care about me. Even if you don't want to." His only response is a clenched jaw and a gaze searing through my bones, bringing a small triumphant smile to my face. "You think feelings are messy." Leaning closer, I press a soft kiss to his cheekbone and bring my lips to his ear. "So let's get messy."

Taking my words as a green light, Callum's groan vibrates over my skin as he takes the reins. His hands grab my hips, firm fingers sinking into the soft flesh. A cry escapes me when I'm lifted and slammed back down, pushing him so deep he bottoms out. My head swims as he repeats the action, filling me until I'm delirious.

"I will never get enough of this perfect pussy," he grunts through clenched teeth as he lifts me and pulls me back down swiftly over and over. Each time his hips jerk to meet mine I gasp, the complete fullness shooting stars behind my eyes. I roll my hips against him, making his pelvis rub against my clit and setting every nerve ending in my body haywire. I reach up for his lips, kissing him deeply as I ride him into oblivion.

"You're so deep," I breathe against his lips. He swallows my moans, pounding up into me as the friction builds between us. "Yes, Callum. *Oh shit.*"

"Who do you come for?" Callum growls, his lips trailing across my jaw and down my neck. I tilt my head with a sigh when he grazes the sensitive pulse point that makes my head spin. Our movements are relentless, chasing our release in a frenzy of need and passion.

"You, Callum. Only you," I pant. I'm so close, teetering on the edge of delicious oblivion. My orgasm is building inside me, drawing heat from every touch, every stroke. It swells inside me, threatening to drown me in unimaginable bliss when the floodgates open. And I'm on the brink.

"Me, only me." His lips graze my ear. "Come all over my cock." At his words, I shatter into a million pieces.

The pleasure pounds against me like the sea crashing against a cliff, wave after wave of euphoria hitting me until I'm spent. "Oh, Callum. Yes, *yes*." His name tumbles from my mouth over and over, my pussy clenching tightly around his cock until he's completely undone.

Callum's release hits him like a freight train, ripping a groan from deep inside his chest as he empties into me. The muscles of his powerful body ripple with the force of his orgasm, his arms shake against me. Looking into his eyes as he falls apart with my name on his lips, I don't stop moving until he's completely wrung out.

My body collapses against his, my head tucking into his neck as we both struggle to catch our breath. We stay there for a moment, just our pounding hearts beating against each other as we pant. Callum presses a kiss to the top of my head. "You are perfection, Dewdrop."

"Why, because I have dirty sex with you in public places?" I ask, only half joking. I've never done anything like this before, it's exhilarating. I'm not new to dirty sex, or even sex with Callum. But never on a public carousel encased in transparent glass. Even now, anyone could walk past and see us, while he's still inside me. The risk makes it even hotter.

"Because we fit," Callum clarifies. He's right—we shouldn't, but we do. "And you have dirty sex with me in public places," he adds with a smirk. I laugh against him, pushing back to look at his face. The smoldering look in his eyes feels a lot like adoration, drawing me in for another sweet kiss.

"This is probably the best first date I've ever been on," I say, shifting off him and sliding my panties back into place. I'll have to spend the rest of the night with my arousal dripping down my thighs, but it's a small price to pay for such a bone-melting orgasm.

"Probably?" he counters in challenge, removing the condom and tucking himself back into his pants. My eyes wander around the magic surrounding us before returning to him.

"I would tell you this is the sweetest thing anyone has ever done for me, but I wouldn't want your head to get too big to fit in the helicopter for the ride home."

"You're the only one my head grows for," he teases, a breathtaking grin spreading across his face as he stands up and straightens the dress shirt I rumpled.

"You're such a flirt," I laugh, letting him help me up and shimmying my dress back into place. Callum draws me against his chest, his hands gripping my hips.

"This is only the beginning," he states, pressing a kiss to my forehead. We stand in our embrace for a nice long moment. I can't remember ever enjoying someone's company like this. After several minutes, he finally speaks, his deep voice vibrating over me. "Let's get home, we have an early morning tomorrow."

The helicopter ride back across the city feels much shorter than the first one, but maybe that's only because I'm more focused on making out with Callum than I am watching the night skyline passing outside the window.

Damn, I feel giddy like a teenager with a crush.

When we fall into bed together, the flirting and teasing for the evening is over. This time is slow, sensual, and feels exactly how I imagine making love should feel. I fall asleep with one thought on my mind.

Could this be love?

CHAPTER THIRTY-FOUR

LEXIE

Anticipation flutters through me as we make our ascent. Takeoff goes smoothly, but my anxiety has nothing to do with our flight. It's our destination that has my nerves in knots.

Callum says they tracked the girls to a shipping container headed to Colombia. I overheard him talking to Roscoe about making a deal with the freight worker to have them reroute the shipment, but they got greedy and switched up the loading records.

Three freighters are currently on their way to Colombia, but he's not sure which ship Charlotte is on. And the ship determines which port we go to. By the determination on Callum's face, he has a plan to get the information he needs.

As soon as the seat belt light turns off, I connect my phone to the plane's Wi-Fi. The moment my phone is connected to the internet, messages are flooding in. They're from Ronnie, telling me to call her as soon as possible. Pressing the phone to my ear, it only rings once.

"Oh my god, Lexie! I've been trying to call you for the last hour," Ronnie gushes.

"My phone was on airplane mode," I explain, sitting forward in my seat. "What's going on?"

"I have a friend who's hooking up with a guy that works at Rikers," she starts, her mention of the prison making me perk up.

"She says that Carl Suco was attacked on his way to the showers. It was brutal."

"How brutal?" Hearing the name of the truck driver responsible for the busload of first graders has white hot rage flashing through me all over again.

"He was stabbed with a shiv at the base of his spine, and one of his eye sockets was shattered. He's never going to walk again and he's permanently blind in his right eye."

Adrenaline floods through me with a wave of satisfaction. Good, a man like him doesn't deserve death—that's too easy. He'll live the rest of his miserable life in pain and suffering like he's inflicted on so many others. I hope he never knows a minute of peace or comfort again.

"Do they know who did it?" The violent gratification barely registers in my mind as it's welcomed openly by my thirst for vengeance. My gaze flickers across the plane, and I catch Callum's passionate stare. He looks at me intently, and something tells me he knows who I'm talking about right now.

"No, they said it was in a blind corner. Whoever did it got away clean, and I can't say I'm mad about that."

"Me neither," I admit. "It's crazy how that happened though."

Is it?

"I know." There's movement on the other end of the call. "Hey, I gotta go. But I just had to tell you."

"I'm glad you did. I'll talk to you later." Ending the call, my eyes meet Callum's again. "Carl Suco was attacked in prison. He's going to live the rest of his life in pain." There's something in the air between us that makes me feel like I'm not telling Callum something he doesn't already know.

"Sounds like he got what was coming to him." Callum's statement is vague and telling at the same time. "People in places like Rikers don't take too kindly to guys who hurt kids. I have a feeling that's not the only time he's going to run into problems."

He did this.

I don't know how, and I'll probably never know exactly who,

but somehow Callum exacted a ruthless justice on the monster behind my nightmares. He's not the one I see when I close my eyes, but he's the cause of it all.

"Good." The word sounds an awful lot like *thanks* coming out of my mouth. "He deserves everything he gets."

I vaguely remember my life before back rooms and men tied to chairs were common occurrences. When we'd stepped off the plane in Colombia and drove through the colorful streets it almost felt like a vacation for a short moment. The house Roscoe drove us to was large, nice, and almost completely empty—a foreclosure I'm guessing. It's pretty secluded, tucked away in the jungle by a long, private drive.

I'd been sitting at the kitchen counter for a few hours by myself when Callum reappeared to collect me. He led me across the house to the back door, through the overgrown backyard with the half-empty green pool, to a detached two-car garage.

Walking into the garage feels a lot like déjà vu. Just like walking into that nightclub, the scene that greets me is shocking. Roscoe and Callum aren't the only men in the room, now there's one more. But he's not a guest, he's a prisoner.

And he's bleeding.

"Please help me, this man is a maniac." The bleeding man's eyes on me are pleading, and a wave of guilt washes over me. He looks so nice, so normal. Still in a shirt and tie, the older man looks like he was snatched on his way home from his office job as an accountant. A pair of wire-rimmed glasses lay broken on the floor near his feet.

Blood stains his dress pants where long metal nails have been brutally hammered into his thighs. A metal clamp clipped to each nail leads to wires connected to something that resembles a car battery covered in dials on the table where Roscoe stands a few feet away. Bloody fingernails that have been removed neatly line a metal tray with the other instruments of torture, making me cringe.

"Again." At Callum's command, Roscoe cranks the dial on the battery. The man convulses as electricity shoots through him, his jaw clenching so tightly I swear I hear his teeth crack. The veins in his neck protrude and his back arches against the chair like he's being yanked backwards. No sound comes out of him; instead it seems like the life is being drained from his body.

Roscoe lets up after an excruciating long moment, and the man's eyes begin to roll back into his head. As soon as the electricity is no longer coursing through him, he slumps like a puppet with cut strings. His head falls forward as he loses consciousness and I step forward to feel for a pulse.

"His heart stopped," I announce.

"Give him what's in that syringe," Callum instructs, motioning for Roscoe to step back so I can get to the small table. Avoiding the fingernails and other assorted cartilage scattered on the different trays, I lift the pre-dosed syringe to read the label.

"This is undiluted adrenaline." It'll get the man's heart beating again, but at what cost?

"I'm aware." Callum's not in any mood to coddle me. "You're here to do a job, Lexie."

Holding the syringe at a 90-degree angle, I push the long needle straight down into the man's thigh until I hit muscle and press the plunger until the full dose of adrenaline has been injected from the barrel. After several seconds that feel like forever, the man's head lifts with a pained gasp of air. His chest heaves, skin so pale he looks like death warmed over.

"Good job, Doc." Callum's praise falls flat. "Now step back so Roscoe can get back to work."

"Is that really necessary?" Callum's eyes move to me at the soft words, a ruthless unfeeling glint in his gaze. The eyes of a killer. Apprehension washes over me, goosebumps raising along my arms. He turns back to the man, his voice cold.

"My nurse here doesn't think you deserve to be in so much pain. But you and I both know exactly what you deserve."

"Fuck you."

"Why don't we tell her who you really are under that cheap suit. What's in the container, Jimmy?" Callum asks, his voice laced with venom.

"Just merchandise."

"What kind of merchandise?" Another zap, more teeth cracking and groaning. "Say it."

"Girls." The answer makes my stomach drop like a ball of lead.

"What kind of girls, Jimmy? Be specific."

"You know what kind."

"I want to hear you say it out loud. Come on, tell me what kind of a man you are. What kind of girls are in that container?"

"Underage girls."

"*Teenage girls.*" Callum's tone turns absolutely lethal. "I have no problem with the sex trade, Jimmy. If people want to be paid for sex, that's none of my business. But teenagers, stolen from their families and forced into sex slavery? That *is* my business. And this time you took the wrong girl. Because this one has parents, parents with money who hired me. And that mistake is going to cost you your life."

"Fuck you, Russo."

"You're a worthless, scum-sucking rat, Jimmy. The lowest form of roach that crawls on this earth. People who mess with kids—depraved, sick men like you—aren't men at all. And even though you don't deserve it, I'm going to let you choose how you die. If you tell me where the container is, I'll consider ending you right here, right now. A bullet right between the eyes, quick and easy. But if you decide not to tell me, or worse lie to me, Roscoe's going to have a field day extracting each organ from your body until your heart gives out. What's your daughter's name again?"

"Lindsay," Roscoe offers easily.

"Ah yes, little Lindsay. Sweet kid, though a little too friendly. You really should teach her more about stranger danger, especially in your line of work. Does she know what kind of a man you are?"

"Don't you fucking go near Lindsay," Jimmy spits.

"Tell me what I want to know and maybe I'll spare her." Any other day I'd be sure that Callum is making an empty threat—he wouldn't hurt a little girl like that. But looking at him right now, I'm suddenly not so sure. Jimmy sees that same brutality residing just beneath the surface too.

"Port of Cartagena." The words fall from Jimmy's mouth like he can't physically hold them in anymore. "The Scorpius. They don't tell me the container number, but it's expected in today at three p.m."

"Security?"

"Three on the ship, four on the ground who move the girls. Semi-automatic weapons and vests."

"What aren't you telling me?"

"Nothing, that's it. I swear on my life."

"That doesn't mean much, Jimmy." The light is fading from Jimmy's eyes as his breathing becomes more labored. More than likely, the electricity is causing organ failure from internal tissue burns. Callum's piercing eyes turn to land on me, his hand running over his impeccable beard.

"I'll let you decide what happens now." My breath gets caught in my chest in surprise. Reaching into his pants pocket, he pulls out his phone to extend to me. "Let Jimmy meet his fate, or call for help."

This isn't the type of decision I've ever had to make. The weight of someone's life in my hands is heavier than I ever thought possible. A few months ago my hand would've reached for that phone in a heartbeat—do no harm and all that. But since being in New York I've seen some shit, and my eyes have been opened to the truth people keep hidden behind suits and closed doors. Nothing is as black and white as it seems.

This is a human life, but not everyone deserves to be saved.

My gaze travels from the phone, up Callum's arm to meet his eyes. I'm sure he can see my thoughts warring with each other. He's probably expecting me to grab the phone and call for help. It's what I should do. Finally, I step forward.

Stepping past the offered phone, I walk the few steps to stand in front of the vile man responsible for so much pain and suffering. The pleading on his face is long gone, replaced by dark contempt. His eyes are empty, even as he fights to keep them open.

"You fucking bitch." He struggles to get the words out, and there's no mistaking the disdain in his feeble voice. His breaths are becoming shorter and heavier, a look of agony permanently etched on his face. The organs in his body are shutting down one by one after being burnt to a crisp. It's an excruciating process, but not a hard one to watch. Not with him.

"This is for every girl who had their life ruined because of you," I say. "You don't deserve peace, and the world will be much better off without you. Including your daughter."

It doesn't take long for Jimmy to lose the ability to speak, his mouth gaping open and shut like he's drowning. Seconds stretch into minutes. I stand over him, watching as the world is rid of a monster. Andie Brentwood's face flashes through my mind with her curly hair, wide brown eyes lit with pain, and two missing front teeth. This is for her, and every other innocent life destroyed by monsters like Jimmy and Carl Suco. They were worth saving.

I've been witness to so much violence and devastation at the hands of selfishness, and all I could do was clean up the aftermath. I've had to patch up women and children, only to send them home to their abusers. Back then my hands were tied by protocol and medical laws—this time I can do something about it. I'm no one's savior, but I can be this man's karma.

I have no delusions that I'm fighting for the greater good or some bullshit like that. I know how twisted it is to hold a man's life in my hands and choose to let him die. Just the idea should make me sick. Honestly, I'm expecting the guilt and devastation to hit any minute, to suddenly have a "what have I done?" moment. But the remorse never comes.

When Jimmy's breathing finally stops and his head falls forward, his half-lidded eyes lifeless, an overwhelming sense of satisfaction washes over me. It settles deep into my bones until it's part of who I am. Pressing my fingers against his neck, I double-check that there's no pulse. "He's dead."

Good fucking riddance.

"Lexie." At some point Callum moved to stand beside me, so close my arm brushes his when I turn to look up at him. He's staring at me like I might break—something I can't blame him for. I wasn't exactly sure how I would handle it either. So far all I feel is relieved. Jimmy brought this upon himself.

"Do you need help disposing of the body?" The words leave my lips before I can think twice about them, and a flicker of concern crosses Callum's face. Or was it confusion? Both are justified, I guess.

"No." It's Roscoe who responds first. "You don't need to touch any of this."

"Okay," I say, pulling my eyes from Callum to glance at the enforcer. His expression is grave as he regards me. It's for the best, honestly. The idea of getting rid of a body is gross, I don't know why I even offered. I was caught up in the moment.

"Come on. Let's get you out of here," Callum says deeply, reaching for my hand—his strong fingers link with mine. I can feel the weight of his eyes on me as I walk out the door without a glance back at the body.

At the man I let die.

CHAPTER THIRTY-FIVE

CALLUM

"I'm fine, Callum," Lexie says finally after feeling my eyes on her for the millionth time since we left the garage. She turns to meet my eyes across the car. "I'm not going to break down."

"You let a man die," I state. "I'd be an idiot not to keep an eye on you after something like that."

"I've watched a lot of people die. And you're not just keeping an eye on me, you're staring," she points out.

"This is different." As unnecessary as she thinks it is, her expression warms at my concern. There's something else mixed with my anxiety, a twinge of regret for placing that decision in her hands at all. I might have pushed her too far.

What's done is done.

"His decisions led him there, he got what he deserved. We have other things to worry about," she says, quoting my own words back at me. The persistence of my gaze doesn't relent, and I can see her softening. "Seriously, Callum. I'm okay, and I'll tell you if that changes. I promise." She's being sincere. If she does start to have a meltdown, I'll be able to read it all over her face the moment it happens.

I'm about to say something, but my phone ringing cuts me off. I've been on the phone from the moment we stepped out of the garage, coordinating the Harris retrieval. Answering the call, I turn to the laptop on my lap.

Lexie settles into the seat next to me as I strategize. Hanging up the phone, adrenaline courses through me as we near our destination. Pulling my gun from behind my back, I bring my eyes to the woman next to me.

"When we arrive at the shipyard, don't leave this car. Roscoe will stay with you," I say, checking the magazine before slamming it back into place and pulling back the slide to chamber a round with a resounding chink.

"What? Why?" Lexie looks from the gun in my hand to me. She's eager to get there, eager to come to those girls' rescue. And she will, I'll make sure of it. But shipments like this come with some grisly reinforcement to ensure the cargo makes it to the destination. There's too much money on the line to leave it up to chance. And I'll be damned if I'll let Lexie step into harm's way, little girls or not. Lottie Harris might be the job, but Lexie is my priority.

"This shipment will come with some kind of security," I explain, deciding that honesty is the best approach in this situation. "I need you to stay safely in the car until it's cleared." Lexie nods in understanding. She's smart, I know she realizes the gravity of these circumstances. Her eyes latch to mine, insistent.

"Those girls have already been through so much, they're gonna be traumatized. They're probably terrified out of their minds, especially of men. I should be there when you open the container, not a bunch of goons with guns." She has a point, something I've already considered. Lexie is a big part of the plan, mostly to find Lottie and get her safely into the car before the others arrive.

"I'll come get you once it's safe. You don't leave this car until I come for you." My eyes drill into hers. The weight of my words hit her, I can see when they register. She blinks at me once, then she nods in agreement. A small weight lifts from my chest.

"Okay, I'll wait for you."

Thank fucking Christ.

She knows exactly what's at stake, not letting her emotions

towards the young victims cloud her judgment. My instructions aren't a power trip, they're what's best for everyone involved. She doesn't realize just how much her safety matters. The last thing I need is Lexie going rogue on me and putting herself in danger. If anything happens to this woman, there's no contract or job that will keep the world safe from my wrath.

"That's my girl." There's a soft edge of praise in my voice, warming her eyes. My pretty pink nurse, with her soft curves wrapped in pastel pink scrubs, and long blonde hair pulled into a ponytail. She's a ray of light, exactly what we need.

Climbing out of the car, I walk around the corner of the metal hangar to where the rest of the team parked. Enzo stands with the hired guns, seven of them total. I've worked with The Ghost Ops team—a private group of mercenaries for hire—on numerous occasions. Their team leader, Russ Castillo, is the best at what they do—it's something we have in common. And I need the best. I'm leaving nothing to chance.

Greeting the team, I update them on the new details we extracted from Jimmy while getting our intercoms set up. Russ instructs his men on our approach, taking this new info into account. We'll be treating this freight yard like a grid, each ghost taking a section. Enzo and I will take the perimeter and work our way towards the center. Once the right container is found and secured, I'll collect Lexie before we open it.

Unholstering their weapons, the team splits up into their assignments. I slowly make my way along the outside of the shipyard, hugging the stacked containers with my gun drawn. My earpiece beeps as one of the other men reports to the group.

"We have a sighting in sector two, lower west corner. Armed with automatic," the voice reports. Gunshots ring out, echoing through the metal maze, followed by male shouts. Turning the corner, I see movement out of the corner of my eye.

Enzo walks around from the other side to meet me in the middle. I slow my steps, allowing him to reach the center aisle before me. Rounding the bend slowly, he visually clears the area before stepping into the opening. Waiting for him to pass the first intersection, I follow behind him. After Enzo passes the opening between rows of containers, an armed man emerges from the shadows behind him. His casual clothing, unmarked bullet-proof vest, and the automatic weapon slung across his chest tell me that he's one of the traffickers we're here to take care of.

His sweaty arms lift the semi-automatic weapon, aiming at Enzo's retreating form with intent in his beady eyes. He's going to shoot, but I don't give him the chance. Raising my own gun, I beat him to the trigger. The bullet explodes from the chamber and enters the side of his skull cleanly, the life leaving him instantly as his body falls. The sound of my gun echoes through the alley of metal walls, making Enzo turn. He watches as I lower my gun, looking at the dead man. There's no hesitation when he pivots to stride back towards me.

"I guess I owe you one," he comments knowingly, eyeing his would-be executioner.

"I'll think of a way for you to repay me. You can start by getting rid of him." We can't have dead bodies scattered around when we bring the girls out of the container. Hysterics aren't part of today's plan.

"I'm on it." Enzo holsters his weapon to unarm the corpse, slinging the machine gun over his shoulder, before dragging the body away by his ankles.

"We're clear. Freight container ACMU 2834661." Tarik's voice sounds in my ear. Perfect. I'm already making my way back to where I left Lexie in the car, my legs moving with a purpose.

"Stand by, don't open it until I give the order."

"Copy."

Relief floods Lexie's face when I open the car door, her expressive eyes searching me for signs of injury. "I heard the gunshots."

"I'm okay, Dewdrop," I assure her. "It's safe for you to come out now." I hold my hand out to her, and she accepts it without hesitation. Helping her out of the car, I make eye contact with

Roscoe over her head where he sits in the driver's seat, gun ready. I nod my thanks, and he's moving to open the door and join us.

Keeping her hand in mine, Lexie's other arm wraps around my bicep. I can feel her nerves, and I can't help but revel in how she clings to me for comfort. She trusts me to keep her safe, an honor I don't plan to fail.

The men back away from the container as soon as the doors open, taking their large firearms and stepping out of sight. Lexie's grip on my arm shifts with anxiety, and I look down at the top of her blonde head. I give her hand a reassuring squeeze and she glances up at me before her shoulders straighten with determination. Letting go of me, she steps away to approach the container. It's almost completely dark inside the metal box, making it hard to see what's inside.

Huddled closely together in the farthest corner, the girls cling together in terror. No less than fifty dirty heads cower, eyes casting alarmed glances at the open doors, squinting against the harsh sunlight. Their whimpers and cries echo and drift out into the open afternoon.

Lexie takes slow, careful steps towards the opening. When she speaks, her tone is soft and gentle. Nurturing. "My name is Lexie, I'm a nurse. No one is going to hurt you anymore. We're here to help you, take you home." She looks over her shoulder at me, our eyes connecting briefly. "I know you're scared. These men look scary, but they're not going to hurt you. I promise, you're safe now."

She takes a few steps farther into the container, stopping to give the girls plenty of space. They shift as a group, clearly unsure as they cling together and eye Lexie uncertainly. Sensing their hesitation, Lexie crouches to put herself closer to their eye level. She keeps her body language open and honest—just a warm woman in her pink scrubs.

"Is one of you named Lottie? Charlotte Harris, your dad sent us to find you." Her eyes scan the group, but it's difficult to distinguish features with the darkness and the unkempt state of the girls. But I notice the dark-haired head that lifts at the name. Lexie sees her too, but she remains calm.

"It's okay, Lottie." She makes eye contact with the girl in the center of the group. Lexie inches closer, holding out her hand. "Your dad told me to tell you he's waiting for you with Winston. We're here to take you home. We're going to take you all home."

At the mention of her bulldog, she steps closer. Charlotte looks at her hand for a split second, the rest of the group watching for her lead. Charlotte Harris reaches out for Lexie's hand, a sob of relief escaping her as she stumbles into Lexie's open arms. She hugs her tightly, sobs wracking her body. Like the tap of the first domino, the rest of the group follows suit. Several girls reach for Lexie's embrace.

Taking her time, Lexie stays in place for several minutes just holding Charlotte and consoling the other girls. Her voice softly asks them questions, if anyone needs medical attention, what their names are. She tells them that my men and I are here to help them, that they don't need to be afraid of us even though we look scary.

When she finally stands, Charlotte tucked into her side, she leads the girls out into the light. The sight of each girl—dirty, exhausted, looking half starved, and so young—the anger and disgust grows inside me. The sick fucks that find pleasure in them all deserve a slow and painful death. I wish I could kill Jimmy all over again, this time without holding back. He didn't deserve the mercy he was shown, his end was far too quick.

My eyes latch on to Lexie, tracking her every move as she slowly walks the girls out. I pull out my phone and make the call. The answer is immediate, they've been waiting. "We're clear. Send them in."

I nod to Roscoe, signaling that it's time to move. Leaning down, I speak close to Lexie's ear. "Take Lottie and go with Roscoe," I instruct her, pulling her from the flock of girls.

"Why? What are you gonna do?" she asks, looking up at me.

"I'm going to get these girls home safely," I explain briefly. "No one can know Lottie was ever here, so I need you to take her with you." She blinks up at me three times as she nods in understanding.

Lexie gathers all the girls together and tells them to stay here. She assures them that all the men here are going to help them get home safely. Despite her assurances, the girls start to cry and protest when Lexie pulls herself away to follow Roscoe to the car with Lottie in tow.

The sound of the approaching chopper announces their arrival. My team keeps the girls contained as the US Navy SEAL team arrives on the scene. I step forward to greet the six-man military team.

"Welcome to the party, Ace," I call to the guy leading the pack. Commander Anthony "Ace" Jacobs, the team leader of SEAL team Four, walks over to me looking every bit the clean-cut Boy Scout he is. His eyes scan the scene.

"You've got quite the turnout," he comments. "I'm counting fifty-seven girls."

"From our intel they range from fifteen to nineteen years old. We don't have names or home addresses, so getting them back to their parents might be difficult."

"Don't worry, we have ways to get that information," Ace assures me. He runs a hand over his blonde buzz cut as a plan forms behind his brown eyes. "The people who did this?"

"They'll be dealt with," I state, earning a nod of approval.

"Alright," he says, straightening his shoulders and signaling to his team. "Let's get these girls home."

"Do you have her?" Richard Harris desperately barks into my ear before the end of the first ring. My eyes land on the girl across from me.

"We have her," I answer. "She's neglected but uninjured. We're administering medical care as we speak. We touch down in five hours and forty-seven minutes. Meet us on the tarmac and have the rest of my payment for delivery."

"Thank God," Harris mutters, and his wife's cry of relief sounds through the phone. "I'll have your payment."

"I'll text you when we're landing."

"We'll be there."

My gaze only drifts to the girl briefly before returning to the beautiful woman cradling her. It's impossible to take my eyes off her. Lexie sits on the sofa, Charlotte's head laying on her shoulder. Tender fingers stroke the girl's dark knotted locks, gently untangling and comforting as the rocking of the plane lulls her to sleep. Her attention moves diligently to the IV drip hanging beside them, monitoring the line flowing into the back of the teen's hand.

Lexie's eyes meet mine, catching me staring. Unashamed, I don't look away. I can't. The small smile she gives me—filled with so much relief, hope, and joy—pierces my chest and runs through my veins like a drug.

"How is she?" I ask, keeping my voice low so I don't disturb the sleeping child. Lexie takes a moment to watch her before answering.

"She's dehydrated, malnourished, and she'll need therapy for PTSD." Her eyes lift to mine. "But she's resilient, and the IV is already helping. Until she gets a full physical exam, there's no way to tell exactly what she's been through. But from what I've seen, that's the extent of it. God, I hope that's the extent of it."

"The girls are worth more untouched. It's all about the money." It's not much of a consolation, but it's something. The disgust and contempt that crosses Lexie's face expresses exactly how I feel right now. But she nods in understanding, looking back down at the girl.

"I was going to examine her, but I don't want to traumatize her any more than she already is. When we land, it's important for her parents to have her properly checked. And by a woman. The last thing she needs is to get home and have a man poking at her."

Peering at Lexie, I can sense the conviction rolling off her in waves. "You can tell Harris exactly what she needs when we land,"

I inform her. Her focus moves to me briefly before returning to the IV drip.

"Okay, I will," she states confidently. My lips twitch with a smile, and I'm suddenly looking forward to seeing Richard Harris again. Just so I can watch Lexie give him orders.

The landing goes smoothly. True to his word, Richard Harris and his wife, Alyssa, are anxiously waiting on the tarmac. The moment the stairs are lowered, Lexie exits the plane with Lottie's hand in hers. I follow them down the stairs, my eyes meeting Harris' before he and his wife are rushing towards their daughter.

"Mom! Dad!" The instant she spots her parents, Lottie is running. Alyssa falls to her knees as she pulls her daughter into her waiting arms, sobbing as she hugs her tightly. The senator wraps his arms around both his wife and daughter in a family embrace, kissing his daughter's head.

Making eye contact with me over his wife's head, the senator murmurs something into Alyssa's ear before nodding for me to follow him. We take a few steps away from the little family reunion to speak privately.

"Any problems?" he asks, making me shake my head.

"Everything went according to plan."

"The wire's complete," Harris says. Pressing the button on my screen, the long number after the dollar sign doesn't match our agreement.

"This is too much. You know the agreement." I set my prices with a purpose. Sticking to the number we agreed on keeps things clean and simple. I'm not going to owe someone or leave a loose end untied just for another comma in a bank statement. That's unnecessarily messy.

My eyes cut to him, his attention latched on his daughter and wife's embrace. Lexie is speaking with Alyssa softly as she cradles her daughter, informing her of the medical care Lottie received before arrival.

"I know," Harris says, his eyes not leaving his family. "I have something else I want you to do."

"Harris, you know how this works. If you want another job, that means another contract."

"It's for this job," Harris clarifies. "I want you to take out the men who did this. And I want them to suffer."

"Consider it done." After seeing the girls walk out of the container, I was ready to exact my own wrath on the sick fucks who were responsible. He nods shortly, his expression grave. With our business done, we rejoin the women.

"How is she?" Harris asks, stroking Lottie's hair while his daughter's head is tucked into her mom's shoulder.

"She'll need to have a full medical exam as soon as possible." Lexie informs the senator.

Harris nods. "Of course," he acknowledges. "Our private physician, Tanya Redding, is on standby."

"Great." Lexie's tone remains calm. "I've seen trafficking victims before in my line of work. It's going to take some time for her to feel comfortable around men again. Including you, Senator. It's important to keep an eye on her, but with female staff instead of your armed men in suits. And routine will help her feel safe again."

"I understand," Harris confirms.

"I know you're trying to keep this as quiet as possible, but she should see someone to work through this trauma. The sooner the better."

"My wife has a therapist we can trust," the senator assures her. Lexie nods, and I can see the relief cross her face.

"Good."

"I knew you were the man I needed," Harris states, holding out his hand to shake mine. He then moves to Lexie, shaking her hand in thanks as well.

"Thank you so much." Alyssa's voice is thick with emotion, her eyes moving between the two of us as she caresses her daughter. "You have no idea. Just, thank you."

"Of course," Lexie says with a nod, gazing at the young girl earnestly. "Take care of her." When she looks up at me, her expressive eyes are misting with unshed tears. Placing my hand on the small of her back, we turn to walk to our waiting car.

"Bye Nurse Lexie, thank you." Lottie's soft voice has Lexie pausing. She offers her a soft smile and a wave before allowing me to lead her away. Tucking her into my side on the drive home, tears stream down Lexie's face. I don't know if they're happy or sad tears—I'm sure she doesn't know either.

CHAPTER THIRTY-SIX

CALLUM

Tossing my suit coat onto the bed, my fingers make quick work of the buttons down my shirt until I'm able to pull it off. Getting out of my suit is always a relief—especially after a work trip.

It's still early but I want nothing more than to climb into bed with Lexie. It didn't take much persuading to convince her to join me after dinner when we got back to the penthouse not too long ago. Colombia was a short but productive trip. I still have some loose ends to tie up for the Harris job, but that can wait until tomorrow. Now that I'm home, I'm ready to indulge in some peace.

Lexie sits cross-legged on the bed, playing with the buttons on her silky pajama top. Her eyes move over me, a thoughtful look on her freshly washed face.

"What do your tattoos mean? Why are only some of them in color when the rest are black and white?" Her curious question catches me off guard, though I don't show it. No one's ever noticed the difference in the ink on my skin before.

My pretty pink nurse, so smart.

"Truth?" I ask, raising my eyebrows in question. Lexie pauses to consider for a split second before she nods, her eyes taking their time to look at each image woven together up both of my arms and spread out over my chest before scattering down my ribs and torso. Every inch of my skin that her eyes touch burns under her gaze.

"Truth," she repeats. Unbuckling my belt, my fingers work to unbutton my pants. "What are you doing?" Lexie asks, eyes following the movement of my hands. I shove my pants to the floor and kick them to the side, leaving just my black boxer briefs.

"If I'm going to tell you about my tattoos, you need to see all of them," I say, indicating the tattoos on my thighs ending several inches above my knees. It's not a lie, but I also want those lovely eyes on all of me. Her fair skin can't hide her blush, but she makes no attempt to look away.

"None of them are visible under your clothes," she points out. Clever girl.

"You like staring at my body?"

"Am I wrong?"

"I do that on purpose." My body tenses when Lexie slides off the bed and steps closer to inspect my ink more closely.

"You do everything on purpose," she murmurs to herself. "Clark Kent's glasses."

"Clark Kent?"

"Yeah, you know, like in Superman. It's just something I thought the night we first met. When you're wearing a suit, you could be anyone on Wall Street. Well, maybe not just *anyone*." Her eyes flicker up to mine. "It's always felt like your camouflage or a disguise. As soon as the suit coat comes off and your sleeves are rolled up you catch a glimpse of who you really are."

"I'm no hero, Dewdrop."

"I know." She says it so certainly. And she does, she knows me.

Standing here, I suddenly feel naked. Exposed. I've never felt such vulnerability before, and I'm suddenly fighting the intense urge to end this. Lexie knows me, she sees me like I've never been seen before. It opens me to weakness. I should see her as a liability, but I can't help but long for her attention. I fucking yearn for her.

Christ.

Her eyes move across my skin, the admiration for the artwork written across her face. My tattoo artist, Gage, is a master at his craft.

I stand completely still, a statue she's admiring in great detail as I stare down at the top of her pretty blonde head. Her hand lifts to brush gentle fingertips over the Celtic knot colored in red in the center of my chest. My muscles jump under her touch, lust surging.

Fuck.

Lexie doesn't even realize what she's doing to me right now, her attention solely focused on the story my skin tells. She looks to me to translate it. My eyes track her as I stand in place, barely breathing. Each breath I take is filled with the sweet citrus scent that's grown to be a part of her. "What's this one? It's beautiful."

Nothing about me has ever been referred to as beautiful before; it fills me with a foreign warmth. Her eyes flicker up to mine and it takes my brain a second to remember her question.

"The triquetra is a Celtic symbol for family. For my mom's side. The roots of her culture run deep."

She nods, her observant eyes taking in the details on my chest. Her gaze moves from the triquetra to the Phoenix on my ribs. I can see her clever mind connecting the dots.

"The tattoos in color are significant."

"Yes."

"How many do you have?"

"Too many to bother counting."

"Do you have a favorite?"

"Not yet."

"Why is the space over your heart empty?"

"I haven't found the right one yet."

"Your tattoos make you look dangerous," she comments, the pad of her index finger running over the cross on my right pec. "They're works of art."

"If I didn't know better, I'd think you want me," I say, tracing her cheekbone and tucking a strand of hair behind her ear. Breath catching slightly, her eyelids flutter at the contact.

"Then I'm glad you know better." She just can't help herself. Her quick wit sends a rush of arousal straight to my already stiffening cock. I'm going to own this pretty, smart mouth of hers.

"Oh, I do know better, Dewdrop. You can't hide from me." It's the truth. Her expressive face displays her every thought and emotion for me to read. Like the desire warming her gaze as her focus flickers to my lips. And there's no corner of the earth she can run to that I won't find her. She's mine to have and never let go.

"Who's hiding? You know I'm a sucker for pretty things." Her hand on my chest says I'm the pretty thing.

"I'm not an impulse buy. Or a pair of shoes you want to try on for a night before taking them back to the store. Once I have you, that's it. No returns." My teeth graze her earlobe, and she shivers against me. My hand in her hair gives a sharp tug, earning me a soft gasp. I take her lips with mine, kissing her so thoroughly that I can feel her heartbeat quicken against my chest. "You're mine, Lexie. I want you to say it."

"I signed my name on your dotted line." Her response makes me want to fuck her into submission. There's nothing I want more than to pound into her until she has no choice but to admit, both to me and herself, that she feels the connection between us. I know exactly how good that feels, having her begging for me while I'm balls deep inside her. But I don't want a hasty surrender in the throes of passion with her simply agreeing to chase an orgasm.

I want Lexie to be mine in every sense of the word. She needs to come to me without persuasion. That just means I have to work harder to get past these commitment issues of hers.

My pretty pink nurse, so fucking stubborn.

"I want you," I state. Lexie's hand lowers to palm my erection through my boxer briefs, squeezing my length. A grunt escapes me at the contact, my hips rocking into her touch involuntarily.

"I know you do. I'm right here, Callum." She can play dumb all she wants, she knows exactly what I mean.

"I want all of you." She can't wriggle out of this, I'm not letting it go. But she's clever, and I can see the spark in her gaze as she unbuttons her top until it falls away from her lush body.

"Like this?" she asks, the innocence in her voice belying the intent in her eyes. Soft blue lace cups her generous breasts, the rosy pink of her nipples peeking through the sheer fabric. The dramatic swell with each breath is hypnotizing. She's trying to distract me, and *fuck* it's working.

"It's a start." My voice is deep with hunger, earning me a knowing smile that goes straight to my already rock-hard cock. Shit, she's too pretty, too alluring. Too damn sexy. My eyes remain glued to Lexie as she reaches behind her back to unclasp her bra, watching as it springs open to let her breasts fall free. Bringing the bra to dangle from her finger, she lets it fall to the floor—those gorgeous breasts bouncing and swaying with her every move.

"Better? Or do you need more?" she asks, looking up at me through her lashes with her blue vixen eyes.

Trouble. This woman is nothing but trouble.

"More." The word is ripped out of me before I can even think, making her smile widen. Next, her shorts are being slid over the generous curve of her hips and down her legs. Her matching blue lace panties are the last to go. Stepping out of them, she stands in front of me completely naked.

My eyes start from her pretty pink toenails, moving upwards slowly. I don't want to miss a single inch. Thick thighs, soft full stomach, defined fleshy waist, beautiful heavy breasts. Blonde hair spills around her shoulders and down her back, bright blue eyes shining at me with a desire that makes me feel like the most powerful man in the world.

"You are—" I rasp, at a loss. *Fuck, Lexie.* Always leaving me without words. "*Fuck me.*" She lets out a soft laugh, taking a step towards me. Her hands go to my briefs, pulling me in by my waistband, her gaze hot on mine.

"Yeah, that's kind of the idea here, Cal," she teases. The laugh

I let out is primal, guttural. While her hands tug at my underwear, mine are sliding into her hair and pulling her in for another kiss. Our lips move together so perfectly. *She* fits so perfectly; she's completely unraveled me. My underwear is swiftly yanked down my legs. Stepping out of them, I'm backing her to the bed. I can't wait another second. I need her, all of her.

Inside her.

Lexie falls back onto the bed and my body covers hers. Scooting her further up the mattress, I'm right there refusing to stop touching her for even a second. Nails scrape my back, her thick thigh hitches around me as I wedge a pillow under her hips. I'm so fucking hot and hard against her, it's almost painful. Her mouth against mine is growing more desperate.

"Please, Cal. I need you," she pleads against my lips, her hand gripping my erection and giving it a pump. I buck against her with a hiss. If she does that again, it's all over.

"Condom," I mutter. But her grasp pulls me back in, guiding me to her entrance.

"I have an IUD," she says, arching against me. "Please." That's all I need to hear. Sinking into her, my jaw clenches as her breath catches in her throat.

Fuck, she's perfection.

I move inside her, nothing between us, and we moan together. Using the pillow beneath her for leverage, I push in deeper, harder. Every one of my senses is heightened—every touch, every movement is amplified. Her gasps and sighs send electricity licking through my veins, urging me on. She meets me with each thrust, driving me wild until I'm completely feral.

"Oh my god," she moans, her legs around my hips pulling me closer. Bracing against my arms on either side of her head, I gaze down at the gorgeous woman beneath me as I pound into her. Her breasts bounce with each stroke, plush curves against my hard panes.

"I know, Dewdrop, I know," I murmur as her eyes drift shut. "Eyes on me." Her blue eyes open to look up at me, her obedience more than gratifying. Gaze locked, I power into her as the electricity builds between us. Each sound of pleasure, each moan and sigh, fuels the primal hunger coursing through me.

"I'm going to come." Lexie's breathless words ask for permission.

"Not yet." I'm not ready for her to come around my cock just yet, I want to draw this out as long as possible and my control can only last so long with her.

"Callum," she pleads, her pussy quivering around me as she fights to keep her orgasm at bay.

"Such a good girl for me," I mutter, her submission plucking at my last strands of control. "Just like that. You're so beautiful while you take my cock."

"I—I can't," she pants, arching against me. "Please."

"Tell me who you belong to." The demand slips past my control before I can think better of it. My need to hear her say it is too strong, I don't care that I'm playing dirty. The way her eyes on me flash tells me she knows exactly what I'm doing. But the defiance is only a flicker between the pleasure and delicious torture.

Shifting my weight on to one hand, my right arm goes under her left leg and lifts it towards my shoulder to push in deeper.

"No—" Her protest morphs into a breathless moan when my angle changes, hitting her G-spot. She writhes against me, eyes accusing. But I remain firm, gaze unwavering as I piston in and out of her.

"Tell me, Lexie." My voice is deep with hunger. Electricity is prickling at the base of my spine, my climax starting to spark inside me. Gripping her hips I drive into her with a fury, making her cry out. She can't last much longer, I can feel her pussy fluttering as the orgasm threatens to overtake her. "Say it."

"You, Callum." The admission spills from her like she can't help herself. "I'm yours." Her words wash over me, dousing me in flames. Hooking my arms under her thighs to lift her hips off the bed, I push into her so hard and deep that I bottom out. Her eyes roll back in her head, hands fisting in the bedsheets.

"Come for me, Lexie," I growl. "Come while I claim what's mine." Lexie's release is immediate, her body bowing with the euphoria that pulls the breath from her lungs.

Nothing is more beautiful than Lexie when she orgasms.

Nothing.

The light in her eyes and flush of her cheeks, her lips parted in ecstasy—there are no witty remarks or denials. The moment she comes around my cock, fingers, or tongue, she's mine. Every sensation, every beat of her racing heart, every gasp of breath—they belong to me. Her eyes, connected with mine, tell me she knows it too.

Her perfect pussy clenches my cock and my own climax strikes like lightning. The sparks collecting in my balls explode, pleasure whipping through me like a live wire. I move through my release, powering into Lexie as I empty into my pretty pink pussy. My groan vibrates through my chest, her inner muscles pulling every last drop of cum from me.

"Oh my god, Cal." Her voice is barely above a whisper, her body trembling against me with the aftershocks. She gazes up at me through half-lidded eyes, a soft sated smile on her lips. Our chests heave in unison, fighting for breath. My hand lifts to brush a strand of her hair from her luminous face.

I love her.

Staring down at Lexie, I'm hit over the head with the revelation. It's undeniable, settling so deeply in my chest that it's a part of me. I don't just care about her, she's the only thing I care about. She's become my first priority and my last tether to sanity.

I lean down to kiss her, my tongue sliding in to taste her. She tastes like sweetness, satisfaction, and *mine*. I could lay here, drinking her in, for the rest of my life and never get tired of her.

"You're an asshole," she mutters, calling me out even as she's still catching her breath. I grin against her lips, a self-satisfied laugh rumbling through my chest. She's right, but that doesn't change the outcome. Catching her lip between my teeth, I give a sharp tug.

"We both got what we wanted."

"That was a power play, Callum. Not a compromise," she argues, her lips moving passionately with mine, even as I pull out of her.

"I always get results. You know that." My arms start to shake over her, the exhaustion creeping in. I've never come harder in my fucking life—each time with this woman just gets better and better.

Lowering onto my elbows, I make sure to keep the majority of my weight off her.

"It doesn't mean anything." I can hear the uncertainty in her voice. There's really no point in denying us anymore.

"Keep telling yourself that," I murmur, pressing a kiss to her jaw. Rolling to the side, I land heavily on the bed beside her. Staring up at the ceiling, my mind processes the realization I've been hit with. Surprisingly, I feel relieved instead of panicked. I'm not shocked—my obsession with my pretty pink nurse has been growing since the moment we met.

"I can't give you what you want from me." Her tone is soft, resigned. She doesn't want to keep fighting what's between us. One step closer.

"What do I want from you?"

"Control," she replies easily. "You're the biggest control freak I've ever met."

"You didn't mind me controlling you a few seconds ago."

"I'm serious, Callum. I'm not a problem for you to handle." What's happened to Lexie that makes her so terrified of being tied to someone else? An abusive ex?

Who hurt her?

The thought makes me want to start demanding names. I'll drown them in gasoline, light a match, and watch their entire world burn with a smile on my face.

When I reach for her, she sits up to look me in the eye. I turn my head to meet her gaze head-on. I'm not hiding from this conversation, there can't be anything left up for interpretation between us. The sooner we get this cleared up, the better.

"I'd never smother your spark, Lexie. I like your fire. I don't want to control you, you're perfect just the way you are." Like the fucking sun that gives life to everything under its rays. And I'm a selfish bastard addicted to her warmth.

CHAPTER THIRTY-SEVEN

CALLUM

Lying in our bed, my head is nestled in my favorite spot between Lexie's breasts. Her hand absentmindedly strokes through my hair and down the bare skin of my spine.

The last week has been spent eating, talking, and fucking. Lexie and I haven't left the penthouse, barely making it out of the bedroom. I make her beg to come, then I make her come until she begs me to stop.

If I'm not sitting with Lexie on the living room couch while she watches reality tv with my laptop, she's on the sofa in my office sketching while I work at my desk. We cook together, eat together, sleep together. There's been a shift towards a romantic relationship. The words haven't been said, but I can feel the difference.

I think about telling Lexie the truth, that I'm in love with her. The feeling grows every second I'm with her. But I don't want to risk scaring her off, and I'm not about to ruin what we currently have. I know we'll get there, I'll tell her when she's ready to hear it.

"Tell me about your family," I say, relaxing into her warmth. Lexie's body shifts beneath me, tensing slightly. I've gotten so attuned to her body it's obvious my question has struck a nerve.

"I have a sister, Samantha. She's two years younger than me," she says. There's something she's not saying, something she doesn't want to talk about. But I want it, whatever that secret is. I need to know every part of her.

"And your parents?" I prompt. She clears her throat softly, adjusting on the pillow. A lock of her hair falls over my face and I can't help but press my nose into her and inhale deeply.

She always smells so fucking good.

"We don't talk." Despite her effort to sound casual, I can sense there's far more to the story. If Lexie's not in contact with her family, something happened to make her cut ties. Anger ripples through me at the thought.

"What did they do?" There's darkness beneath my question, a short temper threatening to be set loose. I know she hears it.

"What makes you think they did something to me?" She tries her best to deny it, to talk her way around having this conversation. I'm not having any of that.

"Because I know you, Dewdrop. You're far too forgiving. You wouldn't cut someone out of your life unless they did something really fucked up to deserve it. You haven't stopped talking to me."

"I probably should," she says softly. There's no conviction in her voice, and I know I don't have to worry. "You've done some pretty fucked-up things of your own."

She's right, I have.

"You'll never be rid of me. What did they do?" The question is met by silence. "Either you tell me, or I'll track them down and get the answers myself."

"My parents are very . . . strict." She struggles to find the right word, not sounding satisfied with the description she came up with.

"Religious?" She shakes her head at my question, letting out a humorless laugh.

"No, they don't believe in God. They don't believe in anything—except the Powerball."

"But you do." I've noticed the way she prays for little things, the way she speaks to God like he's listening at every moment.

"I do believe in God," she agrees easily. "I've seen enough people die and brought back to life to believe there's something after this life." We're getting off track, so I steer the conversation back to the answers I want.

"What were they strict about?"

Lexie takes a deep breath, holding it in for a second before letting it out slowly. "Absolutely everything. They hated wasting things on me and my sister."

"What do you mean *wasting*?" I ask deeply, my jaw tightening. My temper is already flaring, and she hasn't even begun her story yet.

"Food, money, time, attention. Affection." Her voice lacks the bitterness I'm expecting. "Anything other than fulfilling their legal obligation to provide the bare minimum requirements to house, clothe, and feed us were a waste. They kept everything locked down, never spent an extra penny on us that they could save for something else. Something for themselves."

"Locked?"

"Padlocked. The cabinets in the kitchen, the fridge, the thermostat. Only my parents had the keys and asking for any of them was pointless." I can't help the string of curses that leave my mouth. She doesn't seem surprised by them, or bothered, so she continues. "Lights-out every night was at nine-thirty or else we were 'wasting electricity.' All of my clothes were hand-me-downs or pulled from church donation boxes, none of them actually fit me. I didn't even know my real bra size until I moved out and went to get measured at a store for the first time."

Her bra size is 42H, and she's absolutely glorious. I'm taking her shopping tomorrow.

"We got one shower a week, two if we were menstruating. But only for ten minutes or else my mom would shut the water off. She used a timer in the kitchen to keep track. It's funny though, because whatever money was saved by taking cold showers went straight to my dad's bets at the racetrack and my mom's weekly lotto scratch-offs."

"That's abuse, Lexie." What she's describing is neglect and all types of child abuse—and just the thought of it makes me want to go put my suppressor to good use. She nods unemotionally, staring up at the ceiling in the darkness.

"I know," she says with a sigh. "I felt so ugly for the longest time, so unlovable. I smelled terrible, my hair was always a greasy mess. My clothes never fit. I felt like I had to be funny for anyone to like me, like if I wasn't the life of the party, I'd never hold anyone's attention long enough to be my friend. My jokes became my way to distract from the undesirable parts of me." The way she acknowledges it without getting emotional, it's like it doesn't have any power over her anymore. Like she's already moved past it. I never would've guessed any of this about her, so maybe she has.

"What happened after you moved out?"

"I got a job at a plant nursery and worked my way through nursing school. For a while everything my mom said to me was ingrained in my every move. I heard her voice everywhere I went—only bought basic foods at the grocery store, never went shopping for fun. Even though my clothes finally fit, they were plain. I looked in the mirror one morning and something clicked. I was out of that house, but I was living like I was still trapped inside. And if that's how I chose to treat myself after all that time, I was admitting that I thought I deserved it. But I didn't. I knew that it wasn't the life I wanted, I deserve so much more. So, I made changes."

"That's when you met Julie."

"Yes, Julie completely transformed my life. And little by little, I created the life I've always dreamed of. Pretty dresses, skincare, karaoke nights, houseplants. As long as I'm financially responsible, I can have whatever brings me joy. I can be as colorful and extra as I want to be, and no one can ever tell me it's a waste ever again." There's not an ounce of apology in her voice. "I worked hard on my self-image too. Hours and hours of therapy sessions healing the fractured part of me that saw myself as unlovable. I still have good days and bad days, like everyone else. But I'm fucking hot."

"*So fucking hot.*" My agreement rumbles low in my chest, a

primal growl that makes her laugh softly. Turning my head into her chest I nip at her breast through the thin silk of her pajama top, eliciting a moan. Her hands thread through my hair, tugging me closer.

"I used to wonder if maybe I'd never find someone. That maybe the way I was raised was too damaging, something I'd just have to learn to live with." Her tone carries an unspoken *but*.

"But?" I press, unashamed in my prying. I want to know all of it, it's compulsive at this point. I'm so far gone for her.

"But then I met you." Her words make me grin, so stupidly happy I can hardly stand it. Pulling away, I sit up on the bed to look at her. Even in the darkness I can make out each of her delicate features, facial features I've committed to memory and never tire of looking at.

I want to see her. All of her.

The mattress dips beneath my weight when I reach over to the nightstand and snap on the lamp. Her eyes blink up at me as light floods the room, and I can't keep myself from leaning down to kiss her. Her lips are sweet against mine. The hunger growing inside me demands more, pulling and teasing until she's moaning against me.

She spent so much of her life deprived of happiness and love, it enrages me. Lexie is the most gorgeous woman I've ever met. Her personality shines through, she fucking glows from the inside out. She's too smart for her own good, and more fun than most people deserve to experience. The way she cares about people, so deeply—*purely*—never ceases to amaze me.

Lexie West is a brilliant star blazing through any darkness, capturing anyone that she comes across until they're drawn into her orbit with undying loyalty. I gave in to her magnetic pull a long time ago. It wasn't too long before I realized any resistance was as useless as fighting gravity. Now my every thought is destined to orbit around her, the center of my universe.

"You will never have to settle for anything less than everything." And I'm determined to give her just that. There's nothing

I won't do for this woman. "Tell me what you want, what you need. I won't stop until the universe is at your feet."

"Right now, all I want is you, Cal. Inside me. Now."

The familiar buzzing sounds in the studio. I barely feel the bite of the needle as Gage pricks ink into the skin of my chest. Keeping my left side rigidly still under the tattoo artist's hands, I use my right hand to press my phone to my ear. The other line picks up after two rings.

"Boss," Roscoe greets me. "We have a confirmed sighting." Roscoe and Enzo have been tasked with tracking down the men responsible for Lottie's abduction.

Kellen might have snatched her off the street, and Anton Kozlov held and transported the girls. But they're small fish, cogs in the machine. The five men responsible for the sale of girls in this part of New York are all businessmen who hide behind their desks while they ruin children's lives. I won't lose any sleep over their deaths.

"Make sure they're all there, then take them out." I give him the green light. "Take photo evidence when it's done. Harris wants them to suffer."

"Got it. Photos will be uploaded to the server," Roscoe confirms. I can hear Enzo giving updates on movement and location logistics.

"Meet me at my place after you've scrubbed the scene," I say, glancing down at Gage's work in progress. "I want a full report."

"Consider it done." With that, I end the call.

Gage adjusts the light stand to get a better look at his shading, before glancing up at me. He's been biting his tongue since I got here, but he knows better than to ask questions. And I definitely don't need his opinion.

"Finally found the right one, huh?" Gage's question is about my choice in tattoo design, but my answer isn't.

"Definitely the right one."

CHAPTER THIRTY-EIGHT

LEXIE

My hands are too full, so when I reach for the door to Callum's office, my sketchbook falls to the floor. I sigh, putting down my can of Mountain Dew on the side table nearby and tucking my phone into my bra, before crouching down to start scooping up the loose pages that fluttered across the floor. The sound of Callum and Roscoe's conversation drifts through the door that's slightly ajar.

"—everything's been handled and cleaned," Roscoe states. Shoving the papers back into my sketchbook, I can't help but listen.

"Good," Callum says. "I won't pretend that killing those fuckers was for the job. Harris' check was a bonus. People who sell minors like that deserve to suffer; they got what was coming to them."

"It's too bad there were complications," Roscoe says gravely, making me pause.

"You think the casualties could have been avoided?"

"No." Roscoe's answer has my stomach dropping. "But they were innocent, we could've gone when the marks were alone."

Innocents, as in innocent deaths? Callum went after the men who took Lottie and ended up with casualties. And Senator Harris paid him to do it.

Anger and disbelief bubble up inside me. The hammering in

my chest has my fight or flight instincts kicking in. I can't stand here and listen to this anymore.

Leaving my sketchbook where it sits on the floor, I straighten my shoulders before pushing through the door.

"How many?" I demand answers. Both men turn to look at me in surprise, but it doesn't last long. My challenging gaze tells them I heard their conversation.

"Lexie—" I completely ignore Callum, instead turning my demanding gaze to Roscoe.

"How many casualties?" I want answers, my heart hammering in my chest.

"Just two." Roscoe's gruff answer isn't nearly enough, I need details.

"Who?"

"Lexie." This time it's Roscoe trying to dissuade me from the topic, making my stomach churn. The fact that he doesn't want to say it makes me imagine the worst.

"Who?" My voice rises. "Women? *Children?*" Roscoe's eyes cut to Callum, asking his boss for permission. Callum gives no indication, simply staring at me with his jaw clenched, hands gripping his desk tightly. The tension in his body has my anxiety rising.

"The girlfriend to one of the men we hit caught a stray bullet." The knot in my stomach tightens. His voice tells me there's something else, something he's not saying.

"And?" I'm already getting emotional, but I'm not letting this go.

"She was seven months pregnant." Callum's words hit me like a punch to the stomach, my heart stopping in my chest. I turn my horrified eyes to land on him. Callum gazes back, rigid as a statue.

"The baby?" Despite the nausea clawing at me I have to ask. When he doesn't answer, the tears prick behind my eyes. "Tell me."

"He didn't make it," Callum replies heavily. The crushing sadness forces the air from my lungs. "They had to deliver him too soon. He only lived for three hours, there was no way he could survive without his mother."

"You did this?" I ask him.

"It wasn't part of the plan."

"You knew it was a possibility, Callum. You never do anything without knowing every single possible outcome."

"Casualties are always a risk. It's a cost of doing business. Collateral damage."

"Are you really trying to justify this to me right now? This wasn't business," I spit back. "It was murder. Callous, reckless murder."

"I don't have to justify anything to you." Callum's voice darkens at the implication. His need for control is twisting into anger and it's stoking my own rage. "It's the reality of the situation. Her boyfriend made some bad decisions, and his family is the price he paid for them. That woman knew who she was sleeping with, and she chose to have a child with him anyway. She decided to take that risk with both of their lives, and it ended up getting her and her baby killed."

I still, my body shifting from fiery hostility into cold contempt. He can't possibly think that. Callum, the man who holds me at night so I can sleep—who makes sure I drink enough water and watches over me so diligently—couldn't have possibly just said that. Because if this is how he truly feels, then I don't know him at all. This complete disregard for the well-being of others is staggering.

Devastating.

"Is that what you'd say if it was me?" I ask, despair weighing on my chest. "I know who I'm sleeping with, or at least I thought I did. Am I going to pay for your sins with my life?"

"Of course not," Callum replies tersely, bracing his hands on his desk like he needs the support. "I'd never let that happen."

"I'm sure the man who just lost everything told the mother of his child the same thing."

"It's different for us and you know it."

"Do I? You clearly don't value human life; I've seen it firsthand. So why am I trusting you to protect mine? That woman had a name. Do you even know it? Did you even bother to find out?"

"Lexie—"

"Of course not. Why would you bother with details like that, they're irrelevant to you. You're just a machine—a cold, calculating computer only weighing risks for reward and nothing else."

"Not with you, Dewdrop." He steps around the desk, but I take a responding step back.

"I can't even look at you." I shake my head, a tear falling down my cheek and landing on my top. The second tear slides down more slowly, dramatically, making Callum frown.

"Wait, come back," he says, voice strained as I turn on my heel to walk out the door. "Lexie!"

I think I love him, but how can I love a man like this? I believe so strongly in the importance of innocent human life and what they can bring to the world. It's why I chose to work in medicine—to help people. How can I possibly love a man who destroys lives without so much as a second thought? A pregnant woman and her unborn child used as a fuse to blow up a man's life. Callum's not just a killer, he's a robot—devoid of any capacity for human emotion. So how can I love him? And how can he possibly care about me?

He hasn't told me that he loves me, but it's there—between every word he speaks, in every look. It's implied with every bottle of water and stroke of my hair at night. But he's never said it, and I'm an idiot for thinking he does. That he even can. Maybe this whole time I've been looking for signs of something that doesn't exist.

"Where are you going?" He's right behind me, towering over me with each step as I move through the penthouse in search of an escape. I can't deal with him right now. Or maybe ever again after what he's done. Right now it feels impossible to ever get past this.

"Anywhere but here." I just want to curl up in my bed and cry. Alone.

"Stop, we can talk about this." There's an edge to his voice I haven't heard before. It's panic.

"We did talk, and there's nothing left to say. What's done is done, you can't take it back. No returns." My anger has his own words firing at him like bullets. The ammo hits him right where I aimed, dead center.

"Don't fucking say that." The dark edge in his husky voice is raw with conviction. When I reach my room, his hand on my arm catches me. I shake off his touch, batting his hand away. It's a small relief when he takes the hint and steps back.

"Leave me alone."

"Let me in, Lexie," Callum insists, stepping into the doorway so I can't close the door. So I can't shut him out. He's radiating concern, his passionate eyes on me silently pleading.

"You said you'll always give me what I need," I remind him, the tears now streaming down my face freely. "Right now, I need to be alone, and away from you." The tremble in my voice is unmistakable.

A line appears between his brows as he reaches out and swipes a tear from my top lip, his fingers surprisingly gentle compared to how rigidly his body is crowding the doorway. Each muscle is tightly coiled, no doubt fighting the urge to force his way into the room and throw me over his shoulder.

"I'll give you anything. Anything but that," he rasps. I inch away from him, putting space between us. When he reaches for me again, I avoid his touch.

If he doesn't leave, if he keeps insisting, I'm going to cave and let him in. My desperation for him to leave wars with my need for him to wrap me in his strong arms and hold me. Callum is the reason I'm so devastated, but he's also the one person who can take all the pain away.

"I need you to go. Are you going back on your word?" A sob escapes me, and I need to wrap my arms around my middle to keep myself together. I'm about to crumble, and seeing the pained look in Callum's hazel eyes only pushes me closer to the edge.

"No," he forces through clenched teeth, his eyes searching my face intently.

"Then walk away." I stare him down, even when tears blur my vision. Callum moves to reach for me again, but he thinks better of it and pulls back—instead crossing his arms over his chest.

"I'll let you close this door, but I'm not walking away from you." His tone is low, and rough with something that sounds a lot like emotion.

"Please, go." This time my voice is barely above a whisper, hitting him straight in the chest. He begrudgingly takes a step back to clear the doorway, his arms bracing on either side of the doorframe. When I close the door and turn the lock, the sound of his deep voice carries with it the string of curses uttered violently under his breath.

Falling onto the bed, I kick my shoes off before crawling under the covers. No longer trying to hold back, I sob freely into my pillow.

I need to call Mia, or Julie, to talk through the devastating weight dangerously close to crushing me in this moment. I need someone to comfort me, tell me that everything will work out. I need advice on where to go from here, and what steps I need to take to heal from all of this. I need a voice of reason to talk me down from the emotional ledge I'm teetering on right now, dangerously close to free-falling into the knowledge that my life is over. I need understanding and logic against the irrational thoughts dragging me towards a spiral away from the person I've worked so hard to become, and back to the broken person I was before.

But I can't.

I can't tell anyone any of this. Legally, and morally, I can't say a fucking word. Even if the NDA I signed wasn't gagging me, there's no way I could ever drag the people I love into this hell.

The only person I can turn to for refuge is the man who caused all of this.

Instead, I cry myself to sleep.

My phone ringing yanks me out of a restless sleep. I'm exhausted and my eyes are tear swollen when I force them open to reach for the device. A photo of me and Mia on a wild night out lights the screen, her name written across the top. Taking a deep breath, I press the button to answer.

"Hey Mia." I force a cheerful tone despite my wrecked voice. Turns out spending the whole night sobbing uncontrollably really does a number on the vocal cords. "What's up?"

"Lexie." The way she says my name has me sitting up.

"What's wrong?"

"Your sister's here at the hospital." There's something in her tone that has a new knot forming in my stomach. Trying not to assume the worst, I ask for clarification.

"Samantha's there, like, to visit?"

"She's going into surgery; I wanted to call you before I scrub in. You're still her emergency contact." Mia's voice is more serious than I've ever heard it before. This is real, the knot tightening painfully.

"What happened?"

"Looks like a hit and run. Her car rolled; she hasn't regained consciousness." I'm already up and moving. Woah I'm kind of dizzy—last night's episode really did a number on me. It feels like an emotional hangover.

"How is she?" Stumbling into the closet, I'm shoving clothes into my carry-on suitcase before I have a chance to look at what I'm grabbing. Anxiety is starting to build in my chest, pressing against my rib cage like a corset several sizes too small.

"She has a severe concussion. We won't know the extent until she wakes up. The imaging showed massive internal bleeding. She's at risk of paralysis and organ failure. We'll know more after we open her up, but she's stable." Mia's professionalism is impressive as she delivers the update of such an emotional personal topic. I can hear the hospital chaos around her, and I try not to picture my little sister part of the urgency.

The corset strings tighten painfully.

"I'm coming. I'll be there as soon as I can." Bras and panties are being hastily tossed into the bag without consideration.

"I have to get into the O.R." Mia's voice is soft and riddled with restrained concern. "I'll see you when you get here."

"Okay," I breathe. "Thank you for calling, I'll let you go. Bye."

"Of course," Mia responds sincerely. "Bye." Standing in the center of the closet—that looks like it was hit by a tornado—I look around feeling lost. Tugging on a clean pair of leggings and an oversized crewneck sweatshirt, I stuff my sock-clad feet into my white tennis shoes.

Stepping over the piles of strewn clothing, I move to the bathroom to collect my toiletries before adding them to my bag. Zipping the carry-on closed, I rush to the kitchen, trailing the suitcase behind me.

My phone is already open looking for flights from NYC to Oregon. Last-minute flights are so expensive and have multiple hour-long layovers. Overwhelmed and already emotionally raw from last night, the phone is shaking in my hand. Deciding just to pick the best of the shitty flights, and the most expensive, I struggle to fill out the ticket information.

I need my damn credit card.

Grabbing my handbag from the far edge of the counter, I'm digging through it frantically when I hear Callum enter the kitchen behind me. "What's going on?"

Even after shoving everything aside, my wallet is still nowhere to be found. "Where the fuck is it? It has to be in here." I force out a shaky breath, my frustration level rising.

"What are you looking for?" he asks, getting closer.

"My wallet. I can't buy a plane ticket without my fucking credit card." Fed up, I take the bag and turn it upside down to empty the damn thing out on the counter. All my shit comes tumbling out, scattering across the island and falling onto the floor.

"Plane ticket?" His voice is confused, but there's an undertone of trepidation in his question. "Where are you going? Tell me what's happening."

"I need to get back to Oregon." I sift through my makeup bags, crumpled receipts, and packets of tissues. "Mia called; my sister is in the hospital. She was in an accident." It's not here. Why isn't my wallet here? I take a step back to look around me.

"What's her condition?" Callum's question barely registers when my eyes catch on the pink leather peeking out from under the cabinet near the toe-kick.

"Here it is," I hiss, grabbing the wallet. My fingers are trembling as I unsnap it. When I struggle to pull my credit card loose from its place in the card holder, a strong hand is covering mine to stop me.

"Hey, take a breath and talk to me."

"Samantha's car rolled, she's going into surgery," I stammer. "I have to get there."

"You'll get there." Callum presses his phone to his ear, stealing my wallet from my hands as he waits for whoever he's calling to pick up. "I need the plane fueled and ready to go. How soon can it be ready?"

"What are you doing?"

"Good, get it done." He ends the call to answer me. "My jet is the fastest way to get there. It'll be ready in an hour."

"Give me my wallet back, I need it."

"No. I'll give it back once I'm packed."

"What?"

"I'm coming with you," he announces.

"No, you're not."

"Yes, I am."

"It's my sister, Callum. This is *my* family business."

"I know," he states firmly. "I'm coming with you." Holding up my wallet tellingly, he backs out of the room to go pack. I'm not going anywhere without my ID and credit cards, he knows that. He's effectively clipped my wings.

Son of a bitch.

My feet can't stop moving, the anxiety making me restless. If I stop long enough to sit, then the *what ifs* start to take over. And I can't bear the thought of what might be happening with Samantha on the operating table right now. She's the only family I have, I can't lose her.

I end up in my bathroom, standing in front of the sink. Looking in the mirror is a mistake; my reflection is pitiful. Disturbing. My face is puffy from crying under the crusty remnants of yesterday's makeup. Looking at myself, it's a wonder I don't feel as gross as I look.

Turning on the sink, I cup my hands to splash my face with water. The cold liquid feels refreshing against my skin. As each thought about what's happening comes, both with my sister and with Callum, it's forced out of my head. I focus solely on my task as I scrub the last twenty-four hours from my skin.

"There you are." Callum's deep voice sounds as he steps into the doorway. "I thought you'd left for a minute there."

"I can't go anywhere, you made sure of that," I reply flatly, my words heavy with meaning. Reaching for a towel, I pat the moisture from my face before letting it drop back on the counter. My hands are on autopilot carrying out the next few steps of my skincare regimen. Keeping my eyes averted, I turn around to leave the room. But he's right there, standing in my way.

He's always right fucking there.

"I made you a sandwich, you need to eat." Callum's tone is firm. I try to step around him, refusing to meet his eyes. But he follows my movements, his giant frame blocking my path. I can practically feel his eyes on me, burning a hole into the top of my head.

"Leave me alone. I'm not hungry." Lifting my eyes, my gaze lands to focus on the top button of his dress shirt. I don't have it in me to look at his face right now.

"You haven't eaten since yesterday afternoon," he points out. Of course he knows that, leave it to Callum to track my eating habits even when I'm furious with him.

Control freak.

"I said I'm not hungry. You don't get to control everything about me," I snap, the frustration in my voice more than obvious. When I move to turn away, he catches me. One of his large hands clasps my shoulder, the other lifting my chin until I'm forced to look up and meet his eyes. Callum's expression is one of unwavering determination.

"You're angry at me, I get that. You're allowed to be." His gaze drills into me. "But what's not allowed is for you to stop taking care of yourself because you're upset." The message hits home, landing heavily in my chest. It's exactly what my therapist would say—*"you can't pour from an empty cup."* This tends to be a pattern when I'm emotional about something. Self-isolation and restriction—it's how I self-sabotage.

He's right, and I fucking hate it.

"Fine. I'll eat the damn sandwich," I grit out, and I don't miss how the harsh edges of his face soften in concern. I look pointedly at his hands, and he very reluctantly lets go of me. Taking a step back, he doesn't go too far. His eyes are watching diligently as I walk to the kitchen and sit at the island to eat the plate he prepared for me.

CHAPTER THIRTY-NINE

LEXIE

Gray is the ugliest color. I can't believe I've never noticed before. It's drab, bleak, and depressing. Gray is questions that may never be answered. And I need answers.

I've walked these exact halls too many times to count, and I never once noticed. That gray is ugly. Gray chairs, gray fixtures, and a dingy gray linoleum floor. It does nothing to console, comfort, or create hope. It seems like I'm doomed to drown in a never-ending sea of gray for the rest of my life.

Here I am, stuck in this dull, gloomy waiting room at Columbia Memorial Hospital, that I used to call home. The thought that Samantha is somewhere in this horrid building all alone is absolutely maddening.

I've given up on sitting. Instead, I'm wandering aimlessly along the row of hideous chairs, but I never stray far. Callum sits in a chair silently, his attention only ever leaving me to very briefly respond to an email or a text. Roscoe had been on the plane too, but somehow, he didn't end up in this unbearable waiting room with us.

"Lexie." Mia's voice reaches me only seconds before she does. I barely have time to open my arms before she's in them, pulling me into a giant hug. We embrace each other tightly, just her presence already helping to ease some of the weight off my chest. She lets out a harsh breath of relief heavily, causing tears to prick behind my eyes.

"Damn, one hug and I'm getting emotional." My words are muffled by her hair, the tight brown curls tickling my face. The sound she makes is half laugh, half sob. It's a good two minutes before she's finally pulling back to look at me. "Hi, bitch."

"Hi bitch," she repeats with a smile, brushing away a stray tear from fluttery lash extensions. "It's been way too fucking long." I've missed her gorgeous face, with her alert mocha-brown eyes that see more than I want her to, and her full lips that deliver brutal honesty and always make me laugh. Her navy-blue scrubs do nothing to hide her full hourglass figure, and her curls are pulled away from her heart-shaped face by a clip in a half updo.

"I know," I agree. "I almost forgot how much prettier you are than me."

"You're such a liar. Damn, I miss you." She grins. Her eyes look over my shoulder, focusing on something behind me. Lowering her voice so I'm the only one who can hear her, her tone shifts to approval. "*Hot* tattoo guy is right."

Following her gaze over my shoulder, I turn to look at Callum. Our gazes collide, his eyes fixed solely on me. Even now, when I'm so angry that I can barely stand to look at him, the passion in his eyes sends warmth flooding through my veins.

Our six-hour flight was spent in silence, the tension between us growing with every passing moment. Sitting in the waiting room wasn't much better. The constant feeling of Callum's eyes on me every waking minute just added fuel to the fire, causing friction dangerously close to bringing us to the point of destruction. Mia's presence has only dampened the flame temporarily. But no matter how long it lasts, it's a nice little vacation from the complicated whirlwind my life has become since moving to New York.

"This is Callum. I work for him in New York." My matter-of-fact introduction has disapproval flashing in Callum's eyes. His expression is unreadable, but I can still hear the question his eyes are practically spearing me with. *How much longer do you think you can deny what's between us?* "This is my best friend, Mia."

"Nice to meet you, Callum."

"I wish it was under better circumstances." He's turned on the charm, his mask of calm back in place. His comment brings us back to why we're here.

"How's Samantha?" The words tumble out of my mouth a little too fast. Mia's face grows serious with the expression I've seen her use for the families of patients. I have one of those looks of my own as a nurse. It's fucking awful being on the receiving end of it.

Mia lowers to one of the chairs, motioning for me to sit next to her. Callum takes a seat across from me. "She's in post-op. Her spleen ruptured, causing severe internal bleeding that we were able to catch. Her left femur is broken, she's going to need surgery to get plates and screws. But she should recover fully without risk of paralysis. There was minimal swelling in her brain, but there's no way to know the extent of her head injuries until she wakes up." I nod, absorbing and processing the information.

"So, she's going to be okay." I don't realize how much I need to hear her say it until she's nodding.

"She's going to be okay," Mia confirms with a small smile. The breath that leaves me is a sigh of relief, happy tears prick behind my eyes and a little bit of the weight lifts from my chest. I glance at Callum, getting caught in his gaze for a few long seconds. He sits silently, running a hand over his beard while he watches me carefully.

"When can I see her?" Pulling my focus from him, I look back at my best friend. Mia glances between me and the man across from us like she noticed our little moment—it's something I'll be hearing about later.

"As soon as she's set up in her room you can go sit with her until she wakes up."

"Oh, thank god," I sigh, the corset strings loosening around my chest ever so slightly. Samantha's not out of the woods yet, there's still so much up in the air until she wakes up. But she's stable.

The sound of ringing pulls my attention to Callum. He glances at his phone and stands up to excuse himself. When his eyes meet mine, the air between us is charged with everything going unsaid. "I have to take this."

I nod to him, barely making eye contact before turning back to Mia. I can vaguely hear Callum's deep voice answer the call while he walks down the hall in search of some privacy.

"How long do you think it'll be before Samantha wakes up?" I ask Mia.

"I really wish I had an answer to that, but there's no way to be sure. It could be a few hours or a few days. We just have to wait and see." Mia's not telling me new information, I know that's how brain injuries work. But somehow being on the patient side of it feels different—like maybe the rules don't apply to this case. To *my* case.

"I'm so glad you're here. You got here a lot faster than I was expecting. I thought it would take you at least a day to get tickets."

"Callum has a private jet," I explain, knowing exactly how wide I'm cracking open this can of worms. Some things just can't be explained away, and this subject is something we'll have to bring up eventually.

"Of course he does. Hot tattoo guy *would* have his own plane." She reaches up to re-clip her mess of curls back from her face. Her hair has gotten longer since I last saw her, the tight ringlets reach past her collarbone.

"Yeah, I guess I'm lucky he was willing to bring me," I reply vaguely.

"Speaking of Callum, what's going on between you two?" Mia asks intuitively. She has no idea how loaded that question is. There are so many ways to answer, but all of them result in more questions that I can't answer. Not honestly, anyway.

"It's nothing." I hate to lie, especially to Mia, but the truth isn't an option. She flashes me a dirty look, the one telling me she's about to call me out on my bullshit.

"Did you really just lie to me like that? A blind idiot could see the way you two look at each other. Not to mention the fact that he can't seem to take his eyes off you."

"He's just like that." I'm cherry-picking now, and Mia knows it. Shit, she's known me too long.

"So, you're seriously trying to tell me nothing has happened between you and Callum?" It's impossible to lie convincingly to someone who knows you better than you know yourself. There's really no point in trying to keep this up. I've got to give her something.

"We had sex," I admit. Her face lights up like a child on Christmas at the nugget of info, before her brown eyes narrow at me.

"*I knew it!* How many times, more than once?" I knew she wouldn't be satisfied with that one vague bit of info. The girl is addicted to gossip and finding out all the juicy details. Details I would usually tell her before I met Callum and signed that damn NDA.

"More than once." I really can't get into this with her right now, if ever.

"Damn, girl. I knew there's something with you and him. He hangs on your every word. It must've been a good *more than once*. And he's hot too." Mia's both scolding me and giving me props. "I can't believe you didn't tell me. Why didn't you?"

"It's complicated." *Tip of the fucking iceberg.*

"You haven't been telling me a lot of things lately," she says, getting worked up. "Look, I'm not enough of a bitch to try and have this conversation right now. But we are going to talk before you leave—starting with why you never came back from New York." Mia wants answers, and she does deserve some sort of explanation. I just need to figure out what I'm going to tell her.

What I can tell her.

"Okay," I agree. "We'll talk."

"Good."

My sister looks completely different. Outside of the bruises and swelling, she cut her hair to her shoulders and dyed it black. Samantha has always kept her golden-brown hair long and wavy.

As surprising as this new hairstyle is, it's good to see her making changes.

Since she's a few years younger than me, she was stuck in my parents' house alone for a while after I moved out. It's been a long process for her, but she's slowly getting past the trauma from our upbringing. This haircut is one step closer to her finding herself.

They had to remove all her jewelry before surgery, but there are multiple gold hoop earrings in various sizes in the bag of personal items Mia gave me when I sat down at Samantha's bedside. I also recognize a dainty gold septum piercing in the same bag. It hasn't been that long since we last talked, but she's turned into a bad bitch since the last time I had her on video chat.

It's almost five hours of waiting before Samantha's eyes flutter open. I straighten in my chair, pressing the nurse call button. "Hi," I say gently, allowing her to absorb her surroundings.

Samantha's eyes dart around the room, taking in her IV and the hospital equipment surrounding her. Her gaze drifts from her hospital gown up to me. "Hi," she rasps. "What happened?"

"You were in a car accident," I tell her, easing her back against the pillows when she tries to sit forward. "Don't try to move, you just got out of surgery."

"What's wrong with me?" Samantha's voice is just barely above a whisper, her eyelids heavy as she fights off the anesthesia.

"You lost your spleen, your femur is broken, and you have a concussion that caused some brain swelling. Mia is your doctor, she'll be in here to talk to you later," I say, reaching for her hand and giving it a reassuring squeeze. "Do you remember anything?"

"I remember . . . my car rolling. That van came out of nowhere," Samantha responds slowly, waiting for the memories to come back to her. It's a relief that she remembers anything at all; head injuries are terrifying. I was half expecting her to open her eyes with no idea who I am. "Was anyone else hurt?"

"It was a hit and run carjacking. The other driver fled the scene after the crash. The police should be coming by later to get your statement."

A petite Filipino nurse enters the room to answer my page; her ID badge says her name is Tala. I remember having seen her around the hospital when I worked here, but I don't know her personally. She seems sweet, if a little shy, while she checks up on Samantha.

After checking her pupils, vitals, and adjusting her meds, Tala talks Samantha through a few tests, asking her name, what day it is, and if she knows where she is. Samantha passes with flying colors and Tala assures us she'll be back around later to check on her again, before leaving me alone with my sister once more.

"Your hair is so different," I comment. "It looks really good."

"Thanks, I decided it was time for a change. I got my nose pierced too," Samantha replies.

"I bet it looks hot," I announce, making her smile. The sparkle is slowly returning to her eyes—they're blue, just like mine.

We don't have a lot of similar features—I'm short and round, with killer curves, big tits, soft stomach, and thick thighs. My sister is all willowy and streamlined with legs for days and a long, graceful neck. Plus, she's taller than me by several inches, which seems to be the universal rule for younger sisters. Her new hair makes us look even less related than before, but we have the same eyes.

"Damn, I'm so glad you're okay. You have no idea how scared I was when Mia called and said you were being rushed into surgery." My words have her perking up with a look of urgency.

"Wait, how long have I been here?" she asks. I check the clock.

"Almost twenty-four hours. You were brought in yesterday morning."

"Did they find my phone?" she asks, looking around. I look in the bag of her personal belongings and pull out her cell phone. The screen is cracked, and it's covered in scratches, but it still turns on when I press the power button.

"It's a little banged up, but it looks like it's fine." I hold up the device.

"I need you to call someone for me."

"Who?"

"My boyfriend." Her answer shocks the hell out of me. "I was on my way to see him when I got hit. He must be freaking out that I never showed up."

"Wow, you have been making some changes," I add. "I'll call him, what's his name?"

"His name is Noah, but his contact in my phone is under 'Sparky.'" I flash her a questioning look. "I'll tell you later."

Taking a step out into the hallway, I press Sparky's contact. My heart warms at the kissy face and heart emojis after his name. The phone only rings once before it's picked up.

"Baby, where are you? I've been going out of my mind." Concern is Noah's immediate response when he answers the call.

"Hi, this is Samantha's sister, Lexie."

"What happened?" Panic creeps into his voice like he can sense something is wrong.

"She's going to be okay," I start. "Samantha was in a bad car accident. She just woke up after surgery."

"Surgery?"

"She's going to make a full recovery, but we're at Columbia Memorial Hospital and she's going to be here for a while."

"*Fuck*," he mutters, and there's movement on his end of the line. "I'm ninety minutes away, but I'll be there as soon as I can."

"Drive safely, we'll see you when you get here."

"Thanks for calling."

When I hang up, I step back through the doorway to see Samantha drifting off to sleep. Lowering myself into the seat by her bed silently, I place the phone on the adjustable bedside table.

"Were you able to reach him?" Her eyes peek open, fighting the drowsiness.

"Yeah, he's on his way," I assure her, scooping my hair into a high ponytail. She seems determined not to give in to sleep, so I ask my question. "How long have you been together?"

"I've known him for a while, we've been friends since last year. We've been dating for six months, and he started trying to make it official after three. We finally became boyfriend and girlfriend last month." That sounds just like her. She and I have matching commitment issues.

"He sounded nice on the phone."

"Noah is nice, he's the best guy I've ever met." The smile that appears on her face when she's talking about him is really sweet. Her eyes drift past me. "Who's that?"

I follow her gaze over my shoulder. "That's Callum." As if feeling my eyes, Callum looks up from his phone where he stands in the doorway. I avert my eyes and turn back to my sister before we get caught in another staring contest. "He came with me from New York."

"Is he your Noah?"

"I don't know."

"Looks like we both have a lot to talk about."

"I'm not going anywhere. Get some rest, we can talk later."

CHAPTER FORTY

CALLUM

Lexie hasn't left her sister's bedside since she was brought in from post-op. Other nurses have poked their heads in to say hello to her; the excitement buzzing around the halls makes her seem like a local celebrity. That's my Lexie, beloved by all.

About an hour and a half after Samantha woke up, a man dashed into the room with a look of pure panic. After frantically checking on Samantha, he introduced himself as her boyfriend, Noah.

Standing in the corner observing, I overhear Lexie's sister tell her the story of how they got together. Samantha said they met at work, and I'm assuming she meant her job in customer service at the Realtor's office.

It was what Lexie called a "meet cute"—Samantha rounded the corner without paying attention and bumped into Noah, spilling her tea on his shoe in the process. They had become friends, but it's clear to me Noah never had any intention of remaining in the friendzone. From the way he looks at Samantha I can see that he was desperate to win her over, and now he's determined to keep her.

I know the feeling.

As much as I'd like to stay with Lexie at Samantha's bedside, my work doesn't stop rolling in. So here I am, standing in the hallway, ending another call.

Stassi Monroe, a socialite from the Upper East Side, is having an issue with a paparazzo stalking her and sabotaging her charity work. Stassi's parents are loyal clients who own half the real estate in New York City, so this isn't a job I can ignore. But it is something I can delegate, so Liam is on his way over to her apartment to gather more information.

When I turn around to see another doctor coming out of the private hospital room, sent off with a brilliant smile from the same woman who refuses to even look at me, I see red. I'm going out of my fucking mind.

I recognize just how short my fuse is right now, but that doesn't change the outcome. A man could get frostbite from the Arctic breeze coming from Lexie's shoulder. It's a slow, cruel torture to watch her light shine on everyone but me, and an exercise for my restraint not to destroy the people who do get to be on the receiving end of her smile.

I need to calm the fuck down.

Air enters and exits my lungs harshly to force a deep breath before I walk back into Samantha's room. Lexie is where I left her at her sister's bedside, catching up on the last seven months they've been separated. Noah is perched on the edge of the bed while they all chat, chiming in to add details to whatever story Samantha's telling.

Shrugging out of my suit coat, I toss it over the back of the chair in the corner. Sensing movement over my shoulder, I turn to see Mia standing a few steps away. She tucks the chart she was looking at under her arm and walks closer.

"I've heard a lot about you," I say mildly, rolling my sleeve up to my elbow. Critical brown eyes move over me in consideration.

"Really? I don't hear much about you. Or anything else for that matter since you came into the picture." It's difficult to decide if I need to put on a mask with Mia. It's my initial instinct with anyone new I meet. But she's standing here trying to read me— like I'm a tabloid and she trying to determine if the headline is a ploy or not.

"It's probably better that way."

"Is it?" she counters. Before I get a chance to respond she's continuing. "Look, I know you're a businessman—what kind of business, I have no clue—and you're clearly a successful one. I realize there are things I can't know. Lexie would never tell me if she signed an NDA, she's smarter than that, but I'm guessing she did. And I'm sure a man like you keeps his business very private. So I really only have one question for you."

"Alright."

"Do I need to worry about you hurting her?" The question has multiple meanings with various degrees of depth. But the answer is the same for all of them.

"No, never." My eyes move to where Lexie is sitting next to her sister, holding her hand as they chat softly. Looking at them, the picture of sisterly love, is a reminder that I have a few things to do.

There's a problem that needs to be fixed.

Mia's gaze follows mine, her face softening visibly at the sight of her best friend's familial moment. She then turns her gaze back to me thoughtfully. "You're in love with her." It's not a question.

"Yes, I am."

"You haven't told her." Another astute summation instead of a question.

"No, I haven't." There's a brief silence that settles between us as she observes me.

"Lexie is the best person I've ever met. She's the best person most people will ever meet. But in the back of her mind she's always expecting everyone to get bored of her and toss her aside. She deserves a forever with someone who's absolutely obsessed with her. So don't tell her unless you're going to be that forever." Her eyes move between me and Lexie again. "Judging by the way you haven't been able to keep your eyes off her, you just might be."

Standing with Lexie's best friend, her words sink in as we watch over them. My phone buzzes in my hand as I receive a message I've been expecting.

"Keep an eye on her for me. I have some business that can't wait." I consider telling Lexie that I'm leaving. But there's still a lot of tension between us and I don't want to interrupt her time with her sister. She probably won't notice I'm gone.

"I will." With Mia's assurance, I silently step out of the room and make my way outside. Roscoe is waiting for me out front, his expression grave as I climb in the passenger seat.

"Let's go get this fucker."

CHAPTER FORTY-ONE

LEXIE

The quiet is nice. Leaning my head back up against the wall, I let my eyes drift shut to focus on breathing. The last few days have been a lot, and it's not over yet.

If anything good has come out of this horrible accident, it's the fact that I get to see my sister. She and Noah seem really cute together. He's energetic and earnest, while my sister is more mellow and easygoing. It's a good balance. And with the way they look at each other, I can tell they're really in love. That's important to me.

"Aww, look at you. Back in our usual spot, I could just cry. What a Kodak moment." I look up at Mia's voice as she climbs the stairs to the landing. This top-floor alcove in the back stairwell has always been our spot. "I knew I'd find you here."

"Where else would I be?" I tease. "I wanted to give Samantha and Noah some time alone. And I could use a few minutes of peace and quiet." Not to mention a break from the certain pair of hazel eyes that have followed me since I left New York. Callum disappeared a while ago, but I know it won't be too long before he's back to watch me.

"Here," Mia says, holding out a large paper bag. My brows come together in confusion, but I accept it anyway.

"What is this?" I ask, ripping open the sticker securing it shut to see what's inside.

"A bunch of food was delivered to Samantha's room; this one has your name on it," Mia explains, taking a seat on the cushion next to me. "I'm not even sure how it got past the lobby, they're so strict about outside food after surgery."

Opening the bag, I pull out a bottle of Mountain Dew, a large bottle of water, and a food container holding a thick turkey club sandwich, a cup of mac and cheese, and some Caesar salad. A triple fudge brownie sits wrapped in the bottom of the bag with a set of plastic utensils.

I know exactly where this came from, and I can't even say I'm surprised he got it past security. "Callum."

Even when he's not in the same building he's taking care of me. Something that's both touching and painful. I still haven't decided if I'll ever speak to him again, but I could really kiss that man right now. I was dreading another meal from the cafeteria.

"Callum is the reason you're still in New York, isn't he?" Mia asks, the can in her hand fizzing loudly when she pops the tab open to take a sip of her energy drink. Sitting here with her in our old hangout spot on the padded bench in the secluded corner of a back stairwell feels like I'm in an alternate reality—one where I never left Oregon.

"Yeah, he is." Taking a bite of the sandwich, I'm tempted to throw it across the landing. Of course it's fucking delicious, Mr. Control Freak bought it. How could I have expected anything less than perfection?

"I figured," she says, snagging a crouton from my salad. "Do you love him?"

"I don't know." It's a lie and we both know it.

"Yes, you do. You know," she counters. "Just because you deny it out loud doesn't change how you really feel, Lexie. Pushing him away doesn't stop you from caring about him."

"He scares me." I'm not talking about the man, I'm terrified of the feelings I have for him. They make me vulnerable, and there's a huge potential for ruin.

He could break me.

"Could you walk away? If you decided to end it right now, are you ready to live your life without him?"

No.

The answer in my mind is immediate and final. I can't picture my life without Callum in it, and I hope I never have to.

Callum Russo is the most attentive, patient, and generous man I've ever met. He gives with both hands without expecting anything from me in return. With Callum, I know that when his eyes are on me he's not just looking. He sees me like no one ever has. He's completely changed my life past the point of no return—just like he wanted. Callum Russo is a man of his word.

He's also calculated, controlling, and lethal. He always finds a way to get what he wants, even if it means playing dirty. And I love him anyway.

When I turn my head to look at my best friend, I know she can read the answer clearly on my face.

"Damn." The word comes out of me in both relief and disappointment. I've never told a guy I love him before, not when I actually meant it. Not like this. "I'm in love with Callum."

The words feel heavy on my tongue as I say it out loud for the first time. It's weird admitting it to someone else. I can barely admit it to myself.

"I mean, he's not exactly who I pictured you ending up with. Callum is slightly terrifying," Mia admits, and I can't disagree. "But if anyone deserves to be doted on by a super rich, hot, bearded guy with tattoos and a private jet—it's you."

Meeting her eyes I can see that she means it and her words warm my heart. Damn, I miss this woman. How can I go back to New York without her?

Giving her a grateful smile, we settle into a comfortable silence. I lift one half of the hearty sandwich and nudge the container over for her to eat the other half. And just like that, we're simply two best friends sharing a meal in our quiet place.

CHAPTER FORTY-TWO

CALLUM

The newscaster's voice is the only sound in the apartment, and the silence itches under my skin. Lexie sits on the other end of the couch, absentmindedly scrolling through her phone. She's too damn far away from me, physically *and* emotionally. Since our fight she's barely glanced in my direction, and it's driving me insane. The stress of her sister's health only adds distance between us. When I want to pull her in closer, she's pushing me away.

We've spent the last three days at the hospital so Lexie could spend time with her sister and best friend. And I just watched Lexie. I watched her get to know her sister's new boyfriend. I watched her talk and laugh with her long-distance best friend—seeing them together has me deciding that there are more trips to Oregon in the future. And I watch the tormented look in her eyes when she glances at me and remembers what I did—and who I am.

The only moment of intimacy we've had since coming to Astoria was the first night we spent in her apartment. Standing in the kitchen of her cozy two-bedroom, the emotional exhaustion of the last few days had overwhelmed her. When she started to cry, she turned into my arms and let me hold her while she sobbed into my chest.

I can't deny that I felt relieved—because at that moment, I knew it's not over. Not for either of us.

But it didn't last long. After a few minutes, when the tears slowed and reality set back in, Lexie had removed herself from my arms and shoved me back into no-man's-land where all I can do is wait and watch. Every minute that passes is an exercise for my control as I fight my compulsive need to be close to her, to know what she's thinking. Respecting her need for space is one of the hardest things I've ever done.

Not much can scare me, it takes a lot to get me rattled. But fear crept through me, bitter and cold, when Lexie closed her bedroom door on me. The knot of dread that formed in my chest that day never really left, and I have a sinking feeling it won't be gone until she's forgiven me.

A familiar name scrolls across the tv screen, pulling my focus from the woman I love, back to the news. "The Astoria Police Department were stunned when a person of interest was dumped on their doorstep in what they're calling an act of vigilante-style justice."

The weasel's face appears below his name when they display his mugshot. If it wasn't important to Lexie that asshole would be dead, or worse, not in police custody.

Tracking down the man responsible for putting Samantha in the hospital was only a matter of finding the right surveillance cameras. The police report had listed an apartment complex parking lot as the location of the theft where Terence forced a woman out of her parked car. Gaining access to the security footage was as easy as yanking the weasel-faced lowlife out of that dingy dive bar after tracking the credit card he'd taken from the same car.

Terence Bexler was given to the authorities without a few of his teeth, but with all of his organs still intact—something Roscoe is still pouting about. Stopping my enforcer from taking off a few of the asshole's fingers was also a hard sell, but he restrained himself.

For Lexie.

The female newscaster continues, broadcasting the story in her over-enunciated tone.

"Terence Bexler, thought to be responsible for a carjacking turned hit-and-run that resulted in a local young woman being hospitalized, was found cuffed in a holding cell at the Astoria Police Department when the building opened for the morning." There's movement on the couch next to me when Lexie perks up and puts down her phone to listen.

"Wait, that's Samantha's car," Lexie comments when a video of the crash site plays on the screen beside the news anchor's head.

"Along with the suspected carjacker were boxes of information and what the police believe is evidence of Bexler's alleged crimes." The brunette woman on the screen continues. "The department cannot comment on the case, as it is ongoing."

"That's him?" she says in disbelief, glancing in my direction without really seeing me. "It's done; someone caught the carjacker that hit my sister."

"You don't have to worry, Dewdrop. There's enough evidence in those boxes to put him away for several lifetimes," I assure her. It takes a few seconds for my words to sink in and drag her eyes away from the tv.

"Wait, how do you know?" Lexie turns to face me. I look at her, gazing meaningfully into her eyes, and I see the moment it clicks for her. "You found him. What did you do?"

"What I'm good at," I reply simply. "I fixed it." The surprise that lights her pretty face quickly shifts to wariness.

"How did you fix it?" She's smart to worry. But, luckily for my pretty pink nurse, I didn't use my usual tactics to get Terence. Lexie hates violence on her behalf, so I practiced a little restraint... this time.

"The bastard will be charged for his crimes and given the maximum sentence." It's all been arranged. If the explicitly incriminating evidence I provided isn't enough, I've ensured that the local justice system is rigged in our favor. Bexler's not getting away from this.

"So... he's going to prison?"

"He's going to prison for a long time, Dewdrop." Seeing that she's still unconvinced, I concede to her expectant stare. "He's missing a few teeth, but he'll be walking into the courtroom on his own two feet. All limbs still attached."

"What's in the boxes?"

"Everything except a confession. But with the mountain of evidence, I'm sure the Astoria police won't have any trouble getting it," I reply.

"Why?" The way Lexie's looking at me, tells me that her question has nothing to do with the confession.

"Why, what?"

"Why did you fix this?" Her question throws me off. Because the answer couldn't be more obvious.

"He hurt your family," I answer easily. There's something stirring behind those gorgeous eyes of hers, and internal dialogue as her gaze searches my own.

Then she kisses me.

Despite the surprise, I don't hesitate to devour her. *Fuck*, she tastes so sweet. She moves closer, her chest pressing to mine as she climbs on my lap. Her mouth moves desperately with mine, fueling the hunger growing inside me.

A growl resonates in my chest when those perfect tits of hers rub against me. She's so soft, responsive, and pliable. I want to feel every part of her, see every ounce of her, feast on every soft inch of her. The soft breathy moans I'm pulling from her as I devour her mouth are the hottest thing I've ever heard. I need more, I need all of her.

"Are you wet for me?" I murmur.

"Yes, I'm so wet. All for you." Her words send arousal straight to my cock.

"Fuck, I want to taste you again."

"Come with me." She climbs off my lap and holds her hand out for me to follow her. I let her lead me into her bedroom, my entire body aching for her. Every muscle is tensed with desire when she starts to undress me. My hands work with hers to remove my clothes, I want nothing more than to feel her skin against mine.

I stand proudly naked, my cock thickening under Lexie's lustful gaze. She's wearing too many clothes and it's time to change that. My hands move to open the buttons down the front of her little pink romper until I'm able to tug it down her shoulders. The fabric falls to the floor and pools at her feet.

These fucking pajama sets ruin me.

"Come here, Dewdrop." Backing up a few steps, I lower myself to sit on the bed. Taking her hands, I draw her in to stand between my legs. Her hand reaches for my cock, giving me a few firm pumps that has my core tightening. Fuck.

Those gorgeous tits of hers sway tantalizingly right in front of my face, and my control can't stop me from reaching for them. I lift one breast to catch her nipple in my mouth. Her moan vibrates over my skin, her hand stroking me.

"Mmm, damn I miss you," I murmur deeply against her skin.

"I'm sure you do. Especially while you have my tit in your mouth," she teases breathlessly, making me smile. "I miss you too."

"I'm right here."

"Of course you are. You're always *right there*. Always so close." If her hand keeps gripping me like that, this isn't going to last nearly as long as I intend it to.

"Not nearly close enough," I growl, releasing her breasts. Moving back towards the headboard, I pull Lexie onto the bed with me. "Come sit on me."

A look of surprise and skepticism crosses Lexie's face, but she obeys anyway. She tries to be delicate about it, attempting to perch some weight on me while still supporting herself, but I pull her all the way down. I want to feel all of her.

Laying on the pillows, I move Lexie until she's sitting on me, that gorgeous ass of hers on my torso. She leans down to kiss me, her hand reaching between her thighs to relieve some of the pressure I've built there. My hand pulls hers away to replace her fingers with mine. Her moans against my mouth feed my hopeless addiction. My fingers don't relent until she comes all over my stomach.

"Oh my god." She struggles for breath, but I'm just getting started. When I said I missed her, I meant it. And now I'm about to show her just how much. "You're so good at that."

"Does this mean I'm forgiven?" My arms hook under her thighs, my muscles flexing to lift her hips towards my head. My mouth is greedy to bite and lick every inch of her generous thighs. Lexie's hands grip the headboard to keep her balance, long blonde hair flowing freely as she tosses her head back.

"I haven't decided yet," Lexie sighs.

"Then let me convince you." Pulling her back up until her full weight is on me, I revel in her lavish body. Thick thighs envelop my head, smothering me in warmth. She's so goddam hot, I could suffocate under her a million times over and die the happiest man on earth. My mouth reaches her pretty pussy hungrily, my tongue taking time to savor her.

"Callum." I'll never get tired of hearing her say my name. Even muffled from my ears between her legs, it's the sexiest sound in the fucking world. I relax my arms and lower her enough to speak. I can feel her dripping from my beard already.

"Consider this me groveling." My voice rumbles deeply in my chest, sending goosebumps across her fair skin. "Take me back. I'm begging." Then I'm pulling her back into place to enjoy her.

Her pants and moans sustain me. Each time she comes on my tongue is a fucking gift, one I don't plan to take for granted. She shifts against me when the stimulation grows to be too much, struggling against my grasp. But I hold firm until she completely shatters on top of me, clinging to the headboard breathlessly.

Using my grip on her hips, I lower her enough until I can flip us over. Lexie falls onto the pillows beneath me, still gasping for breath. Leaning over her, my fingertips brush the hair from her face to see her clearly. Her blue eyes are bright as they look up at me, and I can't help myself from leaning down to kiss her.

"Please, Lexie," I murmur against her lips, letting my mouth wander across her skin. "Please take me back." Begging isn't something I do, but I will for her. There's no way I can go back to giving her space now—or ever again.

Lexie's hands thread through my hair, pulling my lips back to hers. "There really is no getting rid of you. Is there?" The teasing edge in her tone gives me hope.

"Never." My voice resonates deeply. "You can't run away from this." My lips capture hers possessively to make my point. She responds eagerly, giving me everything in return.

"Good," she breathes, flooding me with pure happiness. "I never liked running anyway." Only Lexie can make me laugh like this, naked, vulnerable, and stupidly happy.

I'm so fucking in love.

"Running is overrated." My lips recapture hers, my throbbing cock lining up with her soaking pussy. She's so swollen and needy for me. "Fuck, I missed you."

Sinking into her with a shared moan, I move inside her incredible pussy like I'm on a mission. We fucking belong together, something I intend to prove to her every day for the rest of my life. But right now, all I plan to focus on is worshiping her body with mine.

CHAPTER FORTY-THREE

LEXIE

I can breathe again. Laying with Callum in my bed, in my apartment in Oregon, knowing that my sister is okay—I can breathe again. There are still so many things that need to be worked out, so much that still needs to be said. But right now, I just breathe.

Callum shifts in the bed beside me, his giant frame dwarfing my queen-sized mattress. What used to be plenty of space just for me feels cramped with the two of us. I'm suddenly missing the California king waiting for us back in New York.

Turning onto his side, Callum places his elbow on the bed and props his head on his hand to look down at me.

Last night was amazing. So was this morning. But every moment that passes just brings us closer to some harsh realities—things I'm not looking forward to talking about. Like going back to NYC, and the death of that poor woman and her baby. Unfortunately, our mind-blowing sex didn't erase all of that.

Per usual, those all-seeing eyes are reading me intently. He can see the wheels turning in my head, can sense my mood shifting. "Tell me."

"Some people deserve what's coming to them, I understand that. But I'll never be okay with innocent people getting hurt," I start. Callum's expression remains pensive.

"I know." His response is an acknowledgment, but not a

promise. That's not good enough for me. Holding the sheet to my breasts, I sit up and turn to meet his gaze straight on.

"Significant others and children are off-limits, Callum. I mean it." Callum's free hand runs down his beard, taking a moment to look at me in consideration.

"There are no guarantees in my business, Dewdrop. But I can promise that I'll make sparing innocent lives more of a priority." It's not exactly what I was hoping for, but I'm realistic enough to know it's the best he can do. Callum doesn't lie to me—he might keep information from me, but his words are always honest. As a man of his word, he means what he says. I know I can trust him to follow through, whether he actually wants to or not.

"Do you really care, or are you just doing this for me?" I ask softly. Strong fingers reach up to gently tuck a tendril of my hair behind my ear.

"You are what I care about, Lexie. I'll do anything for you." Tugging on my sheet, I let him pull me in to meet his lips in a sensual kiss. My hand lifts to caress his cheek and play with his beard.

"Anything?" My tone turns teasing. "Even watch reality tv?"

"If that's what you really want."

"What about drinking Mountain Dew?"

"Don't push it," he growls against my lips. I squeal out a laugh of surprise when he rolls us over until I'm beneath him against the pillows.

Such a control freak, I love him.

"Okay, okay, fine," I concede. "Margaritas then." Callum lifts his head to look down at me, strong fingers tenderly brushing the hair from my face.

"Two margaritas and one episode of *Real Housewives*," he negotiates. The smile I give him is nothing short of beaming. "But if Vicky causes a scene at the movie premiere after her meltdown at Lisa's birthday dinner, we're turning it off."

"Deal." He can pretend to hate reality tv all he wants, but I know he's into it. Every time he says one episode, it easily turns into three without any protest.

The shower turns off in the next room, followed by the sound of the glass shower door. I drop the sweater I've folded into my suitcase to bring back to New York and walk the few steps to the en-suite bathroom doorway in time to see Callum securing the towel on his waist. Droplets of water cling to him from his shower, running down the ink covering his powerful body.

He's so damn hot.

"Okay, look," I say, leaning against my bathroom doorframe and letting out a deep breath dramatically to gear up for my little speech. "I know we have to go back to New York. And I'm guessing with your business it will have to be sooner, rather than later. I signed the contract, so I'll go with you. But I really need a few more days with my sister."

Callum's eyes meet mine in the vanity mirror. He's pulling what looks like a square of cling-wrap from his chest. It's something I didn't notice earlier—I was probably too preoccupied with how thoroughly I was being railed.

"And it might take me an extra day or two to get my apartment packed up and put into storage. I have a lot of stuff, if you haven't noticed. Mia can help me sort through everything. I might also have to force Roscoe to do some of the heavy lifting," I add.

Callum waits patiently for me to get through the monologue before he speaks, the corners of his mouth lifting in amusement. "You done?"

"For now," I respond, watching him lather some soap in his hands and rub the suds on the area of his chest he just uncovered.

"We can stay as long as you need, Dewdrop. Any business I can't do from here can wait." Turning on the faucet, Callum leans forward to scoop water on to his chest and rinse away the soap. "If you love this apartment, you should keep it. If you don't, we'll find one that you do love so we have a place to stay when we come to visit. We can pack up anything you want in New York and have it shipped to the penthouse. No matter what you decide, we'll need a bigger bed."

His words warm my heart, and I swear I fall in love with him all over again. "You want to get a place in Astoria?"

"It's where your family is," he says, as if it's already a done deal. "I have a lot of places across the country, and a few overseas. I'll take you to all of them."

My eyes follow his movements, watching him take the hand towel from the hook to pat his chest dry. I know enough about tattoo care to realize what he's doing.

"You got a new tattoo?" I ask, stepping closer. The towel pauses mid-pat and Callum pulls his hand away with the cloth to reveal the fresh ink coloring his skin. Turning towards me, the image comes into view—with clean lines and beautiful shading filling the once empty space right over his heart. Even with the redness and slight swelling, it's beautifully done. A work of art to match the rest of the masterpieces decorating his skin.

And it's pink.

My eyes flash to his in surprise. He's watching me carefully, his eyes intent on my face as I step closer. "It's beautiful. What kind of flower is it?" I ask curiously.

Lifting my hand to trace gentle fingertips around the delicate petals inked in vibrant pink, I'm careful not to touch the irritated skin. Callum's hand covers mine, pressing my palm flat against his chest over the flower. His heart beats against me, the rhythm steady to match my own. Warmth radiates from him, burning through my hand and heating my blood until I'm on fire.

"It's a dewdrop." His words wash over me, vibrating through my bones. The breath hitches in my chest, eyes lifting to clash with his. The gravity of his meaning is overwhelming. "You've been mine since you signed the contract. But I've been yours from the moment you demanded to see my ID. That ink sealed your fate and now this ink seals mine."

Callum is as powerful as the sea, complicated and unforgiving in his vastness. And I'm completely swept into his undertow.

"You got a tattoo for me?" My tone is one of disbelief as I blink up at him. As always, he's patient while I process it all.

"You're it for me. You're permanently etched into my heart, and on my skin. Piece by piece, you've stripped away my control and tore through every one of my walls. There are no masks with you, there never have been. You're my everything, and I'll stop at nothing to give you the world." Brushing a tendril of hair behind my ear, his hand cups my cheek in a caress. I blink up at him through the tears misting my eyes, emotion swelling inside me. "I love you, Lexie."

I'm completely at a loss. What do you say to something like that? I've never been so overtaken by such adoration and devotion before. I didn't even know I could feel like this, like if he wasn't keeping me firmly in gravity's pull I could soar through the clouds.

It's funny how polarizing Callum's presence can be. His touch is what's holding me together, the only bond keeping my body from bursting into a puff of particles. He's the only one who makes my heart soar.

Keeping my palm over his heart, my other arm goes around his neck to pull him to me. When our lips meet, I kiss him as deeply as his words have affected me. Passion and longing flare between us, but there's something more—the connection of two souls anchoring to one another.

Strong arms wrap around me and I'm being lifted onto the bathroom counter to make up for some of our height difference. Pulling my legs to wrap around his hips, Callum presses impossibly close until our bodies are molded together like two puzzle pieces finding their home and slotting into place. A perfect fit.

Pulling back, I gaze up at him in wonder. My hand on his chest trails up to caress his cheek. Hazel eyes trace over my face as I marvel at the man in my arms. The big, scary Fixer who terrifies even the most dangerous men. Who finds emotions messy, and hates losing control.

Until he met me.

And now, here he is, openly professing the biggest emotion there is. Love.

His tattoos—that used to warn me away from him and hint at the danger that resides inside him—now carry his deepest devotion to me. There's no denying how I feel, not anymore.

"I see you, Callum. All of you. You're everything I've ever wanted, and you're all I'll ever need. My safe place." He's waiting to hear the words. "I love you, Callum Russo." He kisses me so deeply I can feel it in my toes.

"Say it again."

"I love you."

"Again."

"Wouldn't you rather have my mouth doing other things?" My teasing is met with an insistent stare, so I relent. "I'm yours, Callum. I love you."

"Fuck, you have no idea how long I've needed to hear you say that."

"Well, now I have. Do you want to keep talking or . . . ?"

EPILOGUE

CALLUM

One Year Later

As soon as the heels sound in my office doorway, the words coming from the other end of the phone call become of no interest to me. I pull my eyes from the computer to look at the blonde bombshell entering my office. Lexie gives me a beautiful smile, lighting up the room with her presence.

"I'll call you back tomorrow." Cutting off Enzo mid-sentence, I end the call without waiting for a response. I drink her in, a vision in her dark pink gown that displays her incredible cleavage with the open scoop neckline and flashes smooth thigh with the generous slit on one side. Her glittery silver heels sparkle when they catch the light with each step. "You look fucking incredible, Dewdrop."

"You look pretty good yourself, handsome," she says, walking around the desk to press a light kiss against my lips. If she wasn't so beautifully made up, I'd kiss her properly and have a real taste. But she'll kill me for ruining her lipstick if I ravage her the way I want to right now. Standing from my chair, I look down at her as she toys with the lapels of my tux. Black as night.

"Are you ready to go?" Blue eyes peer up at me through dark lashes.

"If I say no, does that mean I get to drag you into the bedroom and enjoy you in this dress?" I ask, tracing a finger across the swells of her breasts over the neckline of her pretty pink dress. Lexie rolls her eyes at me, but she doesn't hide her smile.

"Well, *I'm* going, and this dress is coming with me," she retorts. "The car leaves in five minutes, and your hot ass better be in it."

"Why isn't this back on your finger?" I ask, toying with the diamond ring hanging around her neck. I bought her the gold necklace to keep her ring safe when she's working. The stone is too large for her to wear under the disposable gloves during medical procedures.

"Oh," she says, touching the ring like she completely forgot it was there. She did. "It's not like I even need to wear this for people to know we're married. The first thing you do is introduce me as your wife. I'm sure the whole city knows," she teases. As she talks, she's maneuvering the ring from the rhombus pendant that keeps it secure and slipping it on to her left ring finger. Back where it belongs.

The five-carat emerald cut diamond winks from the simple gold band. I would've gone even bigger, but Lexie insisted that anything above five carats would put her off-balance and make her fall over. I fucking love seeing her wear my ring. It declares to the whole world that she's mine. This incredible woman chose me, and to hell if I'm not going to show her off.

"Better?" she asks, raising her sassy eyebrows at me in challenge. I take her left hand and bring it to my mouth, brushing my lips across her knuckles.

"Much better," I murmur deeply. Desire flashes across her expressive face, but it doesn't last long before the attitude I love so much is back.

"Don't try to distract me so you can lure me into bed," she chides, making me grin. Caught red-handed. "We're going right now; our ride is waiting." Pulling her hand from my lips, she links our fingers and tugs me towards the door. I allow her to lead me into the elevator, happily walking a step behind to watch her round ass sway.

"And you better behave yourself in the car. I'm not redoing my makeup because you can't keep your lips to yourself," she demands as she presses the button to the garage. I pull her against me, my hands sliding their way down to palm her ass. Lowering my head, I let my nose brush along her neck, breathing in the delicious scent of her. My beard scrapes against her delicate skin, sending a shiver down her spine. She lets out a soft sigh when my lips press to the sensitive pulse-point that drives her wild.

"Wouldn't dream of it."

The private car is waiting for us in the parking garage, a uniformed chauffeur waiting patiently to assist us into the luxury SUV by opening the door. I help Lexie in first, waiting for her to slide across the back seat in her gown, before climbing in behind her.

As soon as the car door closes behind us, I'm pulling Lexie closer. She leans back against me, carefully resting to not disturb her curls. My hands move down to caress her stomach, a primal sense of pride coursing through me at the knowledge of what's growing inside—what we made together. We haven't announced it publicly, outside our close family and friends, and she's not showing yet at only twelve weeks.

"How are you feeling, Dewdrop?" I murmur against her hair. The morning sickness has been brutal, making it difficult for her to be around certain foods and smells. Things that she usually loves now make her nauseated. It's driving her a little bit insane.

"I'm fine, just exhausted," she sighs against me. "I don't think I'm gonna make it seven more months without caffeine," she huffs. My chuckle vibrates against her. Being without her Mountain Dew has been the hardest part for her so far, even harder than giving up margaritas. "She's gonna be worth it, though."

"She?" It's too early to know the gender of the baby, but my wife is eager to know what we're having—complete with a countdown calendar to the gender reveal appointment at eighteen weeks. As excited as I am to be a dad—and I'm *really* fucking excited—nothing beats the joy of watching Lexie's over-the-moon elation about our baby.

Every tiny pair of infant socks she buys and vitamin she takes is bursting with joy that spreads to everyone around her. Even Roscoe's started bringing her a special tea to help with the nausea. Only my wife can make such a hardened man go soft; it's one of her many talents. I have no shame in being completely wrapped around this woman's finger.

"It's a girl, I can feel it," she states confidently. "Only I would have a daughter so high maintenance before she's even born. We're gonna have our hands full."

"Speaking of hands being full." My hands slide up her body to cover her breasts, already beginning to swell with the pregnancy hormones. "Your breasts are going to be so fucking big."

"Not just my boobs. Everything is going to get bigger."

"I can't wait."

"I'll feel better once I'm showing. Right now, I just look like I'm really bloated."

"You're stunning." My lips move to press a kiss to the top of her head before lowering to brush against the shell of her ear. "As soon as the ceremony's over, I'm taking you to the bathroom and getting under this dress. I'm going to fuck you so hard and deep; the other guests will hear us over the reception music. You better wipe off your lipstick before the vows, because as soon as they say 'I do,' you're mine."

Her chest rises with a soft gasp beneath my hands, her arm reaching back to hold the side of my face as I trail slow, sensual kisses down the side of her neck. If I can't have her lips, I'll taste any part of her I can get my mouth on.

"Mmmm, it's a good thing I'm already pregnant. It's tacky to conceive a baby at someone else's wedding." I laugh against her skin.

"We're here." Roscoe's voice cuts over the intercom from his place in the passenger seat on the other side of the partition. He knows how I get, too wrapped up in my wife to notice that we've pulled up to the venue.

Of course Lucciano would choose the Plaza Hotel; he's rented out the whole building no doubt. I expect nothing less from the Grassos family.

The uniformed doorman opens the car door, and I exit first to help my wife out of the vehicle in her dress and heels. Hotel staff stand outside the entrance assisting the incoming guests, most of whom I recognize. CEOs, models, socialites—the crowd is full of power and influence.

Smoothing down her dress as we enter the lavish hotel lobby, Lexie's eyes move over the throngs of people in search of familiar faces. Over the last year she's become acquainted with most of the people I know in this city, growing closer with some of them than even I am. I've never been so popular, I definitely married up.

"Just so you know." Lexie leans in to speak softly, her words for my ears only. "I'm so wet for you right now, Cal. And I'm not wearing panties." Her words shoot straight to my cock, the desire hitting me like a Mack truck.

Fuck me.

Before I get a chance to respond, she's smiling at Enzo's wife, Gwen, and stepping away to greet other guests in attendance. Leaving me with a raging hard-on. It takes every last ounce of my self-control not to toss my pretty pink wife over my shoulder and find a vacant room to have my way with her. Forcing my mask of calm firmly back into place, I square my shoulders.

I can make it through the ceremony, even if it means holding one of the frilly personalized cocktail menus over my erection. As soon as Lucciano and his bride are announced as man and wife, I'm claiming what's mine.

ACKNOWLEDGMENTS

I'd like to thank my talented sister, Hannah, my encouraging best friend, Katelyn, my incredible agent, Jill Marr, and my wonderful editor, Hydia Scott-Riley.

And I can't forget to thank my readers, who took a chance on my debut novel and made space in their hearts, bookshelves, and kindles for my plus-size characters. None of this would be possible without all of you.